The Disconsolate

The
Disconsolate

A NOVEL BY
b. elizabeth bell

Cat Over Clock
2022

The Disconsolate
Brandon Elizabeth Bell

This book mentions suicidal ideation. If you or anyone
you know is considering suicide, text or call the National
Suicide Prevention Lifeline at 988.

Published by:
Cat Over Clock, LLC
Portland, OR 97202, USA
Interior Design: M.F. Corwin
Set in LTC Goudy Oldstyle
Front Cover Art: J. Allen
Cover design & back cover art: Brandon Elizabeth Bell

Library of Congress Control Number: 2023908993
Cataloging-in-Publication Data
Bell, Brandon, 1978–

ISBN Hardback: 978-1-7378644-1-7
ISBN Ebook: 978-1-7378644-0-0
ISBN Paperback: 9781737864431

IN LOVING MEMORY

Prologue

Oh, oh, oh! I bloom now with virginal love!
My first love sets me aflame!
This new, new, new love is making me perish!
My promises comfort me,
My denial carries me away.

from Carmina Burana

AISLIN MEMORIZED THE START OF HER ROMANCE WITH JAMES. FIFTY-SIX days after the very first email he sent her, another email came that proclaimed he loved her—in verse. Was he writing about her? He was. Six days after that, he signed "*love, james*" for the first time. She received twenty-three letters in those first fifty-six days.

Although they spent a lot of time together, their hearts and minds lived in the world of their letters. She wrote many in longhand, and he would give her a card for every holiday—perhaps a sonnet by Shakespeare, a poem by Roethke, or long passages from Garcia-Marquez scribbled between the pages of cardstock.

She moved away. The severed physical connection didn't settle into either of them for several months. Their love affair began as an epistolary romance. As the separation created more fire, it became epic. Books existed that analyzed the psychology of epistolary lovers. She began collecting these books and others containing the reprinted letters. They shared the stories over the telephone, read to each other late into the night. From one letter to the next, their connection grew into a love never relinquished. An incurable desire remained that their relationship should emulate those of the greatest writers, but unlike those literary couples—their passions would last forever, and their words carried the promises of everlasting love.

Over time, she realized they were not unlike the greats after all; George Barker and Elizabeth Smart, Franz Kafka and Felice Bauer, Elizabeth Barrett and Robert Browning—all of whose romances began in earnest with exchanges of letters and poetry also ended in sadness and loss. She realized nothing lasts forever.

Four-hundred-and-forty letters full of poetry and short stories, full of adoration and longing, came to her over the first four years. She sent as many back. Eight-hundred-and-eighty letters in total.

The books she studied said that not everything one reads seduces and enchants, but when it does, that seduction is irreversible. She idolized Frances Wilson for her work. For Aislin, James' letters defined seduction. The soul of the epistle seduced the marrow of her bones and then became the very force that changed oxygen to carbon dioxide.

At long last, time and distance wedged between them, and his life took another shape. Slow—unbearable for Aislin—James' letters diminished and changed in content when his first son was born. When his second was born, he wrote her in intermittent spans and without passion, wrote with platonic and formal notions that cooled her veins, changed her blood to liquid charcoal. Soon the longing was part of her, the regret of letting him go lived beneath her skin.

Part One

Vexation, and sorrow of mind, and tears were
his sustenance.

Ovid, The Metamorphoses

Chapter 1 ✦ Aislin

Thirty hours after she drove through Death Valley, Aislin was finally in the bathtub. Blackish-brown dust lined her knuckles, her elbows, her knees. She took the dollar-store scrub brush she bought that day and began to soap up. Bubbles found the creases of her dry skin. Several days had passed since she'd bathed, and without intention, she grew accustomed to the smell of dust and damp anxiety.

A candle burned, its slow light illuminated the motel walls, releasing eucalyptus into the air. Full breaths grew longer, the coolness coated her lungs. Aislin tried not to close her hazel-hued eyes. Every time her heavy lashes met, she saw the sandstorm she had driven through in Death Valley. She focused on the way her body fit within the small tub, the top of her spine pressed against the warming porcelain, her knees bending only a little, and her feet flexing beneath the faucet to keep from sliding forward. Her light brown hair, darkened by wetness, lay across her chest in waves. Strands stuck to her pale-white back while others drifted across the cloudy surface.

When the sun sunk below the horizon for the night, her heart clawed up through her chest in a fit to see the last light. In recent years, she'd less often experienced the warm halo of the sky. The dry sunlight pulled her to it. Just the idea of a trip through the desert met a need inside her. The scenic drive might have relaxed her, could have soothed her. But what she'd envisioned as a time of grounding failed her with the rising of the winds. Now the trip to Southern California was finally behind her—forty-two hours since Gig Harbor and dirt in her mouth most of the way. No preparation existed for the funeral that awaited her near Palm Desert. Was she naïve to think it possible?

The windowpane above the toilet caught the reflection of the motel lights. The flamingo itself was hot pink and the letters cerulean. Radiant-green palm fronds burned from the edge of the "O". With the window open, the fluores-cent's buzz created a symphony with the swishing of tub-water, the occasional sizzle of wax and wick. Before this trip, Aislin would never have considered taking a bath in this type of motel. Cheap. She'd worked at a few and knew how it went.

The corners of the carpets peeled away from walls, exposing stained pad-ding. Over time, the dirt of the windowsills became part of the structure; every shadow gave her pause while she drew the water. She knew how often or not the tubs were cleaned and rinsed. Her mind thought these things through. In this tub, the residue of harsh cleaning chemicals saturated her skin, compet-ing with the dirt to take control of each of her sticky pores. But she needed this soak, needed to coerce her body into relaxation, needed to send all the grime to the sewers.

She didn't evoke it, but the memory surfaced anyway. She closed her eyes and saw the everywhere of it, the scrape of sharp, silica sand beneath her clothes. Minutes latched onto the water down through the overflow pipe. She covered it with her toes to quiet the drain and control the water's escape. Dirt escapes differently.

James was there, too, just a memory. His death was the reason she'd re-turned. She saw his face in the sand, but it would disappear the moment she really focused on it. The love of her life was dead.

The tub-water stilled while images of Death Valley continued to blast her. Although unable to see the road before her, she'd resolved to keep the car going forward. She inched along, careful with the gas. Stopping in the middle of the dust storm seemed foolish to her. But what did she know about dust storms? The winds howled against the glass, threatening to turn it back into the sand from which it came. Aislin imagined the windows disintegrating into quartz dust, mixing with the dry desert dust. She saw the contrast of white on brown. The color scheme had her thinking that maybe a little coffee would cheer her—if she ever made it out alive.

A sudden image of sliding underneath the bathwater and allowing it to take her last breath surfaced as she thought of the word "alive." It was a trig-ger word, like "survive," or like other triggers that she couldn't ever pin down. She pushed the thought away, though not quickly enough to escape a burst of hopelessness in her chest. Images of taking her life had followed her since adolescence, an overshadowing part of her fabric. The tightly folded layers of insula released a desire to die; hundreds of impulses she pushed back down, but never out completely. Aislin kept her head above the water, as she had done time and again. As she would keep doing. A deep and shaky sigh es-caped her inhibited lungs.

Her mind reverted to the dust storm where the false aroma of coffee tried to cheer her. But before she could latch onto the full aroma and rich flavor, the rear-side window imploded, threatening to deafen her with its force. A few raindrops, mixed with gagging sand, followed chunks of safety glass into the car after a large object that she didn't dare look back at. Her ears whooshed and rang. In the confusion, she pushed hard on the gas pedal. Her hands flew up to protect her face. Dust swarmed into the car where it didn't belong. Before she realized the car was moving, her body jolted with pain and her head nearly slammed into the steering wheel. She had hit something big. Sand filled all parts of the air. Did she hit another car? A big rock? Her heart thumped as she wrapped her green wool jacket around her body for protection and waited for the walls of dust to pass.

Aislin huddled in the car for what seemed like a day but was just over an hour. As the last particles of dust settled, she forced her muscles from their tight knots and opened the car door. Everything coated with sand and glass. Her stomach lurched at the realization she would have to get a new vehicle since she'd decided not to pull over. *Hopefully, I took it slow enough to minimize the damage?*

Although far away in a hotel, the storm followed her. She forced herself to breathe again, to push through the sad stillness of her diaphragm. Recalling her desperation to make it to the funeral, she remembered the crumbling asphalt road beneath her feet. It was not the main highway. It led west—turning north before it disappeared into the canyon. Aislin's jaw tightened. Isolation settled over the mangled mesquite brush, descended on the tiny, flattened patch of chamomile, and brought her heartbeat into her ears.

She checked her phone. No signal.

After a few moments of the pounding fear of being lost in Death Valley, she recalled other resources. She had a map. A map on which she could correlate her location when the storm started and then guess where she ended up.

For a split second, she sensed the tub-water cooling down, but the present had no hold on her as she saw herself walking around the lost cause that was once her car. The "something big" she hit turned out to be a dead-end signpost. A smaller sign with an obliterated message lodged itself into the upholstery of the back seat. Her hunk of metal with broken glass on the seats and sand in every crevice shimmered like blue sunstone in the heat. Dust bonded with sweat on her skin and clothes.

Almost an hour later, an unfamiliar growl erupted from Aislin's chest as she jerked the car door open and got back inside. The engine turned over, then the gas pedal made it lurch. *Please, please, make it to the next town.* The map indicated Lone Pine would be her best bet. More sweat moistened her forehead, and she correlated that with warnings of dehydration. Her liberal consumption of water early on only meant it would soon run out.

Making her way past the bases of dry slopes, tears came away with the back of her dusty hand, leaving a trail of thin mud. She sniffled and turned the stereo on, but clenched her jaw against the crackle of sand in the speakers. Turning the radio off gave the engine its own solo—a clank interrupted the emptiness, one that would be her companion, an inconsistent rhythm to give courage through dry, rocky corridors under the echoing blue sky. At under thirty miles an hour for twenty miles, she made it to Lone Pine. She changed her clothes, then washed her face and arms in the mechanic's bathroom before trading her broken-glass wreck for a different sort of wreck.

The tub faucet began to drip. The plink and plunk brought her back to the dilapidating bathroom. She slid onto her knees, feeling the swish of water around her ankles, and began counting the seconds until the hard porcelain hurt her tendons and the tops of her feet. The grit still galled between her toes—there were places she hadn't cleaned.

Aislin transitioned into tabletop pose. Her wrists cracked and released tension, and her knees ached against the porcelain. Yoga in the tub hurt just enough to chase away the dust-storm rerun. Returning to the present, she looked down at the water below her face. The ends of her hair dipped into a bathtub that had become brown, dirty, and cold.

With abruptness, she stood and turned the showerhead on. The hot stream re-rinsed her skin and chased off the chill. The sand and the water swirled down, down, down the drain.

Aislin went to bed clean, engulfed in aromas of eucalyptus and coconut shampoo. But she could not sleep through her first night in Palm Desert. She was back in the city she regretted leaving behind, feeling a tightness grow thick in her chest. It was the same way she felt every time she thought about taking the trip. The entire city swelled shut, and she could never pry it open.

April 14, 2008

Dear James,

Just dreaming that a new baby may be on the way for
you three…

How are things? I hope they are good, and that summer
is not too hot for you. Watched Love in the Time of
Cholera, wasn't as wonderful as the book but had
Benjamin Bratt ;)

How is the writing? I have let any fortunate talent
I may have had slip away and need to awaken it. The
awakening is happening with the magazine and it felt
foreign at first, sort of like writing this letter to
you.

I am sure that little Egon and fatherhood have their
way of bringing inspiration.

For me, no children. Hopefully, more walks around the
harbor. I live in a little apartment by a church and
it feels haunted. The sunsets are outstanding; there
are cranes and bats. I love it.

I look forward to hearing from you if you have time to
write and hope we can keep correspondence.

ever,

Aislin

Chapter 2 ✦ Aislin

T HE LIGHT OF THE MORNING SUN TRANSFORMED THE WALLS OF HER motel room. Aislin allowed herself a slow wake up before dressing and leaving for her next stop. Steam rose from the gas-station coffee. The warm bench outside of the small, aging chapel on Desert Post Lane, northwest of Palm Springs, held her in suspension. Her brown, gauzy skirt whipped around sandaled feet in the sand. She imagined prayers for James forming in the cool darkness behind the chapel's single door. The old-world white adobe was a place that they'd once loved to visit. The desert sun and the perceptible breeze combined with her own nostalgia brought reassurance and comfort while she sat, attempting a prayer for James.

Comforting until it felt contrived.

The interior of the chapel both called her and warned her away. A lump rose in her throat as she stared at the blistering plaster and splintering trim. Everything stuck in time.

She walked back to her vehicle; the lump becoming a sob. Scents of sun and blooming astragalus hitched a ride with a deep inhale of coffee. The bouquet soothed and grounded her on the worn springs of driver's seat but did not prevent further release. With effort, the heavy door closed with a clang, and the uncovered handle dug into her hand.

The key in the ignition of the red rusting truck turned with ease. Beneath the hood roared an engine free of clogged sand—unlike her car, which she had no choice but to leave in Lone Pine. The sturdy trade-in grounded her in the desert. The big tires and imposing metal belonged there, and she belonged in it. There was no clock, and the radio dial had come off in her hand during the first mile, an aftermath of her impatience with the lack of reception. The silver disc, post-life as a tuning dial, shot around the floorboards at each bump, making time better than the erratic beat of her heart. Aislin wiped her face with her arm, allowing her white shirtsleeve to soak up tears that would not be held back. A smudge of coppery blush and mascara stained the cuff. Aislin stared at it in a sort of disbelief.

On the day she learned of James' death, Alen, James' brother and her dear friend, told her she had a guest room waiting at his house. James' house. Alen was a friend; their kinship lasted despite the distance. A friend she shared laughter with, that she considered trustworthy. A friend who hired her to write free-lance for the Athelstans' magazine—given her a second income, one that mattered. A friend with whom she corresponded frequently.

A friend that left her the hardest message he had ever had to leave in his life: communicating the death of his brother, her soulmate, to her empty apartment. His recorded words asked her to come. She was in the will. It clearly requested that Aislin stay at the family home in the event of James' death.

The recorded words relayed it was an accident, something with the control panel. Electricity, smoke. He couldn't shake a bad feeling and couldn't stop babbling to her machine. His recorded words insisted she call him as soon as she got home. He needed to talk. James was dead. She needed to come to California. Im-me-di-ate-ly.

Aislin had held her breath when she heard Alen's recorded words on the machine. She played them again and again before dialing his number. As if by replaying them, she would realize it was all just a joke, and she would hear something that said this story wasn't true. But in the hour-long conversation that followed, Alen's recorded words became real words that prompted her to pack her car.

She arranged time off from the grocer where she'd spent the last eight years. Why was she asked to stay with Jade instead of Alen.... Why James said to stay at his house.... What he could have been thinking.... What he possibly could have willed her.... all questions with no answers.

"I can't explain, but James wished for you to stay with Jade. It's all arranged," Alen said.

"But won't I be in the way? Does Jade want me there?" Aislin wanted to argue that James was dead, and it wouldn't matter where she stayed. She wanted to ask to stay at Alen's, but she would not impose on him. He wasn't inviting her there.

"It would be so good for Jade and the kids if you would please stay there." His voice was like honey made by sad bees. She could not argue against this plea from her sweet, heartbroken friend.

But did James' widow agree with this decision? Alen's courtesy didn't mean Jade would welcome her. And his children.... She didn't feel all that familiar with children.

But these weren't just children, they were James' children.

At the turn of the century, Aislin and James both registered for a short-story writing class. His first story was about gambling. Hers was a veiled piece about Stockholm Syndrome. She recalled the way he wrote every detail of that day:

November 20, 2000

Dear Aislin,

I am in my car on the laptop, banging the keys under my fingers. I cannot stop thinking about you. I have thought of you since the first day of class… it was almost as if I knew you, when I looked at you… the scars on your arm… What do I remember about the day we met?

It is January. Old Professor Henry is lecturing about old Raymond Carver and how the editors are always so brutal, right?

I feel this energy coming, this electricity buzzing the top of my pen, and I turn around and look directly into your eyes. Your body is forward, towards me. I caught you in a stare. You are fidgety and I cannot help that I want to see more of this pulsing movement. The way you parallel a dancer, the way your shoulders tilt. There is skin, and on that skin—an inch's width of lace on the hip. I take you all in, drink you like scotch. I feel my body change and look back into your eyes, and then your eyes flick away, mine following yours to the clock on the wall. I realize I missed most of what the old man is saying, but do not regret it. Class dismissal is the only thing separating you and me. It comes slowly, but when it finally does, I wedge myself in between the rows of seats to be beside you.

"I really liked your story," I say.

You watch my mouth; I am very aware it is moving as I talk because yours is also moving. And I want to kiss it. My chest rises with breath, but I do not feel like I am breathing.

"I really liked yours, too." You sound a little breathless yourself, your voice is weighed with pleasure.

I am shy about the compliment, but I do not want you to know. "Thank you, you gave me a lot of good comments." Your cursive handwriting is tucked away in my bag.

"I really liked your feedback, too." You say, you touch the red canvas of your bag, maybe over the place where the ink from my pen left its insignificant stain around passages including the one about Astaire's movie, The Royal Wedding. I secretly delight that we both want Fred.

"Perhaps one day, I could take you to the races?" I am so shocked these words are coming from my mouth and I wait for you to answer and it takes a year.

"Okay…." you smile, but you look afraid.

You look at my arms, strong and tan from all the hours outside, building. You eat lunch with me and this friend I have. You unpack tuna salad filled with green olives. I can hardly eat. Again, I catch you staring. I stare. You must catch me staring.

I ask you out after the fourth class. You say yes, but just as friends. I know it is more than friends because I have felt you even though it is just words. I have felt you through the winter and into the heated, awful summer. I feel this and it is us. It is autumn; it is us.

But.

We just live in our letters because this other guy exists. Cliff. This boyfriend of yours who seems terribly cruel. But of whom you will still tell me almost nothing.

```
It hurts, but I guess life is full of pain. When we
first met, we drifted and had no goals. I will keep
writing you letters that pale in comparison to the day
we met.

love, james

P.S. Come to Thanksgiving at my house.
```

In February 2000, when she got the first letter, Aislin shared how amazed she was that email even existed. Interactions completed in an instant. They got to know so much about each other: type, type, type, send. She counted all of their similarities; both of them worked full time and were only in one or two classes when they met, both English majors. His father had died, and both of her parents had died.

They were poets, drinkers; they loved the band U2. Sometimes they hand-wrote letters to each other. And his scent lingered on each of his. This fresh sun, shaven, immaculate strength that she craved.

Their first summer brought insurmountable heat. They took refuge in the air-conditioned lobby of the hotel where Aislin worked every function during busy times. Off-season meant few guests. And so James made frequent visits. Propping his tired elbows on the counter, he would tell her about his workday or why he had disappeared for three or more days. She related to him; she knew about wanting to give up, but she also kept coming back.

There in the hotel, they shared stories. Aislin always perched on her stool, queen of the front-desk late shift. The long tales of sadness seemed further behind them when they were there together, like they were someone else's stories. The air above the pool would shimmer in the heat. She was 100% professional while at the hotel, and he had a dominant, cultural formality that brought them closer together while the tension ratcheted between them.

After that summer, their desire to spend time together and Alen's keen academic focus encouraged them to register full time. James switched his focus to construction and architecture, and she migrated to writing and photography.

Their friendship continued, with Alen always in the wings. James read their horoscopes over gazpacho. Every holiday meant Cliff was off with his family on expensive trips she could not afford and that he told her she hadn't earned. And so Aislin said "yes" to Thanksgiving and spent Christmases with the Athelstan brothers and their warm mother, Hana. Aislin found a family with the Athelstans. She and James wrote and wrote their letters. She cherished the ones on paper where the ink smeared beneath years of intense yearning, reading, and re-reading forever.

Aislin shifted her position in the truck, left to right, reflecting with a bit of harsh judgement that she wasn't even sitting in the back row of class that day—anyone might have seen her underwear. But James, for all his apparent formalities, embraced this indiscretion and wrapped himself in the tension of their first meeting.

Aislin closed her eyes and sighed. A flush of heat spread between her legs. She opened them wide, hoping the truck had any AC at all for her. AC like that day in class, raising goosebumps on the small of her back. But things had changed. Now he was dead. It was 89 degrees, no AC.

She cranked down the window to exchange air clogged with rust, dirt, and reality for that of desert flowers, sun, and a small breeze. She lifted her chin toward the dirt road ahead of her, wiping her eyes absently. Her new lodgings waited just around the next foothill.

Chapter 3 ✦ James

HIS FIRST EXPERIENCE OF THE PITCH BLACKNESS SEEMED LIKE IT HAPPENED ages before Aislin's arrival: James began to notice he was watching the blackness turn to gloom, and the gloom itself began to vanish. The sky grew to be the sky, nondescript patterns of light swept in through scattered clouds. Dawn arrived with a gentle breeze he saw in the plants, but could not feel. The sun was there—he was facing east—and he watched the sphere climb over the city. He did not need to avert his eyes and took note of the colors, the texture, and the literal flames. During this extraordinary examination, he experienced no pain nor sensitivity.

He could not feel the temperature rise, although the wrens and doves in the oleander beside him began to sing. For an hour, he sat and could hear nothing but those animals closest to him. A crow swooped into his vision and added to the chorus for a moment. The wings made no sound as they flapped away.

Everywhere James looked, he noticed the sunshine did not look quite sunny. And where the shadow of cacti or the shade of a tree should have been, it was total blackness. Except for the sun and the shadows, everything else seemed to look more colorful. Or was it just that he saw more clearly? He was alone with the wrens for a long time before he decided to go home.

It took him awhile to find his home. He did not recognize the city he had spent twenty-one years in. Eventually, he wandered past a house he had built, and from there he followed the right roads with the right green signs until he was walking on his hard-packed driveway over the cobblestones without a sound, stepping in places the soles of his feet had not connected with in years. From within his senses crept a loss, difficult to place.

Home was empty. There was no noise, absolute stillness. For a while, he sat on the porch and stared at the road. At least outside, the cactus wrens or the sound of a roadrunner paid him a visit; inside was just an unnatural silence, a place where not even the refrigerator hummed. A very faint bark gained his attention, and he remembered his dogs. He made his way to the screened-in back porch and found their three Labradors restless to go outside.

The dogs did not notice him at all, and he found he could not help them go out. James realized he had walked through the closed back door on the porch, walked through the front door. He had not tracked in the dust of his long walk across the wood floors, and no traces of dust wiped off his boots or clouded around him when he brushed off. Wearing boots offsite seemed odd to him. An awareness of work clothes surfaced, and he grimaced at the thought of traipsing through his home, but no trail of dust and dirt or smell of grime followed his path. In fact, he had walked through all the doors without thinking of opening them. He sat down, feeling as if he had no direction. James told himself it was a dream. He said, "I do not have to let them out because they are not real; they're part of my dream. This is all a dream. I am still asleep. I will just sit here, and I will rest better. I do not have to help."

He sat there. He waited for a long time before he heard doors slam and a high-pitched voice calling, "I am so sorry, you guys! I came as fast as possible."

Eleanor Reiner, one of his wife's closest friends, hurried onto the porch, a light, silky, cream scarf trailing behind her. It got caught in the door, wrenching her into an abrupt stillness. She was gorgeous, James noticed, more vividly than before. Her reddish-brown hair was untidy, with thick curls pinned somewhat back from two perfectly spaced green eyes, piercing in their stare. They complimented her smooth, olive skin.

"Eleanor!"

She walked past him and turned only to free her scarf for a moment before re-adjusting her gait. Yet, she was not prepared for golden Freezie who bounded over with all her puppy strength. James went to help Eleanor, but she just stumbled through him, did not acknowledge his words nor his presence. The chocolate Labrador, Indy, fought his way to give her a kiss on the face while Heath—black, but turning grey—sniffed every part of her left pant leg. Eleanor sighed in resignation, suddenly sat on the ground, and just let the dogs kiss her as she took turns hugging them tight. "I'm so sorry about your daddy, so sorry my sweet ones."

"Eleanor?" James tried to ask what she meant. She looked up just then. Her wide eyes beamed before shaking her head and squeezing them shut, as if to undo some thought she did not like.

Crawling towards the door on her hands and knees, Eleanor reached for the handle and slid it open. The dogs burst out onto the slightly withered grass that was surrounded by trees and the formidable wall James had once built. She unblocked the dog door first before watering and feeding them.

With each laborious footfall, James could see her trembling chin. Finally, she just stopped and sat down in the yard, with her forehead on her knees. Eleanor hugged her own small shoulders. "I'm so sorry, so, so sorry," she said. Her shoulders shook with sobs, and James sat next to her, wishing he could just wake, wake up from this sad, sad dream.

Darkness pressed on him again for an undetermined time, and when light returned, he was at his mother's house. She did not greet him. He watched her rise, prepare dough and tea. The doorbell rang, and he watched his brother walk into her house.

Chapter 4 ✦ Hana

A TIMING-BELL RELAYED ITS HIGH PING THROUGH THE KITCHEN; A BALL of pale dough sat ready to knead. The air smelled of yeast, Earl Grey, and sun. It was a morning of genuine autumn. A nostalgic sense for a home of long ago filled the room. A marble board warmed in the window, waiting for the bread.

Hana paused before drying her freshly washed hands. Her old, wrinkled skin spoke to her. To her, these wrinkles stood for time, for years driving south. Being a grandmother, becoming active in her community. Being loved by her sons. These blessings permeated her. A plain linen cloth removed the water from her hands. She pulled out the dough as another bell rang.

"Why Alen, dear, what a wonderful surprise." The sight of him produced a sudden pressure in her lungs. Cell phones made unannounced visits quite rare in the last decade. She opened the glossy, royal purple door all the way. An energetic autumn wind invited itself with her welcome. Fresh herbs thumped against the door twice; the wreath of rosemary and astragalus swirled in with the outside air.

Alen held her eyes for a moment before he stepped to her and held her in his arms. It happened so quickly that the next moment she found herself on the couch with him kneeling before her, his rough hands in her paper-thin ones, then—in awareness of his worker's touch—he released and held onto her knees. His wet eyes brimmed. And before the question reached her tongue, he told her.

"Majka," he said. "James has died, he's in Heaven now, he's in Heaven with Pa. There was an accident."

Alen rushed into a tale of glass and electricity.

"Please slow down and tell me, my son. Tell me," her voice quavered. Once or twice more, she asked him to slow down, to turn to her, to speak with clarity.

Alen nodded, swallowed, and struggled to tell his mother what he had seen with his own eyes. He stiffened his spine as the tears fell. But even with tears, Alen was still the strong son she needed as her heart broke into a million pieces. Her shaking body could not stop from being lost for the rest of time. Her throat gave way to silence.

They held each other like that for only minutes before Alen finally lost it. She presumed he had driven to her in a frantic state and smoothed the cotton shirt down over his tremoring back.

Hana was aware of nothing but his breath, making sure it kept coming, that in the sobs he breathed still, that he was alive and near her. The ends of her pale-blue cardigan sleeves grew damp with his tears. Empty air hung devoid of God or care or anything she recognized. She would not cry; but it did not mean she was not wailing inside.

Inside, she was singing the mourning song of a thousand mothers.

They sat together in her living room, amongst oil paintings of pastures, houses, and rivers. They sat amongst brocade upholstery and light beige wallpaper featuring perfect rows of Fleur-de-Lys, amongst the sun beams that crossed the room. The dough in the kitchen warmed a little too much, melted butter changing the way the bread would be in the end.

Only pieces of words came from either of them for several hours before they drove over to James' home. His wife was, understandably, bereft. Jade would admit no one into the study with her. Alen and Hana returned after an hour's visit with her grandsons. They left them in the care of Father Benjamin and his family for dinner. She struggled with the choice not to take them to her house, but they deserved more care and attention than she could give them right away. She just needed a little rest, and they would be at her side by nightfall.

The shock of this death was impenetrable. Hana witnessed the way the same fate fell on them as fell on her own boys in their youth—the loss of their father.

The room grew colder, and she searched for her shawl. For a moment, she thought she smelled something burning. A trace of the cigarettes her son sometimes smoked before he....

The only other thing they spoke of was of Aislin and her stay with Jade. Alen promised he would talk to Jade about it and give her some time to prepare. Hana sensed drama brewing there. She put the concern aside, trusting Alen would mitigate it and the women would be friendly. Jade was alone out there, and although the past was long, it was better for Egon and Nick to have another adult around. It unsettled Hana that their mother sent them away. She remembered when Edward died, how the three of them had clung to each other for days. She tried not to compare herself to her son's wife, and her grandsons were much younger.

The only warmth Hana allowed her heart was the many memories of Aislin. It had been too long since they kept company.

Late in the night, long after she tucked her grandsons in, she slowly made her way to her own bedroom. Alen was lying in the dark of the guest room, not sleeping. The glint of the night-light reflected off his open eyes. She turned right and entered her room, where she would also not sleep. When she again failed at sensing James, it only strengthened her resolve. Hana would not stop trying.

At first light, Hana woke to frigid air. The sandman shut his doors and turned her away. Hana thought about her life. What did it mean without her eldest? In all ways, she was privileged. She may not have come up with her parents, but she grew up. She may have grown up in a torn country, but she had love and shelter. She lived.

In more recent years, James paid her bills. This act of kindness freed her social-security and retirement income to go wherever her heart desired—and that was back to the people that really supported Coachella Valley and the country that gave her a home after hers tore apart. Every cent went to the farm workers in the southern valley. She hoped it made a difference.

After her husband passed, she prayed she would not fall ill in old age. Moving into a crowded place with shared walls was not a nightmare, but she knew her privilege allowed her freedom and the ability to grow old in her own home. This privilege she had as an elder stemmed from her hard work and her sons' business. When Edward died, she became the sole provider for their family. There was some money from his death, insurance from the house and life policies, plus the nominal money Edward clung to from his own family's estate. But she found they came up short, no matter how much she worked.

Premonitions of school surfaced day and night. In mass, Hana envisioned herself sitting in a classroom. The words law and justice kept surfacing. James was old enough to babysit, and they had the church for extra support. With the help of community resources and James' gift with language, she received a scholarship and found that a law degree suited both her interests and their finances. After passing the bar, she had worked in utility and land disputes for a small firm.

Farming communities knew her when she pulled her late husband's 1965 blue El Camino onto the road and local children ran to greet her boys when they were in tow, bringing paper airplanes or bottle rockets constructed of two-liter soda containers. If there was a case of utility bills, you could find her at Coachella Electric's headquarters or the city commissioner's office, citing the rights of the workers to have bathrooms close by, to have adequate shade and fresh water. To have electricity.

Her firm worked hard to make change. They wished change could be simple. And although small, she believed in their efforts. Anything they could do to help was something. The people who provided the most essential things in life were almost always the most underpaid. Eventually the scales tipped in favor of pro-bono cases, with crowdsourcing and fundraising eventually becoming their lifeline.

And over time, she raised her boys with the help of the church and the Sidran family from their hometown of Vitez. She helped her sons pay for college. But should Hana ever summarize her desires, she had settled for one: to die old before her children was her greatest wish.

Before that, her greatest wish was to have a family. Sometimes wishes would come true; and sometimes life would break one's heart open.

Hana sensed that her departed spouse kept peace in Heaven with their ancestors. Was Edward unaware of James' passing? Long ago, Hana knew Edward greeted her own *majka* and *otac* in Heaven. These were her country's words for mother and father. Majka was what her sons called her, even her grandchildren. They were what she would always call her parents. And since they had never met Edward, she was not sure how that could be true. Yet the truth of it lived in her. There was always hope when Hana thought of Heaven. She did not know where that faith came from, but she latched onto it as strong as grief latched onto her. She fell asleep wondering where James was, seeing his face floating in a darkened limbo.

The day went on to repeat itself in much the same way. She and Alen walked out of their bedrooms, sat with tea and barely any words. She ate little and her youngest son more than made up the difference. They picked up the boys and went to James' house and read in the library. Jade did not show herself.

After a few hours, Hana grew tired, and they took leave. Alen promised Egon and Nick a swift return.

"Alen, could you run to the store and get me some candles?"

"Of course, Majka." He stopped at a hardware store on the way to her house. She waited, bemused, as she never would have picked a hardware store to buy candles at.

The turn signal clicked as he pulled back onto the street.

"You will return to Jade's tonight?" she asked.

"Yes, for a bit. I'm sorry to leave you."

"You need not be sorry. She does not admit it, but she needs you. Egon and Nick need you. We will see each other tomorrow."

He walked her to the door. "See you tomorrow, Majka."

Hana kissed her son and held onto him for a long moment before he stepped off her front porch.

Tomorrow...

A mother always worries about her children. Construction was, of course, a dangerous line of work. But she had always had faith her boys would be as safe as possible.

Death did not know the difference, sometimes.

Pajamas and the bathroom were getting harder; exhaustion and worry set deep into her bones, flaring her arthritic joints. She thought to call the nurse in, but decided against it. Bedtime preparations could wait. It was only six. She pulled her grey afghan off the evening chair with her free hand and it trailed on the floor behind each of her careful steps.

"Time to be with my grief."

In her bedroom, heavy velveteen curtains opened to a low gibbous moon, still almost full. She placed the brown sack on her side table and sat in the big chair with the light off. Two pure-white votives easily unwrapped from a roll of brown paper inside the sack. The untrimmed wicks sparked, and her shadow fell across the wall.

She began to hum.

Chapter 5 ✦ James

I T WAS NOT A DREAM.

Jade never looked so pale. She shook, she drank so much, and her forehead throbbed. James could see his sons' heartbeats against their chests when they were in the bath, when they were sleeping. He could see his mother's pulse through the paper-like skin of her wrists.

And these vitals sounded as clear as his own voice.

He could see these things all day, things he had never seen or heard in his whole life. But the night was different: without light of sun, when the moon was new or slow to rise, when clouds obscured it from the tides, or a flame of fire had yet to ignite, darkness became a veil.

At about midday on Tuesday, James was watching Alen and Hana at her house. James was developing his new habit of witnessing conversations as he faded in and out of lives as light itself did.

Rose, Hana's practical nurse, entered the house with the groceries.

"How is everyone today?" Rose asked. Rose was complete sweetness, but he could see a change in her demeanor: tentative, avoiding actual answers, feelings, and eye contact—all very unlike her. James noted how quickly she unloaded the shopping and gathered Hana's laundry. Since Hana quit driving years back, Rose would check in to see if Hana needed to go anywhere other than scheduled. It was clear to James that, without a routine, Rose became uneasy. Sweat formed on her forehead, her pulse quickened in the silence.

He did not blame her. How do you behave when a family suffers a loss? When a mother loses a son? His heart engorged—riddled with toothpicks.

No one really had anything to say. They needed nothing and thanked her for checking in.

"Cheers then." Her English accent brought the comfort it always did as it was their father's; Rose hailed from the same area of England as Edward, which is honestly why she got the position to begin with. While one of the many qualified candidates they interviewed, her voice made the decision easy.

She exited out the backdoor to her home in the converted pool house. James and Alen had converted it to meet all of Rose's needs. It was clear within her first six months that she would be a loyal partner for Hana, who turned 77 that year. James paid Rose high wages in addition to customizing the 1,700-square-foot space to meet her sensibilities, including a ceramic studio and a kiln.

James promised his mother he would always take care of her. Now Alen would take the responsibility. He did not understand why he must see all this suffering when he could do nothing to alter it. A hitch formed in his throat and he swallowed hard. But it did not leave. Why should it?

Once Rose left, Alen turned to his mother. "Did you see the dust storm, Majka, in Death Valley? Aislin was caught in it."

"Oh my, that is very troublesome. Is she okay? Will she stay with you?"

"No, you know Aislin will stay with Jade as James wished."

James had no memory of this plan.

"And how, my dear, does your grieving sister feel about this?"

"I haven't told her."

"How can you let these women walk into this unawares? Many days have passed since you told me you would speak with Jade. Alen, she is your family. Please, treat her with respect," his mother insisted.

"Well, Aislin knows, we talked, and she agreed to stay," his stubborn brother pushed back.

"Yes, I am sure she did. What else would she say?"

Hana worried over Aislin as Alen told his mother the account of the dust storm. The incredulous and brave Aislin actually drove the totaled car twenty miles.

James took in Alen, the way his eyes sunk in, the way his cheeks puffed a little. With a third beer in his hand, his brother finally admitted that perhaps he was selfishly rushing Aislin down before discussing the matter with Jade. Alen was nervous about Jade's reaction, but settled on being up front.

James' heart that no longer beat, nonetheless, pumped a rush of concern for Aislin's wellbeing. What was the state of her mind—of her heart? Especially her heart. He had not seen or spoken to Aislin in so many years. James could not deal with much more.

Alen stood and went to the kitchen to make a snack. And James noticed that, out of view of their mother, Alen's body was breaking down. With labored breath, Alen wiped his nose with the back of his hand. James stared at his brother's hand in agony. Alen was his little brother, still vulnerable, no different from when they escaped Vitez.

Alen blew his nose and washed his hands. He selected items from the refrigerator that made James think of Jade's days carrying the boys. He ate straight out of the jars, threw things on plates, and screwed the lids on crooked. James watched his brother become clumsy. Inebriated after slamming two beers, an odd, puffy, hollow man stole Alen's place.

That evening, James was home again. He sat with Jade on the bed. He leaned against the wall, watching her brush her teeth.

Jade set up a shrine in every room of the house and was keeping the candles lit at all hours. It was as if she was doing it for him. As if she knew that unless the sun came into the windows, he would be blind, sucked to darkness. But Jade could not see him, so he knew she was lighting the candles for her own reasons. Reasons she refused to discuss out loud with anyone. He considered the bottle of whiskey in the bed. A slim bottle with a small loop at the top poked out of the sheets. Alcoholism is serious; his somber side reminded him, eyes back on his wife. He wanted to lie in the sheets with her, hold her.

He went to her side and studied her in the mirror as she faced it, her toothbrush visibly vibrating, but her hand motionless, so that only the bottom right molars were getting attention. Her eyes were closed. He raised his hand to touch her cheek, and she bent to spit, going through him without noticing.

The phone must have rung, because she walked back into the bedroom and stared at the nightstand. James followed her. After hesitating, Jade picked up her phone. Her thumb slid across the screen. James knew that touch. He remembered the slide of her thumb across his bottom lip. He missed kissing her, holding her.

"Hello," she said.

"Hey." It was Alen. James suddenly loved the fact his wife always used speaker phone. But he could not understand why he could hear his brother's voice. It seemed that he should not be able to, that a phone voice would be inaudible, like the refrigerator, like a screen door closing—among the silence of things. A massage over his temples reminded him he could not really feel his fingertips, just confusion. He did not understand the rules of his new world.

James pulled himself out of analyzing his confounding existence and into another moment of eavesdropping:

"I forgot to mention that Aislin just arrived in town," Alen said.

It was familiar to James to think of Aislin after longing for his wife's touch. He sighed out the regret but once more inhaled it, unable to dislodge the habit or the truth.

"Who?"

"Aislin Birch, our friend from college...." Alen paused.

"Oh, yes. I remember. Your friend. I thought we were going to invite her later, just for the funeral? That part of the will makes no sense, Alen. We both agree that for everyone to gather here to read it is one thing but—Wait... are you saying you called her already?"

"I did. I'm sorry, I put myself first on this one. I just miss her. She's my friend," Alen whined a little.

"She needs to stay with you, then. She shouldn't stay here, with me and the boys. Alen. Should she? Do you really think so?"

"Actually, I think it will be good to have another adult around out there. You're just sorta isolated right now," Alen encouraged.

James wanted to interrupt. Why did it matter where Aislin stayed? Why would he request such a thing? But he could not reach her. Jade had stopped paying attention to his brother. Alen could have said, *'There's a snake in your bed!'* and Jade would have settled in any way. He could not recall the details of his own will. Did not know the role Aislin played. Even if she could hear him, what could he say to Jade to convince her she should let Aislin stay in the house?

"I like how you waited to call me about this, Alen. We had all night to talk about it. I am exhausted. Thanks a fucking ton." Jade threw up her hands, clutching the phone so tight James watched her hand turn red, then white. "Do whatever the hell you want, Alen. You always do anyway!" Alen missed all the theatrics as she hung up and threw the phone on the bed, shaking the cramp in her hand before she slapped her palm hard against the wall.

Jade collapsed on the bed in a sob. James reached out, wished to comfort her, feeling like an alien in his own home as he looked down at the arms that could no longer hold his wife.

She called Alen back ten minutes later.

"It's fine, you know; she can help with the dogs and it will be a distraction for the boys." She seemed to apologize for hanging up on Alen. But James was sure his brother did not need an apology. Alen should have talked to Jade before calling Aislin. That would have been kinder. But Alen was self-centered occasionally, and very aware of the James–Aislin connection.

Try as he might, James did not remember his will. He knew that his own words were the reason that Aislin was staying at his house with Jade. If nothing else, Aislin's arrival at the house meant he could be with her and Jade and the kids all together, even if Aislin staying with Alen was a better idea. A mild pang of selfishness reared when he thought of Aislin staying at Alen's, and he realized he was jealous that his brother's friendship with Aislin flourished while he chose instead to build a wall between them. Maybe that jealousy prompted this mess. Alen's voice pulled James out of his thoughts.

"Thank you, Jade. I think this'll be a good thing. I realize you two don't really know each other very well, but she's really kind."

Jade agreed with Alen as she hung up the line. Her monotonous tone, cooing at her favorite dog to climb into the bed, indicated she stopped listening. She became that way when things were not to her liking. James watched his wife snuggle with Indy and studied her blank stare. Sleep evaded her. Absentmindedly, he perched on the little black chair they never sat on, an old chair they bought for decoration only. After a few moments, he jumped to attention, questioning if he could somehow damage it, if he weighed anything at all. He did not feel uncomfortable sitting on the throw pillows, although the contours were odd. He did not sense the fabric or the shiny tacks and decided to remain, to just be near his wife.

Close to two in the morning, when she finally found sleep, Jade's candles went out one by one until just a sparking wick remained. There was not enough light to see by. Shades of darkness took his eyes until sunrise on the day Aislin would arrive.

Chapter 6 ✦ Aislin

"THEY'RE NEVER GOING TO PAVE THIS." HER VOICE SOUNDED scratchy, distant. Aislin reached for her lukewarm coffee, vibrating in a duct-taped cup holder, as she rounded the final bend. Drinking deeply, she wondered if she even wished for hot pavement to replace the warm, packed sand. Something about the absence of asphalt left the area serene. It was unlike the rest of this Californian urban sprawl, surrounded by low mountain ranges.

A deep pothole forced the truck into a fishtail. The frontend swung 45 degrees before it stopped with a jolt, her body bouncing. The minutes borrowed back heartbeats as she regained her composure. Spit stuck in her throat and her attention froze on the marble mailbox. Her posture stiffened. Everything seemed upside-down. She read the name aloud, "Athelstan," her eyes gleaming in a ridiculous moment of contempt.

Down at the end of a long driveway, just within the northern border of Palm Springs, stood a house as large as the San Bernardino Mountains. A house tiled in travertine. James had lived there with his wife and their children. The columns of the white stone front porch seemed to glow. She knew James Athelstan's residential architecture. She studied and admired it for years. Outside would always be polished, white stone surfaces and porticos inspired by a combination of Balkan and Ottoman influences from his far away birthplace. On the inside, he always used hardwoods with the stone, from beech to cherry. She knew his home, Athelstan House, but only from the impersonal, multi-page spread of a magazine and details from his brother.

The surname carved into the oversized marble mailbox began to carve into her. She was no longer brave enough to accept the invitation. She would stay at the motel. It would suit her far better. Aislin shifted the truck into reverse, turned around, and rolled back towards the main road. The motel whispered her name, calling her back to safety.

Her grip on the steering wheel increased, changing the color of her knuckles, as she caught sight of a glinting brown car with the top down. The driver's bobbed, dark hair caught in the breeze.

The woman driving the brown car twisted the rearview mirror towards her face. Aislin pressed the brake and began slowing to five, four, three miles per hour. Although she barely knew James' wife, she would recognize her from any distance. As the familiar car approached, Aislin wondered what the woman was thinking. *What can she be feeling? How heavy is the weight of James' loss on this woman's heart? Heavy. I am sure it's so heavy.* But she didn't know how heavy— Jade Athelstan and Aislin Birch had not visited for years.

The gap between them closed in, the road swallowed up beneath the tires. When Aislin saw the woman up close, her stomach contracted and distorted. The undertones of Jade's eyes lit up like a cat's in firelight as the vehicles aligned and finally stopped. Aislin half-hoped Jade wouldn't recognize her.

From the vantage point of her vehicle, Aislin inspected the contents of the brown car. The passenger seat held bottles of bottom-shelf whiskey; caffeine-free soda cans rolled from the seat down to the floor, aluminum clanking in a soft, comforting song. Hot soda. Hot whiskey. *How much of that whiskey is she drinking?*

"Well, look what the storm blew in." Jade's cheer came across genuine enough to make Aislin shiver. She accepted the shiver as a sign that this could be a quick visit. She took in the smile, the lips pulled back with effort. This false smile was the only smile Aislin expected from Jade. Perhaps any friendliness shown had only been for James. And James was gone. "Heard you had an awful trip?"

Resigned, Aislin let the words come out. "Jade…. Yeah, I thought I would never get here in one piece. It's good to see you again," Aislin swallowed hard. "I'm so sorry." Aislin wasn't sure Jade heard the last sentence over the random surge of the truck engine, but she might've read her lips.

Maybe Jade said, "Sorry too," but she definitely followed it with, "Let's go."

Aislin made an uncalculated five-point-turn, maneuvering the truck on the narrow road to follow the vintage convertible—where years ago her own hair had flown, where Aislin herself had once sat. Despite attempts to toss the memory aside, it rose back as it always would. Jade's hands gripped the same wheel James gripped the day they'd first kissed. An isolated kiss, but a kiss, nonetheless. Everything about the car was just as she remembered; it shone like new.

She parked the rusted truck just shy of the replicated cobblestone drive that circled the sputtering murkiness of a seventeenth-century Roman-style fountain and led back into the packed earth on the other side.

Aislin stepped onto the vacant earth where her truck belonged. She had no idea if it leaked, but preferred not to find out the 'it's-too-late' way.

Vines whose leaves shook from a welcomed wind grew up the sides of the house. Although it was autumn, the Virginia Creeper's chlorophyll championed ahead, audacious in this climate. Aislin's awestruck eyes looped after the vines and over a carved portico.

In the west, beyond the house, craggy mountain tops met the blue sky, desert blue—vast and dry, stretching out. Aislin looked at her two feet on one spot of the earth and returned her gaze up again, up and out and so far that she swore she saw stars and then looked down again at her feet, her tiny little feet, feeling her bony shoulders as she smoothed the wind out from the ruffling sleeves of her shirt.

The call of a quail brought peace, a connection in all that vastness. She caught it scuttle toward the brush beneath one of three towering fan palms. Beyond the palms, James had built a smooth, Palm Springs Gold wall that would be impossible for Aislin to scale without a rope and anchor. The formidable quartzite structure created a barricade between the grounds and the insatiable coyotes beyond. The bird disappeared and Aislin turned to find Jade parked at the south end of the house, where carriage-style garage doors stood open just a few feet.

Aislin closed her mouth, hastily grabbed her bag from the passenger's seat. Sand slid out from the luggage wheels as she closed the truck door and walked onto the warm cobblestones. A good shake loosened the rest. The sand followed her. She paused long enough for it to slide out and form a small pyramid on one stone. As the pyramid grew, it left her surprised she hadn't become sand herself. After such a long trip and not enough sleep, anything seemed likely.

"Follow me?" Jade rose her voice to carry over the distance between them.

At odds with the surroundings, her heartbeat seemed off. His house may as well have been the moon. Hollering desperate and uncertain, Aislin's mind threatened to induce a panic, but she left the ugliest thoughts outside in the heat.

"Alen's so glad you're here—We're all glad." Jade's voice came out flat as she walked in through the garage before they wound over terracotta tiles in a diversely planted atrium. Aislin remembered Jade was once devoted to her plants. Aislin did not know a lot about horticulture, but she felt something off about the temperature or the humidity of the room. Exiting the atrium through an opaque glass door, they arrived in a grand parlor room. Her uncertainty returned; Aislin judged Athelstan House and all of its grandeur unsuitable for the long stay. It was only Wednesday. A very sad Wednesday and the funeral would not be until Saturday.

The moment she stepped up to a giant portrait of James' family, she sensed the rift grow wider. She no longer fit in here, she recognized, but nostalgia for the way she was once a part of his family rushed through her chest, attacking her heart from between each rib, leaving behind a pulsing, raw scrap. She sucked back her tears and the weight of her lungs increased.

"Where are—Oh." Jade backtracked across the parlor and joined Aislin, staring up at a life-sized portrait of the Athelstan family. Aislin considered the age of the children and placed the commission three years before. An enormous and elegantly carved gold and black-lacquered wood frame held the masterpiece. Shining horizontal oil strokes underneath the light of the wall sconces led to James' face.

With her focus on James' face, all of her oxygen vanished. She didn't answer Jade, who stepped into her peripheral vision as if to protest. Aislin waited to be pulled away, but a peek at Jade's weary green eyes said she demanded nothing. Instead, she turned toward the painting and the two shared the troubled silence of the parlor.

The painter was accurate. He showed James as stoic and handsome, his brown skin-tone executed faultlessly. His nose and brow were prominent. His temples caressed by thick waves of black hair. Below the sweep of hair, wide set and intelligent, deep brown eyes captured the light the artist worked with, giving the painting a most eerie quality.

Aislin's hair rose, and she smoothed goosebumps away. She looked around the cool parlor. Meticulously trained vines, orchids, and succulents interspersed curated works of art as their dead leaves fell to the floor. She and Jade were alone.

Already under its influence, Aislin turned back to the life-size painting. James' eyes, shoulders, and his mere canvas arms became almost three dimensional. His hand rested on his mother's shoulder. Aislin looked at the matriarch of the family. Although filled with pride by the genius of her sons, Hana's eyes still portrayed sadness. Aislin wanted to believe that Jade was a negative influence on the family. But it was only jealousy; Jade had nothing to do with Hana's pain. The wars she had endured in the Balkans influenced her suffering; the years were never long enough to release the grief.

Aislin's eyes circled from Hana's face to that of her other son, Alen. James' brother looked so much like him. Her heart warmed.

She let her eyes travel to Hana's grandsons' faces before they rested hesitantly on Jade's painted likeness. Her thoughts came back into the parlor. She stole a glimpse of Jade beside her, stock-still, staring up at the painting. She was curious, but could not discern the widow's exact focal point. That day, standing in the cool of her desert house, Jade's hair was in a short bob—in the painting an up-do showcased her chiseled cheekbones, the focused eyes added an aura that was far more urbane than Aislin previously imagined Jade.

"Sorry, I'm coming." Aislin finally spoke, her voice just above a whisper. Jade gave her a curt nod and turned her wiry neck away—towards the hall beyond—her gaze immediately detached.

"This way, Aislin. Keep up." They took to a flight of stone steps that actually split halfway up; the marble stairs led left and right; each side guided by hand-carved soap-stone banisters. Aislin's jaw dropped. The splendor of his home in person was far beyond the photos.

The chill in the air displaced her awe with emptiness. They turned to the left. Jade seemed to walk with her feet barely touching the steps. Aislin watched Jade almost float; her motion so fluid, but her frame so thin one would think she could never even climb stairs. Each movement looked like Jade was trying to stay balanced. The cold simultaneously resonated from the widow and echoed off her silence. The stone's smoothness rejected their minced words, colder with each ascending movement. Aislin rubbed more goose bumps away and got lost in how the chill followed them. The density of the coolness seeped through the soles of her shoes. She noted the unnatural sensation that accompanied the low temperatures.

The wall of leaded-glass windows opposite their ascent filtered and directed the light so that a hundred streams of dust danced in chaotic swirls. For a moment she caught the scent of cigarettes with something crude blended in, something that turned her stomach. Jade's feet drifted from one cold step to the next, but never made contact. Never seemed like they connected with anything other than the atmosphere that surrounded them. Mesmerized and overwhelmed, Aislin tripped.

"Watch it there," Jade admonished her guest.

"Sorry." Aislin missed a step and caught herself with her hands on the one right before her face.

Jade just shrugged, "Truly not a good place to fall, dear," and extended a hand to help her up.

With a tone that reminded one of proper manners, Jade seemed out of place with the warm kindness of the Athelstans. Aislin had an increasing feeling Jade would have tried to fit in at any cost. She didn't understand where the feeling came from; it was just a stirring in her guts. Aislin had to remind herself how little she knew about Jade.

Without ceremony, Jade opened a beautiful door to a small, elegant room crowded with antique furniture. Aislin tried to remember it from their architecture magazine, but perhaps it didn't make it into the final layout.

There is no chance I would have forgotten that fireplace.

Aislin took a furtive peak down the hall and across to the landing of the other staircase: there were many doors. Doors of dark woods, most of them doubled. All closed. So tall, their frames couldn't be reached on tiptoe. The candlelight of several altars lifted the darkness, offering photographs of James, incense, and numerous statues of saints. Aislin believed she recognized Saint Francis and smiled because of the Athelstans' love for animals. But when her eyes fell to the names of Saint Jude and Saint Augustine, her body shivered with such severity she could not hide it.

A dark-haired boy with his two front teeth missing bounded into the long hallway from what appeared to be a huge playroom—his brother, shorter and paler, came plowing into him from behind. They fell down laughing, almost as if for show, jabbing at each other's ribs and screaming at each other.

"Nick, stop that!"

"Egon! That hurts!"

The boys collapsed with a thud onto the soft, autumn-colored wool runner that stretched without end along the marble corridors of the upper hall.

The smaller boy looked up in feign surprise. "Hi!"

"Hello," Aislin said.

"Nick, Egon, this is Aislin, she's Uncle Alen's friend, your father's friend." The word *friend* spoken an octave lower the second time.

"Hello," Egon stood and straightened himself out. He nodded his head-full-of-James-hair at her in greeting. "We know who you are."

"Okay. Go back to your room, boys." Jade's chiding tone signaled the introductions were over. Her silky black hair shone under the aggressive hallway lights as she turned back to Aislin. "Dinner is at five-thirty. Do try to be down on time. And change."

The boys' retreat to their room was more graceful than their previous bounding around. Aislin looked down. No surprise to see that besides the mascara and blush on the cuffs, she had spilled her coffee down the front of her cream-colored shirt. She'd stained every other cloth button. The pattern ignited some amusement.

Jade turned to her once more. Aislin's little grin vanished as she looked up into Jade's beautiful, but increasingly hostile, face. "Okay, I guess I'll see you in a bit. Thank you."

Jade nodded, and a small smile came to her lips. She stopped to light an extinguished candle before continuing down the hall without looking back.

Chapter 7 ✦ Aislin

THE GUEST-ROOM CURTAINS OPENED TO A GRAND VIEW OF THE DESERT. She was glad to have this room—gentle tones, beautiful details. A sigh escaped as she closed the door with the softest click of a silver vintage-style knob, complete with its skeleton key. The Athelstans' sublime craftsmanship stood out from one element to the next. She deeply desired to disappear within them all, to slide into the basalt stonework of the fireplace. She could even wear her flowered shirt that matched the chair.... Aislin touched the high, winged back. She ran her hands over the muted reds, greens, and browns of the velveteen. A ripple of nostalgia, weakness, breathlessness overcame her.

I have a shirt that matches this chair! She drew a palm to her mouth as the observation hit with the attention it deserved. For this trip she dug the shirt out of the drawer she buried it in. She couldn't bear to come without it. Once a favorite in college—she had worn it for many Athelstan birthday dinners, and they had affectionately dubbed it the birthday shirt. It wasn't a coincidence that Alen had chosen the pattern for a disused room in Athelstan House. A tingle crept along Aislin's jaw line as she stepped away from the chair, thinking that James would have certainly thought of her every time he entered the room.

A noisy cactus wren shook her free, her almost-tears drying away as the bird gained distance. Drawn to the way the sun poured into the room, Aislin stood by the window. It warmed her through the glass as she took a moment, grateful she was going to be left alone. Aislin broke away from the sunlight and moved with sluggish feet into the gleaming white subway-tiled bathroom. With her shirt soaking in the sink, she grabbed her bag. The walk-in closet held a little padded stool to prop her luggage. She opened it slowly, checking as she unzipped, relieved that the last of the sandstorm was outside on the cobblestones and not on the wood floors of the closet. After selecting a plain brown, sleeveless top, she hung the rest of her clothes up, shaking the wrinkles away as she reminded herself to breathe, breathe, breathe.

Calmer, Aislin stepped back into the room. James sat quietly in the flowered chair. She almost fell over.

A few seconds passed. She studied him, her throat drying with each breath.

A minute passed. Their eyes locked.

"How—wh—I'm going crazy."

James shook his head. "No," he said.

"I'm not crazy." It was more of an affirmation. Perhaps it should have been a question. Aislin's chest tightened; her throat swelled.

He seemed to confirm that she wasn't crazy as his eyes explored hers. His presence absorbed all the light in the room, yet it never grew dark. Two hands, translucent, rested on the arms of the large, wing-backed vintage furniture. His eyelashes rose and fell as he shifted his gaze to his hands, her face, the ceiling.

James. In the flowered chair. How can he be here? Is he really here?

"I am really here."

"I can't believe it." Her voice broke as her swollen eyes dampened. A coldness in her stomach rose to touch her heart, spread to her lungs and her throat. The distance between the earth and the sun became light-years, and the physical properties of the room served merely to support her feet, which were petrified—stone trees leaning into the future. She looked down at them, wondering if she would ever take another step, and James smiled at her, the corners of his mouth almost like mist. He was a person made from mist, but not quite mist.

"Aislin. I am lost, I feel... lost. I feel broken."

And the dead man, who was once her whole life, stretched his hands out before him. He reached for her. Aislin stepped to him, her feet moving without notice. She knew for sure he could—he would—disappear at any moment. This must be a dream.

She gave him her hands, but he couldn't really hold them. She couldn't really hold his. The two of them studied their hands, just sort of... existing simultaneously in space. Aislin jerked her head up, looked into his eyes. Familiar with the wetness of her own tears, she wiped a newly fallen one away, rubbing it between her fingers until it dried. She wondered about his tears. *Are they even eyes now? Can they cry? Will his tears leave tracks? Be wet?*

"Oh." Aislin stepped back and flopped onto the bed. "Shit."

"Aislin?" His ghostly form leaned forward slowly, and he was able to rest his elbows on his knees. She couldn't really see all the way through him, but he appeared to glow a little. He wasn't mist. He was luminous and dust. A mirage? She could never have imagined.

She watched him as shock ran through her. He covered his face with his hands before gliding them through his glossy hair. His hair moved beneath his palms, responded to his fingertips. *It's not a dream.*

She did not know for several moments if she would ever speak again, and so the room became still, quiet. An awareness that they could hear only her breath settled in. The lonely rhythm prompted her to find her words and break the unsettling silence.

"I hope we have some time. Together, I mean. Even if it is just like this, a little time would be nice." She tried not to show how much her jaw quivered and her hands shook as she got the words out. Her eyes twitched as if she had all the cat hair in them. Aislin had been sure this trip would change her, but change was not the same as never again being the same.

"Yes, we can talk. We can talk to each other. Spend time together. I want to do that, Aislin. I love my marriage. I am happy. Was—I guess that is the past? I do not know. And you—you had so many endearing qualities. You were fascinating. I never forgot you for a moment." James finally met her eyes again when he spoke that last sentence.

Looking deeply into the pupils that were still glossy, but somehow caught no reflection. Yes, she heard her own voice in her head. *They are real eyes... they are still so deep, so brown... still filled with that pain, that knowledge of the wretched... that acute perception of passion.* But different—stiff and formal. The way his voice fell on her ears was not the same voice with which he once wrote her. A curious change, indeed; his relaxed and rebellious tones had transformed.

"You are not responding to me. Where are you?" he asked. A slight impatience tinged his voice.

"Sorry," she said. Yet she had to break eye contact. She had to at least try to ground herself. He was dead! She stared hard at the cloud outside the window. Then noticing that it was white, it was in the sky, and nothing more. She breathed in and saw the sky was only the sky. The aether that was inside her was the same as what was outside. *That is a cloud.... That is a cloud. Okay. He's dead, but he's here.* Aislin breathed in deeply. Her heartbeat started to slow, and her throat began to relax. *Ghost or not, this is real. James is here.*

I am talking to James. Her head shook in disbelief. "Do you know how long you'll be here?"

"Until the funeral? Perhaps? That seems to make sense. But I do not know."

"James... um, has she seen you? I mean, has she seen you like this?" Aislin tried to imagine how the now-widowed Jade would react to this... this... James. How would she feel? As Aislin did? As if her whole body had congealed. Would she feel like a quick, cold drip of surrealism had attached to all of her veins at once, inducing an unsteady heartbeat and an almost blurring headache?

"No, I could not reach her—she could not see me. I mean, I guess I am too transparent?"

A dog barked, and they looked over at the bedroom door. They could hear some language through the door, but then the house was quiet again. James' sturdy house, too soundproof to tell who was speaking.

"I see." Aislin put her fingers in her hair, giving an extra tug to make sure she could still feel something, to double check she wasn't dreaming.

Jade cannot see him.

She allowed her hands to drift across her thighs and arms. A check-in or something. "Can you give me a few moments, or two or three? Please, James?"

He nodded and leaned back. The space between them released the air she needed, and a trace of cigarettes combined with the other hot, burning scent lifted at once. Odd how she noticed the odors only after the freshness of oxygen hit. Then they vanished. Just like on the staircase.

With her mind full, Aislin repeated his earlier words. He thought he would only be around until the funeral. She watched the word "funeral" form in her mind. And as she tried to focus on the letters floating and forming words in the space of her mind, she grew dizzy. The smoke lingered again, stronger this time.

He was there, sitting with her, like before. And he almost smelled the same as she remembered. Was he desperate for communication? *He is just sitting here because Jade can't see him. He would be with her if she could. Not with me.* Her heart twisted as the pain of the words started to weave their way in.

No, she sighed and rested her head back on a cool pillow. *Aislin, you can tell yourself he is just with you because he has no other place to go and no one else can see him, but you don't know that. It's just a distorted assumption. Besides, I can tell he's happy to see me. Let me have this.*

She smiled as the weight lifted. *Sometimes talking to your shadow-self is the best way to make progress.*

A curious feeling washed in as she looked at him. Her nausea eased; the room began to still. His presence certainly made her crawl inside and out, yet it was only James. He wouldn't hurt her. She looked around for something to tie herself to, to stable herself. The passing clouds let her down, but the gorgeous bed linens and the four towering posts of the frame became soothing anchors. They sucked her in, comforting, warming yet cooling. They invited her to stay for a while, as James had. She was able to calm her heart and listen to it speak. But no words would come, and her throat was dry.

April 25, 2001

Dear James,

How sweet it would be,
  to fall
 prey to your
   power over me.
i am shaken alive
by
 the sun's hot hands
   showering me in blisters
    that no one will see...
we wanted to steal away
 and stopped short of
  all the desire
  that plagued
 our human minds and
  fought our honest hearts.
Do
  i dare speak of love?
  is not love a disease that
   slides past the lock and seal
   of this heart bruised
  by horrors...?

i will wait not for a second

  to deny your offer to

   buy my soul.

and if i should

  be left undone of my faith—

    i will know that evil had

      the upper hand.

this exemption.... the poem is powerless to grasp value, yet capable of rendering what happens when it is gone. and we will sigh while we whitewash the fence. each person will hear, they all know about the whitewash, about the solitude, yet some of them run into any open arms to avoid it. i don't know what happened... i took three steps as the tears blinded—i was needed, i was a woman who cooked soup, and baked bread....

it all begins again. this side of the fence. December first.... i open the boxes and place the domestics in the greenwash of the kitchen cabinets. my sheets are no longer mine alone... it is exciting and yet when you say exemption, i realize what you mean. what happened to the fantasies? they are still alive and call to you as your eyelids shut out the picture frames and the scented candles flicker out.

it's only a sad dream that will never come to pass.

love, Aislin

Chapter 8　✦　James

JAMES SAT WITH AISLIN FOR THE SECOND TIME THAT WEDNESDAY. IT WAS close to dinner. The sandstorm encounter hung in the air. He hoped she would not bring it up. What would he say, "I am so sorry you had such a stressful time coming to my funeral"?

When she had finally arrived, she found his ghost instead of his permanent silence.

James looked around. Other than setting the stone for the fireplace, he had spent little time in the gold-hued room. Alen's strengths leaned towards interiors. James gave his brother mental applause. The room was gorgeous. He even used their mother's beautiful lacework to decorate the pillows that tied everything together.

James went to the mantle, turned his head from the way the lowering sunlight filtered through the curtains, and touched the masonry as he looked at Aislin.

Aislin in his home.

"You have changed a lot." James looked into Aislin's eyes. He remembered them as being like leaves on a tree, static and wayward all at once. Her eyes looked at everything but him. She seemed to use the objects in the room to tether her to the world. But he could not tether her. She was wrought with an anxiety he was just beginning to uncover.

A quiver in her voice resonated from her throat alone, an emptiness left behind in her torso, a place that lacked vibration, a place that her energy had vacated. Where had it gone? Had she chased it out, or had it fled? Had she dug so deep inside she abandoned her physical form? What stories had her consciousness told? Who was she now? A bird or his dog caused her to jump. She still seemed breathless, but anxiety diminished the passion that used to take her breath away. Different from the woman he knew before: she changed into a woman who did not think she was worth anything, yet she once thought she was strong. He knew she once thought she was someone interesting, someone of note.

James looked away, up at the cornice and frieze, the eloquent slope of the molding, remembering only then how Alen carved the same design in the hearth as in the frieze: triangles stacked like hourglasses. His fingers traced the figures of where he imagined sand flowing, time running out. He sighed his undead sigh and looked back at her.

Time continued to tick for them.

His eyes saw Aislin, both as she was and what she had become. He wanted to hold her, but he knew she would flinch, and he could not bear to see that reaction. The funny thing was that Aislin would flinch. Not because he was a ghost, but because he was too close.

"I'm sorry you're unhappy where you are." The words echoed in his memory. James realized this was a line he wrote to her with empathy before he had proposed to Jade, but while he was carrying the ring around. He knew how it hurt that Aislin kept another lover, so how could he do the same to her? The ring stayed in his pocket as he debated, still waiting for Aislin to speak up and challenge his decision.

He waited for her to fight for him. He wanted it.

His soul lurched when he remembered the day he gave up on Aislin, because she gave up on him. Now he assumed that she never had confidence in their love. Thus, his confidence waned. The decision to move on with his proposal caused a lump to remain in his throat for near to a year. And he hated to admit it, but he could not deny that perhaps the proposal to Jade did not carry the weight it should have—he had loved Aislin so. He still loved her so.

He studied the hearth for a flaw and found reassurance in the perfection of his brother's craft.

Another line he wrote to Aislin was that their meeting had forever changed his life. He told her he was different before he met her, and he would never be the same afterwards. There was a caveat: death. Out of the four-hundred-and-forty letters he sent her, the power of those words over others crashed and landed in this awkward afterlife. They seemed to reach back to a time full of fantasy—full of what-ifs, how-sos, forevers and never-evers. James became aware of the difference in how he conversed with Aislin in death compared to in his youth....

As their time together came to an end, he began to embody the formality that his mother bred into him. Yet, he was still the same man Aislin fell in love with. At the same time, he was not the same as he even was a month before. And as such, did he discover that in death he was indeed the same man as always, regardless of lacking flesh?

Nothing had changed; he loved her.

He wanted to sigh and realized he could not, since he had no breath. Perhaps if he mimicked the motions, anyway.... Just trying to sigh seemed to decrease the discomfort in his throat and chest. It was enough. Finally, he just said, "It is time for dinner."

Aislin jumped up and used the closet to change. When she emerged, she wore a brown, plain-cotton outfit. James watched her smear lip-gloss on, not quite straight. He followed her hands as they smoothed her hair in the antique, gold-framed, full-length mirror and appreciated her small smile.

"You're coming?"

James nodded and waved her on. "I will be down soon."

Alen's forwarded email to James from Aislin:

James, Aislin is doing fine, she's dating a guy named
Louis. Thought you would want to read it…

October 29, 2007

Dear Alen,

Thank God for e-mail. you know, i am really glad
it has not been hard for us to stay in touch over
the years. it's a gut feeling for the future too,
i suppose. So here i am at the Gig Harbor library
waiting for my prince charming, who is going to help
with the harrows of Financing for the Post-College
Life; i really dislike the fundamentals of this math
and wish to implore a new way to build a 'Portfolio'.
i keep telling myself "this is all you need, Aislin,
then you will be set." Prince Charming is eating
dinner. he is going to join me in about 15 minutes.
Prince Charming i tell you, is Louis. so far, he could
be a player. perhaps he would like to help me organize
my finances in order to get down my pants? perhaps i
am just fooling myself when i thought his offer to
assist me would not include going to his place rather
than the library or someplace studious? who knows?
i am cynical and untrusting! where does this fear
of men wanting to use me for sex come from? never
mind, but i will tell you i am having a horrific time
overcoming this dreadful idea. and so, it goes… Maybe
James is gone forever, and you know Cliff always left
me depleted and i am a hopeless romantic by default.
Louis may be the last touch.

love rules my planets… and i am unsure of the future.
i think i need to take a long drive in the desert.
but it's unbearably far. if I could, I would find my
thoughts aligned and my breath steady. the will of my
soul would be discovered. and i would live forever.

that's not real life.

remember that "love is only one of many passions." who
wrote that, Alen?

love, Aislin

P.S. Please forgive this nightmare grammar. Something about writing on a computer in the library makes me feel drunk. it all just poured out of me and i think someone turned off all the red lines.

P.P.S. Oh yes, that dictionary man, Doc Johnson. Passion, passion, smassion.

Chapter 9 ✦ Aislin

ISLIN MADE HER WAY FROM THE LONG HALLWAY, PASSED YET ANOTHER one of Jade's candlelit shrines. She put her finger in the flame for a moment and eased the sting away with a cold blow from her lips and a salve from her tongue. She turned and took a step down the staircase—affected again by its grandeur. As the distance between her and the guestroom grew, so did the questions. What would it have been like to live in that house? Would the life she could have had with James even have gone the same direction? What would their wedding have been like? Soon her thoughts became trampled by the sound of footsteps in the stairway behind her. Every time she turned around, there was nothing there. "James?" she asked, just barely above a whisper.

"Who are you talking to?" Nick asked, appearing from behind a white marble fountain. Still water put off the smell of must and ozone. The laurel tree sprouting from the top clung to life. Rust gathered in the basin, leaving the water a sad yellow. Another fountain had died along with James.

Nick stood straight up and kind of waived at Aislin. He was five. Right behind him stood a nearly eight-year-old Egon. Despite the echoing walls in the immense quiet of the house, he snuck up on her.

"No one. Myself, really."

"We heard you earlier," Egon said. "You said my dad's name."

"Do you have an imaginary friend?" Nick was curious.

"Yes, I do." Aislin answered, hoping to quell Egon's statement. "I do, and his name's Jason, it kinda sounds like James…." she turned her eyes back to Egon, "but it is just silly me and my friend Jason."

"Why can't I see him?" Nick's eyes were the same serious green as his mother's. Her chin and dramatic features were prominent in his face. Egon took after his father's side.

"He's a little shy," Aislin said. But she wondered the same thing.

James appeared behind the boys. "Get them into the dining room, please, Aislin."

Egon noticed her abrupt jump back. Aislin tried to hide the surprise on her face, but it did not go unnoticed like James' voice. Egon's eyes narrowed at her and grew a little dark. He looked around suspiciously and she could see that he not only wore his father's looks, but his serious, inquisitive side. And Jade's severity.

"Come on. He says maybe he will join us for dinner." She extended both hands, and Nick took one with a huge grin. Egon took Nick's other hand instead and lead them down the grand staircase.

Heath greeted them at the bottom, gave Aislin a friendly, tail-whacking-air welcome. Aislin was so nervous she might get covered with his dark fur; she didn't want to pet him. The boys each hugged their big dog and began the charade of leading Heath through every known trick.

"Watch this! Watch this, A—hey lady, what's your name again?"

"Aislin."

"Aaaahhhhs-lynn?" Nick looked up at her to see if he pronounced it right. She smiled and gave a quick nod. "Okay! Aislin, watch this!" He whistled quietly and tapped his shoulder. The dog barked once, jumped, and licked the boy's nose. Then Heath rolled over, got up, turned in a circle and finally hunkered down with his nose between his paws.

All three gave reserved hoots and hollers, clapping cheerfully at the panting Heath.

"Let's go get a treat for him." Egon said and took Nick's hand, who took Aislin's, and they walked in a sideways single file to the lovely kitchen. Once Egon rewarded Heath with a treat from the enormous ceramic pot on the island, his crooked smile vanished. Aislin noticed he was looking at a clock that reminded her of a sundial. It was a swirling, wrought-iron disk with hands made from maple wood. Concrete molds marked each number. The time piece said it was 5:25 p.m.

"Nick, wash your hands." Egon directed Nick onto a soapstone stepping stool and within four remarkably quiet minutes, both boys scrubbed, dried, and entered the dining room.

Precisely as the sun dropped to shine into her beautiful home, Jade entered the great dining room from the west. Her hair caught the light, and the silhouette of her body walked to the head of the table. Once Jade was out of the glare, her face came into focus. She looked at Egon with approval and smiled at Nick. "Thank you for being on time, children."

"You're welcome, Mother. Thank you for providing us with dinner tonight." They said in unison as they took seats across from one another at one end of the long table. While she overcame her surprise at the boys' formal response, Aislin counted fourteen upholstered chairs around the grey stone slab that served as the dining room table. Each was unique in woodwork and subtle shifts of desert tones. Aislin did not hide her delight at sitting in such a grand space.

"Aislin, you can sit by Egon," Jade said. She placed the glass on the table that she brought in with her. The caramel color and added cherry said Manhattan. Jade noticed Aislin looking at it and aimed her chin into the corner where a small bar beckoned. "Be my guest."

Aislin accepted and poured herself a few fingers of peaty bourbon from an impressive selection of both crystal and libation. When she slid into an ample chair, the raw silk sighed beneath her like a cloud while an intended firmness prevented her from slouching. *Oh, nice chair. And this glass!*

She took a sip from the Tiffany Diamond Point highball and caught Nick's expectant stare out of the bottom of her glass. *Oh, no. Please don't bring up the imaginary friend thing, Nick, please.*

But she could see her plea had come too late; Nick was already looking at her expectantly. "Where is your friend Jason going to sit?"

"You've invited someone to dinner, dear?" Jade's still-fake smile failed completely. From the head of the table, she looked back and forth from Aislin to her youngest son, a question forming in her eyes.

"Aislin has an imaginary friend, Mother." Egon said with a cute smile, conveying in a mocking tone what he thought of imaginary friends. Aislin's skin flushed.

"His name is Jason." Nick chimed in with the biggest smile.

Aislin couldn't help but smile back.

Jade raised her eyebrows but said nothing.

The day of the funeral drew closer. Aislin wrestled with her emotions and witnessed the house as an outsider. All meals passed by as eerily as dinner had the first night. Aislin learned Jade had a thing for manners. She believed formal meals would instill proper behavior into her boys. There were places for play and laughter, for shouting and for activities, but equally important, there were places where one must always be quiet and polite.

According to Alen, Aislin's presence helped Jade with the boys and the dogs. Although she found the formal teachings odd, it was more concerning that their mother never tucked them in and spent little time with them. Jade wandered the house, attending to the shrines, sweeping up ash. She disappeared between the intervals of her six-hour candles.

Jade never spent time with the people who came to pay their respects. She requested that her sons and Aislin refrain as well—visitors were just too much. Someone came by once a week and filled the fridge full of measured-out meals for the week. They only made a few servings; the boys ate slowly and Jade and Aislin pushed food around their plates. Hana came by, and they sat in their enormous library together, but Jade was distant, even with Hana engaging her.

Aislin caught Jade making coffee one afternoon on a brilliant espresso machine pulled from a hidden cupboard that was now open; its existence left Aislin curious about other hidden places in Athelstan House. They washed the fancy components and the carafe. Afterward, they leaned against the counters and began the first conversation they ever really had.

"The way I see it is so many of my friend's children never say please or thank you. They never send notes to express they're grateful. I mean, not all of them. A lot of them do, of course."

"I notice that about kids, sometimes," Aislin chimed in, although she noticed it about adults, as well.

"At dinner, the boys will have formality. And maybe it's Hana, and maybe it's just me, but this culture of being polite in my house is good for us all. It provides some structure. This situation with their father is difficult and I would rather let them off the hook, but I think the boys need me to carry on like that right now."

"Yes, it's good to have a routine." Yet, Aislin saw that their routine was awkward, forced one moment and entirely absent the next. The boys' interactions with their mother were ice and fire.

Jade shoved off the counter and took her coffee mug with her. Likely adopted from James or Alen and as big as her head, it bore a long-faded advertisement. Jade sucked the chilled milk with sugary vanilla syrup and many tiny shots of espresso through her accordion, convenience-store straw. "Help yourself to whatever you want," she said.

She walked down the hall and into the gloom of her master suite, muttering something to the tune of "James would want you to be comfortable".

In Aislin's imagination, the master bedroom constructed itself from the ground up. She let her mind run with how James might have designed the window ledges, the material of the walls, a bedframe built by hand. But the image was too much. Abruptly the walls melted away and her reconstruction stopped mid-tile—she'd pictured James along with it—instantly regrettable.

She never again wanted to think of the master bedroom. If she felt bummed that no one bothered to give her the grand tour, that disappointment was now subdued. There was no reason Aislin needed a tour. She never wanted to see the private space that was behind those doors.

James had only died the previous Friday; casserole dishes and cakes arrived from the community and filled up the huge refrigerators in the kitchen. Aislin wondered if these caring souls would taper off after the funeral. More so since Jade was not giving any of them a tether.

"Is Jade in?" Sara Sidran asked, standing at the foyer door with her deep purple suit complimenting her brown eyes. Jade told Aislin she was going to the market and would be back later, but never left. She still hid in the darkness of her suite with the aroma of unidentifiable incense coming from the long hallway in the back of the house.

"She's at the market," Aislin said, keeping up the lie, trying to imagine what it would be like to receive guest after guest if she were in the widow's shoes.

Sara came in without invitation, walking through the foyer and into the kitchen where she set her '70s casserole dish down on the counter. "It's just potatoes and cheese, really, not special."

"Thank you." Aislin put the dish in the freezer.

Sara looked at her for a long time. "I remember you," she said, finally. "You came to my home for dinner once."

Aislin nodded. The memory of the holiday dinner at the Sidran's was one of her favorites. There were perhaps fifty people there. "Yes, you're Hana's friend. I remember your party."

They had a pleasant conversation. Still, Aislin let out a sigh of relief when Sara left.

But lost it only twelve minutes later when two plain-clothes detectives holding a casserole dish introduced themselves.

"I'm Detective Bretti and this is Chas, I mean Detective Lawrence."

"Hello, thank you for coming by. Jade's—"

"Oh," Bretti motioned towards the lasagna, "We actually aren't here just for this. We want to ask a few questions. Is Mrs. Athelstan home?"

"Come in." Aislin pushed the door completely open to give them access to the foyer. "She hasn't been well."

The detectives looked at each other and then down at the fancy floor. She could sense they were uneasy about disturbing the widow. "We understand. It won't take long."

She didn't want to get in the way of whatever their job was, so she took the dish off their hands and asked them to wait.

"Of course, and Miss...?"

"It's Aislin. Aislin Birch," she paused. "I'm a friend."

"Thank you, Miss Birch," said Chas Lawrence as he moved a bunch of hair out of his face. "If you have a moment, we're just talking to a few people about the last project Mr. Athelstan was working on."

"I see. I don't know much. I just drove down from Washington on Wednesday. I have some involvement with their press but know almost nothing about local stuff." She surprised herself at how she made that drive through the storm sound so easy.

The detectives looked at each other. "Okay, well. Don't worry about it, then, ma'am. We'll just wait here for Mrs. Athelstan."

Luckily, she found Jade in the kitchen getting ice cream.

A few minutes later, she watched the widow disappear with the detectives into the atrium. They were only back there for four or five minutes before rushing their goodbyes back in the foyer. They noted the sputtering fountain with a jester before pulling down the long driveway.

After that, Jade's wish for solitude became a soundless echo on the tiles. Aislin kept it for her. She also noticed that no one, not even the boys' playmates, came over for anything other than quick food drop-offs. The house became very quiet. Many people didn't even ask to see Jade and tried to hide their relief that Aislin opened the door.

It's always been too hard to counsel the grieving.

Aislin was not sure how typical it was that Jade refused almost all company. Still, after the detectives came, Aislin kept to the code: she told every caller that Jade wasn't there. The foyer helped to discourage most people from just coming into the house. She opened the door for everyone, organized the meals into the deep freeze or the fridge—one mayonnaisey dish after several kale dishes and then back to cheese.

While the outside world spun on, the sun rising twice since her arrival, Aislin preferred her room or the library. Everyone used the library. There were many crannies to hide in. One afternoon, the voice of Egon reading to Nick drew her to seek them out. Aislin delighted when a pattern developed of reading to Nick herself while Egon read something of his own, keeping a watchful eye on them from the tall stacks in the loft with an unobstructed view of the recessed section that was designed for children.

He looked so much like his father...

But in her room, she could talk to James or deliberate over revealing her secret that James was a ghost in residence. He was trying to persuade her to be silent about it. She guessed this had to do with his glimpse of her long list of cons, although suspected he had a few cons of his own. And really, she didn't want to be silent. Why, when he was there, when she drove 1,000 miles—and through one of the worst dust storms in the history of Death Valley—knowing he was dead, would she want to be quiet? Now he was so real, he seemed even more alive. He was more in touch with her ever-present emotions than he had been in real life. She wanted to speak of it, yearned to tell this secret to someone.

Although most of those real-life events took place ten-plus years ago, she remembered everything that she was too self-absorbed to pay attention to back then. She was forgetting what was important. Sitting there on the eloquent bed and brooding about the past, she was not giving any credit to this—THIS moment as actually being real life. That was an obstacle for Aislin. It has always been real life, but Aislin, dreaming through most of it, lived like it was a simulation. It was only with this recent unbearable death that she realized she was an escapist, but her avoidance made nothing less genuine. She had one life, just ask James.

She tapped her pen.

Mortality. The dust storm was pushing a positive effect on her natural and conscious instincts to survive. Yes, there were nightmares that added to the trauma of James' death, but those would soon pass by and there would be time for therapy. Gratefulness for her life was a plus side, and she would not let go of any plus side easily. Everything was different.

In the last seven years, she had been inconsiderate of her own life. She did not wear a seatbelt; she chewed the skin of her left index finger until she bled, and never mended her wounds too well, leaving traces of blood on paper, pillowcases, or the skin of her cheek while she slept. When she, clumsy as she was, almost fell on the shallow steps of a swimming pool or down a staircase, Aislin often admonished herself for catching her balance: *Why can I not just fall and crack my head open?* The war her instincts waged against her desire for death became the bane of her existence.

The tap of the pen became more rapid, harder against her leg than she was conscious of.

Aislin was constantly and completely irritated with her innate instinct to survive. Since her teens, Aislin would often envision herself pulling the trigger. A voice shouted to jump in front of a train, or to swallow the worst of things. The first time she followed through with it, she swallowed a whole bottle of Tylenol. She was sixteen. She looked at the red cap and thought that all the pain could disappear. Instead of escape, her attempts with pills and slicing her wrist spurred three foster-family failures; it turned out they did not like to take her to get her stomach pumped. A mailman interrupted the time she tried to drown herself in the harbor. That was almost two years prior to James' death. She swallowed hard at how badly time itself hurt.

The pen picked up speed, no rhythm, just her finger flicking it down, down again when it bounced off her thigh.

Early in 2008, she remembered the call like it was yesterday. Exhausted on her couch, after a long week of wheeling 70-pound cheese wheels around the store, stocking shelves, and completing the quarterly inventory, her phone rang. "Aislin, it's Alen."

"I know!" she beamed at him over the distance.

"Hey, I need some pieces on a few buildings up there in Seattle for the press. I'll pay you. You would join our freelance team. We need photographs, too." Alen then detailed the job for the Athelstan brothers' relatively new creative business—an architectural and travel journal. He wanted her to cover the northwest if this initial assignment pleased his editor-in-chief.

"I would be delighted! Oh my god, thank you, Alen!" A wave of emotion swept through her, rekindling faith that she was a talented writer.

She wore a calm pride and happiness to her primary job as a grocery-store clerk so nonchalantly that her boss and the customers noticed nothing but a slight glow they attributed to a restful day off. But she knew her job wasn't just to stock produce anymore; it was also to produce content.

Aislin reviewed the first few issues of the press, looked at the photos, researched the history of buildings. The first assignment was the Saint Spiridon Russian Orthodox Cathedral in the Cascade neighborhood of Seattle. Blossoms covered the trees lining the streets. Hard afternoon showers could scarcely knock off an eighth of them, yet still created dense floral pathways. The motion of walking in practical boots through the damp dogwood blossoms gave her the travel bug. She returned to Seattle season after season for subsequent visits to Pike Place Market and the historic China Gate Restaurant.

The additional income allowed her to reduce her hours at the store, but not much. Gig Harbor's cost of living was only increasing. Travel soon varied up north to Vancouver and beyond the English Bay, covering Victoria and the San Juan Islands. She might tour Puget Sound. Another trip would take her south, down the coast to Astoria. Head inland to Portland to showcase homes of the West Hills, Nobb Hill, or Laurelhurst neighborhoods. Her specialty became mausoleums in some of the Northwest's mossiest cemeteries, such as the Macleay Mausoleum at Lone Fir Cemetery. It was lovely to have a contrast to Coachella Valley's Frey House II and the cemetery with the Athelstan plots. Alen did the introductory piece on the pyramid mausoleums of California, but left the curiosity for Aislin to procure.

The pen tapped slower as memory took over. On a sunny day about three years after starting for the press that Alen developed into a fantastic publication, her lovebirds were having their normal out-of-cage time around the house. Aislin still worked at the store, never feeling quite confident enough to quit her day job, although she had reduced her hours to twenty-four a week—more during inventory periods. Everything was working like clockwork.

While Aislin took a long shower to wash the sweat of the store off, Eurydice spoiled her assignment. She tore the photos into uneven strips and excreted over the remainder of the synopsis. The deadline approached too quickly to replace the developed photos. The postage, also destroyed, made her time, money, and art—worth nothing.

Dropping her towel, sopping wet and in a fit of blind rage, she screamed at the bird. The startled bird flew and crashed into the living room window. The impact forced a small squawk and exhale of air from the bird's lungs as Eurydice's neck snapped against the glass. On the floor, the brown poly-blend of the shag carpet obliterated the tiny face, swallowing the vivid-red beak. Eurydice was completely still. Aislin rushed to the bird, her anger erased as overwhelming guilt and horror guided her into shame.

"What have I done? What have I done?" Next to Eurydice's pocket-sized body, Aislin curled naked on the floor, her towel in the same place as when she had discovered the mess and made the two-yard long strides from the bathroom door to the coffee table. She stroked her head as Orpheus hopped around and tore the last scraps of the postage to pieces. Aislin fell asleep on the floor, tears and snot in her mouth, exhausted from emotion. She woke to feel feathers and a little beak against her skin. And there was Orpheus, the bird that escaped the onslaught of her vicious outburst, softly chewing at her fingers.

Eurydice died by her own hand. Aislin had never gotten their wings clipped, and perhaps a failure to launch could have saved her. Her Eurydice and Orpheus, one disappearing before the eyes of the other.

She waited until early spring to throw Eurydice off a bridge in her little tin coffin. Her tears would never dry, and the calm and faith that had visited Aislin left as if it were just some old friend, staying when they were in town for a conference. Never to call again, never to send a thank-you note. That peace stole away, replaced by a paranoia that was true and deep. The binding knot in her stomach tightened as a creeping conviction took hold: she was not a good person. She removed her rain boots and climbed over the rail. It was cold, but sunlight made its way through a patch of clouds. The clouds drifted; stillness and quiet enveloped her, and she drifted into the decision. The current flowed strong and cold enough to freeze her. She leaned, her right foot followed her upper body, her hands contracted in preparation to release. The right hand first.

"Hey!" The silence broke and sent nearby birds into the air. The urgency in the letter-carrier's voice carried over the water. He grabbed her shoulder, which steadied her remaining foot with so much force her back hit the rail, and she scrambled for balance, the survival instinct kicking in.

In the end she had somehow swiveled around and both feet were stable, toes gripping the edge of the bridge while all white knuckles held fast. Her scream echoed. Face to face with the letter-carrier's glass-green eyes and full lips—his arresting good looks made her forget the reason she was even there, at least for a moment.

Once she was back in her boots and warm, he delivered the rest of his mail. "Can I come check in on you later?"

Her answer came as an unwavering 'yes'. They had sex almost immediately upon his arrival. When he asked her if she was trying to commit suicide, she lied and said she was just trying to get a better look at something the birds were eating. While she didn't feel exactly grateful to this man, she did feel very attracted to him. His posture held something of James'. The man worked on another island and although he carried through on his promise to come back; she didn't answer the door.

His previous visit had created a replacement memory for the bridge. The attempt to use him as a distraction for what she was about to do did not hold. All the pain and anguish came flooding back when he knocked only three days later. But she got up, she went to work, and she saw the sun rise and she noted how it rose again and again. And again. Until watching the sun rise became a liturgy that she didn't know she needed.

Her tapping pen picked up speed again. Would her depression have lifted if she had not left Hana, James, and Alen in her early twenties? Would her struggles have been less overwhelming if she had her people? They were the only family she warmed to since her parents passed, and the only ones who warmed to her in return. She remembered Hana's stews and how, even on a hot day, they were comforting. They filled her fridge for three years of her college life. But any love she found for herself when she was in Palm Desert left her, largely and unapologetically. It wasn't just the food that bonded them together. And now that she was there with them, she understood what the distance had really meant for her.

She was made of all of this. *It is what it is.* Except she did not believe that statement at all. Aislin wanted to take James by the shoulders and shake his dead-self back to life. She also wanted to be at home in her bed in Gig Harbor, hiding from the world.

Truthfully, except for the assignments and days when she dragged herself to work, after the bird died, Aislin didn't leave her house as often. She had a tiny apartment overlooking the vine-covered walls of a church. It was quiet. Orpheus was sad, and she brought home a mandatory replacement to ease his disconsolation.

She adored her lovebirds, Eurydice II and Orpheus, spoiled them from her heart of shame, buying the largest atrium that would fit in the room, filled it with toys and fed them fresh fruits, boiled eggs, dinosaur kale, and a wide variety of seeds and nuts. Dismayed, she'd left them with her boss because of this—this trip, this death, this situation with unbelievable effects. What were they eating now? Were they back to cabbage and store-bought birdseed? She tried not to think about it.

Their new owner was likely not a bird killer, right? It was all she could hope for. A better home than she had given Eurydice I. She knew she was too hard on herself, that she magnified the guilt for the death of the bird. Yet, this self-talk was hard to overcome. Labeling it was only a start. Cognitive distortions were her specialty.

Thankfully, I had that entire drive through the desert to call it what it is.

Silver lining. Catch it while you can.

Reality: it was an accident. Balance: I startled my bird; it could have happened to anyone. Guilt and shame might be BFFs and they routed their tunnels in my brain back and forth, digging the deepest trenches until I was nothing but the belief I clung to. That I murdered my bird. This reasoning and new pathway must be stronger; I must start again. Also, reality: she was a defenseless animal. A beautiful animal. I asked for forgiveness and trust I will be a better person, trust that I will learn to pause before I react.

Her eyes rested on her right hand. It had only been since Death Valley that her index finger had not broken open. That marked the beginning of a huge conflict in her desire to make it to James' funeral alive. After all, she did not stay lost in the desert, indifferent if no one came along.

Yes, something stirred inside that she didn't recognize.

She slouched over the nightstand, freeing her tapping pen to write James a letter. A long time had passed since her addiction to writing James ended. But back in the desert again, the letters were as prolific as when they first met. This letter was to be set apart from all the rest. This letter was overdue, covering a topic she never had the courage to face. Aislin needed to tell James the real reason she'd left Palm Desert.

September 27, 2013

Dear James,

Over ten years have passed since I have seen the red-swollen nose, but it's still before me. I don't know why I never really told you about Cliff.

Some nights, I didn't sleep at all. Every noise on the long catwalk outside my apartment was him banging on the window or pushing his stolen key in the lock. I didn't change the locks because it was a shared apartment. You might remember that Cliff and my roommate Holly were friends. I couldn't talk to her.

The nights he came were long and painful. Sometimes he would be in the bathroom throwing up, so drunk, and I would wonder what would happen if I wasn't there when he came back. But I would stay—lying on the bed in his stink and think of you.

I would dream of the day I would have different circumstances: move, afford a new deposit in a place he would not find. But he would prey. I knew his false charm would destroy a different girl. And for her, I would cry so hard my heart would seize for a moment. If I didn't save them from this monster, who would?

I wasn't a martyr, but a small part of me still loved him as the first boy that paid attention to me in Gig Harbor. Foster homes sent me back into the rain again and again. And here was this rich boy. I followed him to college in the desert. He took my hand, my virginity, but he never took me home to meet his parents.

Toward the end, he cheated so much I was getting an STD test practically every week. The move back to Gig Harbor was the only thing I could do to end his abuse. I sold everything. When I left the sun, I left you. But I was alive.

For years, I was always turning into the next storm. On my way to your funeral, I was caught in another one, a physical storm like the one that took my parents away, but dry and dusty with sand in my teeth ever since. I recall those times with Cliff—I never had the courage to leave him until it was too late, and I lost you to another woman.

Ever, Aislin

Aislin folded the letter and tucked it into the nightstand for later.

Chapter 10 ✦ James

From the passenger's seat, James looked at Alen. He had been dead seven entire days. He missed his little brother; the longing carried a sharpness to it. He craned his neck back to look at the building as Alen pulled out of the bar's cramped parking lot. No pain in his neck where just the week before there was the strain of a long day.

In the restaurant worked a beautiful woman with straight black hair and golden eyes. James watched Alen watch her during every meal. Her eyes found a way to Alen's eyes again and again. It happened this way for five years. The flirting, the dates, the slowly getting acquainted. James did not know all the reasons neither of them would commit to spending any real time with the other. She was not at the hostess station—thankfully sparing Alen an interaction. James preferred to avoid another pained conversation about his death between two people who shared pained conversations about their day to day.

Since college, the brothers ate pastrami together in this place; they served the best sandwiches in the entire valley. It was not really a dive bar; they considered it more like a local relic. The sandwiches really were that good.

When they walked out into the late evening sun to leave, two detectives, another pair of regulars, walked in. James looked straight into their faces. Nothing to hide. They could not see him. He realized he would never again get in trouble with the law. It was something that he would never have to worry about. Not that he ever misbehaved anymore, anyway. And he knew these guys; they had all been eating pastrami for as long as he remembered. James turned forward and paid attention to the present.

The wind may have tunneled from one window through the other and music may have blasted from the dashboard and into the atmosphere, but James only knew stillness and silence next to his brother in the truck. He closed his eyes and imagined the two absent things orchestrating around the cab; perhaps the wind held the vibrations of sounds in its arms, perhaps they kissed, a forbidden affair.

It was not what James would have picked. Glancing over at the album cover, he watched his brother's long fingers delicately place the Nirvana CD into the stereo. Alen turned the volume up and rolled up both windows. James could imagine what that was like: cut off from the interference of the wind, the speakers assaulted Alen full force. But he could not sense it, not a thumping base, not the possible unease of having the volume too loud. James pretended it was Albinoni's Adagio in G minor for Strings, or a concerto played by the London Philharmonic or his recent obsession with chamber and baroque pop with electronic elements and without. And of course the modern cinematic: always to include a soundtrack written by Danny Elfman.

James could have kept the list going, yet a hellish realization stopped him. He was dead in a world he could not hear music in. Could he hear a violin played before him? Would music other than the human voice be lost to him forever? What about a flute, would the breath of a human influence whether the sound could reach him? A harmonica?

He swore to not go crazy thinking of this absence, which created an additional dimension of his present hell. Only when the vocal cords of the living vibrated, was he sure he could hear at all: a bird through the window, a dog in the distance. But it took him seven days to realize this included music. He attempted to think instead of Alen's music tastes. His brother always preferred grunge and punk. James watched him turn up the bass and sensed that Alen took in the energy thumping from his far traveled and well-loved little truck. Alen shared James' loathing of money, but it was much more about waste. Waste or disposal of anything annoyed Alen, so he pledged to keep his truck running until he died.

Alen hummed during a few sections, but otherwise did not sing or speak. James did not really like Nirvana, but he wanted the choice back. The choice to turn it down, the choice to chide his brother for his taste in music. This new jealousy frustrated James—he could not feel the bass to a band he was indifferent to. The desire to know that bass again, to hear the notes... even if it was only grunge forever, he did not care; he wanted it.

He forcibly switched his focus to the absence of the sound of other things like the tinkering of the train or the sound of tires on pavement, things he did not really care about. The sound of jackhammers, L.A. freeways, the dishwasher, the steam cleaner, tile saw, aerosol cans, nails on a chalkboard, the pounding of nails putting on a new roof for days and days. All that was gone. And it was not so terrible.

Alen pulled into the parking lot of the church. He parked and turned the engine off. Nothing changed as James watched the key turn. The silence did not increase. He could not sense the settling of the motor's energy. James could tell from the stereo panel that the music played on. It was so quiet.

It was weird to watch his moonlit brother while under the thrall of this auditory rift. The rhythm in the music suddenly animated Alen. He hit his hands against the steering wheel, flicking his fingers sideways with the beat of the song. Any shame James harbored for being jealous of his brother did not lessen his ache for the music.

They had arrived early. He begrudged his brother a little for leaving Jade and Aislin alone at the house for long periods of time. But the stress was eating at them all, and he granted Alen needed breaks. He recalled Victoria, the girl who worked in the bar. There could be some relief and happiness in Alen's life.

His wake, a celebration of his life, a time to sing, to witness the melting of one thousand candles with far-away gazes. All of this was about to unfold inside. Through the open window, he counted everyone as they went in. They all dressed down compared to tomorrow. Tomorrow, his funeral. Suits and lace gowns with black veils over brimmed hats. The cathedral first. He did not want to think of it, the way his mother would look in mourning clothes. Mourning him. Wakes were lovely, of course, but tomorrow, the way the Catholic tradition had everyone dressing up for the dead was almost a spectacle. This out-of-nowhere slam on the church reminded him of rebellious years.

His brother crossed himself. He wondered why; almost as if they thought the same thing. His brain immediately seized on that assumption: Alen would never slam the church. He was unwavering in his devotion and had been since his youth: catechisms, endless matins. James wavered.

Anyway, where was that god now?

The energy coming from Alen was up and down. James heard something in the way his heart would beat erratically, in the way he would hold his breath while eating everything in sight, noticed the way Alen slept on the couch with his eyes half open, never making it to his bedroom during the last week. For hours and hours, he sat on his white leather couch, more hours standing at the sink with the water running down the drain, James not able to turn it off. It was out-of-character for the man who wasted nothing in his control. In the truck light now, his brother's eyes sunk in. The shadows lengthened his face and his hands shook as he took his keys out of the ignition and put them in his suit-coat pocket.

Alen rummaged around, possibly looking for something. James watched, but did not pay attention. His consciousness flowed from its auditory fascination to other concerns about the afterlife that scared him through. He struggled with the darkness. He sought firelight and moonlight and especially sunlight. Other lights were sometimes detectable when at least one natural light was with him, once he saw the faint outline of a digital clock and tonight, the light in the belfry and a few dashboard lights. Would he ever hear the church-bells ring again? Thankfully, the arriving vehicles distracted him from the painful answer.

He watched the parking lot. As the frail frame that was now his wife climbed out of their oversized vehicle, James brought his mind completely to his family. He watched Alen abandon whatever he'd been searching for and climb out of the cab.

Friday night, the time of his wake, had fallen. The sun had set without him noticing, but the early autumn skies were not to be darkened and the early rising of a third-quarter moon provided the lumens James needed to watch his sons follow their mother inside the church—Hana, Aislin, and Alen on their heels.

Chapter 11 ✦ James

FAMILIAR: THESE CHURCH DOORS. UNFAMILIAR: A THREATENING SILENCE, being derailed by the mere idea of stepping over the threshold. He hesitated: walls might form up around him while the darkness waited to take his sight. What did it mean for him to enter a church for his own wake? Did it mean anything? His knee bent, the ankle flexed and extended, and once back at neutral, his first foot was over. And then the second. The action of a deep breath, the absence of oxygen, the height of his bewilderment as his eyes drew to the candles burning in the next room. He was in. He could see everything. The next moment, James stood observing grief that could not be absorbed; he could not cry for it, run from it, could do nothing but watch it work through the room.

Every candle glowed and light bounced off every set of open eyes. A sneeze echoed, and someone heavily cleared their throat.

The two women he loved dressed similarly, which surprised them both. They knelt on the bench in stylish black linen pants and shirts, but they could not look more different. Although both women were pale by nature, Jade, despite grief changing her appearance, still managed to look sun kissed. Makeup? Perhaps, but unlikely given the rare amount he had seen her grooming herself or even showering since his death. Aislin seemed to look more natural, more at ease, which he found strange in conjunction with his breath going down her neck from beyond.

Jade's fine, dark hair contrasted nicely, albeit sharply with lighter skin and bright eyes. Her features were angular, with pointy elbows and protruding collarbones. Aislin was softer, though not soft; her eyes were sad where Jade's gaze seemed pleading. Aislin's hair, thick and on the blondish side of brown, swept around her body in subtle waves. It hid the thinness of her collarbones and all at once, anyone looking that far down turned back to her sad, hazel eyes.

It confounded James that he could watch them both at once. He forced his eyes away, as if it could change the guilt that crept over him. He had caught himself comparing the two women he loved so deeply. It was foreign to him, after all this time.

Eager to focus elsewhere, James fingered through the pockets of his jeans. A piece of lint provided him so much comfort that longing and nostalgia replaced its insignificance, expounding the incongruity that he could feel the lint at all.

James knew with certainty, on his seventh day of death, that he could only hear living things. The silence of the synthetic caused a rift in what James previously believed was the auditory experience: he continued to dwell on the absence of music. But reminded himself that he could still hear the birds sing, he could hear Egon whistle and his own mother hum as she tried to drown out the sorrow of losing her son. She would not cry. Not his mother, who had brought her family here when the land that was once Yugoslavia again changed to a world of violence and sorrow.

But on the second day of his passing, he had yet to discover many of these things. It took time for James to find his mother's house. He walked down the wrong street, then took only more wrong turns. He was impatient and reluctant to admit a growing change in his senses, his understanding of how things should have been.

When he finally arrived, his majka was humming. It was a few hours before sunset. Her song so acutely narrated a sadness that eclipsed all tears. James watched his grieving mother, more dispirited than he had ever seen her in his life, as he heard the first verse push through her lips. Mostly humming, a few words found sound on the air. Throughout his life, watching her grieve over his father always provoked protectiveness of her. James might have had his defiant years, but he tried to take care of her, never wanting to see her with another broken heart.

She forced the tune further into its story, but it came against her lips as if she wanted nothing more than to just sit silently.

James once knew the words of this song she hummed, but he could not remember the name of it anymore. He knew it was from her people; he knew she had taught him and his brother to sing it when they lived in Central Europe and that she reminded them of it later when his father died. Majka did not verbalize her wish for the words to be lost, but he did not hear her sing often at all after the fire. When musicians revived Sevdalinka into Bosnian mainstream in the twenty-first century, James played them for her, but he never pushed her into listening to it. It was his dream that they might someday collect artists new and old, sit in his library and he would say, "Majka, tell me of the ones my grandparents loved."

Hana was so young when she lost her family and community. Few survived. James bowed his head in honor of his ancestors that experienced the horrors of the Holocaust. Those songs belonged to them. Now, he only wanted to remember all the words he once sung alongside her. They were the scents of the fauna, the voices of lovers, and the sound of water. That was Sevdalinka.

The way music resonated from her throat captivated James. Leaving her that night would have been a second death. As total darkness fell, James feared he would not be able to see, but by some grace, the moon flooded into the windows and her lit candles provided him with the security he yearned for. He did not go outside to make sure the sun rose. To James, nothing mattered more than an all-night vigil with the woman who brought him into the world.

He thought about breathing, how she had given him his breath and his life, and another song sang out in his head, amongst his mother's humming, the violins and angelic soprano of the musicians *Lost in the Trees*. Although this admired song, "The Dead Bird is Beautiful" was an elegy for the composer's mother, and the roles were reversed, the lyrics swam through James, clef notes raising a sob toward his throat. James looked into Hana's face, the words of the song were dust in his drying mouth.

He looked deep into her eyes and squeezed his own shut. James loved that song; but would never hear it again. His tears came, leaving no moisture, leaving no tracks, without becoming tiny molecules of water and salt. Without the sting.

By the time morning swept over the walls of the house, the whole structure shuddering in the slow light, her humming totally consumed him. And it was James who made his way amongst Palo Verde, Yucca Elata, and Fruitless Palms, not knowing what would come next.

The wake brought the attendance of his family and their close friends. Jade sat near Aislin. Nick and Egon kneeling by her side. Hana knelt with care at the end of the row with Egon. Her hand covered the boy's left hand and his other arm rested low around his grandmother's shoulders. James' eldest son's presence seemed to still the old woman's shakes as she took long and even breaths.

"Hana...." Jade reached around her sons' small heads to stroke her mother-in-law's waning shoulder and said her name with a soothing whisper that tugged James' heart.

Alen sat right behind his mother with Rodney, their best friend and loyal employee, and Rodney's family in the second row. Two girls under ten sat by their father and a very tiny baby boy lay close to the chest of his wife, Irene. They were a sight to behold, each beautiful face glowing in the steady candlelight.

He wished he could smell the incense. He wished he could smell the baby and pat his friend Rodney on the back. Rodney Welsh had been their foreperson since the conception of the business. He was a professional and a hard worker. He never said no to a steep roof, and in the early days that always mattered to Alen and James. They needed someone who was dependable and practical about falling off of a building. "It happens," Rodney would say, "but try to avoid it, man."

He listened to the same detectives he always saw in the bar. They lurked in the hallway, chattering about the great food the wife made. *Why are they here?* Perhaps they were friends of Alen's or the Welshes, though James thought their behavior odd. They stopped speaking, and he turned back to his family, no longer concerned.

James closed his eyes. He listened to the breathing, always more breathing. He listened as his mother began to say a prayer and he listened to the Welsh family echo her, to Eleanor's high voice as she chimed in a bit late on each verse, and to Alen as he whispered along. That this chorus of sorrow rose to nothing but wooden beams hit James hard, but he had encountered nothing else that might hear it.

Abandonment washed over him.

Everyone stood after the prayer, but with his eyes closed, he was unaware. Unable to detect the sound of shuffling, he opened his eyes when he heard Aislin's quiet voice say his name.

He rode with them back to his house in his fancy big truck with the windows down. Aislin drove their truck through the lazy palm trees in the lazy breeze that he could not even feel. Jade had bought the truck with expectations. He was to pick up the boys on certain weekdays, a heavy-duty work truck to fit his work-life, yet all tricked out to entertain the boys. Instead, it just blasted noise in the face of quality time. He hated the money and all the technology.

The iceberg of silence in the car between Aislin and Jade prompted his boys to turn the movie on in their giant back seat. They sat staring at the screen, barely paying attention.

October 10, 2005

Dear Aislin,

I write you in October now. And I have to wonder of
my changes. Was it because of the money? All I can
think of is all the ways we spend and do not spend the
dollars. Jade and her ideas. She is always asking for
philanthropic giants and I just want to save it and
rebuild something in my heart. The figures add up as
these books come out. Do you even read them?

All the bidding, more money. It is coming. I
accidentally sent myself a letter I wrote to you. I
was playing some word game and the words refused me.
it was strange. There was something in the rain, as
well, a darkness that found its way between the lines.
Then I slept and you remember rain in the desert, that
is always a good night.

love, James

Chapter 12 ✦ James

THE DAY OF HIS FUNERAL JAMES WAS RESTING HIS HEAD IN HIS ARMS. He did not need the rest and he knew that, but something about the motions of rest calmed him. Eyes that used to be physical eyes were suddenly never dry and did not need to blink. He used those eyes to stare down at the green and black patterns that were the primary colors of the kitchen's massive marble island. Nothing hummed. Once again, nothing buzzed. The ice machine did not make a noise as it made ice, and the ice did not clank as it fell into its frozen basin. He concentrated on the unpolished, swirling pattern.

Honed stone had always brought home the wonder of the earth. As an architect and a homebuilder, James loved combining these elements indoors. He sat up sharply and wondered if it would be his last day to enjoy it, critique it, wonder what he might have done differently. Should he have brought more elements of his far-off home of Bosnia-Herzegovina to this desert? He still wished he had built a fireplace in the kitchen big enough for a hanging kettle.

Jade had hated the idea. She protested and assumed sootiness and James compromised, although he was sure she would have loved it after some time. He could imagine teaching Egon to clean it the way he loved to as a boy—his favorite chore—probably the reason he became a home builder. "See son, this is what it means to care for something so it endures." James could almost hear his son asking questions about mortar and arches. It would have been great to show him how to be a steward. The way to keep things beautiful meant dedication. It meant necessary and fulfilling work.

Their home was already suffering neglect. The time to teach his sons had ended.

Aislin appeared under the carved corner crossettes of the kitchen entrance. She could not always see him when he was there, but this time he sensed she could feel him. There was a look in her eyes as she moved to sit on the wooden stool next to him that said she would be there—that she would not leave him. She reached her right hand out and placed it on the table, right where his hand was. For a moment, he closed his eyes and tried to become real. He did not like that she could see him sometimes, but during others, she was just as unconscious of his presence as Jade was. And the in-between times? Those times grew longer as time passed.

He opened his eyes and noticed both her hands covered his. Crinkles in the corners of her eyes deepened from the pressure of squeezing them shut. A shake resonated from her throat, a silent cry that he sensed was a secret perfected to hide her private misery. He may have been blind to this before, but in this new reality, he picked up on it instantly. Yet possibly his memory of her was incorrect. He remembered a woman he put on a pedestal.

He did not want to make her jump by speaking. She could sense him; had slowly gained awareness and had kept the silence. He knew Aislin tried to comfort him by holding the hand they could not feel. She shared in his apprehension.

"Have you had any contact with, I don't know, anything else, anyone else?" Finally, Aislin broke the silence with a question James hoped to avoid, if only for his total ignorance and fear.

"There were shadows this morning. In the dawn light, I saw them watch me."

"What do you think they wanted?" He sensed her terror at the thought that something otherworldly could be present, which seemed incompatible with her quick acceptance of his spirit. Concerning as that was, he sensed more—humans used love to reason with fear and vice versa. Perhaps it was as simple as Aislin not wanting anything to harm him. Were these shades something that could change this unfathomable situation that they already could not control?

"I am not sure they wanted anything." James was unsure. But he spoke mostly to put her at ease. "Aislin, I am already dead. Nothing bad can happen to me."

The night he thought he was in Hell flashed before his eyes. Of course, she picked up how little he believed his own words. James knew from what he could not see in the darkness of night that anything was conceivable. The darkness haunted him the same way he haunted Aislin. Would there be any change after the living's impending goodbyes? The course remained obscure.

He had thought to ask Aislin not to say goodbye, to tell her he was not ready, to ask her to wait a little longer. But in their culture, funerals were more for the living—not really for the dead. It was a ceremony of memory, of closure. James wanted her to have that. He did not want her to be the only one that knew he was still here when everyone else held the notion that he was at peace.

She will say goodbye to me today. Finally.

He knew it was not true, that she would not have closure, and the expectation that there was closure came from so much denial and fear of death. He knew that when someone died, the 'missing' did not go away. It did not lessen with time. Grief lasted as long as the other person was dead, and although that was not as comforting as the ill-conceived concept of closure, it was more honest. He still grieved for his father; his mother still grieved. But sometimes, when time was just so, and maybe the light or a certain smell came, they remembered that he also lived. James wanted that for his family; he wanted them to remember that he lived.

His death was not the way he imagined himself dying. He should have been on a farm, far from everything. Struggling with fishing poles and holes in his hat. A rowboat waiting at the shore. He would die beneath a walnut tree, and no pain would be present.

He had once written in a letter to Aislin that the birds would sit still that day. His eyes would close upon an old face in an emptiness as great as the ocean of why-nots, could-haves and what-ifs. And his grandfathers would wait for him, and there would be soup from his grandmothers. And then he remembered these were people he never even met.

September 28, 2013

Dearest Aislin,

Today, I feel that peace is not meant to be mine as James Athelstan. I look over at the gathering. You stand like Palo Verde around our family plot. I count how many fingers and legs and eyes and mouths I may never see again—that I was never supposed to see again. I hope I feel differently tomorrow.

I walk over to the Palo Verde. It shelters, although not like an ash or a birch. When I first saw your name, it was in Times New Roman at the top of a short story you wrote and now you see mine in something like Old English on my tombstone. It is most likely not the last time you will ever see my name because if I know you, you will read and re-read this letter that I do not even know how I am writing and I will sign it "ever, James" or "love, James" like I always have.

I get up the courage to come closer and listen to Father Benjamin's voice. He has a lovely voice; wrought with kindness, and I hear no tinge of judgement. That softens my heart. I thought about the day my eulogy would be read and what it might say, but I never imagined the tone of the person reading it.

And I picture this letter, I picture each curl of my writing, each letter painstakingly perfect, but you will never read it because it is all in my head.

Ever, James

Chapter 13 ✦ Aislin

JUST LIKE AISLIN HAD, THE RAIN CAME TO THE DESERT FOR THE FUNERAL. With one hand shielding the drops from her eyes, Aislin took Nick's small hand in her other. He walked up to her and Alen as soon as his feet hit the grass. Slowly, Egon and Hana followed together, their hands interlocked. Jade went to their side, and Hana also took her daughter-in-law's hand. The six of them walked toward the gravesites.

The headstones of significance were side-by-side, one beat by years of hot desert sunshine and the other new and shiny. They had erected a black tent above James' grave so that the rain would not fill the hole. The nylon angles looked fierce against the grey sky. A green tarp protected his father's resting place from trampling feet. As they neared, she could read the ageless epitaphs on each: "EDWARD JAMES / ATHELSTAN 1931–1994 / Beloved Father / and Husband." And a less than a yard away, "JAMES BENJAMIN / ATHELSTAN / 1979–2013 / Beloved Father / and Husband."

Someday, Hana would rest on the other side of Edward, and Jade would be to James' right with their children and Alen. The whole of the Athelstans here. Should Alen have a family, plots were still available. The Birch plot was only for two. No one paid for the plot of an orphan.

She shuddered. When the state buried her parents, she read about cemeteries on an official funeral website: "An 8½ foot front by 17 feet deep will give six graves with headstones."[1] People buried their loved ones by these standards for over 100 years. Today, James.

And there he is.

Across the grass, James leaned against a tree trunk. *Not in the shade, though. The sun has almost left this place, it cannot cast a shadow.* She could tell it was enough light for him. The clouds were thinning, and the storm would not last long. His gaze was off toward the mountain sans snowcaps. He didn't even look over at the gathering crowd before he appeared at her side.

"Should I leave? I cannot decide if I should stay. I should leave."

She shook her head. *No...*

"What? Yes? Leave?"

She looked into his eyes, hoping her eyes revealed to him her desperation, a plea that he would stop asking her questions that she could not answer. *Not here, not now.*

"Just, I will wait... I will stand... over there by the gates."

Through her sadness, Aislin managed a small smile and the smallest nod to indicate she agreed with him. *Wherever you want to be, just please, please do not talk to me now.*

James' hands tunneled into the small comfort of his pockets; he walked away kicking at the taller grasses and flowers that did not stir at his understandable disappointment.

Nick's hand tightened into Aislin's. She turned to see a small face looking up, eyes wet and red, nose running. *Is he looking at me, or for God?* She wondered, but wherever his thoughts were, they changed the moment he seemed to remember that Alen was there, too. The young boy pulled her across the grass to his uncle's side. Alen quickly wiped his nephew's nose, his arm went around the tiny shoulders, and his other arm linked into his mother's.

Hana looked over at Aislin. And although she did not smile, a look of warmth and regard swept across the woman's face. Her strong brow was just as she remembered, and the lines on her face seemed unchanged in the years they were apart. Perfectly shaped lips drew into the smile that melted Aislin's heart; that always made her feel at home. The only home she knew since her parents died.

Dark eyes flecked with light brown shone even under the low grey of the impossible day, pulling Aislin further into the familiar warmth. Hana stepped towards Aislin and hugged her.

"It has been a long time since you have eaten my stew. You need some," she said, and pulled back to look at Aislin, who tenderly held her elbows. James' mother kept her long arms outstretched, five-each of her bony fingers strong on each of Aislin's shoulders, "Look at you."

Hana's voice was kind, motherly. And like earlier that week, Aislin's heart swelled from the hug, the touch. Her tongue thickened with the memory of her own mother and the way Hana always welcomed her to the Athelstan table. Listened to stories about her parents, had sat and taught her lace making and embroidery over Christmas breaks while the boys watched movies and carved nativity figurines from wood as their father had taught them.

Hana always opened her home to people. She loved to cook and feed whomever stopped by her doorstep. And there were many over the years. Her clients, the children of the lawyers she worked with, all of Alen and James' friends. Thanksgivings were potlucks that crowded their small apartment, and after James and Alen had success in business, Aislin heard how the festivities grew in the larger homes.

Aislin noted how the raindrops and her fresh tears distinguished themselves from each other. Cool rain smelled like ozone parted by itchy salt and when it finally touched her lips, she enjoyed an unexpected warmth. Hana took her in with large, glossy eyes. Their happiness to see each other a muddy mix with the surroundings. Aislin wiped her face with her shirtsleeve.

"Come over for food, Aislin dear. Come this week, it has been so long, and I can hear what life has been for you. You can tell me about your home."

"I will," Aislin said, emotion preventing her from more words.

Hana gently released Aislin and turned to Alen. She pulled at her veil. "Alen, help me, dear."

"My pleasure, Majka." Alen turned to help her.

He lifted her veil. Just like James, he had her deep eyes, curly hair, and light brown skin.

And Aislin smiled at his words. They all called her Majka as a nickname. Her mind's eye wrote out the pronunciation for the word for mother in Bosnian, *MAIK-AH*.

Nick began to whine the moment his uncle released him, but Jade jerked the blade of her hand across her neck. A second later, Jade's face softened toward the boy, and he relaxed as Alen finished with his task and claimed Nick's tiny hand.

Aislin studied everyone in order to avoid staring at James, who stood yards across the graves. Father Benjamin began reading from his tattered books. As he spoke, the gentle waves of his voice sent her eyes across the lawn. James sat on the brick wall near the front gates. He was watching his children bury their father. He was watching his mother bury her firstborn.

The rain fell hard on the top of the tent and ran off its sides in a spittery-spattery coolness that should not have chilled her to the core but did. Aislin looked over at Jade, whose lanky black dress hung off her bones. *Which of us will win the competition for weight loss?* Although she had seen Jade eat a pint or two of marshmallow, peanut butter, and chocolate ice cream, there was barely anything else consumed. She knew those calories burned off as Jade cried herself to sleep. She pulled her shawl closer, shielding her skin from the weather.

Aislin wondered, once again, why she was staying with the family.

Guilt frustrated her during the sermon. She should pay attention to Father Benjamin's words or perhaps she should comfort the small child who was still gripping on hands for security.

No more 'shoulding.'

This one wasn't her word. It was a counseling word. "Don't should yourself." Echo talk-therapist. She let herself go back into the book where she first read about this concept. It wasn't about what we should and shouldn't do, and it wasn't about judgment. Do not judge, but acknowledge the moment, how it makes you feel and accept it and move on. No saying, for example, "I should have gone to therapy instead of just reading about it. I should have gotten out of the house more."

No more 'shoulding.' Spacing out on James' eulogy makes me a little unfocused, and I would like to pay attention to the rest.

Father Benjamin began another prayer. "Even as I walk through the valley   of the shadow..."

Aislin lifted her eyes to find James standing in a puddle. Not looking wet, not looking any different than he had hours ago within the green-grey walls of his kitchen. She ached to touch his hair, to cry into him, to kiss his moistless lips.

Chapter 14   ✦   Hana

"IT TOOK ME A LONG TIME TO TRUST PEOPLE, AND I STILL DO NOT know if I do." Hana spoke to Alen as he drove home from the cemetery. She rode to her firstborn child's funeral with her grandchildren, but she had an overwhelming desire to be near her second child. Her second child was still alive.

She discerned that he—being among the few she confided in—better understood the religious struggle of these long years. Alen's thorough study of the history of the Balkans proved he better understood why she kept distance. He stopped asking about her hesitancies and accepted them. They both attended mass regularly, and those walls sheltered her. But when it came to trusting many others in their parish, Hana remembered. Her hesitancy ebbed and flowed over the years, as did her confidence in the world.

What Hana lived through as a child repeated itself, everywhere, in countries across the globe. Humans were so frequently wrong, and yet she wished desperately to trust them. She was unsure she trusted herself. Did it have to start there? She knew it did not all rest with God.

No. Not God.

These days she found herself floating; she wanted to lean on Father Benjamin and her dear friend, a friend from her part of the world, Sara Sidran. She wanted to comfort her daughter-in-law. But her strength ended at calling on Alen. Now it was only he that helped her spend time with her grandchildren. Her heart told her things were not what they appeared to be.

"Be careful, Hana," her mother spoke to her in Bosnian down through the floorboards of the Petars, all those years ago. Her parents were not just hiding their friends that night; they were hiding their only child. "The world is changing, and people are not what they seem. Follow God. Be warned of those who say they have faith but are killing. Should we not return, stay with the Petars, they will shield and guide you. They will love you."

They snuck into the darkness as decoys. That was the last night Hana heard her mother's voice.

On the day of her son's funeral, it sounded as if her mother's words came out of the car speakers. So clear, they hung in the oddly muggy air. She closed her eyes and saw the faces of the people who had shared the hole under the floor. Her parents died to protect them.

Eventually Hana had her own children and raised them Catholic, a choice she made with Edward. Her husband, raised agnostic, believed that Hana's connection to her spirituality would serve the boys well regardless of any religion they chose. But it had also been their choice. A choice for children who wanted to hang out with their mother and did what she did, true. The choice had not existed for young Hana.

She stayed with the Petars and was, by necessity, raised Catholic—a conversion forced by circumstance and war. She was only seven. The conversion went far beyond religion, affecting culture and tradition. Ritual. Initially, her heart could not follow her mother's wishes completely. She did not know who God was and could not follow. Still, she remembered always being grateful to the Petars, and this gratefulness for life eventually allowed her solace in this new religion.

My son is dead, and I live still in these memories.

"Alen, dear, tell me why I am still here."

"Majka?"

"I live through wars and years of civil unrest. I have lost God. I lose my son now. I must know the reasons."

"I want to know too, Majka."

"You will find for me this—this reason?"

"I will try."

So, for the second time in her life, Hana turned her heart away from God and she floated. She knew she had answers to find. Once again, her mother's voice came clearly into the car through the speakers. It demanded that she not forget.

What do these memories have to do with the death of my son?

Hana searched her mind deeply. She went back to the moment she heard of her son's death. She still could not sense him. Something was not right.

It was still not right by the day his burial arrived. Even after putting him to rest, the crushing weight on her chest was still present. She half-hoped it would lift. Edward would be with him now. They would hold hands in the Heaven she knew was still years away for her own soul. They would smile and embrace, would they not?

Hana sensed she was wrong. James had not seen his father.

The weight would not lift because they had not found each other. She stood at Edward's grave often in the years since his passing, and she always believed he was safe. He looked down with his soul in peace and he watched her from the clouds, and those thoughts comforted her. Yet, at James' graveside, she did not believe he was in the same warm place as his father. She reached for Edward, and his soothing light shone on her. But when she tried to sense James—heaviness, loneliness.

Hana shared the rest of the car ride with Alen in silence. She wondered if it had found him too, this displacement, but she did not want to plant these ideas into his head. Her eyes caught the buildings as the car rolled by, each tree, each shrub, trying to survive the sun, thankful for the slightly cooler days of fall. They rolled out of town and into the untouched desert that spanned the miles around Athelstan House.

It was the sudden absence of the nonnative trees, plants, and shrubs that brought her thoughts to Aislin. Aislin was far from her normal life, pulled out of the forested north and straight into this sad time. She remembered feeding Aislin for three years while she went with James and Alen to school. Bean soup was her favorite.

Many years had passed since Hana and Aislin were close, had sat over soup and tea, had talked about James and Alen together. This distance saddened Hana, for Aislin had become like a daughter in those years. She once hoped that the girl would become part of the family.

Aislin sent her cards on holidays, and that was nice, but it was never a replacement for the warmth the young woman brought into a room. Her sweet Alen filled her in from time-to-time. Aislin wrote for that magazine of his, and their friendship lasted the long years. She did not understand why Aislin was staying with Jade instead of Alen; it must feel so awkward for them both.

Hana looked over to her (now) only son, wondering if she should suggest a change in Aislin's lodging now that the funeral was over. She went to speak but just let her breath out slowly against the thickness of the silence. She did not have the strength to break it.

She tried to feel James again. The more she tried, the more the pressure increased on her chest. She thought about what she knew of Chinese Medicine, how grief shapes the lungs. She placed her hands on her chest and she could sense that hers were no longer as they were at birth; they fused together, forming the shape of a headstone.

Chapter 15 ✦ James

H E COULD NOT TASTE ANYTHING, BUT JAMES KNEW THAT IF HE WERE still alive, the earth might stick to his tongue, and he would smell the rain. He was on his elbows and knees by his grave. His funeral was over. Jade, Egon, Nick, Aislin, Alen, and his mother returned to his house in the north. He struggled to remain still. The gravedigger was closing in on him. He could not imagine that it was finally his time.

Since his father's death, he wanted to be cremated. If they had not buried his father, he would have watched the flames today instead. He preferred that to the thought of dirt weighing him down. James shuddered at the image of his own body under hundreds of pounds of dirt, the coffin lid creaking under the weight. Over time, the earth would shift and the stupid sterling silver handles would tone and rattle on their loosening hinges when trucks drove by. Ashes would have given back to the earth; he would have given back—a little. Although in California, they still buried his father with honors for his service in England, and James had done little in his life to follow in the man's footsteps. This was it. Being buried beside him would be the last thing.

He waited there, trying desperately to feel the raindrops one more time. James failed—failed and failed again. He could not even hear the rain—he could not hear the thunder, although the lightning streaked the monsoon sky. It seemed unnatural that this set of rules meant he could not know the sound of thunder, yet could still recognize a voice or hear a whisper. What made thunder different? Or was it only today? If it stormed yesterday, could he have heard it? He lowered his face into a dampened ground, no dew on his cheek, no smell of dust, no smell of rain, no birds. Nothing.

In his senseless cocoon, he pressed his ear to the ground and was at last rewarded with the soft whistle of the gravedigger. His tune was not what James expected, but why should he have judged this man, anyway? Clad in overalls and a threadbare shirt. He supposed he expected Neil Diamond or the Rolling Stones: "Time Is on My Side" had been one of his own private tunes off and on. But he got Alanis Morissette's "Ironic," or not? Now it was, "One Hand in My Pocket." The digger kind of went back and forth between the two. The man was quite a good whistler.

So James stayed there, attempting to feel at peace with the whistle. In a fetal position, he stayed with his left ear to the ground and his right ear to the sky. He could not feel the rain, did not get a single drop of water in his ear canal, and he did not get to shake his head out in annoyance, no earache to follow. Time was just so still; he wanted a cigarette.

When he first experienced night knowing that he was one of the dead, he wanted so badly to know what time it was. James had no way to know time nor place. Blackness surrounded him so deep he wondered if he had not become it. He was the aether of the night.

And certain that he was at last condemned for his failure to be a good Catholic. He had not gone to confession since his eighteenth birthday. He had written of a thousand ungodly characters in their last hours of humanity; emotionally and physically (a kiss is still a kiss) cheated on his wife; had not waited to have sex until after marriage; consumed many drugs; bet belligerently on animal races and sports; walked right into the dens of a crack house and stayed for days, disappearing without telling his family. And in his not-so-distant youth, his family escaped from Vitez because of his father's position and connections, while others they knew and cared for died behind them.

James spun around in the blackness, his left foot over his right, and then back, rummaging through his list of sins; as each one came to mind, he envisioned the surrounding blackness as a chalkboard. He raised a piece of invisible yellow chalk, marking one tick-mark and then another. A tally of sins.

There was a concrete point in his life when everything changed—once his brother was ready for college. Alen's arrival on campus inspired James to clean up his act. Honestly, his mother had shown enough patience in dealing with his experimental phase. The choice changed his life.

Was it because of the money? He remembered all the ways he and Jade spent and did not spend the dollars. The figures added up as his books made best-seller lists, the few children's books, and the historical fiction, as well. The books were still small-time cash, comparatively.

He hated the bidding; he hated the big money. But the bids brought the best jobs, and he was good at placing bids, always had been. Perhaps hating his own success was a sin. Imagined chalk added another angry tally on the blackest of chalkboards. The strokes were hard to imagine for more than a second. He made a hard fist and allowed that invisible chalk to snap and shatter away from all the demons he was falling victim to in the unrelenting darkness.

Where was a comforting memory of Jade in this Hell? James reached into the crevice of his mind, brought her front and center. A phantom reflection caught the sheen of her hair. Jade purchased her own comforts, nice clothes, their beautiful dogs. He lined her up in the blackness with all the things she valued. Himself, the boys, the dogs. She barely put a dent in the money. She sensed his awkwardness with it, his guilt at having it while others died and starved with so much less. Yet why, even in her understanding of his hesitancy and forced separation from it, could she not convince him to donate it?

With repetition, he opened and closed his eyes to see if the blackness was all in his mind. The threatening black that invaded his pupils engulfed his fingers, his legs, his torso. His fortune cut into his veins, ran in his blood where it did not belong. He remembered how at first Jade suggested dozens of charities. He tried, but he did not want to decide. It froze him. There were small donations, contributions to local places, differences that added up. She took the reins, but stepped back whenever his discomfort increased.

They spent some on art and commissioned family portraits that made them both happy.

Alen used a small chunk to start the magazine he always wanted. James wrote his books. He worked harder and longer. He was dead with a label he did not know what to do with. "Prominent."

The money plagued him with guilt. He built with it. They lived in comfort with access to anything they desired. Otherwise, it amassed in an account, while fear and undeserving worthlessness prevented him from claiming it as his own. Losing it terrified him. Could he stop a war with it? Could he rebuild his home country? At least a city?

Hana did not want to return. He put money away for her. Finances were only another struggle after the death of his father, but she went to school and gained ground doing a demanding job. She helped so many others. At least no guilt existed in providing for his mother.

He turned his thoughts back to solving the blackness, but the money flashed. Huge digits appeared as if on an old computer screen. Thousands of reasons for his guilt converted to glowing green numbers pressing on an ocular nerve—out-of-focus dollar signs stayed on like the sun's imprint inside of his eyelids. Fuzzy, jagged lines representing interest on conservative stock investments streaked across a no-man's-land matrix. James shook his head hard to dislodge the dot-matrix hallucination.

I am dead now—does any of this matter?

Death meant that early mornings were full of shadows. They came out of the earth to consume him. James panicked on these mornings, not knowing whether to hide himself, or even how to hide. He spent hours frozen to one spot, his eyes darting around. A tightness in his shoulders and arms should have followed these hours, but no pain settled into his muscles. Still, he remained unsure of why exhaustion took such a hold. What would happen if he just slept? He shuddered at the idea of the shadows finding him in slumber. Fear had power of its own, just as much power over him in death as it had been in life. *So much for passing on after the funeral. It seems these things are only worse now and so is my terror.*

Would he ever see the sun again? Perhaps no other future existed but darkness. Forever to analyze his life, forever to wonder whether donating it all would have changed something. Forever to wish the green imprint of the dollar sign originated from the sun and not some trick of the devil.

Was he Scrooge? He wondered if he would get to meet Charles Dickens.

Or would the blackness stop should he keep walking? Since he recognized walking, the moving of limbs back and forth, he continued forward. And that went on for some distance. Distance unmeasurable, with no landmarks, no difference between steps. Then, with sudden nausea, he sat down. In lotus pose, the contours of his knees shaped his palms, the straightness of his spine pulled his shoulders and the top of his head up into darkness. Where was the sun? James did not move. He could not sense direction nor peace.

Chapter 16 ✦ Aislin

The Athelstan estate loomed against the deepening sky. An ominous contrast featured the once-obsessively maintained marble volutes of the front entrance.

Jade was in a daze after the funeral, half-responding, uninterested. Aislin looked at the boys—weariness on their faces. The weight of the day made Aislin feel like it was eight o'clock at night instead of three o'clock in the afternoon. Streaks of lightning lit the nearby hills from all angles. As they finally traveled west up the drive, a shadow of dense rain clouds followed overhead. It was too ominous.

Once she stepped safely inside, Aislin caught Jade before she disappeared down the hall to her bedroom. Potentially, for the rest of the night. "Can I get you anything, Jade? Do anything?"

Jade stopped to light a shrine. Her eyes blazed in candle fire before she turned back to Aislin.

"Maybe you could hang with the boys? Alen will be here soon. Watch a movie or something?"

Aislin nodded. "Yeah, we can do that."

She left Jade at the entrance to the hallway, not missing the flask that appeared from behind the prayer candles. Three of the tall glass containers depicted Jesus and Mary on stained glass. Aislin helped Jade make runs for more and more candles from a dollar store. Jade had yet to ask her to buy whisky, but Aislin wasn't blind to see it made up a large part of the woman's diet. Aislin was staying away from it, except at evening meals when Jade drank openly. It helped her bond with Jade a little, helped create some harmony. They could share something besides their love for James and their loss of James, both of which they experienced differently. *Especially the loss. I am so sorry, Jade, especially for that.*

Aislin could still not conceive why she could see James and Jade could not. No one else could see him, or if they could, they weren't saying. Maybe she was crazy. And maybe she was enabling Jade's drinking habit.

Aislin poked her head into the playroom where the boys had settled. Egon was reading a book and Nick was playing with a puzzle.

"Do you feel like watching a movie?" Aislin asked them.

Egon shook his head. "No, thank you. Is Uncle Alen coming over?"

"Yes, he is taking your grandma home, but he'll be here soon."

Egon nodded; his eyes returned to the words of his book. She couldn't see the cover.

"Nick, what about you?"

"What's Mother doing?"

"Your mom just needs to lie down for a while. She will be back up after a bit."

Nick looked back down at his puzzle. His hand froze in mid-puzzle-piece placement. She could see he was seconds from crying.

"Nick?" Aislin asked and took a step into the room.

Egon stopped reading and turned to his brother. He gently took the puzzle piece from his hand and hugged him as the sobs began.

"Can you get us a snack?" Egon asked. "I don't remember the last time we ate."

A pang of guilt that shouldn't have been hers to bear rang through her guts. He was just being dramatic; they'd eaten a huge breakfast. *But, shit, that was hours ago.* "Sure, of course. I will find something good," Aislin promised.

She walked down the stairs wondering why in the world no one planned one of those awkward receptions where everyone overeats and sits around sharing stories.

Alen arrived in the kitchen as Aislin's grumbly expletives towards unruly plastic film came spilling from her mouth. She jammed the casserole dish in the fridge and managed to laugh at herself. He started peeling carrots into long curled strands with some contraption from the cupboard. The two of them remained mostly silent during their meal preparation. Then they regarded their masterpieces: smiley-faced food. Mac and cheese balls for eyes, sliced olives pushed in for eyeballs, bell peppers for ears and more veggies for the eyebrows, noses, and mouths. The carrots became hair. They brought the plates upstairs with fresh juice.

"This is awesome!" Nick said, sniffling and wiping his face with the back of his hand. His brother handed him a tissue.

"Yeah, guys. Thanks," Egon agreed. "Alen's always doing this. Where'd you learn to do this?"

Alen grinned at his nephews, "Parks and Rec classes with Aislin here."

Egon looked blank for a second. "Oh. In college?"

"Yeah buddy, in college."

"Huh, weird."

Aislin knew her face wore the same dumb grin as Alen's. "I guess you can learn anything in college." She shrugged.

With full stomachs, the boys agreed to watch a movie. About a half hour in, the door opened, and bright light poured in from the hallway. Nick looked up. "I saved you a seat, Mother."

Jade blocked some of the light entering the room with a bowl containing several pre-popped bags of popcorn.

"Awesome," Alen said. "I totally forgot about the popcorn."

"Aww, thank you, Nick," she leaned over and kissed him on the forehead. She did the same to Egon, who swung in a hammock chair from a huge beam overhead. As Jade walked around the room, Aislin noticed the odor. When everyone had popcorn, Jade folded herself into the five-person beanbag chair Nick barely took a square foot of. With his mother finally present, he stretched out and nuzzled into the pillow she'd abruptly placed between them.

Aislin interested herself in observing Jade; surprised the widow made it upstairs. When Jade's flask disappeared into her own bag of "popcorn" at the beginning of a flash from the big-screen TV light, Aislin looked to Alen to see if he noticed, and it seemed as if he was also studying his sister-in-law.

After the movie, Aislin returned to her room to change out of her funeral clothes. The humidity brought out the staleness of alcohol on the borrowed shawl. *We can't deny this anymore...*

Magic evaporated the clouds; the sun dried the last raindrops on her window, and sunset changed the color of the mountains. Aislin smoothed the wrinkles from her clothes and turned away from the view. Just as before, James sat in the flowered chair. She jumped.

"I am sorry," he said.

"It's okay." She sat on the bed and sighed. "Nick and Egon had a long day."

"Yes, they did." He sat, and the cushion remain undented.

"It's been weird with Jade, whom I barely know and whom my only clear memory of is the longest Fourth of July holiday ever, seemingly a million years ago. And some pictures online. You know, pictures of the kids I always see those, and she looks well, healthy even. Today at the funeral was the first day I haven't seen her with at least a buzz." Aislin leaned back against the cream pillows—all embellished with Hana's hand-crocheted silk doilies—and shook her head, still trying hard to steady her breath before she said the actual words.

"But I can see this isn't new. She's really struggling, James. How long has she been this way?"

"She has always been this way. And she has not. It is complicated. Like when you met her that Fourth of July? She was a secret I hid from you. As I waited for you to leave Cliff, I had another woman. I never told you who it was. It was Jade."

"I knew there was someone else. Secrets you kept from me, things you wrote. You told me it was Jade, but that was later, later when you told me about the proposal. I knew she was the other one you were seeing. I never had the right to care if you had someone else. But we were so young then. You said she has always been this way? She was suffering from alcoholism back then?"

"We were all drinkers."

"Yeah, we partied. But not like this. She's sick, James. And she's a mother, they need her."

"When did it start...? I guess with the bowling alley bids. That was about two months before I died. She has been drinking more and more since we got that bid."

"We can help her. The first thing is to get her to see what you just said. Do you know why she started? Did something happen with the bid?"

James spoke then as if he'd waited a hundred years to say it: "Wow, that is the first time you have ever been direct with me. So, now that we are really talking, how was it you trusted me to marry her when you would never trust me on anything else?"

"No—I... I did... trust you. What?"

"Can we talk, Aislin? Can you and I talk about us? I just—I want to talk."

"Really? Right now? You don't want to talk about Jade?" James looked away, but Aislin continued, "Okay, I'll admit that I want this talk, too. I was better off in the motel. Not that I don't appreciate your hospitality. But it came as a surprise that you thought of me to this extent. Do you realize Alen left me a message...? a voicemail...? telling me you had died!? I remember standing in my apartment, how his voice sounded when he told me you were gone."

He raised his left eyebrow. "Let us get back to this trust," he said. "We are on to something. You trusted me to pick out restaurants, and you trusted me to read your stories. You trusted Alen and I to be your friends and write you a funny horoscope for the paper every month. I picked you up and drove you to work, was a ride to class. We were ALWAYS together, Aislin. You let me drive you to my favorite places and you called me when your favorite song came on. And I called you. But you did not trust me enough with your future, with your life. You would never leave Cliff. Tell me why."

Aislin couldn't answer him. Other things demanded her attention: the lack of warmth from the sun, the rotation of rain, shine, rain, shine; the smell of Jade's scarf mixed with the acrid smell James mysteriously carried; his very movement on his flowered chair, almost invisible, different from how she saw him at first. Unless she was imagining it? The empty chair in the mirror pulled her attention, too.

Where is his reflection? What does it mean that he doesn't have one?

"Why?" James asked again. And it wasn't surprising that his voice came out tinged with years of pent-up frustration. Their situation still stressed him out. In matters of the heart, in matters of love, his sincerity and gentleness were reasons she loved him so deeply. He was kind. He listened. He was James, and she forgave his tone. Their situation stressed her out, too. If stressed was even close to the right word.

She let the past pull her back, but she couldn't tell the story.

Her eyes lowered to see goose bumps rise on her chest. She watched her breath make her ribs rise once, twice, three times before clearing her throat to answer, to give him something. "I really want to say, it wasn't you, it was me. But that sounds like a cliché. I want to say that I did not trust myself, but there were all those moments when Cliff was such scum and I never left him, when I knew you were the one I wanted to be with forever and I stayed with him for years before I finally just moved away from this awful heat—this place—him. I was scared."

"Aislin, tell me," he said.

"I wrote it down finally—here for you on this paper. I have to take a walk." Aislin stood up, pointing to the nightstand.

His eyes widened as they rested on the letter, and for once she thought he didn't notice when she left the room.

Trying to get the air she never got enough of since leaving the Northwest, she let her footfalls and heel-to-toe motion, and her breath be all she needed as she paced the length of the long driveway as the sun dropped further in the western horizon.

When she returned to the room, she sat next to James on the edge of the bed. They sat in silence for an exceptionally long time.

"You never told me, Aislin. You never even told me." He cried, and she sat in silence. She watched how he cried, but his body didn't really cry. "You could have come to me. I would have helped you. We would have all helped you." He cried tears that were not real water. They fell down his cheeks the same way. They slid into the corner of his nose the same way, but they left nothing wet. Left nothing salty.

His truthful words brought forth a sob—tears she had denied from that pain and self-isolation finally heaved forth. She reached for the tissues, wishing she could offer him one, too. Wishing that he was really there.

James went to put an arm around her shoulders, but could not. It could not rest; he could not lean or support her. He returned his hand to his own lap and continued, "He was the reason you could never accept that I chose you... but not because you loved him." James set his shoulders straight and looked like he was sniffling to clear his nose of tears. He made no sound. "And I chose you again—even after you left for Washington. I came for you, but we still could not make us happen. Were you scared that someday I would be like him?"

"No, James. I don't think... I don't think so. I think it was about you deserving someone undamaged. Maybe? I don't want to analyze it."

"But Aislin, I was damaged, too. In a different way, but death follows us both."

"Yes, it does." Aislin knew about James' hard years, the gambling, the drugs, whoring himself out for more. Vitez. And now he was actually dead, and death was really following her.

"Everything turned around when you left, and I had Jade front and center. You were far away. But did you know how close I was to leaving Jade so we could be together? I look back at this, such sadness. I realize we had so much less trust than I thought, we had so much more to work through in order to be together."

"You're right." Light brown hair swept around pale shoulders as she shook her head. Hot tears stung her cheeks again. She settled back deeper and pulled a cashmere throw on top of her. It was cold, yet the sun was suddenly hitting the window after the long and grey day. Yet it wasn't—at all—warm. "I suppose I still do not understand why we never trusted each other. What do you think?"

She used James' voice to disintegrate the memories of Cliff and she tried to focus on her hands instead of that face, one she rarely let surface. "Sorry James, I didn't realize until it was too late that I should have told you how I felt, that I couldn't get out."

"But afterwards, when you let me walk away. Did you really love me?" James asked, his hands trying to adjust his shirt but not creating a single change.

"Yes." She lowered her chin, turning her face further away. She had never told James about the bad in the relationship with her ex. He guessed she wasn't happy, encouraged her to break away. But at the time she lived in fear, she really had nowhere to go. She could not ask James to be responsible for her and the repeating negatives on her bank notes. She feared the loss, and more precisely, the death, of anyone—even someone who was a real danger to her.

She let James walk away. And oh, how she regretted it.

"At least you trust me now," he said.

Their eyes connected.

"How can you tell?"

"You told me your story, Aislin. You are talking to me and I am dead. Finally, you are here with me. At least in death, we have trust." James left behind a faint sheen as he moved, but barely existed between the chair and his new place by the door.

His boys were walking by, shouting about a new book Eleanor had dropped off.

He held his ear to the polished wood. "I will miss them the most, you know. You never thought I wanted to be a father. You thought I loved you more. But..." James turned, straightened to stand at his full height, and faced Aislin again. "I would never have left them. That was the turning point for Jade, and she knew it, too. I felt her relax after Egon was born. It was as if she knew she made a bond with me. She knew we made a solid, unbreakable, concrete slab."

"But I really knew that about you."

"Did you?" He whispered and then stepped right through the door.

She could still smell his dusty pants and the faint trace of cigarettes. After days of visits where he just vanished from the room, she was over trying to convince herself that he wasn't there to begin with. Yet more confused than she was when she arrived.

Aislin commended herself for being so brave. But bravery was just a front. With nothing at stake, no world to protect, why did she even have to be brave? She knew her obsessive streaks finally formed the perfect peaks for all her beating.

Yes, for all her beating, she had finally been granted validation. She told him what happened behind the scenes, behind the doors with Cliff. Those doors were open now, and out flooded the reasons she ran away so many years ago and let her future sway carelessly in a grey and insipid balance, allowing her whole life to become James-less.

Aislin let out a forceful breath, fought off the ache, fought off the shiver. The front of her body wasn't bones and flesh; it was a heart that climbed out and hung on her like a shield—absorbing everything. It left her ribcage empty for years; the hollow grew moldy and stale from the vacancy. Any unkempt home will only crumple. She noticed the far cry of a cactus wren as it followed through to a frantic "Rreek, rreek."

Lose. Lose yourself in it, for if you stop now, the ideas are never coming back. Yes, what is the next step? What do you say to him now? Soon you won't be able to see him.

There was a knock at the door. Alen for a late dinner. "To the bar for pastrami?" he asked.

She thought James looked as tired as Alen, but James was dead. She nodded to Alen, exhausted and suddenly starving.

Chapter 17 ✦ Aislin

N THE WAY TO THE BAR, ALEN LOOKED STRAIGHT AHEAD IN THE TRUCK. "Aislin, it might be good for you to stay at my house next week. It's just an idea."

Relief mixed with uncertainty regarding of her length of stay. She wanted to be close to the Athelstans, but how long did he expect her to stay in Palm Springs? She had planned to stay two weeks and one day, leaving the Thursday after they read the will. But now that James was... well.

How can I walk away? How can I return to a normal life?

Lights from houses glinted in the spaces between palms. Another night had fallen in the desert. She cleared her throat. "Okay, Alen. Thanks."

The look on Alen's face as he stared at the menu and declared he would order an extra bag of potato chips told Aislin that the very opposite had happened to his appetite, as had happened to hers or especially Jade's since the fateful Friday.

The server came to the table: beautiful eyes and the posture of a dancer. Aislin at once recognized her from a photo that Alen shared years back. This was the woman Alen pined for—the woman he dated briefly but could not explain to Aislin why it didn't last. This was Victoria.

Victoria took Alen's hand for a moment, sympathy in her eyes. "I am sorry, Alen. So sorry."

"Thank you." His eyes dropped to the menu, not sustaining the sad exchange.

Victoria turned to Aislin and reached her hand out. "You must be Aislin," an authentic kindness exuded.

"And *you're* Victoria. It's nice to meet you," Aislin returned the woman's respectful greeting.

"Alen has told me—" they said in unison.

"... so much about you," Aislin completed, smiling.

They placed their order with further small talk, but Victoria was busy, and they were both too sad and tired to engage her, anyway.

The food came with another round of small talk. Victoria did not hide her assessment of Aislin. Aislin didn't care. She assessed the woman back. They both cared about Alen. That much was true.

They ate in silence for a while.

At the bar, the same two detectives that came to talk to her and Jade at the house worked on their own sandwiches. She scrutinized their appearance for a few moments and realized they were also hanging out at the wake only the day before.

Why? Don't detectives just investigate foul play...?

Oh!

Aislin's mind swirled with a horrifying notion about why James had not been able to cross.

She took the last bite of pastrami that she could stomach, her hunger having faded after only a few bites. The hands on a standard black and white clock inched by. Eight minutes passed while Alen ate. The edges of the sandwich brushed his lips as he just kept at it. She counted his chewing alongside him. Twenty-five times for each bite. The meat was thick and jerky like. His bites were small and deliberate.

She wanted to say something about those cops. But should she?

Never had she seen anyone so focused on a sandwich.

It was fine, though. James sat beside her, making the idea of speaking terrifying. It was so difficult not to interact with James while in Alen's presence one-on-one. Or to interact. Both stood as options she didn't even want.

Aislin could not read the expression on Alen's face at all. He studied his plate. He ate his pickle and his very last morsel of bread. His eyes rose to hers. She was getting ready to pass him her plate, but something in his face stopped her.

He looked directly at James.

Aislin centered on him. The seconds started ticking. A genuine smile came, a natural happiness, elation. One second. Then memory; Alen's shoulders sinking, pulling back, smile tightening, three seconds. Then the teeth showing as his lips continue to pull back in fear. A rise of his Adam's apple, chest puffing up, five seconds. His eyes blinking, changing from light to dark as his pupils expand. And eight seconds in—the head shaking slowly, then with a few quick jerks, the almost imperceptible tightening of the tendons in his neck and the eyes glazing over, glossier and glossier, his fists rubbing his eyes and strong arms falling to his sides before he just sat starring at his plate.

More seconds ticked by. The clock grew in size, demanding that she measure out her life. His eyes flicked to hers and then down. *What do I do?* James looked at her. She looked at Alen. *Can he see James?* She watched him, suddenly refusing to look at James.

"Aislin...?"

"Alen?"

His plaid-covered shoulders heaved up and dropped. "I... think I have been eating too much pastrami." Alen piled his napkin onto his plate.

James laughed with his head tilted back. It was an inappropriate, boisterous laugh that echoed slightly inauthentic, but mostly it was a bit like a drunk James.

Aislin surprised herself when she realized she'd cracked a smile; it was all she could do to not look at the man—the ghost—beside her.

Then she gave in, made eye contact with James, and his laughing stopped.

"Tell him, Aislin, come on. Tell him you see me, too. That you talk to me all the time and that you have a message."

"No!"

"A message, Aislin, a message," James taunted.

Aislin shook her head.

"No, what?" Alen asked.

Shit. "Here. Have my pastrami," she thrust the plate at Alen. "You should eat. You should listen to your body, is all."

"Thank you," Alen took the plate. He sat it right on top of his napkin and picked up the sandwich and took a huge bite. He chewed some and swallowed a little. With his mouth just full enough to be understood, Alen continued, "But, um, that isn't why you said 'no'."

Alen took another bite of the sandwich before swallowing the first one. He continued to chew and stare at her, and not to even look at James.

"He did not believe it." James spoke, causing her to jump just as Alen's eyes went down to take another bite. "I have been sitting here trying to figure out why he only saw me for a moment, and it is because he does not believe in ghosts. His brain will simply no longer visualize me."

As the last bite of meat went down Alen's throat, he began to talk again. "The reason I think maybe I have been eating too much, or that maybe instead I'm beyond damn tired... it was just for a moment... but Aislin, I think I saw my brother sitting next to you. And I have this feeling—this weird feeling that you can see him still."

Aislin's throat constricted, and she gasped for the air that was simply no longer there.

Chapter 18 ✦ Aislin

"SHE'S CHOKING!" ALEN CALLED OUT TO THE EMPTYING RESTAURANT. Footsteps clattered across the linoleum. Victoria came into view. Eyes huge and pupils dilated. She looked right past Aislin. In the time it might have taken Aislin to take a breath if she were capable, she watched Victoria's expression change completely. Light sparkled in Victoria's narrowing eyes while her mouth curved into a small smile, her head tilted to the right, her lips finally parting with awe.

Aislin realized Victoria could see James, too. Her lungs convulsed and struggled, no longer allowing distractions. She pitched forward, gasping for air.

Victoria dove into the booth and was back at attention. "Are you choking?" Aisling shook her head no.

With a calming and deep breath, Victoria placed one hand on Aislin's back and her other over Aislin's clasped hands. She spoke calmly. "Calm. Envision trees, hear me breathe. Breathe like me, breathe like me." Warmth spread across her back and relaxed her as Victoria's palm traveled up and down. Long strokes helped her diaphragm and lungs remember their purpose. She encouraged Aislin to make eye contact. Her lips formed words. Her voice mimicked calm waves, nourished like the sun.

Looking into those golden eyes, Aislin's parasympathetic nervous system kicked in. After some very long minutes, her breath became more regular. She noticed Victoria inhaled long and deliberately. As Aislin began to mimic her heroine, the tension released.

She focused on the soothing words. The breath. Victoria continued with her slow massage, and her lips continued to move. Aislin could barely hear the message and doubted it reached Alen's ears. Three minutes passed, seven minutes. Aislin was looking into the women's liquid eyes, and she broke that gaze to look at Alen. She looked back at her heroine, still a stranger.

After a few more moments, Aislin saw how Alen watched Victoria. There was still so much chemistry. She ignored their sexual tension and focused on her breath until she recovered enough for words.

"Thank you. I—wow—thank you so much for helping me." Gratefulness flushed her cheeks.

"It's okay. You just take it easy now. Keep focusing on your breath," Victoria soothed.

"How did you learn how to do that, Victoria?" A soft, affecting quality flowed with Alen's words.

"She's suffering from a panic attack. Sometimes if you show someone a normal breathing pattern and connect with them, it can help." He gave a blank stare. "Remember, my master's degree? I just finished clinical hours."

"Oh, your program, right... But does psychology teach you about medical emergencies? How did you know she wasn't choking?" With no warning, his face changed and hardened with accusation.

Victoria started looking at Aislin again, continuing to rub her back. "Hmm? Oh—yes," her head snapped to attention. "Well, I heard you cry 'she's choking'. I was a lifeguard for years and I've trained to respond quickly in school, too. But she shook her head 'no' when I asked her, Alen."

"But she wasn't talking. She wasn't breathing."

"She knew what was happening; she didn't need that kind of help."

"You took a risk. What if you'd been incorrect? What if she was choking on her ice or something and you made the wrong call? You're just a student." Alen's voice rose.

"You were just sitting there."

"I called for help. You could have made a mistake." Alen's tempo climbed as his body rose slightly off the bench.

"Alen, she wasn't choking. Can you please lower your voice?" Victoria's skin flushed.

Just then, Aislin looked up at Alen, her words sputtering out of a dry throat. "I am not sure you should argue with the woman who just saved me from several days of sore throats and high blood pressure."

"You have these attacks often?" Victoria asked.

"Yes, I've been practicing this technique you did. I read about it. The lesson is to tune into the calmest person around when I feel the tension building and match their breathing. But I've never gone through it with someone; relief came so much quicker with your help."

Alen slumped back into the booth and appeared to calm down.

Poor Alen. Aislin knew he'd never liked to be the center of attention. Could she expect anything different from him? Certain she had just witnessed both Alen and Victoria being very aware of James, she wondered what that meant for James and his family. Alen had partially admitted it before giving way to his frustration and bravado—allowing her episode to be an excuse to change the subject.

Alen never believed in ghosts. He believed staunchly that heaven and hell existed, and he believed in purgatory, but he did not think that the living should ever and would ever interact with the dead.

Aislin's heart broke to see him lose familiar ground.

Victoria's eyes glimmered as they flicked over the room. She looked at Aislin before her eyes focused again on Alen. His breath caught; Victoria locked in on him. With everything that was going on around them, it was the first moment she understood—beyond her beauty—what made Victoria so attractive Alen would pine over her for years. She could act under peculiar circumstances. This woman was smart and keen. Eyes of sunshine invoked wheat fields, liquid gold, topaz, another realm.

She recalled the details of Alen and Victoria's many attempts at romance. They weren't friends, they never broke through their enormous sexual tension. Alen still wanted to be more. She remembered that he and James still frequented this bar. In fact, Alen had eaten there just the night before. That he still ate at the same old bar had close to nothing to do with the pastrami. Aislin smiled. Witnessing the awkwardness was refreshing—so commonplace in her world full of dead.

She watched them:

Silence.

Breath, eyes, contemplation.

They both spoke in a rush. Their words came out with heat, yet without anger. Apologies. Explanations. Near excuses.

Silence.

"It's okay. I understand." Alen's eyes shone.

Victoria's voice was calm again. "Yes, I think you do."

Their eye contact remained constant. Victoria laid her hands on the table. She turned her palms up.

Alen, impulsiveness as his ever-weak point, made a move to grab one of her hands. She removed it.

Eye contact broke. His gaze fell to a plate of used napkins, crumbs, and escaped sauce.

"I'm sorry," Alen said.

Victoria reached across the table again. But the sting had landed and Alen kept his arms down at his sides. Aislin heard him wiping the sweat from his palms on the old brocade of the upholstered booth.

Victoria withdrew. "I'm sorry, too." And their eyes again tethered.

Aislin stirred to break apart the unease, and Alen turned his attention to her. She wasn't sure what just happened between the two, but the knowledge of their unrequited feelings was enough to guess there were some communication issues. *Now, who's the one with the psych degree?* Aislin smiled, amusing herself for the first time in days.

Victoria looked at Aislin as well, but Aislin noted the delay—those eyes were not quite ready to break away.

"How do you feel?"

"I'd just like to rest," Aislin said. "Can I rest at your house?"

"Sure. Let's go." Alen fumbled in his wallet for some bills as Victoria rose and disappeared into the back. Aislin found her way to the restroom and back with more speed than she expected from herself under the circumstances.

After he placed some cash neatly on the table, Alen heaved himself out of the deep booth and onto his own unsteady feet. This grief added weight to his strong, lean figure—one would have to know him to see how it changed him. Weariness in his gait left a trail of visible static across the flat, brown carpet. He rubbed his full stomach and smiled at her, but she could see it was hard for him.

In his simple two-door pickup truck, they drove together to his home on the side of the mountain. Alen played an album they both loved. Every note cast itself into a long silence, their memories of James riding on the seat between them. Her finger's edge, the delicate skin near her nail, went to her teeth, but she caught herself in the side-mirror. She clasped her hands before her, not too surprised to find the habit resurface after that event.

Aislin looked over at Alen in the half-light of streetlamps and then turned to watch the earth change from watered curbs to an expanse of jumping chollas, shining silver and white beneath a dwindling halfmoon, black shadows cast against the sand. Alen's skin took on the green of the dash lights. A sad green. She wondered what it would be like for James and his new optical experience.

Maybe he felt like she did the day he told her he was going to marry another woman.

October 29, 2002

*****the moments of life, James. hard to break
the sheltering web that our parents created, but
easy to dig under it. especially if they die. it's just
a fence after all.

Finding the headline news stand
i figured i would learn

  a little about

  the world we live in.

  But i've learned so much

    from you.

  It's the saddest sound

that we've lasted this long

    sadder still that

  i'm praying

      release my soul.

it's nothing like autumn

down here

    and home is so far...

the sculpture in the courtyard...

  if you think about someone else

      it moves

i'm going to have trouble
        giving honest advice.

he never was the man i always dreamt of...
but how could i define that?
ever, Aislin

Chapter 19 ✦ Victoria

Victoria had the place to herself. Scheduled to close, she found it odd to be the only person left in the bar and the parking lot outside. Usually at least two people locked up together, or a regular nursed their melted ice. She shrugged it off. Perhaps she could bring it up with management, but she'd always considered the bar safe.

Ever organized, she took her keys from their special compartment in her purse. The strange night weighed on her. Parts would be completely unbelievable to some. She wanted nothing more than a glass of wine and her couch and maybe some television. A luxury she afforded herself on really tough nights. As she opened her car door and settled into her seat, she thanked herself repeatedly for deciding not to have a roommate.

Many times, she daydreamed of Alen living with her, of sleeping beside him and waking up to him. Maintaining a successful relationship and dedicating her life to her program might seem contrary to each other, but she knew she could have both. Alen was too shy, proud, fearful, or indecisive to keep asking her out. And she was too busy to take the lead. No one else caught her eye, so she abandoned dating.

Only her thesis remained before completing her dual graduate degree in Social Work and Therapy. Finally, the supervised hours required for certification were behind her. The next goal was to land a position in a local hospice organization. The coveted doctoral program loomed like a tower just beyond. Before that, she needed real-life experiences—like this one. The paranormal always seemed to be on the fringes of the work she did. Even when she didn't seek it out.

But this counted as new territory: nothing she ever experienced compared to the last three hours.

The most fascinating thing was not that she'd seen a ghost, but that two people besides her had seen it as well: a woman who was clearly being haunted, and Alen, who was clearly in denial.

By the time Victoria emerged from the galley with their check, they were turning east and out into the darkness. The Athelstans bought the same sandwiches for so long; Alen was adept at stacking the exact change in one pile and her tip in a pile beside it.

Did she dare text Alen? Would the number even work?

She wished they were closer and that he would have called her. She could be there for him.

A great sigh came out. She had been holding her own breath. Apprehension surfaced with the return of air. Alen. She remembered the day he introduced himself to her over his pastrami.

Victoria halted with her keys in the "on" position. She turned the car off. She stepped back inside the bar and sat down again at the booth where the magic happened. The low-wattage security lights remained the only inside light and outside she could see some streetlamps and the oddness of a bright not-quite-half moon casting shadows she was unfamiliar with. She waited in the eerily quiet dining area.

"Alen's brother," she whispered. "James?"

Nothing happened.

"I saw you."

Still nothing.

Victoria placed her hands on the table where the ghost placed his hands. "I want to see you again. Maybe I can help."

For a while, everything was completely quiet.

Victoria glanced around at the empty tables and chairs. She looked for moving objects and wondered if the lights might blink or if perhaps a bottle might shatter behind the bar. These were all signs of paranormal activity.

Her personal course of study had always focused on the effects of the paranormal on patients and life-after-death experiences. Elizabeth Kübler-Ross's work landed at the top of the hierarchy. Victoria knew the signs to look for. She lived through one in her own childhood.

Her first ghost appeared at age eleven. A young, female spirit sat in the window seat and stared straight ahead each afternoon for two months before ever speaking.

When Victoria's mother said they were moving to California, her reason was "we will like it there better," but her words had an undercurrent of fear.

Little Victoria packed with some delight in the days leading up to the afternoon when the girl spoke. That very night, they headed to Palm Desert. Her mother knew that Victoria was being visited, and her mother knew how to protect her. She was intuitive, and now with Alzheimer's, frightfully more so. Aside from this recent struggle, her mother had been right. They had been much happier in the sun. Away from Providence, away from the ghost.

Victoria never forgot the sad girl who shared her bedroom with her in silence for six months. She never told anyone about her. She never repeated what the girl said to her on moving day.

"Hello. Can you see me? Maybe you can just hear me?" This was a man speaking to her—in the present restaurant. His voice yanked her by her hair out of her past and into the dimly lit here and now.

"I can see you and hear you."

"Hello, Victoria."

She never spoke to the sad girl. Paralyzed by fear and excitement, she had absolutely no idea what a girl of eleven could offer to the dead. But she was speaking to this dead man. She had even said she could help. *Why would she say that?*

"Hello, James."

"I know we kind of act like strangers sometimes, but I think it is just because this place is so casual to us, our place going on twenty years. Alen and all your flirting that goes nowhere, I never knew how to act around you." He looked around the room. "It has not changed much, but we do not really come here for the food anymore." He winked at her, and heat rose to her face. He kindly changed the subject. "Thank you for helping Aislin tonight."

"You're welcome." Victoria realized with relief that Aislin tied herself to James and not to Alen. Alen mentioned his friend with admiration on one of their dates when the Pacific Northwest came up. Victoria never knew if there was competition. She shook her head at the thought of jealousy. It wasn't the way towards building friendships or holding other women up.

She let out a deep sigh, wanting to be better than that. James didn't react and probably assumed her sigh was in response to something he said.

A transparent older version of Alen sat across from her; she wondered what kind of man he was. Now that he wasn't really a man at all. *Did he feel like a man? Did he feel human? Could he hurt? Be displeased? Happy? What did he actually feel like?*

Thinking she could make something out of this experience once her professional reputation grew, Victoria was suddenly eager to learn everything about the way this man existed. What was his reality?

"Tell me what happened to her. I am positive you saw me earlier."

"I heard coughing. The cough became distressed, and I thought perhaps

I could help. I approached the booth and saw you. She was having a panic attack, and I saw your brother and he looked freaked out. I sat beside her and I just went through my training."

"How did you know with certainty she was not choking on that pastrami? I know Alen already asked this of you, I want to hear it again."

Listening to James speak lent more to the experience than Victoria expected. His accent was mild, but it was noticeable. He was very formal in the way English language speakers can be when English is not their first language. The omission of contractions created an unfamiliar tone that resonated as haunting. If he hadn't been a ghost, she wouldn't say this quality lent to an atmosphere of otherworldliness—she'd never even caught it before. But he was one. James was a ghost that didn't use contractions. She smiled at the difference—his brother used them.

Alen told her some of his history on their first date. They moved to California at an impressionable time for Alen, who spoke Bosnian fluently, but his English had almost no trace of an accent, and none of the formality James exuded. But James carefully cultivated this formality, even practiced it. She sensed it was more important for him to maintain than she might ever understand.

"I asked her. That's really the first thing you're supposed to do when you think someone is choking. Ask. She shook her head no." Victoria finally got around to answering the question she had grown tired of.

"You came back inside the restaurant because you would like to get to know my brother better? Be warned that he is very devout in his faith. He will not rock easily, and you may have a battle on your hands if you break through. To think he might believe he saw me! Let alone believe that you and Aislin see me. But you see all this. He is too complicated for you."

"I'm pretty complicated," she said in response. His insinuation stung her; he didn't seem to notice *that*.

In the window's reflection, she glimpsed her own eyes. The way they caught the light made her hair stand up, and the air became colder.

Victoria stared at James; the layout of the booth interfered with his reflection. More than curious about his physics, she made a mental note to check for his mirror image. When and if he stood, would she be able to see him in the mirror behind the bar?

He seemed to know things he should not. She had more questions. "Why do you think I came back for him?"

"I think somehow, I could hear it when you spoke to each other."

The mystery was ebbing for Victoria now. Psychology. That is the only reason that James knew what he knew. First, she came back in to beckon him and second, he just saw their attraction, their body language. It was still there. Third, he knew his brother—and he knew the past, which included her. James knew about all the things that got in the way. He knew why Alen came in and just stared instead of taking her out. But she had her reasons not to get involved. And James did not understand her the way he thought he did.

"You're observant."

Victoria jumped in response to the raucous laughter that spilled from James. She remembered hearing it earlier in the restaurant and realized that there must be irony somewhere.

"You have no idea. No idea..." James' laugh trailed off, the outburst giving way to his discomfort.

"Well, tell me what you see."

So he did. He started at the very beginning. He opened the shadows and the sun to the stranger that Victoria was. He told her all about the sounds he heard and did not hear. He told her of his mother's all-night vigil. He told her of his mother's past and about his guilt for leaving her. James told Victoria his afterlife's most perplexing and shameful secret:

His former lover could see him, and his widow could not.

Victoria soaked in every bit of information from James that she could before he disappeared. She wanted to take notes in the worst way. As soon as he left, she scrambled behind the counter for a notepad. Her pen flew across the paper, writing every detail she could remember. She tore off the sheets, tucking them into her purse.

When she looked up and across the bar, she flashed back to the prior week. Another pair of her regulars, two detectives, discussed the death of a man. She'd normally ignore their disregard of proprietary information and tune them out, but when the pace slowed, sometimes their stories kept her entertained while she wiped down the shelves and bottles.

"It was such a mess," said the more talkative detective, who she always called Chas. "The cage still stunk when I arrived, even with the glass gone. I was praying for a breeze, oh man." He paused with dramatic effect to wave at his pleasant face. His thick hair fell into place. "The expert analyzed it later. They said the panel shorted out, and the guy was dead by electric shock *before* the wrecking ball hit. It was such a mess. The cab was bloody, and the panel fried. Didn't you read that report?"

The other dick—the one everyone called Bretti—dropped his voice to a whisper, but Victoria didn't miss a word. She liked his crisp voice; it reminded her of a teacher she knew from the plains. His forehead creased up and down with the movement of his lips. "I skimmed it. But I was curious this morning, so, I was reading the report that wasn't ready to read instead of focusing on the one that was. But I'm glad I read it. It's not a final report; but the coroner confirmed the time of death was before the ball struck the cage. So that part is solid." He dropped his voice even lower, "There was also an order from the mayor's office to re-check all equipment at the site."

Victoria's interest piqued.

Mr. Chas-lovely hair finally dropped his voice, too, "For sabotage?"

Victoria caught a curt nod from the corner of her eye. Bretti replied, "Any kind of vandalism. It could have just been some kids messing around at the site."

"But I heard there were threat reports to the mayor demanding he stop construction."

"Yeah, those don't add up. We should look closer. The threats came in about the project's popularity and not long after ground broke, the circuit blew. He was electrocuted and smashed when the controls went out."

"There could be someone responsible for the shortage. The one that made all the threats, perhaps? Did anyone make threats to the developer or just to the mayor?"

Bretti shrugged, "No idea. I guess we ain't done."

"I guess not, damn it. This shit can't ever be easy. Let's get back." Chas picked up his black baseball cap from the bar and covered his curls.

Late into the night, Victoria's head whirled between thoughts of Alen and the implications of the detectives' conversation. How concerned were they about foul play?

Chapter 20 ✦ Victoria

THE MORNING AFTER TALKING TO GHOST JAMES, VICTORIA COULD not stop thinking about Alen. The years they flirted were many. She loved the time they spent on their few dates, and sometimes, just seeing him in the bar made her flustered.

She sent him a text.

"Do you want to get a drink?"

She didn't even know if his number was still the same.

"I'll be there at six," he responded immediately.

That afternoon, she planned what she would wear when Alen arrived at her house. She chose a short, green cotton skirt and a soft white button-up shirt with a longer back. When Victoria opened the door, he was the most unkempt she could imagine. She had sort of expected this: a man grieving. Yet she had never once seen him a tad less than pulled together, even after a day of hard work—both brothers always had pride in their appearance. His blue-striped work shirt was half untucked, his curly hair was wild.

"Victoria." His voice was breathy.

"Come in, Alen."

In her small apartment, her style was minimalist. A few plants in white pots sat on top of dark tabletops. He joined her on the only option: a blue loveseat that faced a large bookshelf.

"My brother is dead."

"I am so sorry." She wondered if he'd forgotten their conversation or if those words were on repeat in his mind.

"I saw him, Victoria." Alen's face paled, and he hid from her in his palms. As he took his hands off his face to look at her again, a few greasy curls straightened in his fingers and sprang back to his forehead when his hands fell to his lap. "I don't know what to do."

"I talked to him for a while last night."

Alen placed his hand on her arm and shook his head. Victoria took a breath. She counted to three.

"Alen, he is really here."

He touched his temple with his left hand, his shoulders rounding into his chest. "No. I don't see how that is possible."

She waited again, letting the seconds tick by as he slowly relaxed into a more neutral posture before she reached out and stroked his back.

"It's going to be okay," she whispered, leaning close to his ear.

He turned to her. His lips hit hers with heat and greed, and hers did the same. During their second date, she played this scene out in her mind. Wishing things between them didn't have to be so serious and cordial.

As soon as he unbuttoned the last button on her shirt, she quickly raised her skirt around her waist and rose onto him, her legs on each side of his, her mouth finding his again and again for the kiss she fantasized about. He caressed her back and her breasts, her stomach, her arms, moaning with pleasure at the heat between her legs.

After a few clothing adjustments and the addition of protection, Alen went into her. For years, they'd built up such raw sexual tension that when she came, she basically exploded.

Her education taught her to expect specific reactions. Alen reacted the way a "normal" person should react to interacting with a deceased family member. Alen was real. Having sex during a period of grief was good.

Of course, he was also plenty spooked. But with Alen acting as her studies suggested he should, she was confident and secure. They acted in their most wild state. Her living room vanished as their insecurities and fears about James gave way to adrenaline, pheromones, and hormones.

All of this behaved like a warm blanket of science for Victoria, and she was happy to continue with it for as long as it felt right for them. She could not say if it would last, but she led him to her bedroom. They curled around each other in more sweat and lust until they were hungry. They played footsie while eating snacks and couldn't keep their hands off each other.

He didn't stay the night. Saying goodbye involved another half hour of making out and whispering the benefits of staying and going before he wrestled himself away from her—family obligations winning out.

The following afternoon, James appeared in the middle of her living room. He faced away from her, staring out the window.

"How was your night? Do you think you could call my brother over to chat?" When he suddenly spoke and turned to her, she jumped and a shudder traveled over her. It took a few moments to get past the sense of invasion and fear.

He cleared his throat, and she remembered he had asked her something. She sat down. Could she do it? Was she ready? James acted as though she had the constitution to pull it off. Why else would he have come to her? Why not go to Aislin?

"It was about time." He grinned because he must have sensed their intimacy had finally gone to the next level. But his smile was not something that could break the tension. James had been handsome, but she could not see it anymore, not in this state.

About an hour later, James' broad hands lay translucent on his translucent jeans. He perched on the edge of a white dining chair at her mid-century metal kitchen table. His hands rested on the table. They did not sink through it. The surface somehow supported him, like the chair, like the floor. She watched him until she got a deep chill. The shiver relieved her of the deadpan silence and uncomfortable shame she felt for staring.

She noted that James still acted like a living human. His emotions and his brain were unchanged. She could show him more respect. He was not to blame for her discomfort.

Alen arrived. He took his time getting to the kitchen, looking around at things as though it were his first time being there. The archway between the zone of safety in the living room and the kitchen was as far as he could go. His work boots were unlaced and dirty, teetering on the transition strip between grey carpet and beige linoleum. She couldn't help but frown at them.

"Alen, can you kindly remove your shoes?"

He looked from James to her and to his feet. "Oh, sorry," he said, "I'm sorry."

Victoria sensed his hesitation. He looked at the ground but didn't take a step. Whether it was of soiling more of the floor or getting closer to James, she was not sure. She slid a chair to him and then busied herself getting water before she leaned on a counter facing the Athelstans. Alen's beard was coarse and patchy, uncombed. She had hoped intimacy would motivate a little self-care, but reminded herself of what he faced.

James was also unshaved. How long would he remain with that shadow of stubble? The two-day-old growth of beard from the day he died never changed as Alen's grew wilder.

"Alen, I am so happy to see you," the sentence came out as a whisper, but it was loud enough to cause jumps in Alen and Victoria. The quiet of shoes shuffling and her glass clanging brought enough comfort for her. She tried to put aside her desire to be present during this intimate reunion. She pushed her weight off the worn, laminate countertop.

"Why don't you have some time alone?" she asked.

Alen's "please stay" came out at the same time as James' "we would like your company."

The men smiled at each other. She nodded and resettled, her emotional insides realigning with her goal: research on life after death.

But the brothers could barely speak to each other in their first real meeting and it took several more chaperoned visits before Alen started asking his brother questions about what it was like to be a ghost. With each answer, James exhibited he was just James. Scared, see-through, but the same brother he had grown up with, the same brother he missed and wept for.

Midway through the following week, they stood around her living room. It was the fourth meeting she was chaperoning. Alen was so overwhelmed, he went to hug his brother—the hug failed. Victoria watched the strain in Alen's eyes during the encounter. Her heart bled for him while trying to retain every moment. The back of her mind nudged out a small warning that this experience might teach her why you never get involved with patients. She was mixing her professional interests with her romance.

"I'm not okay with this," Alen landed hard on her couch, "but I can't help my awe and wonder at getting to be with you now, James. I don't know what's before us, but I will do anything for you."

Now the words that the little girl said in her childhood home echoed in the back of her mind, affecting her in ways they never had.

Chapter 21 ✦ Aislin

Afternoons passed. Many of them found James and Aislin talking for hours in her room, bringing them to her second Saturday in Palm Springs. Rarely did Aislin find herself all alone in the vast house, but Jade and the boys were out. Aislin did not know if they were together, or if the boys were with Hana and Jade had holed herself up in a dark bar or knelt praying at the church. *Probably not the last one.* Jade's religious order now seemed to stop at the altars, no matter how Alen nagged her.

On her way downstairs, Aislin stopped short, noticing one altar covered with ashy fragments. A black curl flaked apart beneath the light pressure of one fingertip like burnt paper. She brushed it away on her pants and noticed more ashes on the floor. The air carried traces beyond what the candle gave off. She shook her head, unsure of what was once whole.

At the giant kitchen island, a stolen pen and stationery from the first motel she stayed at on this long and tiring trip stared back at her. She wrote a letter and hated that it could be a goodbye letter. What if James could not leave the city? Anything out of the ordinary might cause him to disappear. Aislin had to prepare. Sought something to control; writing gave her that.

She reread the third goodbye letter of the week. Absentmindedly tracing the crown of the hotel logo in black ink again and again. Obsessed that any finalities or different circumstances would cause a crossing over. If he crossed, her chances to be with him would be lost forever.

October 6, 2013

Dear James, I know there will always be more to say, and I think it is time to share some of that now.

I feel desperate and sad, and the fact that you have noticed how different I have become—that was huge to me, and I feel a great connection, after years of hiding, that feels so peaceful, I actually feel understood and perhaps, even ready to be seen.

In these last days, even in your death, I have looked to you for guidance and strength, and you have not let me down. I admire a great deal about you, and I know others admire you, too.

Although much has changed in your demeanor than existed in our youth, you are the same man. You reverted to a polished exterior to match what you see in your mother, to match her world, but it's not fake, it's created from reverence and has become your fabric.

Just as the worlds you created in your letters to me were part of your journey, I see why you made the choice to revert to what you knew before that wild grew into you. . . . The tortured adolescent within you transformed into a man that commands great respect, and I know it's by the way you treat others in kindness that this respect is extended.

I refuse to forget you, and I will never try to erase any of this. From time to time, I will let you remind me of my capacity to be totally enchanted. I could never steer my heart away because, to me, you are totally amazing. For so many years, I have thought of no one but you. Know that you made me happy, just by calling me, being my friend when the world pulled back. And now, the sadness of your death becomes overshadowed by the miracle of your spirit.

I hope you can see that many have loved you. And I hope that as days pass, you begin to see that we'll all keep you in our hearts. I am wishing you so much happiness, wherever the thereafter takes you. . . and the strength to discover it, even with all these shadows looming.

You confirmed I helped to bring happiness to your life. I have been waiting to hear that since I left the desert. My heart is open, cultivated of friendship and shared, finally, in some of your most desperate days. That I could see you in the end, in the very end. . .

I hope this friendship we share means as much to you as it has for me. I will never forget you, and I shall always love you, James.

Love, Aislin

She read over the letter again and for a third time. There was no turning back; she could see James fading into the room out of thin air. Hiding the stationery would not be an option.

Options, strangely, were gone. On the new path her life took, she moved past things that normally would consume her. Moved past regretting that it was not towards Gig Harbor. Past regretting that just the day prior, her boss took her lovebirds to live with his niece in Seattle. And past regretting that her apartment was now a sublet to an unfamiliar voice, that the window that looked over the church might be dirty and spotted with saltwater.

James was there. And even though she worried he might disappear at any moment; how could she leave him? Everything changed the moment she saw him in the flowered chair. She began making the arrangements to stay on after Alen saw him, too. How could she leave Alen? Aislin resigned herself to this hot place. This hot place where condensed seawater did not make trails on the windows, where she could not get up in the morning to lose herself in fog for hours, and she could not find a lonely bench in the rain, not anywhere. There seemed to be no unoccupied place in this city.

James was on every bench.

No regrets.

She sighed and slid the letter over to him. *I must seize every opportunity. Any minute might be our last.*

"Another letter? Oh, Aislin." Her name was a sad song in his throat, a thick and high note, a warble. His hand reached up to touch her back, but she couldn't feel his fingers. When his hand dropped, her eyes closed tightly against the world, and she waited for his voice again. When James moved around a room, he never made a sound. He did not scuffle, and his shoes never squeaked on the floors. It kept Aislin's senses on alert.

Aislin kept her eyes closed. James could stay or go, and she would not know unless he spoke to her.

"Alen just pulled up."

She opened her hazel eyes to his deep brown ones. "The beach!" Her whole body smiled. California beaches were so different from the Pacific Northwest coast; she longed to rediscover the sun and sand together in a penetrating warmth.

"I am going to go with you. At least, I think I should be able to go?"

"Alen's idea for you to see the ocean again is just perfect." She reached to touch his hand with reassurance; they both turned their heads away from what they knew would fail.

James looked at her again. "When he broke down and eventually told Victoria he could see me.... I wish you had been there. You know... when he first spoke to me? I thought he might run away screaming. But now Alen and I talk to each other like nothing happened, right? As if I am still alive."

"Wow, I'm so sorry, James. That's so hard with Alen. He loves you. He's excited about this trip. And he's overwhelmed. He's treating this like a vacation. I don't know what that would feel like. How he must feel, but I can imagine because of my parents—if they came back...." Her voice cracked with emotion, a lump in her throat growing uncomfortable. "But—it is good that Victoria's coming with us. It's good for him."

"Oh?"

"Seeing them together is heartwarming. And Jade warmed to her, too, I think."

His face turned away again. She thought she saw some unease, a shadow of darkness at the idea of Victoria. She changed the subject back to his earlier concern.

"Why do you think you won't be able to leave the Valley?"

"I do not know."

She set her chin in her hands; elbows propped on the beautiful stone.

James put his hand over the stationery, her perfect cursive almost visible through his translucence. She wondered if he could feel the coolness of the stone, but suspected not. This time, he closed his eyes.

Aislin shuddered. She wished her body were different, that she could control her display of emotional disturbances. She took a deep breath. "You know as well as I that things happen for a reason."

"I know as well as you."

They both nodded. She closed her eyes but made herself open them again quickly. Perhaps she should not close them so much while she lived; she could miss too much.

Aislin went to get her bag.

Alen met her in the Champagne Room. This is what she called it. She named all the rooms in any house after the color of the walls—a habit inspired by her childhood home had also become an element in her Athelstan Press articles.

It was midday, and the sun was in the window. Everything was catching light in the way the world does when you first realize the sun is getting lower on the horizon and fall has come. It was also shining on James.

Alen was at the window, trying not to look at his brother, but also trying not to be rude.

Aislin understood. At least, she thought she did. She wasn't James' brother. Her heartbreak could not be compared, and she had even more time to get used to this. Looking at James would always be difficult.

"Alen, I am so sorry," James said. "I never meant to leave you, and I never meant to rattle you. I did not choose this, this ghost thing."

Aislin loved how James used her words for it.

"I don't know if I can do this."

"You can." Aislin altered the quality of her voice to soothe him. "It will be like vacations you used to take together. The sun and the ocean will be good for you, Alen."

Alen shifted from foot to foot. His palms came to the windowpane, his body leaning into the structure, his hips swaying from side to side, and he gently nodded his head. "Yeah. Yeah."

He kept nodding for a moment, and Aislin worried.

"Oh my god, James. What about Jade and the kids?" Aislin's heart sunk. She had not thought about them at all—just about the ocean, about being away with James.

"It's just a few days. The boys have soccer again. With that and music lessons, there is a lot to keep them busy. Hana has plans to keep them at her house. They're excited about their time with Majka." James said, a regretful, yet contended, look in his eyes. "Victoria and Alen did some meddling." He winked at his brother.

Alen appeared more at ease. "Aislin, they will be fine. Eleanor is coming to stay with Jade. Girl's weekend." He looked at his round watch. The reflection of the face beamed onto the wall instead of flashing in James' eyes, but Alen didn't notice. "We should go, it's getting late."

Aislin trusted they were right and said nothing. Family knows best? Yet the phantom sound of Jade's swishing bottle followed them out the door. Aislin avoided eye contact as they said goodbye, sensing that they were doing Jade a disservice and hoping she was wrong.

Once in the car, she let a heavy sigh escape. She would not challenge it, but she had a feeling the Eleanor story was indeed that, just a story. Jade rarely accepted visitors, even Eleanor, who had stopped to talk to Aislin as she left one afternoon:

"I am glad you're here," she said. "I am really worried about Jade. She's been… different lately. Not just heartbreak different. You will let me know if I am needed, won't you?"

Aislin assured the woman she would, knowing deep down it was already true. Jade needed Eleanor, but the comment surprised Aislin, and she did not know how to facilitate any further.

Hopefully, Eleanor was staying the weekend. And if not, did Jade prefer solitude to Aislin's company? Maybe Jade just needed a break. They were both getting a break. Aislin let out a hopeful sigh.

Chapter 22 ✦ Victoria

"**O**H YES! SHOTGUN! THANKS SO MUCH. I GET SO CARSICK RIDING IN back." Victoria's little song of appreciation melted the tension in the car as she clamored in with a sleek tote bag full of reading material.

Alen's breath caught when she got in—shiny eyes and a loud swallow followed. Victoria's look was librarian-esque but with a sexy twist that she was happy to see appealed to Alen. She wore a light green tailored suit coat and matching pencil skirt. The golden of her eyes danced with the shiny diamonds of her violet scarf—opposites on the color wheel. Long, black hair draped her shoulders. Beneath the coat, a fitted white shirt opened to the perfect place on her chest. There was more beneath that, and she suddenly wanted him to see her right then. Her palm rested on his leg, and there was heat beneath it.

Her anticipation of him spurred an awkward chatter. "So, whatcha guys think? Ready to go out there and have oysters on the beach, escape this heat and get hit with a breeze that will remind us all how great it is to be alive?"

With a little extra pitch, Victoria continued talking to hide her statement of being alive. She spoke quickly and paused very little, rambling about the beach house, and asking questions that Alen answered monosyllabically. She hadn't been to the beach in so long and the last time had been so lovely. It was just her and her mother and the stillness that only comes from reading an excellent book. That holiday was far from what was overcoming her at the moment. She worked herself up enough that she had to stop and take a breath.

But no one else knew what to say and in the heavy silence, she grew self-conscious.

Suddenly hyper-aware that she was the only one speaking, Victoria completely dropped her running commentary. It was quiet in the car for two minutes, then five. Each of them watched the road go by. Victoria turned and looked at James sitting behind Alen, he looked at her for a moment before reverting to his long stare out the window, his irises flickering in the sunlight as his head moved, muscles appearing to contract but not contracting. His translucent eyes caused her to shudder. For someone who was not solid, he penetrated the entire desert with so much austerity; it was as if the landscape was punishing him for existing. Grief stuck in his face as cactus needles in skin. James turned back to her, and she quickly turned her head to the road before them.

She noticed Alen struggled to pay more attention to his driving and less to her clothing as the traffic thickened. She appreciated his reaction.

Victoria extended her perfect nails toward the radio dial, withdrew, then reached for it once more and turned it on. Some alternative band came on, the song brought up no memories for her; the voice was unrecognizable. She heard Aislin in the back seat, talking to James. She could see Aislin in the visor mirror, flirtatiously talking about some memory at a restaurant or bringing up a favorite band. Items that tied him to the land of the living.

Alen let out a deep breath, and she wondered how long he had unconsciously been holding it—a sure sign of a body under pressure. They all breathed, except James. Unless you watched him. He still looked like he was breathing. And often he would appear to sigh so hard, yet of course there was no sound and no air passing through his lips. His nostrils flared with no oxygen. He was a physical phenomenon.

Now that she was sitting, Victoria realized how everything hurt. Exhausted by the current ghost, exhausted by revived words from a past ghost. By her mother, by Alen. All their stories. She rubbed at her neck for a few moments, but it did little to relieve her.

"I'll find us something to listen to." She twisted the dial for a while, unfamiliar with the rental. Eventually, she found the public radio station. She and Alen laughed along with the programming they were familiar with. Tension disintegrating out the window with the weekend trivia show. Grateful they had this station in common, she forgot all about the two people in the back seat for the first time in days.

As the credits aired, she overheard James' voice, saturated with sadness. "I cannot accept that I will never hear music again. If it is true, then this is Hell."

Victoria realized he was referring to his auditory rift and realized the conversation came up because James could not hear the radio. Victoria and Alen had forgotten. She reached to turn it off but stopped when she saw Alen in a kind of oblivion, already distracted by the next program. His cheer made her drop her hand. Damn them. She had a feeling Aislin didn't need to work at tuning it out. James appeared to be the only thing in her existence.

Victoria took a deep breath. She placed her hand on Alen's thigh and settled back into the car seat, her eyes closed on autopilot. Maybe she could catch a nap. Alen's hand rested over hers and she sighed in contentment. The list of reasons for exhaustion added up: wariness, extra shifts, reading, thesis prep, and her past week as their mediator.

Regrettably, instead of sleeping, her brain analyzed Alen's stories. Some of his stories were of vacations together with his brother. The ocean was their favorite, and he wanted his brother to see it again before he moved on. He didn't remember the last time they had been there as a family—Egon had been five? Coronado Island had provided a weekend of magic. A fairytale vacation that was also stifling, with Jade being so into manners. Alen wasn't sure Nick would even remember it.

In the last years, James worked around the clock most months. Family vacations dwindled. The kids and Jade kept busy with school, swimming in the summer and soccer in the winter, cello and piano happened year-round with private lessons.

She jerked around in her seat to say something about going down to Coronado Island and saw Aislin and James' hands resting together on the seat between them. They weren't holding hands because James was not corporeal. But they were trying to. Victoria gasped, Aislin and James looked up from their daydreams to the revulsion they would surely find on her face. Her jaw open and crooked, eyes narrow. She quickly faced forward and looked outside for something else to focus on. Alen was still oblivious, laughing out loud at the multiple-choice options on the show.

The ocean liners and rigs came into view. Victoria worked to ease her distress and appreciated the landscape and pristine houses. She did not, however, let go of the judgement forming in her mind against Aislin.

They rented a house by the water off of Second. Alen pulled up and parked them in the middle of the energized feeling of the California beach city. Victoria turned to smile at Alen. James stood on the curb outside Alen's window, looking straight down the street toward the rest of Long Beach. Her will to smile, disturbed by the absence of the car door opening. But she acknowledged something important—James wasn't haunting his house, or the scene of his accident. As Alen suspected, James was still, after all these years, haunting Aislin.

But if there was any relief, it was short-lived. The tiny voice of the girl in Providence took over Victoria's contemplations. She had to see more if she was to learn what she had to do. Was it Aislin holding James back? Were the detectives right about sabotage?

She asked herself what Alen knew about hauntings. After all, until this, he never even believed in ghosts.

Chapter 23 ✦ Aislin

After a long walk on the coast, Aislin kept wondering what James was up to—but she was trying to meditate. One whole week passed since the funeral and she was taking a day to "relax" alone while Alen and James spent some quality time on the beach together—Victoria tagging along behind them.

In her room at the beach house, Aislin sat for a while with her eyes closed and her feet beneath her, conscious of the blood flow getting slower and tighter. She thought about James and how it might be for him, not knowing this type of pain anymore. He could now sit on his haunches for an unsettling amount of time, and he never noticed if he was lying on his hand or his arm was at a weird angle when they lounged on her bed. *That was unreal. Them lying together on the bed.*

Nine years prior, the only night they shared a bed space, they also took in a production of Carmina Burana. She had already been in Washington a year, but she missed James terribly. No letter could fill in for him in the flesh, and he said the same.

```
Dear Aislin,

There is always a way. There is an opera in San
Francisco.

with love, james.
```

They made a secret rendezvous.

Aislin always remembered the night of the show. The night she and James got drunk in their hotel room in San Francisco was the night she ruined her chance to be with him:

"Another shot?" he asked her.

"For us both, yes, let's toast." Aislin poured out a few fingers each of Laphroaig, their all-time favorite—if you could have an all-time favorite scotch in your early twenties. "To Carmina Burana!" she shouted in her shouting voice, all warmed up from the liquor.

"To whiskey!" James said.

"Everyone loves whiskey and scotch!" Aislin got louder.

"To snips and snails and puppy dog tails!" James started singing. "To bows and rice and everything nice!"

"Rice!!?? That isn't how it goes!!!" A laugh exploded from her.

"Well then, how does it go?" James dropped a playful fist on the arm of his chair.

But she could not remember. They both tried. They surmised quite some humor from forgetting the rest of the rhyme, and they drank more and toasted more, but they never mentioned it again to each other. Individually, they carried so much guilt from that night.

Their room was in an average hotel. They planned on different beds. But after all the drinking, they ended up crawling into one bed together, and she had not thought so much about kissing until it was happening. She tasted him, tasted the scotch, touched his back. They were so close together. And then they were thinking about Jade, and the kiss was over.

James kept sighing through his pinched face. But she froze.

"We can't."

"Yeah." He rolled over in a huff.

She listened to him breathe. And when he fell asleep, that sound slowed, and she just kept listening. She could see his curls in a mat on the pillow in the glow of the alarm clock and the next thing she knew, the sun shone brightly into her face. Aislin sat up, disoriented for a moment, until the sound of the shower registered and her eyes settled on a fresh pot of hotel coffee.

After skirting around each other in the room, they said goodbye to each other at the terminal. People bustled around in their own drama as the two of them prepared to board different flights to different homes. She looked into his eyes and the fire spread once more. He held her close during a long hug, but would barely look at her after they let go. She could not believe she had stopped them from finally making love, from finally being together.

James was a capital man. In all ways, even this one moment of indiscretion would not change him in the eyes of most—if the story of the secret kiss even left the room. It never left the room. Even Alen never heard of it, and what a moment of exclamation that may have been! She still thought about his reaction. Dreamt she knew his words:

"Well, are you going to leave Jade? You should be with Aislin...."

This was all before there were children.

Back around the time when Nick was born, Aislin obsessively scrolled through photographs on social media, yearning for a photo of James. She assumed Jade did not humor James. She resented the lack of photographs of him, and she resented Jade's lack of posts concerning him. Comment upon comment about Egon and Nick. The children were the center and the core. Every so often, she would hear a bite about the weather. "It's finally raining..." or "The temperatures have plateaued at ninety."

As Aislin aged, her understanding of others matured, and she learned that many mother's worlds centered on their children and Jade had been no exception. She was an excellent mother. Even her current process of grieving and drinking would not undo a life devoted to her boys.

As she learned bit by bit how very often James worked, wrote, locked himself within his own worlds, she realized how unfair she had been to Jade back then. The photo opportunities were scarce, and his absence had little to do with the mother. James wasn't in the photographs because he was busy making money. The Athelstan Estate didn't grow without hard work. James was a hard worker. Her heart softened toward the widow as her so-called meditation became just a long rumination.

She could think for twenty pages and never progress on her own story. She remembered and lived the past—internalized everything.

"No more 'meditating' this evening," she said aloud to herself and just sat to focus on her breath. This act relaxed her, whereas meditation as a concept often put too much pressure on a person struggling just to get through. *Start small. Just breathe, just start with the building blocks of the nervous system.*

She took another long look off the back porch, brushed her teeth, and crawled into the bed.

Once tucked in up to her chin, she stroked the sheets, their dampness soft and comforting. The hominess of the ocean's humidity wrapped around her; she settled into it.

Aislin replayed the scene where they tried to remember that nursery rhyme.

These days they could turn on the internet and read the whole child's rhyme in a matter of seconds—in the palm of their hands, even. Times had changed in so many ways.

She had grown to despise the rhyme because it falsely labeled roles and attributes for genders. *If nothing else, it can serve as a good example of what not to teach children and how to encourage a greater span of love and acceptance for themselves and others. I'll have to ask James what he thinks about that....*

Aislin let out a sigh as her heart ached for the whole world.

Chapter 24 ✦ James

James found himself on Aislin's bed—somehow summoned. He smiled at her and wanted so badly to bring her near and hold her like he never had the chance to, and now never would. He thought of Marquez's *Love in the Time of Cholera*.

She did not jump; she was past jumping when he appeared. He loved her, but his heart was in a mortar, and the pestle worked it without a break.

"That nursery rhyme did finally come to me the next day, long after you had gone," she said. "Did the boys ever learn that one?"

"Actually, I remember talking to them about it not too long ago... not too keen on it. I told them they can like anything they want, and they are made of stardust. We are each made of stardust."

"Yes! Stardust... I love that!"

God, how I love when her face lights up that way.

To make her smile more, he told her how he told his boys he would never require them to like something just because of their gender. "In the end, I admit they were the ones that schooled me on that topic!"

Aislin laughed with him, the light in her eyes shining their approval of his clever children. But after a moment, that light changed, and she looked at him with a new expression.

"James, I can't believe that you are gone now. You're gone but you are not."

"I know. It is like we have a whole new chance to be friends." A flush tried to rise in his cheeks, a bloodless, colorless flush. *Can she sense this heat inside me?*

"You speak of friendship when we're in the memory of that night?"

"Do you forget how many years it has been?" It surprised James they were going to talk about the long-ago desire. Although only moments passed since he wanted to draw her to him, he was not sure he wanted intimacy. Confused

about whether this feeling was due to his marriage, or by the passing of time—
James rubbed his eyes. Maybe it was just death.

He looked up again and tried to read her eyes. There was no getting to
their depths. He had no knowledge of where she was. Still, if he were to guess,
which he hesitated to do in all his life, but if he had to, he would say she was
still madly in love with him.

They sat together in silence for some time, the twilight fading. Both stroked
the sheet, but their eyes focused on his hand and how it did not sink through
the bed the way it sunk through her.

She looked alert suddenly, a question in her face. "James, could you tell me
about the will? I am so nervous about it being read, about Jade, too. How will
she feel? Does she know the truth? All of this is just days away. James?"

He averted the plea in her voice, her body, avoided how the whole thing,
legs and arms and head, begged him. She moved away and drew up those
legs, propped up a chin that was as wayward as his, but much smaller, finer,
smoother, solid. The eyes that found him were brimming with need.

A cat he once lived with perplexed him like this. He would want to pet this
cat so badly, but it would always stay just out of reach—knowing, sensing his
desperation to hold it and find comfort in its softness.

He moved to the chair. What else was he to do?

Why could he not remember the reason she was in the will?

The will.

The book rights and all James had ever written; all the family histories....
He did not remember why, but he remembered these things involved Aislin.

He remembered Jade saying nothing about it at all. Did she only care about
the money? Why did he care so much about the money now that he was dead,
anyway? Was this detail enough to have increased Jade's anxiety and her propensity to indulge? Was it the will and not the bid?

"Aislin, it—I do not remember, exactly. I am sorry. It has something to do
with my books?"

"Thank you for trying."

He softened and returned to her side. She held her hand out, and he almost
shrank from it, but corrected and hoped she was unaware. He put his hand
out, too. Then the two of them, it seemed to him, were almost truly touching.

Jolted into darkness, James gasped and reached out to nothing. The ceiling and the walls, and Aislin and her fingers and her hands—vanished. Without even the bed, he found he did not know if he was floating or standing on the ground. There was no sound in this place, no churr of a wren. His eyes rolled and his thoughts swirled. He could not feel a quickened pulse or heated cheeks, and he did not feel his heart pounding in his chest. But he wanted to know why! Why was it possible to have all these thoughts and emotions— why when he could feel absolutely no physiological effects?

If he were to be doomed for an eternity in Hell with severe psychological torture, he would cross that bridge where it began. He granted this blackness could be torture if it lasted and lasted. But only a few moments had passed. He lifted his arms and tuned into the air. Was it indeed holding him in suspension? Could he move from this place two steps to his left? How about to his right?

These questions all eased his panic. But his heart did not slow. Blood did not exist.

He could not say he was stepping, as his determination of solid ground was indistinct. James did a turn. Was he hanging in air? Suspended like a puppet? Could he pretend he was Fred Astaire and dance around? Pretend his feet climbed a wall or hit the ceiling? *If I were Fred Astaire....*

But the thought of the iconic dancing, singing actor did not stay with him—for the next moment he was looking at his lonely, shadowed face in a mirror. The eyes that looked back at him looked decades younger. These eyes were unaffected by sun and time and the knowledge of the wretched and war, unaffected by the end of his life. The boy that looked back did not seem to know his fate. He looked relaxed. A James from another dimension.

He did not recognize this James. Did not know him.

James did not speak to himself. What could he say?

Could he give a warning to this apparently younger version of himself? If this was not other-dimensional James, could this be a James from the past...? He could warn of the heavy ball that would swing out and casually crush out his heart in the desert heat. Yes. Warn yourself.

But move his lips and his tongue, he could not. They would not budge, words would not form, and although it made sense to him, it surprised him he could speak at all. Without speech, would he be able to help his brother? Was being in the darkness and then being in front of this mirror a sort of passageway to his final resting place?

Aislin. Jade. Alen.

Egon. Nick. Hana.

Would he ever see them again? Be able to be so remarkably close so as to watch the rising of their chests? See his Jade waste away from the bottle and his mother of old age? These things would happen if he were alive as well, he knew. And he did not know if he wanted to see any of it happen. At least in death, he may not know their fate. He could not know; he could project. Perhaps Aislin was there to watch after Jade...

The eyes in the mirror did not confirm or deny any of his questions. *Damn this.* He did not need a mirror self to tell him he was responsible, in part. He knew it. But he also knew better. That very propensity to drink ran back generations. But he digressed.

It was not the matter of the disease that made him cringe; it was that he could not help her, and he knew Aislin was not there to help her, either. He had no magic to fertilize such a seed in her mind. And Alen could not help Jade. James was going to have to live with the fact that she was beyond his help. He was suddenly so infuriated with this passive, younger version of himself that he lashed out at the mirror. It transformed into smoke and the universe once again pitched him into deep darkness.

Live with the fact.... He hung his head after realizing that, once again, he blurred the lines of life and death.

❧

With that thought, as if the universe heard him, James appeared back into the bedroom where he left Aislin. But he could see nothing; night had fallen outside the windows and over the ocean. The room was vacant of her smell and vacant of her energy. *I cannot smell or see. I cannot understand how I know anything, how I even know that I am in her room now and was nowhere before.*

Yet he knew he was in the right place.

His family would never want for anything material. They had everything. He had certainly seen to that. Thus, there were consequences. Jade's drinking. He expected a reactive twist of the stomach but suffered nothing.

The easy in-and-out style of this rental, combined with its ocean views, was a luxury the traveling band could afford. There was no reason they should not all be comfortable. Even if he was the very opposite of comfortable, that was not new to him. *Death was not comfort. It carried regret.*

Since traveling to Long Beach, the many oversights of his existence in the world of the dead were tallying up more and more chalk marks. Even after these bizarre segments of darkness, he continuously caught himself thinking that he held real presence with his friends and family. James did not want to keep another list. He just wanted to rest.

A reflection of another letter reminded him how far he had come. In his

Aislin days, his emotions were uncontrollable. He lost himself in sprawling Los Angeles for days. He was everything he did not desire to model for his own boys.

Nothing was sacrificed by recreating himself, by going back to his early years. He became the boy his father and mother raised—he was who they meant for him to be, not a strung-out twenty-year-old drifter.

But the pain was real, and their paths had to collide. He knew his experiences were vital to growth; it was destiny for Aislin to hear his stories. She existed as the confidant he trusted. And perhaps the darker letters drove away the woman he loved, perhaps his acute perception was too great for her and that is why she left him... but he knew better. Her words could be equally dark and their perceptions intertwined. And now he witnessed how she tied her worth up in her decision to part with him. Aislin's regret remained pungent. Yet for them both, all of it was necessary.

December 15, 2003

Aislin,

My heart—

Any box I ever built to protect it fell apart or
burned to ash.

I am silent as I skulk around the house. Alen notices
it, too, and he watches me. My brother, trying to
engage me. But I tell him I do not feel like eating.
I need to get out of here—to return to the streets. I
need you. Thanksgiving was horrible. the time without
you weaves sticky webs around me and leaves the
carcasses of what a giant spider finds unappealing.

After six months, it has become clear that you will
never move back to the desert.

Except I am here. I hope I am the part of your mind
that has never rested. I am the unending connections
that tie the world together. Which is why I have
always struggled. It is because I am really listening
to the haunting noise that crawls in the silent night…
Are you really paying attention? I know I let you get
away.

ever, james

Chapter 25 ✦ Victoria

THE BEACH HOUSE WAS MOSTLY QUIET. ALEN DRIFTED OFF THE MOment they said good night. At one point, she heard the door to the ocean open and close, Aislin's footsteps climbing the stairs. Water ran and everything was quiet again. A few minutes passed. The faint whispers of Aislin and James entered her consciousness, but soon all inside sounds softened and Victoria could only hear the waves and the traffic on 2nd Street. She watched the occasional set of headlights reach the ceiling through a small gap near the curtain rod.

It was a danger that everyone was becoming comfortable with James being around. Victoria worried the most about James, though. She could feel he possessed the same consciousness that he did as a living person. She feared that his interactions with his brother and Aislin would cause him to become stuck where he didn't belong, whether that was with them or in the darkness he feared. Many moments came to pass when it seemed he forgot—that they all forgot—he was a ghost.

She wanted that to stop. He needed to cross.

Victoria did not feel the situation was fair. She knew that the mourning period that was supposed to follow his funeral was in danger of permanent delay. Certainly, the heartbreak would be far greater when he left for the second time.

The memory of meeting Jade the week before entered her mind. In the grand parlor, Victoria took the widow's offered hand, and held it for a moment. And although the tone of her voice was warm, Victoria sensed that beneath the pain she could see on the surface, something deeply unstable was happening within.

"Alen's mystery woman is even more beautiful than he boasts," The teasing of Jade's brother-in-law pinked his cheeks, a sight Victoria relished.

"Thank you." Victoria blushed as well, trying to act comfortable while her senses were calculating. If she were to commit to Alen, she wanted to know what she was getting into.

Victoria always observed with her sixth sense—it did not shock her to see an intense grief split Jade's fabricated smile. The crack widened into her everyday life. Spider veins around the nose were red and raw, her skin seemed dry and she looked like she was aging rapidly compared to the newspaper photo of the family together. Victoria's heart sunk as she realized Jade could not hide something from a stranger that she might have thought, and certainly hoped, she was hiding. During the brief embrace that followed, Victoria also smelled it.

Beneath the booze and the grief, there was something else buried in Jade that Victoria sensed: something mocking, perhaps a feeling of contempt. The secret they kept about James could be getting to Jade. The woman likely picked up that they withheld something. But even if that was it, Victoria wouldn't tell anyone. She was steadfast in keeping James a secret. The knowledge benefited no one.

The children beckoned from a hallway, and Jade invited Victoria into the rest of the house. Alen introduced her to the dogs and suggested a tour. Victoria kept her tentacles out, reaching and probing. The more she dug, the more grief she encountered. She prodded, as Jade gave a tour of the house. But Victoria could not capture it. In each room they visited, the deeper struggle behind the widow's sorrow spun into the cobwebs of the high ceilings.

She finally let her psych eval rest and took Alen's hand for comfort and escape. Before the tour was over, Alen had largely taken over and Jade fell to the back of the group, finally disappearing down a hallway, past a shrine smelling of cheap wax and burnt paper.

Did she have the responsibility to talk to Alen about it? The boys seemed to respond normally to losing their father. But there was no hospice team to assess this family: no red, yellow, or green label to request professional guidance. And to complicate things, as a mandatory reporter, Victoria could not let the mother with alcoholism stray far from her thoughts.

In their modern room at the beach house, Victoria tried to fall asleep beside Alen. She relished the movement of the blankets as they slid back and forth over her body with his even exhalations. Making love to him filled her with a growing satisfaction. She placed her hand on his arm and sucked in his warmth.

James appeared in the room, but faded out slowly. From what she understood of his reality, he might sense he was in his brother's room, but without natural light, he could not see.

She could make him out in the gloom although he lacked a shadow or substance. Victoria wondered if he emitted his own light. A shiver passed over her entire body, goose bumps prickling her smooth skin. Her heart pounded in her chest, and she held her breath until the apparition faded.

He unsettled her.

This was not natural, and she wanted more than anything to find a solution, to abate the voice in her head, the growing warning. She wanted him to cross over and leave Alen in peace to mourn and cope. That was the real reason she would not tell Jade; it would just make things that much harder for the grieving woman.

In the car on the way to beach, Aislin was tender and overly considerate toward James. Victoria realized she wore a sort of sneer when she witnessed them try to hold hands. She was not entirely sure why, but Aislin got shorter towards her after noticing. A curt "Cream?" instead of a more gracious "Do you want cream?" for example, was something that Victoria caught onto quickly, not that formality equaled politeness, more of an observation of tone, body language, and normal tenderness.

Victoria picked up on Aislin's utter desperation for James to stay in their world. She could feel the desperation for anything *James*. She knew James picked up on it as well. With their past, they must have both agreed they were getting a second chance together.

They weren't getting a second chance.

They were increasing their spooky factor.

Victoria wanted peace.

Peace for the mother and brother.

Peace for the grieving widow and the fatherless children.

Victoria decided not to share what she had overheard in the bar. At least, not yet. Alen spoke with the coroner himself. He knew the timeline of his brother's death. He knew his project was unpopular. The detectives were just speculating. Weren't they?

Her strong suspicions that a murder would expose a darkness that they could not escape skewed her normal forthrightness. She would rather Alen spend his time healing than become obsessed with a possible, but unlikely, case of foul play. Victoria realized this small omission was a lie that took his choices away. It made her wonder about her own motives in their relationship. If she wasn't being honest with Alen, what was she doing? Protecting him? But from what, exactly?

Just a few days ago, Alen was staying the night at her apartment. He wiped his eyes and nose with most of a box of tissue and Victoria learned more details about his family. His father was a British diplomat and his mother an orphan whose parents were both casualties of the Second World War. Alen interrupted his own speech, trying to find a tissue to wipe his nose and puffy eyes. She handed him a box. He hid his face behind his hands as he sniffled. "I don't cry every time I tell this story."

Alen sat before her on the foot of her bed, cross-legged, an elbow rested on his knees. He shifted and allowed her to see his face with one hand propping up his heavy head, and the other tracing the seams of her quilt. She reached and smoothed the hair of his arm.

He seemed to look around the room for a moment, and she wondered what he thought of the décor. Although it was small, it was easy to keep clutter to a minimum, and that pleased her. The walls remained the classic white of every rental. In soft and attractive sky-blue pajamas, she perched on her memory chest at the foot of her bed. The skin of her arms chilled with the night air and her neckline was fluid, often showing a glimpse of more. His eyes turned back to hers.

"Lašva Valley. Our home was northwest of Sarajevo, but I do not know how many realize the war was everywhere in the region. It was a miracle we could get out. My father lied about our identities. He secured fake documents." His voice broke, and she noticed his color rise. "We made it to sea. Past the graves, the bodies we drove around on the street. Everything was wrong. Vitez was a ghost town...." He looked at her suddenly. "My brother is a ghost."

Victoria reached and once more smoothed his skin, his hair. She reached out to keep one of his hands in hers.

Alen cleared his throat. "Peace here in California lasted only a few years. My father died in an accident, too. A fire caught—a fire burned our home when we went with my mother to see some movie. I don't even know the name, but I think James could tell you." Alen gently took his hand back. His chest rose as he sucked in all the air from the room. Finally, he just let his eyes settle on the blue pattern of the quilt.

She could see his neck muscles bulge and pulse. Victoria rose to the bed behind Alen. With the heaviness of James' death, his father's death, and the wars of former Yugoslavia hanging in the air, her hands tried to work out his muscular tension. Tears continued to slide down his face. He was silent for some time, eventually turning his face to her. Each time they made love was more poignant than the last.

The night grew long by the ocean. The thick curtains smothered Victoria as she remembered Alen's choked narrative. She thought of Hana and her sons at a movie while their loved one tragically suffocated, trapped inside their home. *How were the Athelstans successful with all they underwent?*

Was it possible the fire was foul play? Initiated by war criminals that followed them back from Vitez? She dismissed the thought with an almost imperceptible headshake. The atrocious political parties involved in this war of the early nineties were not likely to follow refugees across the globe—unless there was a long-buried vendetta against his father's involvement. She detested that much speculation.

Victoria did not sleep for many hours. She was aware of Alen's breath, fascinated by the sheets sliding over their skin. The clue was under her nose and she was almost upon it....

"My father died in an accident, too," he'd said.

A connection to their father was unlikely.... Why else would the detectives need to dig further? Was the mere mention that it was unsolved putting unnecessary thoughts in her head? Who made the threats to the mayor, and how could she find out?

As if in response to the question, the words of the little girl in Providence lit up Victoria's brain.

She sat in the darkness, coaxing a revelation into being: *Meddling is only going to make it harder for the family.* With that thought, the girl quieted down. It was a sign of agreement. The resolution to ignore that part of things solidified before exhaustion took her mind into a dreamless night.

Chapter 26 ✦ Aislin

WHEN JAMES DISAPPEARED FROM THE ROOM IN THE MIDDLE OF THEIR talk, she found she could not breathe. And once again, she tried to focus on the room. That is a lamp and that a chair, and so forth. Gasps followed and begged for improvement.

Aislin could only guess why, but Victoria was no longer interested in helping her. Asking was too much—confrontation undesirable. But this abandonment was not subtle, and Aislin still hoped for the woman's steady breath to guide her. She saw the strange, golden eyes. And she listened for the breath. But, of course, Victoria never came, and nautical twilight took its last breath of sunlight before the darkness of astronomical twilight swallowed the very last rays and brought in the night. Aislin looked outside, streetlights reflected falsely. Cities that never slept stretching for miles in all directions. Finally, calm, she rested her head on the pillow but couldn't sleep. *Damn the rotation of the earth!*

The moon, just renewed, beckoned her outside beneath an unbelievably clear city sky. The tide was out, but not completely. Each wave that came in filled the loneliness of the room she left behind. She sat for hours, knees settled deep in the sand, feet spread so her bottom made its own imprint as well. The black ocean waves took her in. They aren't empty. *They are full of life. Like James. Can he still hear the waves?*

She let herself drift within the surf. A cradle that held her in dark arms lapped at her consciousness and protected her. The focus eased her; only the waves came and went. Washing in peace and washing out desperation. The ocean was her friend back home, and she had spent Washington nights the same way on the shore at Iron Springs. The crashing waves kept her going. She thought of choosing a new meditation with the waves, something that would keep nourishing after she turned her back and went to the desert.

The moon dropped into the western horizon when the numbness in her legs became a sensation over the sound of the waves. Aislin raised her hips and adjusted her body into child's pose. As her weight shifted, the sand gave way beneath her body like flowing hourglasses.

Are we running out of time? Did he disappear because of this maddening thing with natural light? Confusion flooded the weird conditions that came with this afterlife. Why had he not returned with the moonlight?

The long meditation halted—he was back with her again. James, her personal ghost. Yet he wasn't there all the way. She wondered if the moonlight was too pale, too far away to give him enough light to see by.

I will always love you. No time can change that. No pale moon.

There was so much wrong. She sighed deeply and fatigue caused her to practice an incomplete sun salutation to the moon.

The house stood before her, windows wide and black. The darkness seemed to be everywhere, but it was just a little light that she needed to make it to her room, just a glimmer. She entered through the gaping door on the back porch, padded across the damp rug, and found her way through the dark hallway. When she opened the bedroom door, the moon greeted her through the floor to ceiling windows. Her lonely, pale friend.

She fell asleep in the chair making wishes at the moon and stars, telling them stories of her mother and father. Crying.

Pounding interrupted a dream in which she was at Athelstan House. She had to sneak out because Jade had just pulled into the driveway. James was not dead, and she was going through his things. She was eating their food.

"Aislin!"

Oh my god, now Alen is going to catch me.

"Aislin! Are you awake?"

And yes, she was awake. Escaped from another one of those dreams where she was visiting James and he would either hold her or send her away. And in this one, she was stalking him. It was creepy. She shook it away.

"Hi, Alen." Her voice came out hoarse as she opened the door to let him into her bedroom.

He sank into the warm chair she had spent the night in.

"How are you this morning?"

"Tired." She rested her body on the edge of the bed, her posture slackened. Aislin thought he looked a little more rested.

"Victoria made coffee."

She watched the corners of his mouth rise a little, taking her heart with them.

"My sweet friend," she said, and placed her arm around his shoulders as they went downstairs.

And so, just a week after the funeral, they greeted Sunday just before sunrise. Happiness eluded them, teasing with dogs running past and kite boards sailing over the water. Existence was long, the way she imagined two old men on a neighborhood sidewalk playing an endless chess game on a wooden folding table, the small wobble in the leg corrected with matchbooks for their pipes. She could see full oak trees overhead, creating the perfect shade for a summer evening. James would never be one of these men.

And these men played differently than the way she played with James' kids. Nick and Egon played a game so fast, Egon swiping the queen over and over and Nick eager to figure out a better strategy, yet still too inexperienced to see the big picture. It was different on those slow, cracked sidewalks. Aislin imagined someday when the boys became old and grey, they would slide the pieces across the board, occasionally knocking down the rook with the wrinkle of a tremoring hand. Their lives would pass by with each slow movement; spotted fingertips alight on a pawn, disengage, land on a bishop.

Action is a tease to the senses. Progress is a joke. Except this was not a chess game. This was the fate of the man she loved. He disappeared for longer and longer intervals.

Downstairs in the kitchen, glass doors were open to the ocean—new clouds asked the water to match the sky, swathing the water in shadow. Victoria served the coffee from a carafe, everything set like a tea party. Matching mugs, cream, and sugar bowls. She poured for Aislin and asked her how she took it.

"Everything. A lot of everything. Please."

Alen took his coffee black and sank into the biggest chair in the room.

Aislin looked outside to see orange grow on the horizon, coaxing brightness from the surface. Glassy stripes of orange and black transmuted and altered its shape. A small flock of seagulls flew down the shoreline.

"Funny how the furniture is so oversized and comfy. It almost makes you want to stay in instead of going to the beach... and the bed linens and these doors. I feel so spoiled...." Victoria sounded like a radio that was turned on for background noise; she kept talking without pause. Aislin was too tired to focus on every word. She tried, but the ocean called her, and the coffee already needed a refresh.

The progression of sunrise changed the corners of the house. And with this fresh light, James appeared on the stairs. The miraculously thin wooden treads were walnut and rectangles of grey carpet. There were no risers. She could see the wall through James' ankles, his calves, his pelvis, ribs, his shoulders, the top of his head. James, the love of her life, ragged and tousled, the same as the day she'd arrived.

Halfway up the staircase, the ghost looked out the open doors to the shore. He hugged himself, palms cupping his shoulders. His jaw clenched as something beyond the doors drew his attention.

Alen's voice came like a cheery bell, "The sun is up." He looked around for his brother.

Their eyes finally met, and James descended the staircase. The absent risers left the impression that he was walking on air—or floating. He walked over to his brother, shoulders easing down and hands dropping. He may have wanted to hug him and realized he could not, so halfway there he just stopped walking. His fists balled up and energy rolled off of him. Frustrated tension.

After shuffling around with some trinkets on a little table, he grabbed a bar stool and sat facing the open doors.

No one spoke. They watched the sun instead.

But Aislin couldn't stand the quiet that had descended on the group. "Why don't you two enjoy the beach before you go home? I was thinking of staying on; if that's okay? I can get a rental car and drive back in a day or so. I just want some time alone. And you have things to get back to."

No one answered.

Alen stood, turned from the room and walked onto the deck. James faded, and Aislin's breath caught. Although he regularly vanished, she remained unprepared for the reality that a person could be in the room one moment and gone the next. It defied the definitions she created for things; the ones taught to her, even the ones she always ignored. *James' disappearing breaks the world.*

She looked at Victoria, whose mouth hung open. Aislin pulled her jaw back together and swallowed hard. The striking woman's gaze dropped towards her coffee mug; the steam hit her cheeks. A flick of light glinted off her eyes. The energy changed, and Victoria's body language caused Aislin to retreat to a safer distance.

A rift dividing her from allies—*But why?*

With rounded shoulders and a knotted gut, Aislin followed Alen outside to figure out the silent treatment of her proposition. She put a hand on Alen's back. "What is it?"

"Why are you asking me to leave you? Don't you want my company anymore? Times have changed so much for us. I mean, I understand about Jade...." Alen trailed off. She knew he was sensitive to her issues and didn't want to hit her with anything.

Earlier in the week, when she'd closed a book on her life back in Washington; subletting her apartment, giving her precious birds away... she wasn't wholly ready to accept it. This trip helped her remember how close the ocean was to Palm Desert. Only a few hours in the car... But how could she move away from the ocean? Alen didn't know all the ways it kept her alive. Maybe only the poet Pablo Neruda understood the ways she was indebted to the ocean's lessons.

Staying at the beach meant healing, going back with Victoria and Alen meant finding a job and forcing herself to move forward when she wasn't ready. It meant facing the move back to California. But had she actually decided it? Or had she just gone through the actions to make it happen? Regardless, it left her anxious. The beach was nonthreatening. She opened her mouth to tell Alen all of that, but different words came out:

"Alen, you know I want you around. I just can't bring myself to leave the ocean right now." She made eye contact with him. "Also, I don't want to get in the way, and Jade... well, staying there with her... it's harder than I thought."

Alen's eyes widened, and he swayed. He understood. James picked Jade. "I hadn't thought about it that way, all the emotions it must bring up for you. He picked her. I get that, now. I'm sorry. But I don't feel okay to just leave you behind." He dropped his voice. "I wish I could say that James would be here with you, but he's in and out, Aislin. You will be all alone."

He looks so, so tired. He was just hiding it before, somehow. A trick of the light. Catawampus. All of this.

She didn't know the answer and shrugged. Alen turned so he could see Victoria inside. She watched him make eye contact with Victoria and noticed his lips were slightly parted. But after a moment, Alen's eyes darted around the room and found James gone. His gaze fell to the wooden slats of the patio.

She placed her hand on his shoulder. Her old friend. His heart losing structure with each grieving breath.

After a long embrace with Alen that warmed her, she returned to the kitchen and stopped to say something to Victoria. But all the words seemed wrong and nothing came out.

"We'll catch up soon," Victoria said.

Alen joined them around the kitchen island. "Are you sure you will be okay alone, Aislin?"

She nodded, shrugged. *Maybe.* "Yes, I'll be fine, Alen," she smiled to appease him. "It's just two nights and one day, really. I will be back early on Wednesday."

Alen accepted this with a nod and disappeared up the stairs. She gave another glance at Victoria, who looked like she was pretending to read the paper, stepped out the door while stuffing a house key into her jeans. For hours, the coast took her footprints. Some were sucked away at once where others might remain until high tide, but each of them would fade, each of them embraced impermanence—one of the many lessons in the sea.

March 11, 2000

dearest James,

forgive me my friend…. i got so, so lost, next time
the plane crashes. or the boat… well, perhaps this is
why we go back and forth and i can never be there.
really there. i try to reach into pandora every day…

it's the way you tell me that you love my skin.

the way i think of what you could be doing in the
darkness.

it's the way i can't escape the trap i set for myself.
and i never seem to tell the truth.

yet i always hope to see you at the hotel. and that
hope never dies

ever, aislin

Chapter 27 ✦ Aislin

THE OCEAN WAVES KEPT COMING. THEY KEPT WASHING AWAY SAND, and they kept bringing in sand. Tears kept coming, they kept washing away salt, and they kept bringing in salt and… relief? She only wished.

James was okay. They believed in love.

And she loved James, and she could still sense his presence.

She didn't like their story, unfinished as it was, resolution out of reach.

Coldness swept across her shoulders as she leaned towards James' imperceptible arm. He should not have held her up, yet she did not fall through him. She massaged the overtight muscles of her core. Beneath her fingertips, the muscles were stone, her center carved from marble rather than flesh. These muscles built a wall of protection for her abdomen. They ached with anxiety. They were solid, tense, guarded—a shield against the instability and unknown of her past, present, and future.

"Nothing is working out the way you planned." Words spoken in tones just as imperceptible as his form were worth worry.

"Did I really have a plan?" Aislin asked him.

He nodded, "But you changed it."

She shut her eyes and wished for her lovebirds and her couch, the way its old pillows folded around her, sucking her body in with their own sense of care.

I can't focus.

As cold air swept around her temples and her head relaxed, she was grateful without measure for James; his gentle, not-quite-contact head massage was effective, sucked away the pain—albeit arresting in its mystery.

Hours later, her phone rang. She watched the phone light up with Alen's name and then sent the call to voicemail. Maybe she just needed a little space from Victoria and things would be better when she returned. *I hope so.*

Aislin wasn't sure what Victoria thought was going to happen. The woman's very cheerfulness, high-strung nerves, and overconfidence were building around something. *I don't trust Victoria. Why don't I trust Victoria? Alen loves her, it would be so nice to love her, too. To have a sister, of sorts. I want Alen to have what he needs. And if she makes him happy....*

Yet, there is something about her... the more Aislin thought of it, the more it was as if Victoria was trying to get James to leave. Along with Jade's less-then-warm attitude, Victoria contributed to her desire to stay at the beach alone. Aislin wanted to make friends, but she saw the disapproving glances and felt the opposite was true in Victoria. Aislin just wanted James' fears to subside, for him to stay with her and Alen. No frightening shadows, no darkness. She hated to ignore Alen, but she was just too tired to talk.

Back in her room, sandstorm dreams crept into her mind. The sounds of the waves outside swept away the terror, thwarting it off to another day.

Clouds obscured sunrise on her fourth day at the beach. What light could find a way reflected off the ocean in melancholy yellow. The waves swallowed any color left and brought it deep away from the surface, while the clouds continued to build with ceremony. The deck of the beach house allowed a perfect view of the grey sea.

A quiet day at the beach alone. Aislin sat with her knees to her chest, holding a glossy architecture magazine, but not looking at it. Several drops of rain hit the window behind her head, splashed onto the skin of her arms. She let it tease her, remain puddled in the folds of her limbs. With its slight sustenance, it consumed her. She did not turn when her ears picked up a dying engine that sounded so much like a boat. Before she could get out of the rain and go inside, the triggers forced her mind backwards, involuntarily recreating the day her parents died....

...the front door, the screens. After a few moments of shuffling, her mother called, "We'll see you in a bit, honey." The backdoor slammed shut, the boat motor started. It was a ten-minute trip up the small harbor to get groceries. They did it once a week. Teenaged Aislin sat reading in her favorite harbor-facing window like she always had. High gusts of wind gave her pause in her book, but more absorbed in the story, she only raised her eyes for a second at the torrential rain and wind. She kept reading. An hour passed by... maybe it was longer. Lightning peeled across the sky, thunder broke her out of her literary trance as it charged the air with negative ions and a subsequent crash. Sudden noise, almost like a train, shook the ground. She looked at the clock. Over two hours had passed. Perhaps she did not hear them return.

At the base of the stairs, she saw the lock engaged on the back door. No trace of the boat, nor the sight of their arms full of groceries, nor their smiling faces down at the end of the dock. There was only rain.

"Where are they?" She enjoyed the cool glass on her forehead as she rested it for a moment, peering hard to find the boat in the rain. The charge of the next lightning strike struck so close, she could almost see the split air particles. Thunder shook her away from the window. A deep quiet consumed the house for a moment before another horizontal rain—like the one she had ignored upstairs—hit the house. She retreated from the rear windows to the darker interior of the front of the house. Through that window, a Washington State Police car. Its muddy wheels left tracks on the round stones of their drive. The ranger fought off the rain with a coat over his head while raising his hand to the doorbell. She still remembered the moment she made eye contact with the ranger through that window. She ran out the side door, carrying in her heart a fear much deeper than the storm and escaping the message he carried for her in that face of grief and pity.

It took three days for anyone to find her hiding place in the boathouse of a vacation home, and by then the state had no patience. Fourteen years old. Orphan. Many foster homes before she blindly followed Cliff to the desert for college. Too sad, unreachable.

Climbing out of the memory took effort. She brushed the raindrops away. A million drops hit the sand and the wood, each one feeling the desires of an empty paper cup. With tears choking her path, she wound through the beach house and then to the shower. She wept into tanning hands, back pressed against the shower wall as unstable legs held her body at an awkward angle. Water and mucus took her breath, yet she found herself unable to stop the sobs. She had not remembered the day they died so vividly in years, and she knew James' death and the Death Valley storm created a path to her memories of deep fear and sadness.

Two days crept by since she had last seen James. All of Tuesday passed without him. She bought and lit candles so he could see at night. But he was a no-show; her loneliness went unmeasured. The area of knots that she once knew as her stomach flexed, relaxed, and flexed repeatedly. She remembered how his eyes had tethered to the setting sun the last time she observed him. James. Her favorite thing to observe.

But all tears must stop. Soon we run dry. She sobered and finished her shower; thoughts collecting with the water around her feet. It was time to go back to

Palm Springs. They would read the will that afternoon, a reception to follow.

As she drove east, James appeared in the car beside her. Her nervousness melted. A smile tugged at her mouth as he hummed 90s pop rock.

She drove for an hour before James disappeared again. As she came around the last bend in the valley that opened to the desert, she saw a dust storm rise in the rearview mirror. Her throat began to constrict in that familiar way, and she accelerated in a panic without regard to road safety.

No more dust storms. Not ever.

The space between the car and James' towering front door was closed within minutes. She slammed the massive door on its state-of-the-art hinges, but it barely reverberated beneath her sweaty palms as she continued to push against the door. She had not looked twice at the dust devil to assess its threat. Had not even slowed, but she was sure it was miles wide. Once the click sounded, she slid her back along the cold, carved mass. Coming to a stop on the parquet floor, uncomfortable breaths forced her rib cage out and out again.

Her eyes darted around the room, but she did not hear anything. She swore she'd sensed the sound of sand hitting the house. But everything was so still. The light at the closest window was brilliant and the palms and the bushes in the yard were immaculate. Still. They didn't stir in a frenzy of wind, nor did they sway.

Retracing her steps, Aislin recalled shutting the door with little resistance. No wind whipped behind her, and the air was clear of dust. The sun shone; she had a shadow with every step. "What a fool I am..." she whispered as she raised her hands up, letting her fingers just hang in her hair. The pressure built and pulled on her scalp. No sand there either, not like before. A cactus wren broke the spell of silence.

I'm losing my mind.

She forced herself up and to the window—a look outside told her the truth. Her clean rental caught the sun, the cactus wrens continued. No dust storm at all. Calm. She had made the whole thing up from the sight of one typical Californian dust devil. Anxiety exploded from her.

An uncontrolled step back from the window caused a crash into the central pedestal. On it: the replica of the beautiful Stari Most Bridge. James built the model in his final year of college. Made of tiny wooden slivers, it was the project that more than inspired his life's work and the confidence to move forward in his career. The fragile woven wood would do nothing but splinter to pieces upon hitting the tile—she lunged for it but misjudged her space and flew headfirst into the wall.

Chapter 28 ✦ Hana

ANA DID NOT LOOK FORWARD TO THE READING OF HER SON'S WILL. James let her know he was writing one, but she refused the conversation. She could never understand how he could have been so nonchalant about such a subject. She knew that Alen and Jade shared the sentiment. All of them shirking James. "No. No, James, just keep this morose activity to yourself."

She shuddered. Her bare arms prickled at the vehicle's cold leather interior and this topic of wills. Nick and Egon's soccer field came into view; she focused on that instead. Her head ached from thirst. Hana drank deeply from her water bottle to help ease the tension. It was amazing what a little water could do.

After the game was over, the boys climbed into the backseat with her. Alen and Victoria were in the front. She leaned her neck back to rest. Nick dozed as soon as he finished his juice box. Egon sat in the middle. His empathic nature, much like her own, replaced his excitement at once. Egon always knew when to comfort, and he took her hand. They rode a few blocks in silence before a horrible image of Aislin drowning jolted Hana upright.

"What is it, grandma?"

"Alen. Go to James' house now."

"Majka?" His shoulders and hands surrendered, the tension fleeing from him as he uttered the one word that always brought safety.

"Alen, you have to go for Aislin."

"Why Majka?"

"Aislin."

"Sorry, yes, I heard you. What are you talking about?" He glimpsed her unblinking eyes in the rearview mirror.

He pulled off at the exit and onto the shoulder.

"Why have you stopped, Alen?" Hana said with a rare annoyance towards her son.

He turned around completely and looked into his mother's eyes. "What is it, Majka?"

"I had a dream that she was drowning."

"Drowning?" He flinched.

Hana automatically thought of suicide. *Would that not be the best way for Aislin to join James? Her son and his long-time friend, together forever?* The feeling of how much Aislin might wish for the same fate consumed Hana.

Victoria made an audible gibberish sound and reached for her phone to call Aislin. Alen stilled her with a brush of his hand as his mother continued.

"It is not about the drowning, but danger of some sort. I sense she is alone and in trouble," Hana said.

It was funny how her son knew her to be intuitive, but never had it been life or death. When he finally listened to the words she was saying, and perhaps remembered she had a sense for things, he stopped questioning her and navigated back into the traffic.

Hana knew how her boys loved that girl. Hana, like her boys, always felt so close to Aislin. Her heart adopted a daughter. And when the girl moved to Washington, James could not hide his misery from his mother, but Hana also wished for her return. All the recent conversations and Alen's concern for Aislin reconnected Hana with the girl and quietly reopened up the portal through which her extra senses worked.

"I believe we should call an ambulance, Alen. Now."

Hana watched Victoria get her phone out, but she just stared at it for a moment.

Alen said, "Victoria. Call 911."

In slow motion, Hana watched Victoria turn back to her cell phone. She dialed and kept the phone on speaker.

The dispatcher wanted details about blood, fire, drowning, overdose, breathing; knowledge Victoria did not have. "Oh, I think she's not waking up. I don't know. . . . I am in the other room with the kids. My boyfriend is with her now."

The words came out odd and echoing, like listening through a tunnel. Victoria lied, but she had to lie.

The vision interrupted her thoughts again. Hana's eyes shut tight and her hands reached up to her head to a tender spot. Not drowning, but bleeding. Blood drowned her connection with Aislin.

When the subsequent vision ended, Hana opened her eyes. Alen rushed through traffic quickly enough to match Hana's urgency. As they drove at the max of the maximum speed limit, Alen focused only on the traffic. He would not allow himself to share the thoughts about what they would find at the house. Her sons were often like that. Trapdoors full of emotion.

Hana tried to shift her old bones into a more comfortable position. The slick seats of the modern car caused her to slide around with Alen's quickened pace. She gripped the door handle and one grandson claimed her other hand. The other child slept.

Seeing Nick sound asleep seemed to be just the grounding Hana needed. She took a deep breath and let it flow out. Controlled, purposeful breaths brought her back into alignment with her typical self.

Engaged in her grandchildren again and free of the gripping vision, she watched Egon pick up the empty juice box off Nick's lap while she assessed her youngest grandson. Slumped into his seat with a twisted frown and balled up little fists. Relieved he did not awaken, she wished she could bring comfort to his restless little face.

"It is okay, Egon," she said. "We will all get there in time. Aislin will be okay."

"I know, Majka." His response came hollow though, and Hana felt it in her hollow parts, too. The deafening of her heartbeat hit her ears.

She rearranged their hands so she could hold on to his better. Let go of the handle and patted their clasped hands. Their bodies relaxed into each other. Her Egon might be young, but he had always had his grandfather's wisdom, and so much like his father, too. The spitting image at this age.

Hana allowed herself to grieve for James as a little boy, as well. It seemed like a foreign thing to her leading up to this point.

She recalled his last birthday on autopilot throughout each day. A rare joy had filled him that day. The library glowed yellow from a haze-filtered sun. His gramophone was playing a record she danced to with his father. He swept Jade into his arms and around and around the furniture.

That smile surfaced for Hana. His smile and the way his eyes crinkled at the laughter of his children. A close shave with oiled curls. The way he had unknotted his tie and messed up the collar, living in the worlds of a professional and an artist. No more dancing to those nostalgic songs and breathing in the smells of sweat mixed with his sandalwood aftershave.

No more birthdays.

Egon patted her leg. He could sense her grief. She thought for a moment that maybe the afternoon was traumatic for Egon. The emergency call on speaker phone combined with the intense emotions was a lot for her—let alone an eight-year-old boy. And did Nick bring this into his subconscious as he slept?

She did not know, but at last, she settled on a silver lining. It would prepare Egon to make calls like this in the future. After all, life was unpredictable.

Chapter 29 ✦ Aislin

THE AIR WAS COOL AROUND HER HEAD AND TORSO, BUT AISLIN DID not register the rest of her body. Her eyes took a moment to focus. The unfamiliar room became her swimming pool. She was abnormally still. Beautiful lighting in all directions, rich wooden walls, a closed door leading into the foyer. *I'm in James' main entrance hall.*

Rising, she looked around the room. It was full of different art than the grand parlor where the family portrait hung. She noticed the wren's call. There were always cactus wrens. Little brown jobbies, her mother called them... LBJs. Chickadees, sparrows, wrens, even a baby robin could be an LBJ.

The bridge!

The sculpture of James' amazing bridge splintered into one thousand pieces. With clarity, she replayed the seconds rushing to save the replica. She remembered the panic dashing and the dive to correct the falling pedestal, but she did not remember failing.

She watched the body on the ground: her own body. Watched her own chest rise and fall. She sank next to herself on the floor among all the wooden pieces.

No discernible damage marred the pedestal. Her eyes focused in and out and back in again. *Hard stuff, that wood.* Her head was bleeding; splinters of wood from the bridge stuck in clothes clinging to limp limbs, in her hair, in her blood. *Bleeding, bleeding a lot.*

"Oh!" Her hand flew up to touch her head. Another gasp followed: the body she was watching did not move. She looked at the hand that just touched her head. *I am just like James.*

She studied herself, the wound with the blood. Here it was, the moment she'd been waiting for her whole clumsy twenties. An accident that had an end. *Finally.*

But the elation she expected about this finality didn't match her next charged realization.

She closed her eyes. This wasn't an accident with an ending. Knowing what she now knew about death—that existence could continue with the same heartache and within the same existence—she wanted to retract every death wish she'd ever had. *Am I too late? I want no part of this. I don't want to be a ghost. I was finally starting over.*

The air grew colder, and Aislin lost her place in the foyer, sunk back into her struggling body.

Chapter 30 ✦ James

HIS HEART SPLIT FOR THE THIRTY-FIRST TIME SINCE HIS DEATH AS HE AP-peared beneath his nine-foot-tall doors between the foyer and parlor to find Aislin kneeling by her own body. The red muscle that was no longer a muscle continued to split open. Each second a new pathway connected to an intensely emotional past—each nerve sparking as it wove its way back through memories: his father, trying to cover his brother's eyes during their escape from Vitez, kissing Aislin for the first time, kissing Jade, seeing the pink flesh of Egon's head when it first hit the oxygen of the hospital room. His heart and head kept splitting with each revisit.

In the blink of his translucent eyelash, the faint outline of Aislin kneeling beside her body sunk back in. Her breath filled up the walls of the room that held such beautiful art, which held his bridge in splinters across the high-polish parquet floor. The wood squares interlocked beneath her head. He watched Aislin's blood pool onto the sheen beneath the sconce lighting and soak red the tiny pieces of beech that once represented the Stari Most Bridge of Mostar in Bosnia and Herzegovina. They would always be stained. Soon the blood would dry and become brown. No one would ever put his bridge back together.

He watched as the splinters changed from beige to deep red. In the next second, James was back on the banks of the Neretva River. It was his fifth wedding anniversary. He wished his mother was there with them. But at that time, she felt no desire to travel back to her homeland. The land before him—stained. The bridge that was once destroyed—rebuilt. During the wedding planning, Hana deeply wished to introduce him to family, but the Sidran family was the lone, plausible host. He shook the memory away.

His mother had only ghosts there. He was a ghost.

His bridge was stained. He shook his head. This was Aislin's blood. Each drop would be in the river forever with all the blood he remembered from 1992. He would never forget.

James replayed the disbelief, relief, and unease of watching Aislin's spirit-self merge back into her limp body. She had not even looked at him. He took her hand and did not forget for a moment that he should not be able to hold it the way he was holding it; he should not be able to feel the hair on her knuckles the way he could. The bed of her fingernail was slick with blood from the darkened stream her body rested in. James bent his lips to her wrist and let them sit there, enjoying the warmth. He absorbed the meaning of her warmth—it meant that she was not dead. Counting the times her pulse thudded against the heel of his hand, he let the warmth of her forearm affect his cheek as he settled into the curve of Aislin's body on the floor. He kept his lips on her wrist, pulling in her scent, immersing himself in the heat of her. He curled around her on the floor and waited for her to come back to life.

She is still warm; she is still warm. How is it I can even feel this warmth?

December 11, 2001

Dear Aislin,

I am in life and it is dark and poisonous, like the
way of your smile, the sway of your arms in the sun
and what your laughter does to me. It aches.

    Thank you for the greeting card… how are you?

I hope you like your present. i made you something in
my shop, a model, from my architecture class. it is
just too much to wait for you to see it.

Writing is going well this week. There's an agent
that asked to see my book on bridges… I need to see
you, dream to hold you once more. I have a feeling you
won't be staying here in the desert.

    — be careful, Aislin, you just don't know your
worth

    but perhaps someday I will show you.

perhaps,

        love, james

Chapter 31 ✦ Victoria

I**N THE DISTANCE WAS A HOUSE WHERE HER NEW LOVER'S FRIEND WAS DY-**ing. Victoria knew it with conviction. Goosebumps spread up her arms. It was weird being around another person who sensed things. She wondered if Hana also saw James, but was not speaking about it.

She hadn't even considered how difficult it would be to report an accident with zero details. She wasn't much of a storyteller, and she wasn't a liar—trivial or otherwise.

The rest of the drive down the long desert lane was unbearable. She locked and unlocked the car door and fidgeted with the visor. She counted the few cars that passed.

Alen reached the dusty driveway, and they heard the sirens when he finally stopped on the cobblestones. Victoria bolted from the car and up the travertine steps beneath the portico, pushing the unlocked, towering doors inward.

"Aislin?—Oh Alen!" the scream died on her lips as she knelt beside the limp body. Victoria realized she had prevented herself from getting to know Aislin because of her own ideals, because of some little girl in a house on the other side of the country over twenty years ago. Now perhaps she would never get the chance.

She felt for a pulse.

Victoria took the chill all the way to the bone, even when Alen's sweaty shoulder pressed into hers.

But the pulse was there. Aislin's chest rose shallowly. There was plenty of blood. No pills. No fire. No drowning.

A med tech finally knelt at Aislin's side. It was a blur as directions hit the air and the stretcher clattered against the hardwood; small red trails appeared across the parquet. Victoria half expected Aislin to rise off the gurney as it wheeled away, but her eyes remained shut.

Alen, Hana, and Victoria stuck to a story that they found Aislin unresponsive and that they called immediately upon discovery. Victoria thought she had handled the call very well. She pulled the emergency call back to her mind. There was one thing she was very conscious not to say: she didn't mention that Aislin was suicidal. Alen disclosed his friend's struggle in private, and she didn't want to betray his confidence. Although there was much Victoria didn't know about Aislin, she knew that suicide attempts often required hospitalized observation. She knew about mental health and how it was still changing in society; it was a slow change. She would let Alen find out what happened.

She wanted to brush off the apprehension that omitting Hana's vision from the rescue team caused. It was strange that there even was a vision to consider, but the world was full of mystery. There was a shadow in every corner, and she saw it. She didn't feel alone anymore, and that was her normal. Maybe it was being in the presence of someone else with gifts that made her feel off. She had only ever known one person with psychic abilities: her mother. *I miss my mother right now. I need to go see her.*

They had lied. Omission of truth is a lie. But how do you explain that your new lover's mother drifted to sleep in the back seat of the car and dreamt that someone was in danger and you called 911?

Maybe it mattered that they hadn't waited to confirm Hana's dream before calling. Maybe those crucial ten minutes tipped the scale in favor of life. Aislin could live or die because of the decision to believe in a dream. In her life, Victoria never thought she would be with other people that believed the way the Athelstans did. They seemed to be so open and willing to believe in any possibility. Including Aislin, who Victoria wished to separate from the Athelstans completely. There was only heartache to be had.

Victoria acknowledged having a little guilt about her agenda of moving James on. Her preoccupation came at Aislin's expense, but for the betterment of everyone. Aislin would have been her friend, might have been interested in the same things, could have related. Honestly, Victoria wished she could change what happened. She grew momentarily flustered and wished she had been more open to Aislin before they left the beach.

Rational thought always prevailed, however, and she would not change her belief that James must go.

Hana could be her friend, too. Even though they weren't telling Hana that James was in spirit form, she sensed Hana knew something. It wasn't fair that

Hana did not have more time with James. But Victoria hated how James was there at all. She couldn't help it. James' ghostly existence was causing turmoil, omission, deception, and perpetuating lies. And Victoria still heard the voice. The words. Could see the terror in the little girl's eyes.

On each of the occasions Victoria had visited the house, something odd about the family's current activities struck her. But nothing stayed with her more than the odor on Jade: a mixture of not showering and liquor. Then, the small things, like the boys being babysat by Aislin or even herself, and the sudden hiring of a nanny. The odd altars that were set up in every nook or cranny altered the grandeur.

It wasn't until watching Aislin's blood soak into the cracks of the parquet floor and the white grout of the front porch that Victoria acknowledged the different losses Alen would experience with the absence of his brother. Their teamwork, their career partnership: these things would never be the same for Alen. Each time he built something he would always wonder "What would James do here?" or "How might James build this entrance?"

From the portico, Victoria watched Jade return to her own house amid confusion and an ambulance leaving the drive. She left the car on and door ajar. Alen ran to intercept her screams of "Egon?" and "Nick?" as she rushed toward the moving ambulance.

"They're okay! It's okay! They're inside with Hana." Alen caught his sister-in-law and hugged her close.

She pulled back with a jerk. "Who's in there?"

"Aislin—."

"Oh," color flooded back into her cheeks and a nonchalant response came out of a mother now angry they did not inform her about an ambulance in her driveway. She rushed to her boys, who had stayed with their grandmother in the library while the paramedics helped Aislin.

Alen drove while Victoria rode in the back seat on the way to take Hana home. His rapidly aging mother looked exhausted, and asked them to reach out to her about Aislin's condition as soon as possible. It was difficult to leave Hana by herself. Her care for Aislin was palpable.

The next stop was the hospital. Alen focused on Aislin's condition, and his silence weighed on Victoria, although no more than her own critical mind. For no reason, his driving aggravated her as he made slow progress of the streets.

Logically, everything they did was textbook perfect for the type of deception known as concealment. She never imagined this in her multiple fantasies of Alen. By beginning their relationship in agreement with relational transgressions, they were condemning themselves to more of the same behavior. James was a special circumstance, but she was certain that allowing deception led to believing it was acceptable and might pave a pathway for it in everyday life.

She longed to speak her mind but held back because they lied for a good reason. It was just a tiny lie to the dispatcher, just a tiny lie to Hana when they offered sentiments that James was in a better place. Why did Victoria feel so neurotic about these lies? Calling the ambulance before they even arrived had been a gamble. She persuaded herself that lying to the dispatcher was necessary. They had not done it to deceive each other. They could talk about a clean slate when they knew Aislin was safe. And was it obvious that Aislin had just fallen? It could have been pills. There may not have been any at the scene, but maybe she swallowed them earlier and then passed out and hit her head? What better way to be with James than for Aislin to kill herself?

Victoria tapped her fingers unrhythmically on the window and turned to Alen to say something about Aislin, then stopped herself. Would Alen want to hear what she suspected? Would Hana?

Victoria might be his lover, but Aislin had been friends of the Athelstans for over a decade. She was in the deceased's will. Victoria was going to have to tread lightly.

Victoria realized, once again, that she was dismissing Aislin as an ally, but her top priority was Alen. With Aislin's mental health history, it was not a far-out idea she would go to great lengths to be with James. All she really knew about Aislin was that she spent the last ten years depressed. Alen had divulged many stories about Aislin and James. But there had to be more to Aislin's despair than one man. *He's leaving something out.* Her assessments sped on. It did not surprise Victoria that a woman with Mrs. Hana Athelstan's history was psychic: trauma and loss caused a heightened sensitivity.

Alen and Victoria finally arrived at the patient parking lot when the certain silence of the car lifted.

"She left her body."

Victoria jumped at the voice and Alen's hand bounced on her thigh as his body jolted in surprise.

James is back. I wonder where he was...

"She knows what happened, but she will not return until she has your apology." James' voice was a phantom on the air, and she wanted a dial to tune the eeriness out of his voice.

When Victoria and Alen whipped their heads around to see him, they hit into each other over the center console. They rubbed out the sensation and caught one another's eyes for a long moment. It was a soft moment when all the strain and sadness of the morning drained into the asphalt to be absorbed into the earth beneath.

They remembered they had company.

Victoria's surprise to see James was temporary and replaced quickly with familiar unease and judgment. She didn't want to look back at James and see his translucent hands and face, his unnatural existence. She closed her eyes to prepare herself.

"You look different," Alen observed.

"Oh, do I?"

"Yeah, less... Uh. Dead."

Victoria looked to see the more-or-less corporeal man.

James looked like he was going to speak, but only shrugged.

Alen extended her a tender touch, and she could feel him tremble.

A few minutes' worth of heartbeats passed before James broke the silence.

"We had best go to her." James was now giving orders in his overly formal tone.

He is the oldest, Victoria reminded herself when her annoyance grew.

Why would Aislin need their apology? The statement struck a nerve. *Apparently, James can sense that I'm not feeling the love.... Ugh. I hate that I'm not feeling it either. I wish they could just understand that James' being here is so bad for everyone.*

Victoria focused on breathing calmly as they wound through the corridors to a second ER waiting room. She and Alen looked disheveled as they inquired at the nurses' station, then settled in for a long wait. James went unseen by the hospital staff. His sudden opaqueness tempted Victoria to reach out and touch him. When she finally worked up the nerve to try it, he abruptly stood and announced he would visit Aislin's bedside and report back.

Victoria never guessed a relationship with Alen would have come with this much drama. She found it interesting that she had held off, although their attraction for each other was palpable on the first date. They had hit it off then, laughed and even kissed on the second date, just a short kiss. The third date had been full of heaviness neither of them had the courage to pick up after. Perhaps they had over-shared. And now that they were finally together, grief surrounded them. Alen paced to the far end of the room with his mother on the line, leaving Victoria in terrible need of comfort.

This hole was filled later, but not by Alen, as she would have wanted. She got a call from Jade saying that the nanny was sick and could she come take the boys to their private soccer lessons. The Athelstan family needed her. Not sure she had time to feel needed or why it was so important to her, she would make time for the grieving family, regardless.

The reason Jade could not take the boys was apparent by the way she smelled as she ushered them toward Victoria with juice boxes and water bottles bigger than their forearms.

"Here's a few dollars for dinner, too, if you can stop with them somewhere. Not fast food. Can you stop with them somewhere sit-down?" Jade thrust a crumpled bill at Victoria.

"Sure."

"Thank you." Jade closed the carriage-like door before Victoria pulled away.

She read a chapter from her psychopathology book on a blanket in the grass while Alen's nephews practiced with their private coach. Looking up at the blue sky, the gorgeous fall day stood as acceptable compensation for her support. The thud of the heavy text falling from her lap made her jump. She left it where it was, not able to read it with the girl's voice in her head, anyway.

Victoria thought of the $50 bill smashed into her pocket. She wasn't sure where they usually ate, but it was just as well they go to their uncle's favorite spot.

Chapter 32 ✦ James

HE WAS NOT HAPPY. THE TRUTH WAS THAT HE WAS NOT SAD, ANGRY, enthralled, nor hopeful. James put his hand through Aislin's and watched it sink down to the white sheet.

He could not feel or see any difference between what he looked like from one moment to the next. What did it mean that a dead person looked less dead? What did it mean that it shocked Alen and Victoria to see him?

He tried to identify his feelings. Maybe it was anger. It was confusion. That was the right word. Frustration was closer.

Aislin did not seem to be reacting to his presence. He hated it. It had never happened. It was ironic that hating that loss of affection made him feel like a bad person.

Frustration.

He looked down at Aislin. The doctor stitched her head up, a tiny, curved needle in a steady hand. The IV in her arm and the ventilator giving her life. He wondered if she had stopped breathing on her own and when. And if she would breathe again. More than anything, he desperately wished he could just speed up time to a future with her healed and walking down the street again.

He wanted a cigarette.

Aislin began to convulse, and the nurses held her steady as the machines responded with a barrage of warning bells that James could see and guess at, but not hear. Her blood pressure was tanking. Her oxygen and pulse diminishing.

She squeezed his hand as if it was flesh. And then she was still.

A doctor—the one that had been stitching—watched as her heartbeat flat lined. He watched as the other doctor went through the resuscitation attempts: charge, clear, charge, clear, charge. When the stitcher's lips parted to call time of death, Aislin squeezed James once more. The monitors kicked back to a healthy forward-moving status. The doctor lowered his watch and motioned for his assistant to wipe his brow. He corrected the slack in his suture to follow through with his commitment.

Time was a funny thing in James' new world, but in the hospital, it was worse. James tried to measure the days in nurses' shifts. He thought about their long hours, their tennis shoes on linoleum, the grey dullness of the keys recording health stats beneath two sets of five perfect fingernails. Aislin's voice brought James back to the present.

Once again, so much time must have passed that it changed everything. He was by her bedside in a different hospital room. Her head had developed a bruise, but he thought she looked better. She appeared to be sleeping soundly, but he knew he heard her call out his name. *Where does she call me from?*

He lifted his eyes from her still face. The sterile white walls and a curtain shut them off from whatever else occupied the space. Natural light reached their section, filtered by inert curtains hanging around the beds of other patients. If machines beeped and the whoosh of ventilators powered failing lungs, James could not hear them. No one spoke.

James paced the perimeter of the rectangular section. His eyes traveled the windowpanes, rested on the clock, then continued assessing the architecture. He was grateful for the person who designed that wing of the hospital. His eyes went back to the clock; the minutes ticked by. Aislin did not stir again. No echo of her voice filled the silence. Her breath and pulse appeared to be normal; IV fluids filled her with things he hoped made her comfortable. He did not know if she had gained consciousness, but she still drifted where he could not reach her.

She had called him from a vague distance. He could not pinpoint her. Was she under the protection of her spirit guide? He did not know. And he did not know until that moment he even knew what a spirit guide was. The knowledge felt bitter, as if his own guide was somehow lost or stolen from him.

Alen and Victoria appeared hand in hand through the drawn green curtain, their coloring altered beneath the fluorescent lights. Alen's strong shoulders appeared rigid, his light-blue shirttail half untucked. Victoria held his hand, her knuckles almost white as she leaned into him, walking off kilter in her desperation to be close.

"I am glad you are here." They did not seem to hear him.

James suspected something was happening between his friends, but he did not know what. Another memory surfaced, an old memory of Vitez. He bit his tongue. Did he imagine the sound of teeth clicking together? There should have been pain.

Maybe they cannot see me...

Alen went to Aislin's side; put his free hand over her hand and slumped into the only chair. James deaf to any sounds of his own movement. Victoria stood beside him, and after a moment moved both her hands to Aislin's leg, her head bowed, shallow breathing. Alen looked at his abandoned hand for a moment before leaving it to a rest, lonely on his thigh.

James watched them from across the bed for some time before speaking again.

"Speak to her so she knows you are here. If she has your apology, she will wake up."

Victoria blinked up at him and crossed her arms over her chest. "James. Where've you been?"

Alen's eyes went from Aislin's sleeping face to his brother's face. James wondered how he appeared to them. Corporeal? Transparent? Their observations of his physical presence piqued his curiosity.

Silence.

"Someone, say something," James said.

"Answer her question, go ahead." Alen's tone, unfriendly.

James shook his head. "What question?"

"Brother, where have you been?"

"Time is funny for me. I do not know. I keep jumping around. Time moves forward and I do not know how I am where I am. The last thing I remember before standing in this room is watching a doctor stitch her up. I do not know if she has even gained consciousness yet. Darkness takes me away. Days and hours gone. And when the room comes back to me, then I see her again, you again. I pace these halls for days, but I see no one else. Time has passed and things are different. I have been lost.... Tell me, has she awoken?"

"No." Victoria scowled. "What happened to her?"

James raised his palms up and stepped back from her. "I was there at the beach with Aislin, but I do not know. I left on and off, and then we were in the car. Then I came in and out... I do not know what happened at my house, nor how she fell."

Although he did not like her tone, James tried to understand Victoria's emotions. He watched his brother lean back, one hand not leaving Aislin's and the other one busy rubbing his eyes and ear, his hair. James tried to be polite to Victoria. He could not understand where the tension was coming from, but it seemed mutual between her and Alen. The time had passed for them to figure it out and get over it.

"What else do you remember?" Alen asked, his tone easing off.

"I was with Aislin in the car on our way back and suddenly I was kneeling beside her in my foyer and it was like I could feel her. She was so warm, she was bleeding. I saw her outside her body. She sank back into it. I held her and it was as if I could feel her flesh and I wondered if she could feel mine. Then, I was in the back seat of your car. And I disappeared again and then, back here as if I never left. How many days has it been?"

"Three, James. Three exceptionally long days." Alen's voice eased away from frustration, but neutral was not the tone he would reach. His tears stuck in the pitch, raising it as they threatened to fall. *My brother, crying. Again.* James' heart split.

"It is okay, Alen. It is okay to be scared. Aislin's coma is dark. I cannot break through to her. She floats in the black, a world I see other than when I am with you. What concerns me most about her now is that she must realize that she wished for an accident her entire adult life. And now, an accident has taken my life, and another threatens hers. She could not protect the fragility of her body. Now tell me what is making you so upset."

Alen's chair rocked forward with his body weight in protest to the way James' tone shifted from sympathetic toward demanding. James looked at him with compassion, his eyes funneling into Alen with purpose, calmness.

Alen leaned back with a sigh, disarmed. "It's right that you know what's happening, James." He took a moment to smooth out his pants. Alen put his elbow onto the arm of the chair and let the hard metal create an indent. He sucked air straight into his lungs, exhaled and inhaled again, and James could barely take another tense moment. *What is so bad that my brother fidgets and cannot be honest with me?*

Finally, Alen spoke. He did not make eye contact at first, and stared instead at Aislin, then at her beeping machines. "Victoria thinks you need to cross over, James. She says Aislin is keeping you here and that you should 'depart'. I might be the reason you linger here, too. I keep leaving Jade and the boys all alone. There're just so many things to be upset about," Alen said.

"Yes," James nodded, looking from Alen to Victoria, and down to Aislin, "there are so very many things."

Victoria cleared her throat. "It's not that I blame them, James. The fact that they want you to be here makes sense. But their clinging will not help them heal from the heartache of your death. You are dead. It's going to be so much harder for everyone a second time. There are reasons the dead should stay dead."

He could sense Aislin stirring somewhere inside him and tried to focus on

Victoria.

But he could not focus: heat struck him with a blazing drum mallet. The devil had strapped his body onto his chest like a hollow bass drum—banging and marching into the underworld. In this intense heat, an empty rib cage housed sparse cobwebs, and in places protected from the drumbeat, a silence had taken over. The drumstick tried to invade the emptiness of his heart, but beat as it might, it did not know how to keep a rhythm; it did not even know how to strike the head. The emptiness was stillness. No vibration welled from his stagnant diaphragm below. Life could not find a way. He wanted to scream. But screaming would not help.

He dismissed her desire to cross him over as quickly as the intrusion of the inept percussionist. Immediately, the heat disintegrated, leaving bitter ash in his mouth.

"I think I understand why Aislin is becoming leery of you, it is clear you wish I were not here." He dropped his gaze from Victoria and looked at Aislin's face. Wishing for her bright smile, he asked, "Can we please focus on her waking up, for now?" He heard the question come out, but did not feel his vocal chords move. No vibration of his voice crossed his lips. He placed his hand on Aislin's arm and once again watched his fingers sink through her to the hospital sheet.

Three days later...

James ignored Victoria's semi-cloaked disapproval of his relationship with Aislin. He had no desire to discuss emotions with her. It was becoming clear that her professional training was exhaustive. She was not just a student; she was obsessed about her work. Nothing could change the fact that Alen and Aislin wanted him to stay. He knew they did not want him to cross over. For now, he did not care that this displeased Victoria.

Hana, Jade, and the boys needed Alen. In that, at least, Victoria had a point. He did not like that she used it as a chain to yank Alen around. James did not understand how it was any of her business until he saw the way his brother looked into her golden eyes. He knew by this look that everything concerning Alen now concerned Victoria. James detected the bond between them. If she made his brother happy, she was important.

Another three days passed. They stood around the bed in which Aislin slept. His brother, always good looking, now beyond tired, scared, and sad.

James came around the bed and rested his hand on Alen's shoulder. "It is okay," he said.

Alen's muscled shoulder was familiar—warm, strong, and like a treasure. Or something. He could hardly believe his head. Describing something as a treasure? But how could he feel his brother's shoulder under his hand—when he could not *feel* anything? It had not just passed through; it sat there, resting on flesh.

Alen twisted around in his chair. "James. What the hell? I can actually feel you!" Alen's mouth opened and closed and then he swallowed so hard James could hear it.

James stood solid, tangible, and corporeal. He noticed Victoria only for a second as she fled the room. He could see Alen grow still. His heart seemed to have stopped, and the air was suffocating. Alen stopped breathing.

"Breathe, Alen!"

James shouted at him. Unaware, at first, of the motion of shaking his brother's shoulders until Alen's spine hit the cold metal chair under his own strength and realized he was *moving* him—trying to get him to take a breath, trying to save him.

Alen caught his breath. "Stop! Stop, James..." his voice came hoarse and labored.

"Oh, thank God, thank God you are breathing." James behaved like someone in a panic, yet most of his panic was missing.

Alen's breath came out harsh, his color changed from lack of air. "Oh, Mary, Mother of God. You were touching me. You shook me."

Chapter 33 ✦ Aislin

When Aislin awoke the next week, the sub-suns enchanted her—i.e., the emergency lights that poured through the door and lit up her hospital room at night. She was bored. Really bored. And she had never known boredom. She'd always had her brain and heart, woven with unequivocal emotion, never too focused, full of everlasting entertainment, grief, and lost battles. Also, she loved books. And these sub-suns were just lights, regular fluorescent lights. *Oh, I miss the sea, the sun.*

And she had a brain hemorrhage.

"It will take several weeks…" the doctor told them. Sudden movement could cause the hemorrhage to bleed or burst. The likely outcomes: immediate death or permanent coma. The best course was to wait until it shrunk. Slowly, her blood could absorb back into her vessels. Slowly and with luck and stillness, the body could correct a hemorrhage.

They moved Aislin to acute care and with that came a private room. Thankfully. Because, if the hemorrhage weren't enough, concerns for her mental health arose as she continuously spoke with James. The pain meds made it a struggle for Aislin to remember that no one else could see him. Combined with anti-anxiety and anticonvulsants, the meds worked together to make James seem more real than ever.

She watched Alen at the little impromptu desk made from an extra over-bed table. He contacted everyone in James' will to arrange plans to meet at Athelstan House after her release. When he made the last phone call, he rested his head with an "argh," dozing off with his head in his arms. The table sloped under his weight.

His beautiful, brown skin had always been Alen's eye-catching feature. It was becoming sallow, broken-out in several places. Creases on his cheek from sleeping that way remained for hours due to dehydration. His untamed hair grew over his eyes. She wished to right his upside-down life. Normalcy. He thrived on a schedule and routine. Wednesday and Sunday Matins. Working at the magazine or building something new, installing a window, taking his nephews to their soccer games.

Her new life: lying completely still, trying not to cry, cough, laugh; trying not to talk too much. The nursing assistant helped her one steady step at a time into the washroom. She had come a long way since only being able to use the bedpan in the first five days when the risk was highest—it was necessary for two aides to roll her and keep her spine and neck stable. Albeit snail-slow, walking showed improvement. They did everything they could to help her keep basic occupational skills.

Some of her marbles were lost and others scattered. James and Alen spoke of her when they thought she was sleeping.... she excelled at pretending to sleep. The nurse would always say how great she was at getting so much sleep.

Anyway, she had always been a good sleeper. Maybe she slept too much before this, missed too much. Although she eavesdropped often, she still didn't understand all that was happening. *It must be this morphine drip. God, if they could just give me so much less...*

"They will release her when the risk of it rupturing again is closer to 20%. With any luck, it will only be a few days," Alen said.

"Yes, the blood formation is decreasing, and she is coagulating normally. These are good signs and more than they hoped for, quite honestly. They expect she will make a full recovery." James kept his voice so low she strained to hear him as he narrated to Alen before the doctors even made their rounds.

Aislin's heart hurt for Alen. He had not loved many women, and she could see that his affection for Victoria took to the bone. The woman had gone, returned to her studies with obsession and fear, overwhelmed that James had become almost real, but it was just for a moment—then he was back to ghost.

She wished Victoria could give one of her educated, paranormal opinions. But she didn't wish it a lot. She could surmise on her own how James had saved his brother from choking on his own tongue from fright. His spirit was strong; anyone could see that. Well not, anyone, she remembered. Other than Alen, the only one at the hospital who could see James was a woman on morphine for days. Aislin doubted everything. But the journey off medications was finally underway. When the tapering gave her more awareness to keep James' presence to herself, Aislin began to feel hopeful about her recovery.

Alen never complained about all he missed, but she knew he missed it. She thought about her apartment again. Did her habitation of it make it her home? It was never home the way her parents were home, or the way Hana's had been home, but it brought comfort.

"Hi there, dear. How are you feeling?" a nursing assistant asked.

Aislin learned not to be jumpy the day she woke up with the cage on her head. The strict instructions to stay still drove her, so although she also didn't hear her regular nurse's entry, she didn't flinch at either woman's voice. *Calm, calm, calm. That's my middle name.*

"I am tired." *No, that's my middle name.*

"Pain level?" The aide, one Aislin had never seen, began writing Aislin's vitals from the monitors. A manual blood pressure check often followed the electronic one. *Pulse, pupils, oxygen, temperature, respirations.*

James appeared at her side. "Tell her you are a new woman."

Aislin's eyes bore into him. "I told you, don't—Oh, pain is about one hundred today." Aislin grimaced, "Sorry." She had told James a hundred times not to ask questions while in the nurses' presence. But perhaps it just seemed like one hundred times. *Why were all the numbers suddenly a hundred, anyway?* She let out a sigh and a pain-induced tear rolled out with it. "It's more like an eight," she conceded and took some deep breaths.

"There, there." Her nurse explained some med adjustments and injected them into Aislin's IV. She gave Aislin's hand a tender pat before retreating into the arousing and bright hallway. Aislin's eyes dropped to the IV in her arm. The little section of her blood that was always left behind shifted in the tube.

Time for another deep breath.

She looked around for James again but there was nothing. James receded again to a place Aislin feared, could not follow, yet wanted desperately to reach through and pull him back to her. She could not even get out of bed.

She looked back at Alen; he did not stir. Exhausted. When Ronnie, a patient assistant, came back to bring her to radiology, Alen still had not stirred. Aislin was growing fond of Ronnie because of his tattoos and humor. He quietly checked on Alen before he wheeled her bed into the hall. *The hallway of excitement!*

"That's right, ladies and gentlemen... here we have Aislin Birch. Aislin has been living at St. Mary's now for just over two weeks. She has her own private view of the drop ceiling tiles, a fancy sprinkler head, and one tiny scrap of sky. Aislin keeps her friends close but...."

As Ronnie chattered on with endless, entertaining words, Aislin tried to keep still. She let herself laugh on the inside, and he could see the smile on her lips and in her eyes, but she took the whole "stiff as a corpse" part of her healing journey seriously. Because, if there was one thing that Aislin Birch was, it was serious. Eternally serious, emotional, and scared. *Will I come back from this the same? Will I drift into darkness like James?*

She went through all the familiar motions of getting into the tube and waiting, listening to the rapid-fire camera. MRI this time. The intravenous contrast was getting easier to tolerate, the waves of nausea shorter and shorter. They rolled back down the hallway and through elevator doors as her mind whirred about variant lights, moans, and smells.

"How long have you been in California?" Ronnie's voice shattered her drifting thoughts.

"James died."

"Aislin? How long have you been in California?"

"Oh, I think 31 days."

"You think 31? That's a pretty exact number."

"Yeah, my friend, my so…. James, he died."

"I'm so sorry. Well, I am going to leave you now. Here's your call light. You make sure you sleep for a while, okay Aislin?"

"I will." Aislin closed her eyes. "Ronnie?"

"Hmm?"

"Where's Alen?"

"I'll find out, okay?"

Aislin smiled her thanks and her eyelids fluttered before sleep swallowed her.

February 14, 2001

Dearest James,

I cannot believe we so recently met. When I read your letter about your story in my bag, I knew you saw right through me and my heart was captured. is there some symbolism that I am going for by writing you on valentine's day? a saint. i know the saints mean the world to Alen. I wish I had a saint in the same way, but I have an emptiness there, a retched religious emptiness that was hollowed out the day my parents died. but your family fills these holes in me, even when I am told they can't be filled.

i fill myself endlessly on pastrami staring at you across the table and in my stomach is a hollow cavern that wants.

love, Aislin

Chapter 34 ✦ Victoria

ALEN HAD NOT CALLED HER FOR DAYS, SO WHEN THE PHONE RANG, SHE was unprepared. She half-hoped he would forget about her. Victoria brooded; she lifted her shirt over her head in the unusual heat of the evening and eased her body into her cool sheets. Her dark hair fell around her face, and she wished for Alen to brush it away. She listened to the final vibration before the call went to voicemail. She wasn't ready.

The apartment complex was quiet, unusually quiet. The silence reverberated, had her looking around for more ghosts. She expected they would begin coming out of the walls at any time.

She was tired, but had to get going on the thesis proposal. After closing her eyes for twenty-two minutes, a wave of peace washed over her and she headed to the library. She had not been there for weeks.

As she exited her building, another idea surfaced. She should call on Hana and Jade. Maybe Jade would want a babysitter. She would not return Alen's calls now, but that didn't mean she couldn't help the family. On the last step of the staircase, she shook her head and sat. She set her books at her feet after checking for gross items and pulled her phone out. The "new voicemail" icon on her phone stared back; she deleted it. "Delete" was not really delete until she emptied that box. She appreciated a small sense of control.

She only had to touch an Athelstan's phone number, each one in alphabetical order under A.

There was no entry for James. A chill settled under her skin.

You're an unwelcomed stranger.

Her mind skipped back to babysitting. On several occasions, while Alen devoted what little strength he had to getting Aislin better, Victoria had watched

Jade's kids and checked on their dogs. Alen spent the rest of the time with his brother and after the day James touched him, he just fell deeper in. Aislin was almost a sister to Alen, and Victoria suspected she was James' true love.

Why do I care about her so much?

She had to get more distance. She reorganized her books and walked to the library.

The conveniences of living within walking distance of campus made her smile for the first time since returning to her simple apartment. Not smiling was rare for Victoria. No matter what rolled her way, she usually beamed back into existence. She guessed it was in part due to her personality, but otherwise, she had a deep understanding of how fortunate she had it.

Coping was her specialty, even without her mother's wisdom. These last six months, Alzheimer's completely prevented wisdom from formulating. *This time last year, she would have talked to me. She would have the answers I seek. Was this story even too bizarre for her mother? I have my own problems too, but he doesn't ask about my life... ever.*

It was impossible to open the door of her study room. She lost her breath after climbing the three flights of stairs for the first time in several weeks. But that didn't really seem to be the reason it wouldn't open more than an inch. A peak through the crack confirmed that at least one tower of books had come down. After five minutes of pushing, she gave up with an exaggerated sigh.

Victoria took a seat in an almost-empty campus bar. Her elbows tentatively rested on the filmy, U-shaped counter. Low lighting did its best to hide the unwashed surfaces of the TV and the dust motes on the year-round strings of lights. Her first margarita slid down cool; the ice soothed her body. It was not the library, but it was happiness in a different way. The way the salt fell onto her tongue with light pressure.

Life was exhausting—and she was losing precious time, falling so behind she was going to need to discuss things with the dean if she didn't get back on track. The silver lining was that James could inform her future work... It wasn't her story, and she knew that. She knew the story belonged to Aislin and the Athelstans, but she desperately wanted to study James' effect on the family—which meant leaving Alen. Victoria didn't know what to do. She could not have Alen as a lover and a thesis, let alone a subject of study beyond that. She acknowledged her delusion that romance could become permanent with Alen. The connection they made had a stronger pull on her psyche than her studies. It was bridging intolerance.

But, if she had diagnosed him correctly, he was now so deeply affected by his brother's ghost, he would never be stable. Victoria would rather die alone than live the rest of her life with a ghost in residence trailing behind them and appearing during her private moments. If that wasn't enough, sometimes he appeared in his favorite old booth in the bar. He didn't seem to notice her at those times; he haunted like a residual haunting, fading in and out without interacting.

She set the margarita glass on the table with more force than she intended, and the clatter brought a wave of stares from a couple at the end of the bar.

Victoria closed her eyes and let her favorite season wash in. She had created a safe space with a method called biofeedback. She had memorized it long ago, and no longer needed to listen to the recording to go to her place of relaxation: autumn. The seasons weren't accurate in this part of the world; thus, she was grateful for growing up in the northeast, grateful to have solid memories on which to build an effective and personalized biofeedback session that she could summon in any situation. She repeated her own words silently to herself when she needed space and calm:

The sun set in the western sky and the warm globe pulsed around buildings of brick and glass. Just below the rooftops, a row of oak trees put their new clothes on, just hats and scarves for now. Everyone anticipates the donning of brilliant red, yellow, and orange coats on the day green gives way to glamorous fall.

She let the words carry her into fall and let go of everything else.

"Another margarita on the rocks?" she asked as the bartender walked by. He rolled his eyes at her; she didn't care.

For a few moments, the biofeedback and the margarita gave her the sense that she was calm and in control. But it wasn't long before uncertainty ebbed back in. She thought of James constantly. The lights in his eyes were there when she closed hers. The image of him grabbing his brother's shoulders and shaking him followed her everywhere. The way he breathed but didn't.

Victoria ordered a double shot of tequila.

The day James had become corporeal, she had hysterically hailed a driver. She spent two days isolating herself in bed with a Deepak Chopra book *Life After Death*. Clinging to its pages, she didn't know what she hoped to rediscover or how it might relate. But she needed spiritual comfort, and that book had always brought it.

James had become solid. A solid shape that had shaken her lover by the shoulders with desperation. Victoria dumped the shot into her half-empty cocktail. The memory of James physically shaking his brother was all she could think about as she sucked down the rest of her cocktail, leaving no trace to a watered-down fate.

The next day, noon-like light streamed through the window, bright and unfiltered. Instead of panic and the uncharacteristic desire to escape—a familiar resolve visited. It wasn't like her to run away, and she would not start now. She suddenly vowed she would change things; she could engineer this situation.

I will cross him over. Then, everyone will be at peace. And the girl will leave my head. I will also have peace. But first, I will visit my mother.

Chapter 35 ✦ Aislin

ISLIN WAS FORTIFIED AND DANGEROUS AND LOSING THE ABILITY TO reason. Because this is how you feel when you dream. And as a patient, she embodied a state of dreaming. And it was mostly of the past that Aislin dreamt. In this state of mind, she relived what had been wasted. She heard the seasons of her heart that she had not given the time to, the sensitivity to, or the will to—become sharply magnified. The dreams were still part of her, dreams of being lost, dreams of sandstorms, dreams of James...

On the same bench outside the same chapel that she visited on her first day in Palm Springs, Aislin watched Dream Aislin turn to the page titled "Desire," page 487, with the pressed rose petals, and all at once, they fell to the concrete. She watched them blow away, over the grey and into the hot sand. Some of them stuck there at an angle, looking like fish fins churning out of the earth. In a field and then a pond, fish went into battle with the ants. Neither side could ever win. Battles could never be won with old rose petals. The fish and ants disappeared. Aislin closed the book on Paul Hoover's idea of desire.

She held onto a hopelessly romantic state and the sky even seemed to bleed with an ethereal romantic filter. What else could trigger the sledgehammer of failed romance other than the sight of the rose petals in desert sand?

She walked over the threshold and into a familiar chapel. A voice called from behind, but she ignored it and entered the room. James was inside a coffin and his eyes were open. She walked up to it; the voice got louder. She couldn't hear the words.

With unseen aid, James flew from his resting place with great force and as she watched the body fly into the first row of pews, she ducked as something else propelled over her head from the open door. She never saw what it was because she ran out of the chapel screaming for help. *Someone is trying to hurt James.*

Aislin bolted upright in the hospital bed. Instantly, the dream pushed out of her consciousness and she regretted the pain that mere movements caused. She took advantage of the moment and looked around to see the sun filtering in and the monitor's steady lights. Alen's chair sat empty, as did the chair next to her bed.

James' chair.

James. Something seemed off about her memories of him. Everything seemed off about everything. It took several moments for her to remember where she was.

Yes, I hit my head.

It was probably a good sign that it didn't take too long to remember everything, including the little, tiny brain-bleed that caused so much of a fuss.

I'm lucky to be alive.

I'm lucky to be alive.

I am lucky to be alive!!

Aislin's oxygen stopped short of her diaphragm for a few moments and tried to relax. She tried not to heave. *Okay, okay. It's okay.*

She lowered herself down onto the bed and let the tears flow freely. She hoped she would never forget this gratitude for her own life force, as fear and hope mixed into her soul and consumed her. Whelmed by the flood of change, she cried until once again she drifted into sleep.

Aislin didn't know how much longer she could have handled the sounds of the hospital, the creepy dreams it gave her, the smell, the cries from the other rooms. Staying in bed for hours and hours.

After so much sleeping, she returned to Athelstan House, healthier and in much less pain. Hesitation prevented real happiness: there had been no hospital visits from Jade, no real invitation back—what might await her there? The fact that it was November furiously scribbled on the outskirts of her mind, an ink pen scratching on paper until it went dry.

The water fountain had dried up, leaving mud caked against the once-pristine marble. That was the first thing Aislin noticed when she returned to Athelstan House. The second thing—the dead and drying leaves of the plants in the atrium. As she returned to her room upstairs, one steady step at a time, she noticed more signs of neglect. More signs that the widow needed help.

The big house didn't seem so big while confined to one space. It was the Champagne Room again; the silk and the doilies decorated the world about Aislin's head as she tried to focus on the novel by Bram Stoker. The Athelstan House library was extraordinary by design. In way of reading: architecture and classics, children's books, unique horror (including collections from Tartarus Press), small collections of poetry from as early as the sixteenth century, particularly England and the Balkans. These were great, of course. Aislin tried to fight her shallowness, but she just wanted a series of simple mysteries to preoccupy her mind—more of the less complex variety. Like a Nancy Drew. Or maybe a Harlequin romance. Alen brought her an illustrated fourth edition, *Dracula.*

Thanks, Alen. It's beautiful.

She kept it close, but she couldn't bring herself to enjoy it. Sighs escaped and the words "thank you" never came out enough. She was back in that house again; it was less relaxing than Alen's would have been, but he seemed to have forgotten his previous invitation. He'd already given her so much time and devoted many resources to her.

James was not around. She questioned if he was staying away from her on purpose, but Alen had not seen his brother, either. She was both scared and confused about his absence.

The mysteries of the will that James couldn't remember were going to be revealed in just a few short days.

November 18, 2004

Dear James, we departed San Francisco last night. My
feelings this night, closer to you than tomorrow….

I guess there are always times when one must reminisce
about all that has passed- though I cannot stop to
enjoy them or force them from my mind, rather they
engulf me with sadness. why sadness so? why not relief
or the insight that yes, indeed I have always loved
this ghost of my past and shall forever on. I can
accept this as betrayal of my heart, yes. but I would
rather accept it as tried and failed. this does not
mean we can be together. it means far of that. I can
have free thoughts and free will.

I am obsessed with telling myself that you are crazy
and that it would have never worked. I wasn't strong
enough. and would I even be today? the favorite coffee
house—the indifference of a ride out into the desert,
feeling my neck hot with a sinful kiss. this kiss that
lasted only a moment, and that I did not evoke or
embark on. it is so hard to hide from memory, and that
is why I write to you.

I do falter so in my love for myself. I think not of
another while in the memory of your embrace. I simply
wonder of the past and with this wonder, I am greeted
with dense melancholy. with the root of darkness
washing over this heart. grated thin this night with a
fine razor. tempting me to delete what was once love
in a Marquez book. tempting me to love myself for
the creativity I can put forth today and not yearn
for that I put forth while your own craft endlessly
inspired me. I would not listen so now I pay with not
worse than my life YET MY MEMORY! alas… it is never to
be freed. and should I have it?

  [freedom]?

would I deem the common phrase 'better to have loved
and lost then to have never loved AT ALL?' I dry
tears from my eyes, yet my heart swells with them…
unbeknownst to the passersby, the wrangling of my
soul. the sweetness of you and I. Never a day to
relive without catching my breath with such force.
I am strong and proud of my stature this day. I
stand knowing we drew a line, but torn apart by the
knowledge that line will affect us permanently. Happy
I tell you, I had to be honest, thus. I had to be
true. and I love you for reading this. What changed us
forever has happened and I know you will move on.

ever,

Aislin

Chapter 36 ✦ James

THE RISING SUN BROUGHT MEMORY UP FROM THE LONG DARKNESS. Early the morning of the reading, Alen and James sat for some time and talked in the study. The familiar hunter green walls and uneven temperatures seemed to help regain the pieces lost since his death.

Alen admitted he had still not read the entire will. He told James how much he hated it. So many pieces came back to James with the new day and Alen patiently helped James as best as he could. James remembered Jade's overly stoic posture the day she signed everything, signed it without really reading it. It was around the time she started really hitting the bottle.

Later, the sun was climbing into noon, James stood on the other side of his library beneath the spiral staircase, thinking about his smile. He missed his own reflection; how expressive people always said his face was. He imagined the spread of his smile over his face now, but he couldn't really feel the muscles of his face move like they had when he lived. It seemed the dominant sensations actually present after death centered on emotion. With less focus on the positive ones, unfortunately. Plenty of psychology stated that smiling could lift one's mood. He worked on it a little more, like a muscle with atrophy—it just needed more attention.

Aislin seated in a down-filled burgundy chair. Anticipating events that were about to fold out before him, he wished for her to look up and see him smiling.

His once-favorite chair made him smile. For a moment, remembering the way it braced his back and how perfect the cushion was on his thighs and posterior. Never again. He shook his head and grimaced, unable to keep up the smile charade.

It took a painstaking hour for Alen to help her downstairs to the library that morning. James watched his brother walk with her, prepare breakfast, walk the dogs. He watched his brother's life change so much in forty-nine days.

Everyone ate breakfast. He followed Alen around as he brought Aislin some breakfast in the library and a book of essays off the shelf for her to read. Alen went off to complete more tasks. When the lawyer, Richard Clary, arrived, Jade instructed him to wait in the library, not realizing Aislin was there. Richard was familiar with their home and showed himself the way.

"Oh, I'm sorry, excuse me, I wasn't aware this room was occupied."

James watched Aislin's pupils dilate. He heard her heart accelerate.

"No, stay," she said to Clary. "I mean, you're more than welcome to come in. I'm just reading."

James heard the man's heartbeat increase in turn.

He knew Aislin could not sense him. He stepped out of the soft shadow by the door and drew closer to them. With cruelty, his head filled with the sense of smell. At first, he could not place it. But as Richard drew closer to Aislin and finally stretched his hand out to shake hers, James realized he smelled their desire for each other. His stomach flipped. He was sure he could not smell that. It was certainly just a sense. He could not smell anything.

Richard stood tall, dressed impeccably. He let his hand stay in Aislin's for a long moment. "I've heard so much about you, but James didn't tell me you were so beautiful."

She shot that smile, and James' senses increased. Richard looked at Aislin. He stirred, flushing. Finally, Aislin took her hand back.

"I am so sorry. I have no idea what came over me. My apologies, Ms. Birch."

But Richard seemed to be spellbound, and as the sunlight poured into the enormous room, it illuminated Aislin. Her skin and eyes were luminous, her lips became full, and James desired her as strong as the days he was twenty-four. He went to her then, yet Richard held her eyes with his own. She could not see James. She did not seem to sense his presence. James placed his hand on her knee. To his own eyes, he looked solid; he felt complete and whole, and all the blood rushed through him.

"No need to be sorry." She smiled that smile—the one James always wanted to see.

"I'll just take some time to prepare, if you don't mind my intrusion."

"Not at all." Still smiling, she turned back to her book. At the top of her next page, an essay by Theodore Roethke continued. James read over her shoulder. Roethke: always with the right words for the moment.

Perhaps that was the reason he collected random copies and notes from his favorite poets and bound them into zines. James always needed to be surrounded by the right words. The ones that fueled him, made him, taught him, brought him laughter, or deepened a somber mood.

"Can you see me?" he asked Aislin.

She did not respond, her soft and mischievous smile persisted, and he sensed she was no longer reading his lovingly curated collection of Roethke. She was just staring at the page in a daydream.

James turned and watched Richard. He respected the man and could see why Aislin appeared to be attracted to him.

Watching Richard brought forth a memory from five months earlier. James and Jade sat with Richard in the study.

"Mrs. Athelstan. It's time to sign the will. Are you ready?" Richard asked.

"Yes."

"You understand this document is not contingent on your signature, but that by signing it, you agree not to contest any part of the Athelstan estate as it stands in this document in the event of James' death?"

"Yes." Jade took the pen from Clary's hand without looking at him, signed and dated the last line, marked "spouse."

Richard showed himself out the study door and descended the grand staircase alone.

James and Jade sat in silence for about ten minutes before he brought out his Laphroaig and turned out the overhead lights. It was still daylight, and he wanted to relax with her, sit on the porch, and watch the sunset. He poured them both a glass, but she did not pick hers up.

"Did you read it?"

"Not all of it, skimmed most of it."

"Is there a part that upset you, specifically? I know I took some silly liberties. But you know I just want you and the boys to have a full life experience."

"The only life experience we need has you in it. It has you home for dinner and at soccer games, swim meets, recitals. It has you putting some effort into our interests, too." Her eyes looked wild.

It was a punch in the side. He wondered why and when she started being hateful toward him. It was new to him, but the feeling had obviously been simmering in her. He had worried that the part about Aislin and the money for the book would upset her, but perhaps his wife had never even read that part of the will.

Jade's voice broke through his considerations. "You spent so much time with Richard creating this spectacular fairytale of what we are supposed to do without you, but we were without you the last three months. And we will be without you when your next project starts. And the one after. Why should it be any different if you're dead?" Jade drank her whole glass with a grimace.

Her footsteps fell hard against the dark wood, and the heavy door slammed. When she left the room, she did not look back.

He stayed behind for an hour, troubling over what she said. The words made him dizzy.

He finally searched her out. The sound of voices guided him into the library, where the boys read one of his books. When his eyes met Jade's, splotched makeup spoke for her. He settled into the recessed section of the room with them, surrounded by colorful zafu, poufs, kilims, ottomans, and oversized stuffed animals. The largest A for Athelstan reproduced the spirit of Animalia, by Graeme Base, stood like a family crest on the walls of the nook.

With abrupt clearness, he recognized how inaccessible he had become. He had forgotten a vital role in his life. Father. Husband. Buried in making the money and writing, James had neglected his family. And if he was to be honest, it was not just those things: his mind, his heart, and his many creative projects had not always, and not even regularly, involved Jade.

When the advice came to create a living will, James was beside himself with delight. It was a chance to focus on the morose parts of his heart, the deep-down parts where Aislin was buried. He dredged her up from where he had hidden her, breathed life into a long-dead romance. Just writing her name gave her power over his world. He began going over their old letters and emails; he dove into the memories.

Aislin would write him:

```
James,

I am just writing; I haven't written, not a sentence
of creativity in months, a little poem that can't be
called a poem. Here the torment of understanding a
little heartbreak. Is it easier to analyze the self in
third person, second? first? Couldn't decide. i hope
married life is good.

love, aislin.
```

A letter to Aislin after his first child was conceived went like this:

```
Aislin, Jade has grown a belly, and I fear what grows
inside. My senses say it is a girl and I will not know
how to protect her. I will be the father watching from
the porch, untrusting of any boy that offers a hand,
and she will, of course, detest my overprotective
sensibility. I have much to learn to be a father for
```

```
this is not the way to raise one little girl, is it?
if it is instead the hair of a boy, I will worry he
will suffer the same sorrows I have suffered and I
will shut him in his room with books and tutor him
myself, and never let him leave. Yes, you see. I am
terrified and have much growing to do. love, james
```

But Aislin was just a memory. He dropped his chin to his chest for a moment and asked for another chance to make Jade happy.

James needed to make some changes for them all. His new project on the old bowling alley would be a huge payload from the city, but after demolition, his foreperson, Rodney, could coordinate the rest of the work. The four of them could take a vacation—should indeed take one. He did not know why he still worked so hard. They had all the money they needed.

He reached out for her hand, and she let him take it. He tried to show her how sorry he was with a soft expression. In her rigidness, he knew immediately that it would take more than a wordless apology. Would his smile ever again melt her resolve? How many months passed since he had genuinely shown interest? He could not deny it now that the evidence squirmed before him, a disemboweled earthworm on a sidewalk. James never knew why she hid her feelings of neglect before that day. He wondered why it was the first time he heard of such displeasure, yet never asked her why.

He watched her with her highball, the easy way the bourbon went down. It was not an acquired taste like when she forced the Laphroaig; she was very accustomed to her poison. A new concern tumbled through James' mind.

The day he learned of Jade's discontent faded away. It was just another memory he could never change, filled with unmendable actions and promises he did not keep.

Uncertainty abounded in James' heart. Yet another event was about to unfold that he never wanted to witness. And although he went into the event with restored memories, nothing could really prepare him for the reactions to his living will and the reception to follow.

His home library began to fill with the people he missed. He watched each person come in, one by one, thought of something they had once said or a way they had made him feel. The memories of each of them flooded his heart until they became all the light in the room.

February 21, 2001

Dear Aislin,

Our meeting is like a shadow on the moon, there is stillness and angles that you cannot touch, and I bring myself into smiling at your face and it means nothing and everything that I breathe. I too cannot believe we just met....

Thank you for letting me take you to dinner. I always love that restaurant, the server that has clicking spoons in this apron, he walks and my brain chases him with cello and then there is stage lighting as he steps to the bar and that reaches your face and you are glowing like a saint: and my heart... i cannot even tell you what my heart does.

who told you that you cannot be filled? do not tell me or they might find they can no longer walk. I can guess who it might be, but I would never be so rash as to risk upsetting you. I cannot stand to think you might ever be mad at me

love, james

Chapter 37 ✦ Aislin

FINALLY, THE OVERDUE CALENDAR DATE ARRIVED.
She sat and waited for the room to fill. Everyone mentioned in James' will had required attendance. There were about thirty people filling the rented folding chairs and a hodgepodge of chairs from all around the first floor. Her head was still swimming in pain, but heat flashed between her legs and she could feel her nipples harden.

The Athelstans' lawyer—James' lawyer—was attractive. His velvety grey tie, his striped shirt taut from the pressure of his muscles. Aislin skimmed his waistline and the curve of his hips from her position at his left. He stood at the podium. Of course, the library would have a podium. *What grand estate can get by without a grand piano and a podium?*

The lawyer's blond curls tumbled across his forehead as he turned his head. His eyes fell into hers and she watched him breathe her in. It was finally her turn. The lawyer's southern accent covered one nuance of the will after another over the course of nearly two hours. James was a slight control freak, and he held some radical ideas about how his fortune might be spent. His ghost faded in and out of the room that day, laughing at some parts as the memories returned. He was getting a kick out of small things, like sending the boys to awkward boarding schools overseas and having Jade stay in a monastery in Indonesia for a month. These were all just "recommended spending habits."

The lawyer kept a straight face through it all.

Aislin blushed when she realized James observed her admiration of Richard. The simmering feeling of romance and sex she gleaned from his fancy tie, and just the way he'd said hello, made Aislin feel alive again. The way she wanted to hold on and bounce around in his lap, her legs wrapped around his waist, wearing nothing. She leaned into the fantasy, her back pressed into her chair, comfortable down-fill sucked her into the way she imagined him. She allowed the vision of her lips touching his with hunger.

Contact with someone who wanted her—whom she wanted—was still a desire, a real desire. On this rare day, with people all around her, after head trauma and everything shitty, she was having a sexual fantasy. The short exchange of pleasantries and snapshot of mutual attraction sparked a wetness between her legs. She closed her eyes to enjoy where her mind went as she listened to Richard's voice spell out what James was asking her to do. Her focus stayed on the arousing encounter where the lawyer's hands made her writhe on his lap as she held fast to the grey velvet tie and her fantasy properly replaced Richard with James and then Richard and back to James once more…. Their hands all over her breasts, her body. But Richard's voice was the one in the room now. And how were his words going to change her life?

"'Section 29: James Athelstan hereby bequeaths to the person hereinafter named part of his personal literary estate excluding the children's genre: this includes his fictional works; his non-fiction works, and any correspondence to or from the trustee Aislin Birch. Hana Athelstan's literary estate includes the books handed down on his father's side for generations detailing the family history in England; and those diaries of his mother's—previously given him by Hana Athelstan; there are five sets of one-hundred letters written between Edward and Hana Athelstan that are part of this collection.

James began work on a historical biography of the Athelstan family, and should he pre-decease its completion, Section 29 of the Estate of James Athelstan appoints Aislin Birch to complete this project with access to the materials. Once the work is complete, return the materials to the Archives of the Athelstan Estate. This includes a share of $80,000 per year to be distributed monthly for a maximum of three years.'

Do you accept?" Richard concluded the section.

Aislin was so enthralled in her fantasy, she did not realize he stopped talking.

"Ms. Birch…?" Richard's throat cleared politely. "Do you accept, Ms. Birch?"

"Yes." A pant escaped her parted lips. "Everything, yes."

Everyone in the room was watching her. She held her composure, waited for the lawyer to continue to the next section and for everyone's eyes to leave her.

Okay, that was embarrassing…

Aislin readjusted the large blanket on her lap to avoid looking like she was readjusting herself. The wetness between her legs reminded her how human, how beautiful, how wonderful it was to feel desire for someone. When later that night, if she touched herself, she would do so to remember that she could still feel something greater than the finite heartbreak that lasted too many years. Would that she could truly experience the pleasure of biting an apple, the pleasure of seeing the ocean, the pleasure of reading a poem, of enjoying another person's touch. *Would that I could, and I suddenly feel that I can.*

After Richard read her part, Aislin tore herself away from her fantasy, and watched Jade, watched Alen and Hana. Clary read four more sections before clearing his throat to make his closing remarks. "I know Mr. James Athelstan's brilliance isn't lost on anyone today. The lack of seriousness in some parts of the will is undeniable, but please be aware Mr. Athelstan's intentions were never to insult anyone's grief and healing process. James did not mock death, nor did he intend injury to another's tradition of honoring the dead. The prospect of making this document overwhelmed him and he approached it with humor to get through it and be able to face the thought of mortality. As you might remember, he lost his father at a young age. I hope you each will reflect on what Mr. Athelstan has bequeathed you and consider how much each of you meant to him. He regarded each of you as his friends."

Although she could recall many discussions about death with James, Aislin was sure they were not commonplace with most people. Death could be hard to talk about, and unless you had a reason to discuss it, well, her culture had largely veiled it and it had become taboo for many. Be this an unconscious or conscious choice, it fascinated her that many grew up without discussing it freely, even if they experienced the death of a loved one at a young age. So.... she supposed that what Clary said was true, from a certain point of view. She wondered if everyone had at least one person with whom they confided their feelings on the subject.

No one had discussed her recent brush with death. All she knew was that she wanted more than anything to live and to feel everything.

She realized she would cry again. The sun filtered in the clerestory windows and highlighted a row of seats. She recognized Hazel Birmingham, the editor-in-chief of the magazine, and the Welsh family. Father Benjamin stood in his robes in the back of the room. He seemed to wait for something or someone.

Everyone was quiet. James surprised everyone with the extensive content of the will, and what surprised them further was that no one knew many details, save Richard.

Hana came to sit by her, pleased with her son and his "legal novella," a term that spread through the crowd due to Richard's respectful and well-crafted messaging.

Hana talked with some pleasure. "How are you feeling?"

"Better, every day I get better. There are some side effects."

"Oh, dear, yes, earlier you were so far from us."

Aislin blushed. She could not lie and blame her indulgence in that fantasy on her head injury, but she nodded, unsure of what to say. "I'm still a bit dizzy and spacey." That much was true, at least.

Hana returned the conversation to the book. "I am glad my son thought to continue the book. Often, I have thought it would be nice to chronicle many of my memories. I am relieved and pleased to have help with this. It is too lonely to do this alone. Aislin, thank you. Thank you, for helping my family write our legacy."

"Oh, Hana." Aislin's chest rushed with gratitude and sweetness. She took Hana's hand. "Thank you. I'm so honored to be involved, and so touched by this. I feel like it's been so long, we hardly know each other anymore...."

"Better now. We will get to know each other much better again, do you agree?"

Aislin smiled an agreement but before she spoke again, Jade came over to ask Hana if she was ready to eat.

"Yes, dear. I will join you." She gave Jade her full attention before turning back. "Aislin, goodbye, for now." She patted the blanket.

"See you soon, Hana."

Biographies were always being commissioned; it was commonplace. Aislin never understood the need for all these secrets even with the chill of circumstance, but nothing had ever been a secret. The contents of the will remained unknown to Aislin due largely to James' inability to remember. Jade, Hana, Alen had all intentionally avoided the will before forced to read it because James died. Jade, who had signed it, had really only skimmed it. The circumstances were too heavy—what family wanted to discuss a living-young-man's will? Aislin sighed as it all fell into place. Everything she thought was a secret was simply avoidance.

Aislin watched the Welshes. A sun beam highlighted the cloister of chairs they occupied. Rodney and Irene were speaking in soft voices, but Aislin was close enough to hear them. "James allowed drama by staging this reading," Irene whispered, her voice tinged with frustration.

Rodney put his arm around Irene and pulled her close. "It wasn't staged, dear. You know it was an accident. He never meant for us to see his will."

"I know, I'm so sorry." She turned, buried her face in his shoulder and muffled the sound of her sorrow. James gave the couple a six-digit inheritance. Irene was overwhelmed.

It became understood by all in the room that James had thought the whole thing to be more of a creative project than something that would ever happen, that he never thought his death would be so imminent as to not write a real one. But death came and let this little circus play out.

Richard spoke to a man who wore a too-small button-up shirt paired with clean khaki carpenter pants. "At some point James intended to rewrite this with the seriousness such a topic deserves."

The two appeared to know each other. The man addressed as Thomas in the reading nodded. "That he didn't get the chance to rewrite this is tragic... and his boys, what they must think...." Thomas and Richard both dropped their eyes.

The mood in the room became tender and quieted any judgements that might have formed before. Everyone present reflected that James provided for each significantly. He imparted each with a very personal touch, yet not revealing anyone's private matters to the rest of the audience. It spoke to how closely James knew and cared about his employees and friends. His career took him from his family life, Aislin conceded, but she also noted how he spread himself thin—always on some level engaged with those who touched his life.

Jade led Hana from the room, their arms linked and pace matched. Jade's body leaned in close and softer than normal. Aislin didn't miss the glance Jade threw back at her. It was a bit territorial, full of some jealousy Aislin did not expect, not after so many weeks. Aislin expected it when she first arrived, yet Jade had welcomed her. She troubled over it for hours. She could come up with nothing that quite matched Jade's temperament. *Why now? Was it the will?*

Aislin stayed in her chair, worried she would get bumped into. She wasn't her most stable, but she was content. James was there. They watched everyone. Nick came and sat in her lap, and they flipped through some books. James stood next to her with his hand on the wing of his favorite chair.

She enjoyed that a reception was finally being held in his honor. Friends told stories. Alen had busied himself playing his brother's favorite symphonies on the gramophone.

James mentioned he could not hear it.

"It's Gustav Holst, *St. Paul's Suite.*"

Nick looked up at her. "Is that who Uncle Alen is playing on that victrolella, record thing?"

"You're thinking of a Victrola, but that's a gramophone." Aislin corrected. "Uncle Alen likes this symphony, but 'The Planets' is your dad's favorite by this composer." Aislin said and hugged Nick closer.

James asked, "How do you always remember this stuff?"

Aislin kept her eyes diverted from James to stop from crying. The swell was already rising into her throat. She hated not responding to him, conversing with him. Hated that they hid his presence.

Egon appeared before Eleanor with his guitar. "Will you sing something for my father?" he asked. Alen stopped cranking and lifted the needle off the record.

Eleanor used the back of her hand to wipe her blotchy face. She accepted the guitar while pulling Egon in to kiss him briefly on the head. Egon quickly wiped his own eyes as he stepped back from her and sat on a close-by chair.

"I know you liked this one, James." She cleared her throat and hummed to get in key, looking up at the sky, sucking in air. She began the cords and sang Cohen's *Hallelujah*.

"I can hear that," James said. "I cannot hear the guitar, but I can hear Eleanor, and her voice is perfect." James walked close to Eleanor and stood before her, swaying and kind of shaking. Aislin wanted to go to him, hold the nothing that was air, hold the James-ghost-intangible.

All those words meant she would only be holding herself.

Eleanor played other songs, some on request. She held everyone spellbound, her green eyes sparkling with the tears she held at bay for the music. For James.

Egon played his cello for a while, arresting them all with *Hallelujah* again. At his brother's encouragement, Nick reluctantly left Aislin's lap to play the piano. James drifted towards them, invisible tears choking him up.

After a few hours of drinking scotch and nibbling on finger sandwiches, guests eventually left Athelstan House, ready to rejoin the world outside the thralls of the heartfelt, never-the-less, overwrought will.

Back in her room, Aislin cried. She was so tired, light years away from who she thought she was. She reached down into the sheets and blankets and let her finger slide on the slickness of her. Was her life missing human touch for any other reason except for James? She carried a photograph of him. She had memorized a letter where he described how much he wanted her:

"I know you are even warmer inside. I imagine our legs wrapping around one another. I wish the time we spent together was magical in a way only intimacy can create... unforgotten passion."

And the words just went on about what he would do to make her feel good and she had copied it by hand and kept it for insulation. In the bleakness of her life, how rarely she had been intimate? So often as a teenager and then in college with Cliff and then just three one-night stands in ten years: Louise, the banker; the mailman that saved her; and Eric, the stock boy in his early twenties that had come home with her in a fit of passion after slaving over inventory for a whole Saturday. The summer heat had filled the loading docks with his scent and the night of his last shift—he had filled her with himself. He left to go back to college the next day. Aislin never needed to see him again.

Pining after James was what she knew. She thought of all of them then. She thought of the occasional nights she masturbated along with the scenes in movies or gripping his printed words.

So, since she could not touch James, she focused on touching herself. Her fingers pulsed in an earnestness that was new and hot. Richard came into the vision briefly at first but faded from her as her love for James became the familiar knotted twist in her arteries, gnawing at her ribs, consuming her with its impossibilities. There was a newness within her body, and she wanted James more than she ever remembered wanting him. The heat swelled between her legs, her fingers not stopping their intense circles for a moment, allowing her to climax, writhe her hips on the bed, and revel in a pleasure she was free to repeat.

She spent her time trying to plan the next part of her life from the comfort of the Champagne Room. James remained at bay, but the healing power of time rose the moon twice more. The air felt frigid the night it was soon to rise again. The AC was suppressing the lovely way the sun spent its day warming the west side of the house. So tired of being cold, she decided to close the duct. Searching for the vent in the room, Aislin only made it a quarter of the way around the space.

"What happened in the library?" James' voice—a flirtatious elongation of vowels filled the room and replaced the coolness of the air with a fierce heat in her body.

"Oh! James. Hi."

He's always sneaking up on me.

"I never thought I would see you turned on by someone else."

"Me neither." All that heat increased at the mention of Richard, and she saw her fingers gripping his grey tie once more. Aislin smiled.

"It is not something that I like, yet it is. The way you flush and glow, I like that," he said.

"Well, it's not common." She carefully climbed to her feet from the floor—

the vent was no longer a concern—she was no longer cold. James sat in the flowered chair and she went to him.

He tilted his face to hers, and she looked down at him. He held his hands out like the first day she had seen his ghost.

But unlike that day, they made contact.

Their eyes lit with hunger. An ache pulled them closer together. He was able to run his hand over her back and she felt every finger as more than a cold spot or a vacuum—pressure, not warmth, but pressure. She pulled him to his feet as he rose to her. She found his mouth and as many seconds as possible passed before she parted for the air that he didn't need. Aislin bit her lip. Their torsos flush, ribs and sternum and pelvis and breasts. His translucence perceived as solid as her solid, his hardness known to her—stirring wild, magic thoughts through her mind. Her impassioned breathing filled the fading light of the evening. The last moment of nautical twilight brought the brightest stars of astronomical twilight—so quick was the night to rob her of James and plunge his world into darkness, sacrificing their new kiss to the air.

"Oh, how I'm hopeless!" A choked noise escaped.

After he left, she was alone. When she returned to bed, her self-touch changed. Her hands, exploratory—purposeful—aimed at waking desire and not just consoling the lonely.

October 29, 2002

Dear James,

I felt this great sense of glory

one moment when we were one,

although no words were spoken.

last night these clouds

drifted in and caressed me.

they were your hands

recreating the world,

recreating my life.

and i could only lie there,

breathlessly… my head back, eyes closed,

waiting.

love,

Aislin

Chapter 38 ✦ Hana

ANA SAT ON THE FLOWERED CHAIR IN THE ROOM HER YOUNGEST SON designed. Aislin reclined on the pillows Hana was proud were on display. Crocheted lace was a dying art, yet this room was proof it could blend with a modern feminine décor.

"Do you remember how to crochet them?" Hana asked.

"Yes, I've made a lot of them over the years. They took over my apartment." Aislin laughed and blushed, "Actually they make up much of my décor."

"In your Bohemian land, I am sure they are perfect."

"Lace is quite Bohemian. I'm surprised you remember my style."

Hana relaxed back into the chair, enjoying her visit with Aislin. Witnessing that sparkle again and laugh together lifted her mood in a way she was becoming unfamiliar with. She had worried. "I am sorry for my absence in the hospital. I... I feel quite an unease there."

"It's okay, Hana, really." Aislin's words created a smile in her heart. She knew she had a pardon. "And I got your soup. Thank you so much. The hospital food was fine for a while, but when I started feeling better, it was... well... your soup was amazing."

Hana always loved feeding people and was glad she had sent plenty of soup with Alen.

She looked around the room Aislin had been calling home for several months and sensed only the designer's intended style. Not a trace of spirit or personal trinkets. The girl had not settled in. It was Jade's home, and Hana discerned the disconnect between Aislin and the house.

"What is next, dear? What is best for you?"

"I would love to rent a small apartment. We can set up and get to work on your book!"

Hana longed for the work to begin. "I have those letters from Edward, James' father. The letters he wrote me before the war and the letters I wrote him. During that time, the letters are love letters. Later, they become instructional... and..." Hana lowered her eyes.

Aislin waited.

"You see, when the first strikes came, Edward tried to get us to England, but that fell apart, and he found a route to the States. We can write of our escape from Vitez. He took many risks, my Edward."

"It would be an honor to tell that story. Let's start as soon as I'm in my new place. And we can write at your house, too."

Hana nodded and dropped her head. "I miss my dear James." She could not help but say it, her throat caught on his name. Looking at Aislin was full of memories of her son leaving his delinquent path and finding himself and his family again. "I know you helped him back then. He credits Alen for it, but I suspect there was more to the story. It was also you. Thank you."

Aislin dipped her head. "Hana, you know I would do anything for either of them."

"Yes, Aislin dear, I know."

They said goodbye.

Hana smiled on her way out the bedroom door until the antique wash basin-turned-shrine in the hallway caught her attention. She scowled at the disarray, ashes littered the bowl and smeared across the peeling finish. Green wax piled up on the surface; it yielded an unpleasant smell. It was unusual for her daughter-in-law to have things out of such order.

"Are you ready to go downstairs?"

Hana turned towards the sound of her eldest grandson's voice. Her smile returned to her body as she gave him a warm nod and offered her arm. "Come here, my child."

Hana and Egon walked down the shiny marble stairs, one step at a time.

"Majka?" Egon said.

"Yes, my dear?"

"Do you think Aislin can talk to my dad? Because, sometimes it sounds like she's talking to him."

Hana took several moments to think about what her grandson was saying. How might she respond to him? His question explained so much of what she felt. "Let us sit down, my dear."

"Right here, Majka?"

"Yes, here, please."

They sat down together; his eyes as big as saucers as he made sure she was steady. The words came tumbling to her once more. Aislin 'would do anything for James.' She had phrased it like she still could, had said it in the present tense.

"Are you okay, Majka?"

"Yes, fine dear. You know your father has passed, and he has gone to heaven. He is now with his otac in heaven, right?"

"Yes, Majka," Egon nodded slowly.

She smiled at him and squeezed his hand. "Okay then. Let us just sit here a minute while I catch my breath. Your otac sure made a lot of stairs."

"He did. I like these stairs. Are you sure you're okay? Should I get Uncle Alen?"

"No, no. I am fine, Egon. We will keep going here, Majka just needs a moment."

"Okay. Do you want some ice cream?"

"I do. I do, indeed." The cold marble stairs pained her tailbone. The house was always just so cold. She stood up slowly. *Oh, how the cold hurt.*

One step after the next, relief hit as she reached solid ground. She did not consider the weariness that climbing them meant when her journey to see Aislin first began.

Finally, she settled with Egon in the much warmer kitchen, and he fetched them ice cream sandwiches. In a half-second, as if Nick could see through walls and floors, or smell the ice cream from his playroom, her youngest grandson bounced into the room. "Hey, where's mine?"

Egon and Hana shared a friendly chuckle.

And although Hana warded off Egon's question, guilt poked at her for the redirection. It was not the honesty she always sought to have with her grandchildren. And she normally talked to Egon about all the things he brought up; she wanted to be there for him. It seemed unfair for him to face the thoughts alone. But this was her son, and the idea of him as a ghost spoken aloud troubled her insides. Her lungs changed shape once more and took a moment to relearn what breath was.

Hana sent a text to Alen through that vast and chilling house that he might fetch her home.

Not that she did not believe Egon. Soon she would ask him about it, she would let him talk. For now, she would wait. Messages to her Edward went unanswered. *Where is my young James?*

Chapter 39 ✦ Aislin

"Hello?" there was a knock at the door that came with a tiny voice.

Aislin started. She realized she slept through the night for the first time since being at Jade's again. No nightmares. She panicked for a moment that she did not have clothes on, but then remembered how chilly she was after her "self-care" session. She never did find the vent...

"Come in."

Nick entered. He came in and climbed into the flowered chair. Then he sat on the bed. His knees tucked under his chin and his little face peaked through his dark hair.

"Are you still sick? You don't look very pretty anymore."

Aislin's self-confidence drifted a bit, but she kept up a smile. "Yes, I still have an awful headache."

"I'm sorry."

"It's okay, sweety. Don't worry about me."

Nick watched his fingers work at a thread on his pajamas.

"Do you have any books?" she asked.

Nick nodded with a gleam in his eyes. "I have one about wizards."

"Is it about hobbits, too?"

"Yeah."

"Go get it."

"Okay!" Nick bounded off so quickly, Aislin braced for the shock of the bed bouncing. When none came, she knew that finally, finally, she was healing.

A half-hour later, Egon appeared at the door and eventually made himself a comfortable spot leaning against the bedpost. His feet wound around his brother's ankles. Both boys listened to Aislin's voice as she plodded along, armed with a huge dose of ibuprofen until Frodo and Samwise separated from the Fellowship that swore to protect them.

Alen found his nephews asleep on the four-post bed, where Aislin was at-tempting a small stretch that wouldn't disturb them. Egon and Nick looked so tired. Circles shaded deeper beneath their little eyes each week. Losing their dad was hard; thunderclouds seemed to hover overhead with the imminent threat of drowning the family, sweeping them down the canals and into the far-off gulf with debris, sand, and other abandoned souls.

After Alen carried the boys, one at a time, back to their rooms, he returned and looked down at Aislin, who saw him through her watery eyes. Her mem-ory of looking at him with the cage around her head was still sharp. With the recent removal, this was the first time she felt normal in weeks. She just wanted to look at him, to feel the contrast to looking out at him. She let out a deep sigh and smiled. For weeks, four bars around her head, attached to a chest harness and an additional halo-type headband, helped stabilize and heal her injury. She did not miss them, yet she was grateful.

"Well, it seems like you are their new best friend." Alen's hushed tone filled the heavy silence. He sat on the edge of the bed and placed his hand over her ankle. "How are you feeling?"

He squeezed gently. Her smile was weak.

Their eyes locked, and he put his other hand over hers and patted it gently. He was strong, but she knew he was tired of being strong.

Since Victoria left Alen, he did not lift his chin. And, it was as if James died twice—his spirit stayed missing for too many days, the absence was hard on Alen. The days were long, but the nights were longer. He didn't look for strength from Father Benjamin, nor for comfort from his grieving mother. He did not pray. Aislin worried about him.

"Aislin, all I do is hammer the walls. I hired another accountant, no more math for me. Don't worry."

"An accountant?"

"Yes, and another office manager. And I promoted my foreperson into operations. I have more time now. Less paperwork, more hammering. I love the hammering. The building of a new home. The wood. The stone. Carving, making something beautiful." He hung his head. "Building was something James and I did together. It was always better than running the business. It was only James who loved that shit."

He looked around. She shook her head. "He's not here."

Alen looked at his hand on her ankle, released it. "The mayor commis-sioned the last project, the one where the machine swung its massive weight backward and crushed the cabin and its operator. Crushed James. They cleared it, Aislin. The police have taken the tape down and said we can keep working. It's time to move forward." He buried his head in his hands and aggressively shook it, his hands matting his hair. "How can I do that, Aislin? How can I work on this job?"

When he took his hands away and looked back up at her, his face was wet, and his hair matted in small sections against his forehead. She rested her hand on his shin that was folded up toward her on the bed. A tissue box was all she could offer.

He chattered on and on, told her everything that was happening. That week, Alen took his breaks at the house, rotating between Jade, Aislin, and the boys. The hottest times of the day pulled out his stories, one-by-one, the rooms filled with hundreds of memories of his brother.

One evening, Alen found them all together again, the boys fast asleep. He gently shook them and asked them to go down for dinner early. Their mother was downstairs. Pizza tonight. It was a Sunday; the days were growing shorter, but it was still warm outside.

"James died on a Friday when we were at work. I don't eat burritos anymore."

"What?"

"There was blood all over. He was crushed. I will never forget the blood. At least not until consumption and old age take my memory."

"Why burritos?"

"Huh? Oh, my breakfast came up in the job-site office, you know, it was so early in the morning, the sun wasn't even up. They even forgot to turn the work lights off until that evening as the sun faded."

"Oh," Aislin said.

"Aislin, I don't know how I can walk back in there."

"Can Rodney handle the demolition without you?"

"He can...." Alen looked far away. "Is it fair for me to abandon him?"

"Alen.... yes. It's not about fairness. Do what you can do. If you don't want to go back there, don't go."

He looked straight at her. "I'm a coward."

"No, Alen." Aislin moved to hug him. But he quickly withdrew.

"Where's James?"

"I'm not sure." James' absence troubled her even more since they had touched. She flushed.

"I need him, Aislin. I need him to tell me what to do." She thought he was going to cry, but he got up and sat in the chair. The box of tissues from the nightstand and the vampire book Aislin abandoned accompanied him. Alen leafed through the pages, looking at the illustrations, not reading it any more than she had.

Her thoughts floated from James to Dracula and back into the Champagne Room. She was falling asleep again. She watched Alen settle deeper into the wing-backed chair. The tissue box fell to the floor as his eyelids dropped and he fell deeply asleep. His resting head centered on the biggest upholstered rose. The petals and leaves held him in a peaceful dream that might have been about elves or something far from the sadness of this house.

June 16, 2003

dearest Aislin,

 how is life? the world we live in, and cannot escape

… i belong in the desert… and it does not belong in
me… so it goes. i cannot escape the decay of boats in
the salt flats and the way they travel in my dreams.
can you?

 i spoke with Majka on the phone. it has been so busy
lately and i do not see her enough… and what a way to
honor her… it hurts in deep places

i try to be graceful and separate myself from the
choking beads of sweat.

 and to see you again at sunset… could you not appear
although you have just left?

i am wondering where you are and why you are not near
me anymore.

i wish you respite from the heat that I love and you
shun. i wonder what it is like there today.

with love to gig harbor,

james

Chapter 40 ✦ Aislin

Mindful that somebody was watching her, Aislin rolled over in bed and opened her eyes. Light sparkled within the beautiful organza of the canopy; tiny little threads of silk caught the candlelight from the hall. It was the first night she slept on her side in too long. As her eyes adjusted to the gloom, they fell on the faint outline of someone in the corner. Her breath caught. Alen was asleep in the chair, just as she last remembered.

The figure wasn't James, who often came and went in the night—it wasn't James whose other worldly existence wrangled her heart. It wasn't James who kept watch over her like a soldier that came and went when he could not even see. *Where is he now?*

"This is how it starts," said the voice. "First you lose your husband in a freak accident, and then his former lover comes to stay with you. This is how the end of your life starts. How you lose your happiness."

Jade. It was Jade's voice from the shadow in the corner of the room with glittering champagne walls; in the corner of a room where Aislin never even wanted to be.

She drew in a sharp breath and winced at the sharp pain in her head as she rose onto her atrophied arms too quickly. *Why was Jade allowing me to stay when she feels this way? But how else can Jade feel?*

Aislin looked for her in the dark, but the widow's silhouette had moved, and it took a moment to find her again. She stood in the doorway. The hallway light flicked on. Jade was lit from behind. She had a gangly silhouette, just as unfriendly as while hiding in the shadows. Aislin couldn't see her face.

Jade said, "Get up."

Chapter 41 ✦ James

Ⓙ AMES APPEARED IN THE CHAMPAGNE ROOM AT FIRST LIGHT AND LOOKED at the crumpled bed sheets, empty of Aislin.

Alen opened his eyes, James turned to his wife in the doorway. The light from the candles of the hallway altar still glowed—accentuating her quivering chin. She looked incredibly pale and thinner than James remembered. Heartache spread through his chest.

James waited for Alen to notice that Aislin was not in the bed. When at last he did, he jerked up. Then, they noticed Jade; she swallowed hard and licked her lips. Every muscle in her body looked tense as she took a small step backwards. Questions hung in the air; yet patience would win this morning. Alen allowed space and time. Jade would talk when she could talk. In that moment, anyone could see from her trembling body that she was barely holding it together. James knew his brother wished he could snare just a hint of happiness from a movie or from another person's life and give it to his sister-in-law.

In the hall, Jade's shadow came at the bed and split at the edge of darkness. Alen's face bent to creases. Although James could not distinguish the glaring wattage, he knew the track lights were on full blast. Alen rubbed his eyes. James wished the silence to end. He could not read minds and was becoming very impatient. The bathroom was dark. *Where is Aislin?*

After an unreasonable amount of time, Alen rose and took Jade's hand. His brother stood in the same shadow, in the same stillness, just out of the same glare of the hallway light James recalled as obnoxious. Why Jade wanted to install track lighting in the hallway, he would never understand. It was modern, unnatural, unlike the rest of his designs. And although he could not see the track lights anymore, the memory of flood-light effect was still fresh.

The candles seemed like the only kindness that morning; the sun was still too low. He could not completely make things out.

Jade held Alen's hand. The hands on the clock kept turning. Eleven minutes had passed since James entered the room. Alen and Jade stood motionless under the glare of those awful lights. Jade's knuckles whitened, but Alen did not take his hand back. All the hands had played their parts, and yet had parts to play.

Thirteen minutes. James noticed a loud exhale, and it occurred to him that Jade had been holding her breath. James no longer thought about breathing. Alen noticed her exhale and smoothed his sister-in-law's back. In her black silk pajamas, she blended into the sharp shadows of the doorway. Alen guided her out of the room and held her at arm's length to look her over.

Alen was still not aware of James when he joined them in the hall. Their grandfather clock chimed on the quarter hour.

Skin wilted and darkened beneath his widow's eyes; James knew Jade had abandoned eye makeup; the shadows were biological. He had overheard Jade telling Alen this one night as he watched them eat through a half-gallon of frozen yogurt. They were trying to be healthy, get a little extra protein in. Probiotics. If the circles were dark beneath her eyes that night—tonight, she looked like a creature from beyond—at least as the movies portrayed them.

But they said James looked just like he did the day he died. Was he a creature from beyond—or perhaps that was what lurked in the darkness?

The hands on the clock kept moving; twenty minutes had passed since he had found Aislin's empty bed.

Jade lifted her pale fingers into the light and just pointed down the hallway. She pointed down past the brightest part of the hall and her finger shook there, with barely any latitude, getting heavier as it quivered, until her hand was down at her side again.

James followed Alen's eyes until they met his. They began at the low trajectory, skimmed the floor to the tip of James' work boot. Then the rest of his leg and above that was denim and a belt and a t-shirt that fit smoothly over strong shoulders. Ascending, Alen would see his brother's chin and crooked smile and above that his eyes. James watched as Alen took him in, his hair disheveled and a few months past cutting—just like on the day he died. His brother's face was a mixture James could not read.

"You can see me, finally," James whispered.

He was unsure if he was talking to Alen or Jade, or both. Jade sustained her desperate hold on Alen's hand, but had the meaning behind her grip shifted? James tried again. "Can you see me? Are you seeing me now, finally?"

James caught his breath, realizing he might look more alive than Jade did, standing there, three a.m., gaping at her dead husband, having a breakdown. He may have been transparent, invisible to most, but Jade had lost so much weight, she was disappearing. She struggled in silence beyond Aislin's head injury, beyond Hana's loss of religion, beyond his children's uncertainty of when they should play and when they could laugh. Beyond them feeling bad if they did not miss their father every minute. He knew the struggle so well himself. Jade's struggle reached beyond Alen's self-absorbed loss of Victoria. For Alen had James back, and so did Aislin.

James could tell his brother's eyes were still adjusting from the dark of the Champagne Room to the glare of the hall. He peered into the dark recesses of the shadowed hall beyond James. Due to his difficulty existing in the dim, James may have left them at any moment. He watched the closest altar falter. Candles that burned out one-by-one would not be replaced in a time like this.

James had never held such reverence for the sun as it climbed with each advance of the clock-hand; it filled the darkened corners of the marble staircase from the cathedral-like windows of the east wall and claimed its stake on the other end of the hallway. Though, to the living, it would not be bright enough to compete with the track lighting. There was a momentary relief that he would not miss whatever was about to happen.

Jade's eyes lingered on the floor, where there was another foot, another pant leg. This was a worn flannel pant that extended into the gloom. It took a few moments for him to realize it was Aislin.

Alen must have noticed her at the same time. He tried to pull toward her, but Jade gripped his hand with a force fueled by fear. Aislin was unconscious on the floor, and now in the panicked silence, James could not know for sure if Jade could even see his ghost at all.

Jade's fear was lying flat out with Aislin on their hallway runner.

"You'll never forgive me," her voice croaked out in a whisper. "We got in a fight." The last words a whisper so flat and emotionless their black aura hung in the air.

And Alen just stood there, letting Jade's intense grip cut off blood to his fingertips. He let her grip hold him back for reasons James could only guess at but was impatient with. Uneasiness filtered into his heart as the implications swept up the hall, leaving him with the sensation of goosebumps that his arms could not physically have. It was only seconds, but it seemed to be minutes, and Alen was barely resisting Jade's hold on him.

"Alen, move!" James tried to intervene; not even sure anyone heard him.

Alen stayed back. James looked at Jade, thinning and weak. Jade had lost so much of her strength—could she even hold his brother back if he really wanted free? Alen was afraid.

Aislin moaned. Jade jerked in surprise; the movement strong enough to knock Alen off balance. He regained it and placed a careful hand on Jade's shoulder; he looked into her eyes and tried the trick Victoria told him about. In a softened tone, Alen repeated, "It's going to be okay. It's all going to be fine." Then he slowed his own breathing. It did not work at large; James sensed the erratic rate of her pulse. But apparently it was enough for Jade to believe it was time to check on Aislin.

"I am going to her. Now. Jade," Alen said as he kissed the motionless woman's forehead. Only her fingers moved when she released him. He shook his hand out as the blood returned.

When Alen reached Aislin's side, his head turned back. "Jade, what have you done?"

Jade's shadow spread like a whisper towards them. Her eyes shone with concern and regret. She turned and leaned back against the wall, sliding down until her rear came to rest on a rectangle of cold travertine. She drew her knees to her chest, expression blank.

Staring. Silent. Still.

Dread built in James as the meaning of Jade's words slithered into his head. Everything hit him: from fear of Aislin's state, to a strange relief that Jade could not see him, to a horror when he realized Jade thought Aislin was dead.

He could hear his brother's voice in the hallway, saying Aislin's name again and again, but his own thoughts were caving in on him. The lives of his loved ones snowballed into disorder. And he did not know what to do.

But if Aislin never woke, it would destroy Jade. How many years of therapy would she need? Would the boys grow up with no parents if it were manslaughter? How would Jade get through? She was more fragile than anyone saw; she had shed so much more than color, shed so much of her light, so much weight, so much laughter. Jade shed and shed. How could they continue to let this shedding go untreated?

James looked at Aislin on the ground. He looked at his wife now with her head in her hands. If he were not already dead, his heart would have stopped beating.

November 20, 2001

My Dear, Dear Aislin,

it is almost time for thanksgiving. will you come
again this year and fill our house with your magic
laughter? Majka says to write you with haste and
scolds me for waiting so long. she made you cabbage
rolls last week and i forgot them. she might leave me
to sleep in the cold tonight.

it is possible. Alen might hose me down and the dogs
might take turns licking my popsicle fingers until
frost bite spreads up my arms and the blackness finds
my soul disappointed it is already blackened.

it is so cold in the desert this time of year. i need
your body to warm me and i cannot keep but shaking now
thinking that someday… there might be a way.

ever, james

Part Two

... She
Wails the long night, and perched upon a spray
With sad insistence pipes her dolorous strain,
Till all the region with her wrongs o'erflows.
No love, no new desire, constrained his soul

—*Virgil, Georgics*

Chapter 42 ✦ Jade

Several months before, the ringing phone in the silence of James' executive-style home office made Jade jump. As she pulled her mind out of James' upcoming month's work schedule and the boys' soccer and music lesson schedules, her stomach turned. He would miss every game and the recital.

James' previous promises were erased the moment the mayor selected the Athelstan bid. She reminded herself he had put the bid in before the promises—before the talk that took all that inner and liquid courage. And although he told her it was not a straightforward choice; she knew he was too proud to say no. She knew too many of his men's livelihoods depended on jobs like this. So, she heard the words before he said them...

"I am sorry, Jade, but we have to take it. Our design is the one the owners and the mayor want, and the only one that replicates that dilapidated building."

Jade finally picked the phone up on its tenth ring. The answering machine wasn't working. Her brow creased. Who the hell lets it ring that long, anyway? When she looked at the caller ID, her spit stuck in her throat.

"Hello?" she said.

"Jade, every other wrecking ball in the city is out of service. There's just one left to take care of and the project will have serious setbacks."

"Okay."

"When's the demolition of the bowling alley scheduled?"

She gave the caller all the details from the schedule.

"It's pretty straight-forward. The electrical short will cause the equipment to malfunction. It won't hurt him, but there will be a jolt that will cause a bit of whiplash."

Jade was quiet for so long that her accomplice cleared his throat.

"Hello?" He made sure she was still there.

"Yeah."

"Okay, so this will meet our individual goals. It's nice being a terrorist with you."

Jade didn't know what to say. She returned the rotary phone to its fancy pink-marble and brass stand. Upon first contact by the mad historian who wanted to preserve the stinky bowling alley, she had listened with apathy. She knew the owners of the bowling alley personally; she understood the increased quality of life that the project would provide for them. The mayor's project incorporated all the present businesses into a new establishment that James won the bid on. It would be clear of smoke, but hold the style and design of the 40s, a time when the bowling alley was beautiful, clean, and new. The current owners lacked the finances to restore and remodel their dilapidating business. Taglines like "Frank Sinatra bowled here!" were just not enough to compete with the entertainment emporiums of the twenty-first century.

The director of the Palm Springs Historical Society, John Murray, didn't care about the current owners. He kept calling her. The heyday of his favorite stars and their hangouts was fading, and the buildings were being replaced. He could barely cope with the dozens of letters coming in from octogenarians demanding preservation of their town and history. Murray resorted to removing these "destroyers of the past" in the midnight hours with his bare hands. He hated developers and once he got the Athelstans' home phone number, the harassing calls were constant.

Murray's advanced knowledge of excavators and demolition machines enthralled Jade. It was James talk: he loved describing machines. She craved Murray's comforting reassurance that the developers followed the wrong agenda. She agreed with his pitch that their own agendas were both, in their singularities, more important than having another shiny new building in Palm Springs. At the same time, she knew James designed an authentic retro plan—she loved the model. It really looked like its mid-century photos. But regardless of all the historian's shortcomings and unsupported claims, Jade caved on the third call of that day, perhaps the twenty-fifth call overall, while sucking on the ice of the afternoon's fifth bourbon and ginger.

Then, almost holding her breath, Jade waited for James to say something about trouble at work with the historical society. No word came. No sharing, no exciting job-site updates. In retrospect, she knew that his non-sharing had come at her request. When James accepted the bid, the choice wounded her, and she declared the project none of her concern. He had shut her out due to her own stubbornness. But it didn't make it hurt any less.

It wasn't supposed to kill him.

The air emptied out of the study. Jade couldn't hear anything above the whirring and spinning within, as the sound of her heart collapsing in on itself took over the world. The historian who knew so much about machinery failed to anticipate that his electrical sabotage could be delayed. It was. James already had the wrecking ball in full swing when the power shorted out, causing the guide panel to fail and the ball to strike the cage. It would have killed James, but it electrocuted him first. She waited for the coroner's report to come back, but the men onsite said they could smell the electrical fire. Authorities suspected the sequence spared James from the pain of the glass cage shattering; and likely he did not experience the impact of the heavy pendulum at all.

Jade didn't shift from her spot at his desk for a whole day.

By that point, he should have been home with mild whiplash, and she should be feeding him chicken soup. When he felt up to it, they would go to the beach—just the four of them—and he could take his time to recover....

As the sunset, she opened his bottle of Laphroaig and drank straight from it. Pain shot through her stiff legs as she got up and took the scotch to the window. She had never liked the taste, but the extreme peat flavor took her mind to a faraway place.

In the bottom of the ceramic pot on the windowsill was a stash of leftover pain killers from kidney stones and surgeries past. Jade pulled one from the old plastic bag, chewed, and swallowed the chalkiness down with another swig from the bottle.

Several people came and went from the office that day. Several people sat with her and held her hand. More people whispered out in the hallway. The words "shock" and "long recovery" touched her ears. Everyone determining her future, their prognosis planting a seed she would not even need to tend.

Jade, inconsolable in her silence, didn't speak to anyone. Her boys came over and hugged her. She kissed each on the head and sent them away, James' face instead of their faces. She sent her children to Father Benjamin's house, unable to leave the study, unable to look at them. Her mother-in-law, the ever intuitive, eased their protests and protected them the way she always seemed to know how to protect children.

Hana didn't see this coming.

Jade's rage leached into the roof, permeated the wooden desk and the chairs, soaked the deep-green, damask velvet wallpaper until the insulation beneath held it like a sponge. Seeping it back into her or morphing into shame or grief to feed the endless cycle. She leaned her forehead against the warm window, pressing hard into the glass. Then her palms, pushing, hoping to break it, praying it would give, and let her fall into the cacti below.

The panorama from the attic story of their home stretched for miles, the tumbleweeds sat dry and alone out there. Out there, the suffering echoed her suffering. Her eyes refocused on the water spots from the recent storm, putting the view from her late husband's study into a blur. The doors opposite the windows led out to a balcony. And if she jumped from there, that would do it. It would be better than breaking the glass. But she was never one to jump.

She released the pressure from the window; it wasn't going anywhere, anyway. This glass was stronger than the glass of the cage. This glass her husband had installed with his own two hands. The round, dusty imprints of rain accused her from their vantage points, each screaming, "How dare you? How could you? You killed him!" in a thousand condemning voices.

The desire to embody the earthy flavor of the scotch was overwhelming, she wished she could become it, wished her bones were made of it, that she could taste it at the source—as if traveling to the Isle of Islay would somehow dampen the truth.

Officials summoned Jade to the morgue. Alen identified James at the scene, but they still asked her to go as some sick formality she did not understand.

Her exhale drew a form in the chill of the quiet morgue. She looked down at James' eyes, his cheeks, out the swinging doors to the shine of the security guard's badge, and back up at the coroner, before throwing a tentative glance at the detective with the accent she couldn't place.

There were many things in the room to look at instead of James: the green swinging lamps, the doors of the body lockers, the clean beyond clean of the floor. Her nails and at the burnt parts of hair on James' hand and at the reflection of the lights on the metal table next to it. But Jade could not return her eyes to his face, to the deep cuts from the glass on his collarbone, and the smell and the blackness that seemed to be his now, again at the hand sticking out from the sheet on her side of the table. Nor to the sheet over his body, that lie over his naked center, that hid his sculpted abs, that covered most of the shoulders that were always so strong and the way his left and right feet bowed just a little. She could not return to the motionless of it all, to the heart that lay inside the chest that did not pump, to the diaphragm that did not rise, to the blood that did not make him hard and love her, and hold her, and make a baby with her. It would do none of these things.

Jade could not return her eyes to the coldness that was her husband. Still lying on metal, chrome on wheels holding his weight, his body on this and not in the soft sheets of their bed where she would have to sleep without him. His body on this table, not a bed, not a couch, not their semi-grassy California desert yard with their dogs, not under the sun on the hammock between palms, not in the boys' bed reading a story or in the library. Not with her, not beside her. No.

She nodded to the coroner, and she said, "Yes, that's him. That's my husband, James Athelstan." And then she did not look at anything but the door and then the stained tile of the hallway as her feet took her over it and out more doors and into the sun where she was alone and just staring straight into it, reacting with a dry heave to the queasiness of her empty stomach.

On the way home, Jade drove to the place that was becoming her place. Standing under the glaring lights of her ubiquitous liquor store, in the back room of a gas station off the route of fellow moms. How could she face them at all? A sudden and cherished stillness took over her mind as she decided on her poison. *It would be better to just drink poison.* But she was never one to die in agony.

She found the Laphroaig. It was on the top shelf and was fifty bucks. Would she let her drinking habit get in the way of being perpetually, comfortably unemployed and spend the years drowning in expensive scotch? No. She didn't care how it tasted. And the Laphroaig reminded her of James. It reminded her of his long pours and longer hours writing and designing behind his heavy, wooden study doors. *Damn the Laphroaig!!!* After all these years of sliding it over her tongue, she was done trying to like it.

She blinked under the fluorescent lights and adjusted her weight over her heels in a squat. Her eyes sank to the stained linoleum, to places unmopped for decades. Above a stain that looked like blood was the Wild Turkey. Beside it was a store brand. *Perfect.*

The plastic collapsed slightly under the grip of her hand. It was a bourbon. All bourbons are whiskies, but not all whiskies are bourbons. Something about corn. She didn't know if she cared about this detail that cracked James up whenever he rehearsed it. He would apply the same thing to dogs and Labs, insects and butterflies. She missed him. She didn't care about anything. The light shone down on her. Failing fluorescent gasses led her to the soda aisle. Not to be confused with other isles like the Isle of Islay, a place where she could have gone with her husband, watched her children run on the moors, explored megaliths. Not to be confused with her favorite vacation place, Coronado Island.

No.

She was selfish, and he was gone. There would be no other types of aisles. She had been thinking about this scotch too much, and she vowed then to stop, to kill her wistful longing for Scotland and the life that could never exist.

Jade made it home without crying. She left her plastic bottle on the floor of the car and led her visitor, Aislin, off the dusty road and into her home.

A babysitter. Good grief, Alen, if that's what you want to believe, that's fine. But my boys need you. They need their dad. They don't need this girl.

Chapter 43 ✦ Jade

AT THE CHURCH, ONE HUNDRED CANDLES BURNED. GOD'S COLD STARE drove down Jade's back in the pews; his eyes followed her from each stained-glass window. She looked up at the cross where Jesus hung with turned down lips and closed eyes. His eyes were not closed, though. They saw right through her. The wake seemed to last for hours, and Jade could not escape the church fast enough.

Late that night, Jade was preparing another camp-out in James' study. Aislin had driven her and the boys to and from the wake. Too many hours kept passing between the time of his death and her present moment. She needed some time to just sit and be with his things. Exploring, she pulled up a false bottom in one drawer, never realizing it was there before. She frowned at a stack of bound letters. Some of them took triangular shape. Others were flat rectangles with hard-worn edges. She pressed her thumb against the velvet ribbon in hunter green—James' favorite color. She tugged a letter loose and opened it.

This letter was from Aislin. It was old, but only a year before Egon was born, long after Aislin had moved away. Printed on computer paper, the URL was almost obliterated by curled edges. Deep creases indicated he had refolded it again and again. She pulled out a second one and realized all the letters were from Aislin. Jade did not keep her grip on them and touched her heart as they bounced down off her knees and hit the floor with a substantial thud.

At the wake, she remembered her regard for Aislin. The woman helped her with chores and feeding the kids. After a few days, she even brushed the dogs. It was nice. She almost believed Alen was right about Aislin. She had also helped those detectives get out of the house quickly. When the detective started with, "We know you're not feeling well, today." Jade played the about-to-vomit card like an Emmy-award winner. She genuinely appreciated Aislin keeping the house quiet and all those people at bay.

Yet, here were these letters. The woman came to steal her life.

All week, Aislin helped to light the altar candles, and weirdly, knew without being asked exactly what saints to buy at the store. Jade worried about

Aislin becoming suspicious. Saint Augustine's presence was not helping the guilt subside.

None of the saints were helping.

Jade wanted Hana and Alen's religion to be hers. She wanted the Saints to forgive her and watch over her and her boys. Not only did the Saints not help, but they did not care.

She burned the letters one by one on the altars. In the days after, she watched Aislin sweep the remains of the letters off the altar, not knowing what they were.

The boys were desperate with questions about Victoria, who, after the funeral, showed up with Alen almost every time he came. She tried not to, but an angry tone came out when the boys asked about Uncle Alen's girlfriend. Jade wanted to like Victoria, but she was taking Alen away. Taking him from the boys. And Alen was sneaking around, whispering to himself constantly. The abnormal behavior began the night of the funeral. He was different when he ate with her, didn't really talk to her. He looked around the room a lot, rarely right at her. Jade hated everything. She hated being alone in the huge, empty house.

Alen left for a trip to the beach with his new lover and Aislin. She lied and said Eleanor would stay with her, but never even sent the invitation.

The accidental death of her husband was something she knew everything about. She turned over the facts of what everyone else knew. There was obvious evidence of sabotage for those with a trained eye, but it was apparent the cops were too hot to care.

Questions about vandalism during her interview with them gave her the impression they had no solid leads. They weren't asking the right questions. The lazy days of heat lingered and spilled into their investigations. The donation she gave to the historical society, along with any other clues, sat below police radars as they readjusted AC fans before priorities.

She thanked any saint listening for assigning such odd detectives to her case: one of them seemed overly squeamish about vomit and the other one seemed reluctant to even bring James up. In this one way, her candles were working. She could not believe they never returned to question her more thoroughly. With any luck they would stick with vandalism and blame the whole thing on bored teenagers.

St. John Paul II Feast Day came, and she sent the boys to Eleanor's house. Where else could they eat all the papal cakes they wanted but their Godmother's? She tried to dress up to join them but worshipped the porcelain god instead of the Polish saint, instead of eating pierogie and potatoes with the dear friend she was pulling away from.

Everyone else was at the hospital—waiting for Aislin to wake up. Jade alone, once again, looked at the blood in the foyer, wondering who was going to clean it, who might ever get the stain out.

Jade went to the college library where Victoria studied. They asked her to grab a book and pick up a note from a professor for Victoria. A huge favor, but Alen was just trying to get Jade doing something, anything, without saying as much. Jade was sure Victoria knew of a classmate more poised for this type of errand. But she did things for her brother-in-law—that was totally her thing. She did not want to be at the hospital, and Victoria helped her with the dogs. She had even taken the boys to soccer when the new nanny caught a cold, so Jade owed her.

The nanny just meant that Jade could drink more, it meant she didn't have to drive the boys herself. The nanny was just an enabler. They had never hired a nanny; Jade barely remembered the last "real job" she had held.

She decided on a nanny a few days after Alen and Aislin took off to play at the beach. Her boys. They needed someone to take them to school now that they returned. And school meant they needed help with homework. Jade could not help. But the cross was hers. She carried it; drank from it; prayed with it. A flask with a subtle, yet sparkly, cross sandblasted into the side of the silver. It was antique, or maybe it just looked antique. It wasn't a crucifix, but it was hers alone to fill and drain and fill and suffer and refill. And perhaps she would get lead poisoning from this vessel. A fitting end. So she needed the nanny.

When she realized Victoria used a private study room, she flushed with curiosity. *Do they know something about James' death? How could Alen leave me alone so often, unless he suspects me of something?*

Jade found nothing about herself in the girlfriend's research room—except books about death. It was creepy; wrong. A cold, uncomfortable spark jumped inside her. Fury and dizzying possibilities danced in her head. She read book title after title, biting her lip. Her breath grew into shorter bursts. The spark extinguished, turning the remains into a smoking coal in her stomach. She opened to a bookmark in the chapter, "Death Does Not Exist," and then a sentence, "... nobody can die alone because the deceased one is able to visit anyone he likes."[2]

A book titled *Twentieth Century Book of the Dead*[3] sat alone in the center of the desk. A peeled jacket cover exposed the book board beneath. She peeked at the sub-chapters inside, *Are the Dead Named?* and *Evolution of a Death Machine.* She closed the cover and her eyes, but her eyes jolted back open.

"What is all this?" She tossed the book down and stepped back without looking. Her discarded pile of books tumbled over, causing another stack by the door to spill. She managed to get the door open to leave, and as she turned to close it, another stack fell. This stack knocked over the trashcan, jamming the door.

Exasperated, Jade tried to fix it. Her shoulders and arms lost their strength. But the will to exercise or stretch her body had died with James. Her muscles were tight. Pain jerked into every joint. Just moving the heavy subject-matter out of the way caused tears to scorch her face with their salt and heat. She pulled the door shut and heard more items fall behind it. With heat and panic threatening to explode her insides, she left the books in disarray. A green light from a desk lamp followed her from beneath the door, casting its lonely spirit out onto her black suede boots.

Jade fled through the stacks; the angry ghosts of the books she'd scattered chased her. The stacks went on forever. Staircases twisted and creaked with every footfall. Jade became Snow White running through the forest. Shadows fell across the library's gold and red carpet. More artificial light came in through the windows than from the dreary interior. She ran all the way outside the building and to the parking lot. Nearly twenty students watched her throw up on the asphalt, heaving from exhaustion. Out of shape—and away from the bottle for at least four hours. No one asked her if she was okay.

Behind the wheel of her car, a tidal wave of grief and shame brought her to side of the road. So much for driving anymore. If she was not drinking, she was not coping. She did not want to tell Alen she failed in her errand, either. But he was calling.

"Jade, hey, do you want me to hang out with the boys?" he asked.

She needed him to come over so badly she could scream. "Yes, if you're not busy. I know they want to see you. And, uh, Alen? I couldn't get Victoria's stuff." Jade got ready to make up some story about the room being locked or getting a flat tire or the paper with the directions blowing away.

"It's okay, she can get it herself."

"What? Why? What happened?"

"I don't think we'll be seeing each other anymore."

"Oh, Alen, I'm so sorry." Jade could hear sadness in his voice, extra sadness. She bore the responsibility for his brother's death and could not prevent another woman from breaking his heart.

"It's alright."

"Well, if you want to talk about it...." Jade offered.

"Sure, maybe sometime. Let me pick up some food and I will be there soon." She ended the call with a deep sigh of relief. She hadn't even needed to lie to Alen about throwing up in the university parking lot—and they would get him all to themselves, at least for dinner.

Aislin woke up. But she stayed in the hospital until, for "healing purposes," Alen sent Aislin back into Jade's house. The invalid slept in the pretty, gold-lace room that was suddenly referred to as the Champagne Room.

Time passed as slowly as a tree trunk thickened. She could not recognize her face in the mirror. She didn't recognize herself in her children. Hana's absence, although chosen (because how could she even look the woman in the eyes?), tore her up like another excavation.

Jade really missed Hana.

Jade longed for James.

Jade missed Alen, who increasingly could not seem to look at her. He had some secret to hide, but it couldn't be that he knew hers. Jade mused over the fact that Alen and Aislin were involved with each other. It didn't matter that there was the girlfriend, Victoria. Did it? People were disloyal. And Victoria hadn't even stuck around. Jade liked Victoria, mostly. Except for the books and taking Alen's attention away, the few times she visited had been pleasant. Was Aislin the reason? Jade gritted her teeth with resolve. It couldn't be that Alen was involved with Aislin. The invalid could barely turn her head. But Alen was being secretive about the reason Victoria left him.

When would Aislin just leave?

November 1, 2004

dear James,

You once told me, some years ago, that there is always
a way. And so, with those words i will continue to
state my impossible, far-fetched plan; I suppose it
is time to tell you that suffering this cannot even be
described with the word "hard". I am glad that was the
end of your sentence, terrifying, truly, i can hardly
say more.

it is not going to end the way that i dream that
it will, and perhaps not the way that you dream it
either. In a few Wednesdays, the 17th, I will be going
to San Francisco to a hotel by the airport. I will
leave at noon from Washington; if my impossible far-
fetched plan is out of your range, I will await your
words. but it is only a short plane ride. we could
take in a show; it is hard. i know that Jade is there
with you… would wonder where you dared to venture.

i may however not survive that long, scorpions in my
stomach and my heart beating abnormally. i wonder what
you would have said to this long ago. at least it is a
hotel with some class, anyway. not the illustrious one
of my employ in Palm Desert.

of course, it is impossible.

i am reading Gabriel Garcia Marquez, Love in a Time
of Cholera. It is by far the most amazing book i have
read. If you have not, you must, James. you will need
it, grow from it… live it even perhaps…

i must return from lunch now. leave the quiet of the
library and wait to go home. i will make enchiladas.
and think of Wednesday, how it could be.

I dreamt of your name deeply imprinted on cream
papyrus, following a sweet message. all of these years
come flooding back to me.

ever,

Aislin

Chapter 44 ✦ Jade

JADE PACED OUTSIDE OF AISLIN'S ROOM. IT WAS EARLY, THREE OR FOUR o'clock. The door was open and Alen was sleeping in the chair. She had to know what the hell was going on. Why was Aislin always whispering and stopping the moment she walked into the room?

All of this had to stop, or Jade was going to explode on the next person who spoke to her. In the dark hours just before dawn, she decided to wake Aislin up.

Jade waited for Aislin to join her after giving the rehearsed "this is how the end of your life starts" speech. She grew impatient in the hallway, eyes adjusting to the light, her foot tapping and tapping.

She might lose her upper hand if she made a joke, but she almost couldn't help saying something about Aislin's plaid penguin pajamas and bedhead. She looked down at her own tailored, black-silk pajamas and grew taller. Every little thing about Aislin was a bother to her senses.

Jade frowned. "Hurry," she said.

Aislin only then seemed to accomplish an acceptable speed, as if she were slow on purpose before. "I don't have time for theatrics."

Aislin finally joined Jade in the hallway. Once again, she wore a look of secrecy, deceit, and surprise. Jade watched her Adam's apple descend and rise, saw her pupils dilate when they should have shrunk. It was infuriating to watch; it was like the woman was in love.

"You have to not be here anymore!!"

"Okay, I get it. I do. I will leave."

"It's like you're always bumping into things. You're always talking to yourself. You and Alen. But you're not, you're talking, and you suddenly stop because I walk in. It's not normal talk-to-yourself talk. I see you. What the hell is going on? What the hell do you know?"

Aislin jerked her chin up. Jade fell silent, expectant. She stared at Aislin for a long time, with no idea what the woman was thinking. "What the hell are you doing here, anyway?" Was all she came up with. It was the question on Jade's mind almost all the time, besides *howthehellcouldIhavedonethat? whatdidido? howcanIlivewithmyself? whyisshehere? where'sthefuckingbottle?*

"Aislin. I want you to pack and leave."

"I'm still on bedre—"

"I don't fucking care about bedrest. Right now. You're gone." Jade didn't care about the injury. She wasn't sure she ever had.

"Okay."

"Okay. Then get fucking moving."

"Yeah." Aislin started back to the Champagne Room.

"I'm not a bitch, you know."

Aislin looked at her and raised her eyebrow. Her eyes were infuriating.

"I want you to leave. Your stay has ended."

"Yes, I am going. I just—it's not recommended I be on my own yet."

"I've had enough of you." Without even thinking, she shoved Aislin down the hall. But all her anger couldn't make up for how tired, scared, and sad she was. She had little strength since losing her husband. "You're keeping something from me. Tell me!" The way she heard her voice threw her for a moment. It came like a monster.

"I am not hiding anything."

Each time Aislin spoke, Jade pictured a diminutive mouse, cowering, hiding itself. Jade wanted to be a cat, she wanted to pounce. "What are you lying about? You and Alen? I can tell you're sharing some secret. They may have asked you to write a book about us, but you keep your hands to yourself, Aislin. Alen doesn't need you. We don't need you." She pushed Aislin a little further down the hallway, and the girl stumbled.

"Say something. You little slut, you home-wrecker. Tell me why you're here. What are you hiding?"

"I came because that's what James wanted."

"And how would you know what my husband wanted?"

"He told me."

Now Jade knew Aislin was hiding something. James hadn't told her anything.

That fucking will. The words coming out of Aislin's mouth were more than Jade could handle, and she lunged at Aislin, knocking her to the stone floor. The thin rug did little to pad such a fall.

Jade looked down at her for a moment, the hall light not quite reaching Aislin's lovely face. *Lovely, if you were into pitiful as a fashion.*

"Oh, so fragile. You poor, little, broken orphan."

Aislin didn't move.

"Look at you." Jade jostled the plaid-penguin lump with her foot. Nothing. She bent down and could not discern Aislin's very shallow breathing. Without the wherewithal to check for a pulse, she mildly shook Aislin's shoulders.

"Get up, you bitch. I'm not done talking to you."

Jade let go, allowing Aislin to slump on the ground.

"It's been so many long years. My kids are growing up. Once, once you sat in the seat where I sit and you kissed the man that I love. But you didn't let go. I know that now, I see how it was. I've read the letters and burned them. You two didn't let go of your little romance, not really. I know that for years he loved me second to you. I know how he would have left me if you said the words. But I didn't know all of that back then. Yes, I had a feeling. I kept you close."

Jade settled to the ground and held onto the edge of Aislin's stupid shirt cuff, not understanding the desperation that was building up in her words. She tugged at it with longing, her tears stung. *Even my tears sting....*

"I extended friendship because that's what he wanted," Jade said. "But that way, I could also watch you. And I thought you seeing my life would still your desire towards him. It would heighten your ethics. I guess mostly that it did. And he stopped speaking about you, and over time you were a distant memory. Even when I skimmed over that part of the will, I didn't care. I didn't know what was gonna happen. I thought James would live. I mean, people make wills all the time and live 'til they're a hundred."

Jade stretched out on her side by Aislin. A horrible pit grew in her stomach, grief, and guilt—and Aislin. Aislin on the floor, not moving. Jade felt the words flow out of her mouth. Some awful confession of a sort. Yet she didn't want to stop talking. She wanted to be free. She shook Aislin again, and the girl did not move.

Aislin's head flopped sideways toward the shadow when Jade gave the shoulders a good little shake. From her position on the floor, Jade could no longer see Aislin's entire face. She kept talking anyway. "I never could have imagined what I was capable of. What I could conceive with just one mad man's convincing, with a little too much of the bottle. You know? And now you... you will expose me. One way or another." Jade tugged at Aislin's flannel a little harder. "Come on. Get up."

Jade heard a soft rustle and a creak behind her. She turned her head and could see Alen readjusting in the chair. But there was Aislin, who was not readjusting, who was not getting more comfortable on the floor. She shook her shoulder a little. Looked back at Alen; he was still asleep.

She waited.

She shook the shoulder a little harder. Still nothing. "Shit. Aislin, too. I killed Aislin, too."

Jade rose on unsteady legs and turned the lights up even more. The glare settled into her. Its harshness matched her harsh reality and all that life had become.

A coldness settled down her spine and into her stomach. The cold was different this time. Before, with James, it was an accident; it wasn't really her fault. But Aislin was breathing thirty minutes ago. Thirty minutes ago, her nemesis was on her way to recovery, planning a new life here in the desert where she would write a book and preoccupy Hana enough for Jade to go on "vacation" with the boys. She stood in the doorway and waited for Alen to wake up.

Five minutes passed, and he still slept. The sun was rising.

She leaned forward. Alen was sound asleep.

Aislin was dead.

Alen was sleeping.

She swallowed hard; her saliva became a sharp stone.

She might be able to lie.

It might have been an accident. But Alen—Alen would be heartbroken. And she wasn't a bitch. Hadn't she just told Aislin that? The coldness settled in; Jade had already begun to freeze inside. That coldness spread. It wrapped guilt around her bones, one at a time. The guilt found her heart, the coldness with it, traveling with its icy fingertips all over her soul. Guilt left frost trails in the muscles of each of Jade's limbs until finally she stood under the track-lighting she once had so cleverly lobbied for, frozen in a harsh, unforgiving light. There were no saints in the light with her. All her prayers had failed. Her two feet, and legs, and torso held her upright, but she was sure she would soon fall.

Chapter 45 ✦ James

"Aislin? Aislin? Wake up, Aislin!" both James and Alen spoke out, their voices discordant in a sad *a cappella*.

Her eyes blinked open and focused on Alen. There was a breeze in the hall and one of the Labs came to the top of the stairs, whining and sitting by Jade's side. James longed to scratch Indy's head, curl into a ball with his dog and shut out the worlds that he walked in.

Had Jade seen him? He had asked her himself, but sensed his voice only echoed throughout their halls without affecting her. The shape he made in his afterlife resisted a shape her eyes could see. His voice rang in his ears, demanding validation; did it even reach her? It was not clear if she could hear him. Did he dare believe she reacted to him?

James hoped *yes, please*, while also praying she had not seen him. It would be better if she did not know, especially after all this time. Certainly not after what was now transpiring with Aislin. He looked at Aislin. Lying there, so still when they so recently became physical. Touched. She had been so vibrant—healing. But here, skin paled. The memory of her spirit hovering in the foyer came back to him in a rush. It was all James could do not to scream.

"No, don't move," Alen said, as Aislin rose onto her elbows.

"I'm okay." Aislin turned her head back and forth with care.

"Still, you know, head trauma." He looked back at Jade; she had already left the conversation. Her mind left the hallway, her eyes glazed over, the lower whites became puddles of salt. "What happened? Can you tell me?"

"I remember some of it, some." She put her hand on her head. "Oh, Alen."

"Does it hurt?" Alen and James asked her at the same time.

"It does." She rose a little more. "I feel woozy."

"Should I bring you to the hospital?"

Aislin closed her eyes for a moment and took a deep breath. She opened and closed them. She raised on her elbows a little more. "No, I... I think I'm okay. Can you help me sit up?"

"I don't know, Aislin... are you sure?"

Aislin nodded. Her color returned a little. Alen conceded. Once her back was up against the wall and far enough from Jade, Alen sat in between them.

"Jade said you fought? Are you sure you're okay?"

Aislin forced a smile and nodded before putting her head on his shoulder. James noticed Alen drain of color. He did not know if his brother could handle anymore. Aislin patted Alen's hand, took it in hers, and rested them together on Alen's knee.

James reached out to touch her forehead. She tilted away from Alen and into his hand, and he knew she relished the strange sense of coolness he could offer her. At least it was something.

November 19, 2004

Aislin,

Ah, it's been three days since San Francisco

        I love Northern California; I love the rocky
coast. How do you think things have changed? I feel
bland as of late, as if I have never had sugar or
spice. I am terribly sorry for the way things went. I
know why you feel all the ways you feel.

My dog needs surgery. I never have had surgery for
my kidney stones, but I remember a weird cyst they
removed from my side. I would pay any money for my
dog's care.

please, tell me how you feel. should I still write?
have you changed forever? I will never be the same as
I was before you.

I am in Seattle beginning December 19th for a
contractor's business symposium; it is three days
long. I will be just across the bay… you are amazing
and will always be one I love, and never truly tasted.

love, James

Chapter 46 ✦ Aislin

 FIGHT? HOW COULD SHE GET INTO A FIGHT? SHE SAT QUIETLY WITH the cool of James on her forehead, holding Alen's hand and trying to remember.

Should I go to the hospital?

Aislin became present, burying her emotions for a moment to see what injuries were new, which ones exacerbated by their fight. That word again. Fight. Her last, and only, physical fight took place after her parents died. She grimaced at the idea of being set back in her recovery process.

James broke the silence. "You guys, will you look at Jade?"

Aislin looked around Alen at Jade's face, catatonic at the bright edge of the harsh track lighting.

The lights hurt Aislin's eyes. "What's up with this lighting?"

Alen and James ignored her question.

"I am trying to tell you there is something wrong with Jade. But I do not think she sees me."

"Then what the hell?" Alen's voice echoed down the stone stairs. "We've all seen death. And Jade is strong; this makes no sense."

The three of them looked at Jade's ashen skin, her eyes sinking into her skull. Aislin let out her obligatory sigh. Jade stirred a little, adjusting her head, tilting it against the wall. It looked like she was looking right at James.

"Are you sure she didn't see you?" Aislin asked.

James knelt before his wife, placed his hands around hers, tried to grip her skinny knees, tried to touch her. Jade reminded Aislin of a prepped canvas stretched to its limits. A basecoat waiting for stars or a moon, waiting for a flower in a vase, seeking the very color that peace would be. She showed no change, no signs of awareness. *He's not physical with her now, like he was with me.*

Aislin held her breath while she watched James with his wife.

Jade stirred, silent tears still coming, following the same pathway, falling, falling. More tears falling. Alen exhaled loudly in response.

If it was words Jade wanted, none were born. A sticky sound came from her throat that kind of sounded like an "i."

"Well, she had a ton to say a few minutes ago," Aislin said, as the event came back to her. She held her head in her hands, looking away from Jade and behind her, behind the fogginess of being knocked out. *No, she did not knock me out; I was conscious.* She was conscious, and Jade had been talking.... She moved her head too quickly and a pain that was more in her heart than in her head struck her. *What had Jade done?*

She could see the heat grow in Alen's face. He wanted her to share what she was thinking. Her silence aggravated him. *Could she argue with his frustration? No, he's so clueless, having awoken to this nonsense. He's fussing over us, not knowing the truth.*

She sat there with Alen, with Jade. James pacing and squatting at intervals before them all—wondering, mystified.

Aislin was struggling with the pain in her head and the damn-bright lights. *I can't stay here in the house anymore. I have to go. James, what will happen to us now?*

Never had Aislin experienced this, this flatness from the sky that crushed the earth she stood on. Crushed like James had been crushed. Crushed under the weight of neglect and communication lost. A one-dimensional pain where she walked like a zombie, not fully realizing what she had witnessed and what had happened.

Until she did.

Bile rose in her throat, and she swallowed it back. How was guilt fair? Well, what if she had run off with him long ago? Let him kiss her and enjoy the salty taste of him within the San Francisco fog? Would he be dead now?

Jade.

She wanted me to die!

A few hours before, she watched Jade get smaller and smaller as she descended the stairs beside Alen, presumably back to her own bedroom. Where would Jade hide her secrets?

Aislin arrived in the gloom of the green-walled study and poked around for a while. She rested a bit, flipping through ledgers. "Ugh," the bile rose again, and she swallowed.

Alen stood in the kitchen staring into an empty glass.

"Alen, I think Jade has something to hide. I can remember, little by little, the things she said to me in the hallway."

"Aislin, what are you talking about?" Alen eyebrows knitted together.

"Well, I felt very weak after Jade pushed me. I couldn't respond. Every time Jade shook me, the pain was overwhelming, and I was so nauseous. But she must have thought I was totally unconscious because—she was talking."

Alen folded his arms and leaned toward her over the island. She slid the ledger to him.

"I just came from James' study, and I found some things in his desk. The only thing in a drawer that locked with a skeleton key." *Conveniently hung from a knob by the knee.*

Aislin shared Jade's words and realized it was the beginning of a something they would never return from. The bile rose again, and she turned away from Alen, fear and uneasiness flushing at her ears and eyes and everything as she swallowed even harder and refilled his empty glass while pouring herself some, too.

Alen lost a lot of color. He took the glass and set it down without looking at it. "I need to talk to her. I need to hear this myself."

Alen had successfully led Jade to her master bedroom, both walking in a catatonic state. Alen's request that Aislin come to James and Jade's room for interrogation sunk in from the surrounding air. Aislin agreed. And once the door was open, she was inside.

Aislin looked around the master bedroom. All purple, all plush, all velvet, brocade, and lace. Her eyes saw the walls, the chairs, the blankets. There was no TV. She never wanted to see the inside of his bedroom. Though the house was only six years old, it looked like it had been there forever. Details in every room represented the artistry from bygone eras. Each element crafted by the studied artisans and masters over whom the brothers presided. Athelstan House was another character in their lives, providing a lovely, archaic backdrop to their painfully wrought drama.

Just days before, in an upstairs bedroom of this very house, she was kissing James. She could still feel his lips, still feel the pressure of his hand on her back, on her bare skin just where her shirt ended. She could *feel* him.

But things had progressed into such a state that instead of enjoying implausible, afterlife pleasantries—she was sitting in a room James had shared with his wife.

Chapter 47 ✦ Jade

It wasn't the end. She rolled over in all her velveteen bed covers and vehemently wished it was the end. But she'd never considered suicide. Never in her life, even her wish to break the glass or jump on the day he died weren't ideations. Discarded thoughts. Not even now in the total ruins of it. Or maybe things had changed.

No.

The new question: how to run away and keep within James' damn constraints? Luckily, the will conceded her traveling and she could go under that guise. Hana could take the boys from her, or perhaps Hana might want to go along, or maybe it would be good if Hana took the boys from her. Her heart surged. *No, that would never be good.*

When she rolled over a third time, she came up to a room of two faces that weren't there before.

Alen and Aislin staring at her from the side of the bed.

"Jade?" Alen's voice wrought with concern, the only emotion he held for her anymore. Their friendship, broken with no repair in sight. She didn't know when that started, but she knew it was her fault. She was pushing him away just as much as he pulled. Except he did not know there was such an ugly reason behind the pushing.

She clutched the delicately crocheted edge of the black sheets. It was no longer a strong grip, and after months in which her diet comprised mostly ice cream and bourbon, the weakness reminded her that her muscles had changed. It wasn't a good day; it wasn't a day to face anyone. As she maneuvered the sheet over her head and sank down into the blankets to escape the four questioning eyes. All the secrets would surface. Tears came, a thousand tears just like at night, but this time, she could not hide them.

"Jade, I am so glad you're awake," more from Mr. Concerned.

"Do you remember anything? You've been out of it for quite some time," Aislin questioned, with the audacity to sit in her bedroom.

She would never invite Aislin into this room. It was a place for her and James. It wasn't a place Aislin should be! She shouldn't be here, and she shouldn't be digging into the family history. Why would James give her the right? Why did Hana accept the idea with such—Oh my god, Aislin is alive?

Jade pulled the covers back and turned her head to see Aislin.

Somehow, an absence of judgement reflected from Aislin's eyes. Beneath the linens, Jade pinched herself. She closed her eyes, opened them. Aislin still sat there, intense. Jade maintained the connection, almost retching at the memory of all but confessing in the hallway. She swallowed back. What did Aislin remember?

Alen put his hand on Jade's forehead. After a moment, he smiled and seemed satisfied. "We had quite a scare with you two."

Jade nodded.

Aislin smiled at Alen and put her arm on the back of his chair as she leaned back. She seemed fine. *How is she fine?* Jade didn't trust what was happening. Alen's posture was alarming. He leaned into her space, far forward with his elbows on his knees and more of that pity on his face that she recognized in his voice. "I understand that stress is one of the biggest killers, but you've lived a pretty posh life, sister. At least since I've known you."

Every hair on Jade's body rose to defend her. "Wha—?"

"No, no. No need to get worked up, Jade. But I have a few questions for you."

She was beneath her linens and in the comfort of her own home, but the walls were closing in on her. The ceiling coming down. The heavy drapes grew thicker. She shrunk into the mattress away from their dense fabric, attempting to hide from the way the dark panels caged her. And deeper, inside the walls of her mind, her confession to Alen, strangely imminent. Confession had never, ever been her plan. So why had she lost it in the hallway? Jade started and looked around the room. The only way out was through the garden patio or the main door. *I'm trapped.*

"Alen," Aislin began. "Jade looks really surprised to see me."

"Jade?" Alen asked. "Why don't you tell us why you are so surprised to see Aislin?"

"Will you two get the fuck out of here? I am not playing whatever insane game this is. Leave me the hell alone."

"Okay. But wouldn't you like to tell us more about what you're capable of?" Alen was still leaning forward, warmly patronizing her, as if it would comfort her.

She could not understand what was happening. Jade wished she could re-member what happened after she woke Alen up. How much did she drink? She presumed her drinking was under control, that she was fine. Functioning. She was not at risk of losing her children. Drunks black out. She remembered things, usually. But maybe she blacked out? "Why can't I remember what happened?"

"I don't know, Jade. One minute we were having such a fine fight, and you pushed me down. I blacked out for a moment. Sensitive head, you know? When I woke up, you were mumbling to me. Then Alen got me up to sit next to you. It was as if you saw a ghost then. Did you see one?"

"A ghost? What ghost?"

Silence in the room.

"... Oh... God...." She couldn't stand being made a mockery of. But it was weird, because it was almost as if Aislin wasn't being cruel. She asked because she genuinely wanted to know if she had seen James' ghost. Jade shook her head. "No, I didn't see a ghost."

The relief in the room was palpable. "Oh, my God. You two. This is too much. I ask you again to please leave!" Jade's voice was rising and shaking. Her throat tightened, and the pressure built behind her eyes.

But they just sat there. Alen still leaning close and Aislin leaning back in her chair with a book on her lap.

It wasn't just a book.

It was Jade's banknote book.

Jade eyed the book and considered trying to take it from Aislin. She didn't have the energy. Instead, she pushed the covers off, untangled her legs from her twisted pajamas, and slowly slid on her butt to the edge of the bed. She steadied herself as she stood, hungover, which was becoming rare for her the more steadily she drank. A five-foot shuffle got her to the chair by the win-dow before she practically crashed into it. A fallen pillow took the brunt of a kick and their monstrous curtains whispered and swayed in response. *So be it.* She gripped the French Victorian armrests. She was so mad; the chair wasn't even for sitting in. It was an antique. But if she worried about falling through the bottom, that fear dissipated when Alen started speaking.

"We put you in your room early this morning. Aislin told me that when she was coming in and out, you were talking to her. It sounds like you already started a confession, Jade, and we see the payment to that historian. The one that harassed the mayor... logged two days before James, ah.... Please tell me what happened. Please don't let me think you had anything to do with my brother's death." Alen's voice cracked with tears.

Upon a closer look, she noticed signs of recent crying. Jade looked away and just stared at the travertine floor, traced a small crack under their ancient bureau.

"Tell me!" Alen screamed.

Jade's head snapped up. Alen had never raised his voice that way. *Alen is yelling and now they're claiming James is a ghost? What the fuck is going on?* Jade looked from one face to the other and back.

"He's here," Aislin whispered. "He wants me to tell you he forgives you. He says he will always love you." Aislin's voice lifted a little, wrought with pain. "James wants you to start at the beginning."

"You liars!" Jade screamed at them both. "How many times must I ask you to get out?"

"No! My brother and I want to know. Tell us, please, Jade. Why is there a payment to the Historical Society?"

"It's not a payment," Jade thought for a moment. "It's a donation. For recompense."

"Recompense?"

"The director was harassing me, every day. A settlement offer, a donation was the quickest way to make him go away."

"I have the call logs, too." Aislin, who did not belong in her bedroom, held up a piece of paper.

It could have been call-logs—or not. It could have been anything. Jade couldn't see in the dim light. She got up as her alter candles started going out. She lit them all again, one by one, with a long match. No one spoke. Some needed replaced. It took a long time. Jade's body was stiff, each movement tinged her muscles like a bee sting.

No one spoke during the ritual. Jade tried to think of lies, but it was too quiet, and she was too tired. She thought the silence was weird. They watched her light each one, her actions a sacred liturgy.

"He can see in the dark because of these nice little altars you have every-where," Aislin spoke nonsense about James.

Jade sucked in a sharp breath, the foreboding grew within her. Her steely eyes saw Aislin, as if for the first time in weeks, and realized the woman was not just staring doe-eyed at nothing. Something else stirred. Jade sunk back into her chair. She hated how comfortable it was, and how it sat there for five years as only a prop for pillows at night. She drew her legs to her chest, rubbed her chin against the black silk, circling the bone of her left knee. The fabric, cool to the touch, lent a bit of relief to her clenched and aching jaw.

There was no way Aislin and Alen were really asking her all these ques-tions and telling her that James was a ghost. Alen didn't believe in ghosts. This was a dream.

Tears shone, the candle grabbing each one until tangled trails of pale light were a part of her skin. "Why can't I see you, James?" The hope drained from her soul. A lifeless nothingness replaced the air of the room, no longer a thing that brought life and no longer a thing that was comforting.

Alen ran to Jade. He knelt at her side as she sobbed and rocked. The weeping consumed her, uncontrollable for over an hour. Jade understood that her actions caused not only the death of her husband, but entirely severed the bond between them. This bond, once made from concrete poured into perfect forms, incorporated with children's photographs, glass, and cacti blooms—was replaced by concrete poured into a form to make a headstone.

A headstone that decorated a grave empty of its soul.

Her husband's spirit roamed the earth. He roamed on without her. He wanted this inquisition, and so she told him everything. And at the end, she was just a ball of soaked black silk in a pretty chair.

Chapter 48 ✦ James

Alen's plan got a confession no one suspected. No one could breathe. James was the first to realize that the three people who normally could breathe were all holding their breath. Alen at first grabbed Jade's thinning arms, shook her once, and screamed out that she was lying.

But she was not.

After his outburst, Alen let go and turned away, his hair sticking to his face with the salt of tears and sweat. He collapsed to the floor, weeping in anger, weeping without hope. He looked up at James and held onto Jade's leg in a desperation that James understood completely.

Jade pulled back into her ball.

Aislin went to Alen across the room, but James could see she needed to sit down. The only place to sit that was close to Alen was James' bed. He watched her tentatively touch the bedspread. Her hand only resting for a moment before she gave in to her physical needs and sat down. His insides sank and somersaulted. And he knew hers must be, too, for she would hate being in his bedroom. She remained progressively still, progressively sober.

Minutes passed. Maybe five. Only the sounds of mixed breathing and crying could be heard until Aislin stood and cleared her throat. She walked towards the door and stopped to lean her back against the wall, let it hold her up.

Jade crawled back to the bed and Alen left the room. His brother wandered the hallway, his shoulders rounded forward and low, and his eyes lined with rawness. Aislin followed without purpose.

Alen poured water for everyone. Jade refused hers. He left it on the nightstand and retreated into the darkened corridors of Athelstan House.

James guessed it was a good enough place to disappear from.

Aislin went outside and James wished her breath. He could not follow her out into a world where he could recognize neither the sun nor the moon. And by degrees, he watched his arms fade away—his body dissolved in a current of shadows. Blackness obliterated his eyes.

Jade's robbery, her selfish betrayal consumed his flesh and pain erased him from his home.

A week later, Aislin moved into her own place. She drank tea on the floor, purchased a mattress and tea set for the small studio. Between watching her sip tea, sleep, or paint in a whirlwind of lavender and periwinkle, James remained by her side. Except, of course, for moonless astronomical twilights and check-ins on Hana.

Sometimes he could think of a place and then go there, sometimes he had to walk, other times, it did not matter what he wanted, he just was where he was. Aislin was just where he was.

And there was another exception—the afternoon he returned with Victoria.

"Victoria is outside. Can she come in and talk for a while?" James worried over Aislin's reaction.

"Why? Victoria's ignorant." He knew Aislin's wish to put distance between herself and Victoria, but he did not expect harsh words.

"It would be great if you heard her out. She has beckoned me to Jade's side. She wants to see if she can cross me over." James' not-heart permeated hope and shame. He knew Aislin could read his emotions.

"James, this means you will leave in their presence. Should Jade be the one to say the last goodbye? Should Victoria bear witness? What about Alen? Shouldn't he be there?" Aislin turned her head away.

"I do not want to leave any of you, Aislin. But I am afraid." James reached for her shoulder and stopped. "I fear what is next. Can you not see? She has researched so much about this. This is her passion. She says I have nothing to fear. I need to hear that. Victoria has good intentions. Please see that, or just... trust me." James realized he was pleading with Aislin to consent to the meeting. He needed her support.

"I agree with her, a little. I mean, I want peace for you, James. Not this. Not this fading in and out. You've become scared, resistant, and so sad. It's difficult, but I want to have this conversation. I want to know what you're thinking," Aislin sighed. "Sure, have her come in and explain her good intentions to me."

Victoria entered the studio. She hung her coat and hat on the rack on the back of the door, installed with grit by a previous tenant. He noted she kept her purse. She looked around but said nothing about the lack of furnishings.

"How do you do, Aislin?" Victoria said, and nodded to James.

The formal greeting took them aback. He second-guessed his plan, but he did not know what else to do, so he just started talking. "Victoria seeks to protect us from heartache. My mother especially discerns this unsettled state with Alen. Everyday cracks wider with an enormous breech in peace."

Victoria opened her purse. "Inside, I have a few charms said to protect the dead while they are passing. I promise I am only here to help the family heal. To help Alen. You have seen us. You know what we have is special. So, James, if you will come to Jade's, I can bring peace between you two. I know that your affair with Aislin is holding her back from forgiving you."

Aislin stood up and James rebuked, "Aislin and I did not have an affair."

"What about the letters? They were all over the house when I went, half charred scribbles by the candles. I found a few still bound on the floor under an altar. In a velvet ribbon. You obviously cared for these letters, James."

Aislin sat down and looked at her hands. James could see she already knew about Jade burning her letters while he remained oblivious to the whole thing. He buried his face in the crook of his elbow, some invisible heat and sweat flushed on his brow. The affair was an affair when you talked about it, but he never did. Not really, and he never thought Jade would go through his desk. But he never stopped loving Aislin; the letters were proof. That he sat by no action of his own in this apartment instead of with his children, mother, Alen, or Jade—further proof.

"They're old letters," Victoria said. "Jade knows that. She knew of your relationship, of course, and she was grateful for the disappearing act, Aislin. But you came back into their lives on James' bequest at a bad time for Jade. Now she needs your apology, James."

Victoria placed her hands on her hips. "Moreover, if you can feel release, you can move on and everyone can start healing. You no longer belong in this world. Your presence has etched the pain into Alen's face. When you leave the room and he doesn't know if you will come back. His heart breaks not knowing when and if you will die again. This way you can say goodbye, I know you were robbed of that before." Completing her speech, she let her arms drop to her sides and softened.

James suddenly wished he had listened to Aislin. Victoria did not know the whole story. "You cannot know how this feels."

He broke into a series of violent shakes, a sobbing and shaking of his transparent form, where he could not feel if he was moving or if he was still, if he was crying or if this was just an act of crying, an act of deep guilt and confusion manifesting in unphysical convulsions.

After some time, James could converse with the women in the room again. Victoria and James decided to meet at his house on the following Tuesday. He would say goodbye.

"Okay, you can leave now." Aislin stood and abruptly opened and closed the door for Victoria. She turned her back to it and slid down against the surface until her forearms rested on her knees, her hands going to her hair. The scalp still sensitive.

"I hate this. That woman thinks that this is all about an affair. We hardly had an affair." Aislin snapped her head back up.

"She doesn't need to know everything to see that my being here hurts everyone. I was not there for Jade. And Aislin," he reached down for her and she stood. He cupped her cheek in his palm, could not feel her, but did not go through her. He leaned in. "I love you."

"James...." she closed her eyes and drew up to him; their lips touching briefly before she pulled back. "But... I... I don't understand. And I think it's because Victoria tries so hard to make us believe her views that she's more readily blinded."

"What makes her blind?"

"She doesn't know what Jade did to you! She's obsessed."

Aislin was obviously, albeit understandably, beyond comprehension of why he still wanted to protect his wife. Why he still needed to go to her.

There was nothing else he could say.

July 31, 2003

James, there is so much under the surface of your
words…

 well, you are proposing to Jade, you tell me on the
phone, and you tell me in letters. I can see her
eyes glisten with delight over the gain of you, over
holding your hand and waiting.

you dear, are the wonder-all. so full of life (history
that is part of our souls) is the story about your
family. there is Majka… giving birth to children and
then there was you.

i am so proud of you for the work ahead of you. i know
that you will make a great writer. i will always be
that hopeless romantic. always, i fear.

i have moved to my next story and work is in progress.
i shall send it to you when the scars are healed…

it's clear and blue and sunny and the sky isn't
falling in Washington, only my regrets for leaving you
are rain for ants.

love,

Aislin

Chapter 49 ✦ Hana

THE AIR IN HER KITCHEN WAS STUFFY, AND SHE COULD NOT CATCH HER breath. Her lungs kept seizing, changing. Too many nights passed since her eldest son left her world. Her family hid their disharmony behind false smiles under the weight of war. Heavy cannon fire. Missiles dropping in the library. The crumbling of stucco.

The sun shifted in the early morning, and Hana could feel the air change. What might have been warmth from a rising sun sent her for her afghan. Within these chilly mornings, the bones of her fingers ached and curled around the edges of the grey yarn. The scallop and fringe work withstood her grip as her fingers swelled with arthritis.

The den dropped ten degrees, and she knew her son was there. Layers of wool wrapped around her shoulders, the pillows behind her billowed and bowed, and the plush of her hand-knitted non-slip socks guarded her from the change. Hana pulled a soft, grey snood over her cold ears.

She had paid a visit to Father Benjamin that week, and in their meeting, she told him the fear in her soul. Benjamin was a friend of Alen's and he would always treat her with a kind regard.

"I worry...."

"Go ahead, Mrs. Athelstan."

"I worry James is not in heaven, Father." Standing up near the pulpit suddenly made her vulnerable. Her eyes jumped around the old structure before flowing up into the great heights of the ceiling. She wished the towering ceiling of the Cathedral paved a path to her husband instead of God. She found her voice as she looked at Benjamin's face. "He is not with his father. And I do not know what to do." Hana's gaze lifted again. As if, after all this time,

Edward knew the answers—as if he could still hold her and let her know their family would be okay.

Father Benjamin gazed at her. "There is a place in a mother's heart where she knows all things." He patted her shoulder, turned her towards the pulpit where Jesus hung on the cross. "James was a good man, Mrs. Athelstan. And I didn't have the privilege to meet your husband, but I know he helped to raise two men that I respect and am very proud of. My heart is heavy with your loss. Is there anything else you wish to share?"

Hana wished to share of the temperature drops in her den, of the certainty that James was a ghost. She found she could not speak. Was it a coincidence that Benjamin brought up Edward just as she wished for his presence? The long rows of candles on the pulpit mocked her and teased her with shuddering variations of darkness. This gift had blessed her in her youth. Premonitions. Like the day Aislin hit her head, and she knew.

Maybe Benjamin had them, too.

Had James come to tell her something?

Hana never gave into paranoia, but Aislin and her younger son increasingly tiptoed around the subject of her firstborn. And that might be expected, except for the mannerisms they brought with them. The possibility of James' drifting as a lost spirit and the wellbeing of her daughter-in-law were constant companions.

For a moment, she became the interest of a clergy member before he ducked through a darkened door in the wings. His eyes glowed in the reflective glint of candles, breaking the spell of catapulting thoughts as they watched each other longer than comfortable. She came back to Father Benjamin just as she heard the door close.

He waited for her to speak, offered her a seat.

But as uncertainty overwhelmed her, Hana would rather flee from his probing eyes. The only thing she could think of was the church betraying its people in what seemed like a lifetime ago some days. Other days, these flashbacks left her hollow, like it was all still happening. She could see the persecuted. The ones that resisted. And in fact, it still happened in many places.

She no longer trusted the priest. Today, the memory would fill her with conviction to protect her legacy.

A spark of fear caught in her throat, and she cleared it away. He would be greedy to pass James on. Father Benjamin would fervently chase the spirit of her son all over the purgatory that the church had abandoned. The eagerness of a priest after the supernatural was too much. Hana shut out that reason she had come. She would need to find James on her own. It was foolish to speak about anything but Alen.

"Father, Alen's out buried in a heavy tar. This stickiness pulls at him; he has it on his hands. All of his tools fall from a rooftop and he cannot patch the holes. On his own, how can he repair this roof or himself? He looks out at a sea of sand from his perch. The sun bakes his soul. Blisters form on his nose and his ears. I cannot stop how it eats him through. What can we do?"

Father Benjamin held her hand. "It takes time, Hana. I will reach out to him. Thank you for coming to me. The Church is here to support your family. Alen has always been like a brother to me. Is there anything else... about James... that you want to share?"

Hana shook her head, uneasy, but grateful for the earnest listening of one of Alen's long-time friends. Even if the priest could not hide his aptitude for the supernatural—it was still just Benjamin and he and Alen had been friends from the start.

Amongst the Prince-of-Wales feather, boxwood hedges, and purple beef-steak plants, Father Benjamin gave his blessings, and they said goodbye. Hana took a deep breath of the headier aromas of the roses and the clematis climbing up the shady wall. Walking away from the church, there was a curious uncertainty she would return. And as she turned the corner, from the corners of her heart, sprung a desire to explore the Muslim Romani traditions she had practiced as a young girl.

In her den the next morning, she waited for the cold air. When it descended, she pulled her scarf near. Gripping the familiar edge of the afghan, "I love you. For each day I live without you, James, I will wish your soul peace."

The ring of the telephone pulled her from the chill. Aislin was ready to write as soon as the week was out.

They could write about Adil and Mara, unrequited lovers from eighteenth-century tales. They could even explore the world that had inspired her mother and father's literary dreams. For the first time in a long time, she allowed the books on the tables of her parent's tiny living room to flood her memory. Poetry by Luka Botić and Aleksa Šantić—verses by the first woman Bosniak poet, Umihana Čuvidina, scribbled in the margins from memory as spoken word was the way of her poems.[4]

Hana let herself explore the hidden memories of her parents reading these pages out loud.

Chapter 50 ✦ Jade

AYS PASSED....

She spent long hours just sitting on the back porch. Days with the sun in the sky like summer, a pleasant summer, not a normal Palm Springs summer. Because it was November. The whispers of winter came with holiday decorations in stores, but never affected the actual weather. The desert continued to bloom under this sun, but Jade was no longer someone that bloomed.

Aislin left. Jade breathed easier without her under the roof, but not much. She appreciated sharing her house with the nanny over Aislin.

Next: boarding school. It was, after all, in the will. Egon and Nick were likely to hate her or love her for this act. Did she deserve love? She knew they deserved normal. They deserved an excellent school and routine and all the things that didn't involve seeing mommy have yet another breakdown. And she had to dry out or someone would find out and take her boys. It was the only option.

Drying out after drinking for months and the recent prescription drug abuse thrown in the mix would not be pretty. She was happy to keep drinking until everything was in place. *Why change for them now?*

After all, Alen kept his word. No more questions. No more cops.

One weekend afternoon, Alen and Aislin showed up. Rather together or separately, Jade did not know, but they came out back at the same time. Jade had just popped out back to visit with the boys and was ready to leave them back in the hands of the so-far capable nanny. The dogs were running around, happy that Alen was there and that the kids had been in the yard with them all day.

Alen asked the boys to go get some snacks and set up a board game, their choice; he would be there soon. They retreated, debating KerPlunk, Clue, or Uno. The nanny on their heels. Alen explained the reason for the visit. A promise was to be made. He looked awful. Weight accumulated around his neck. His skin had grown waxy and his hair coated with oil. Jade couldn't look him in the eye.

James was in the study, too, so they said. His motive was to protect her, so they said.

Jade lamented the sun and begrudged the absence of her boys and dogs as soon as she passed over the threshold of her porch; there were no more rooms left for Jade to take refuge in. They climbed the stairs together. Gathered around the desk, Jade took James's chair and looked up at the two people who were not her friends.

"Promise me, Aislin," Alen pleaded, pressing his open palm against Aislin's heart and breathing his request into her ear.

After the third rejection, he was going deep. It looked like Alen was going to kiss Aislin, and if it was part of his plan, Jade didn't want to watch. They had a weird relationship.

Jade turned away for a few moments and looked out the porch window. She watched a wren hop onto the railing. She turned back to get her hot toddy. Alen remained whispering in Aislin's ear while she gripped his wrist—his elbow still jutting out from her chest at an awkward angle. Jade could not hear Alen, but whatever he was saying was making Aislin cry. Aislin kept her eyes shut. And she placed her other hand on Alen's wrist, maybe trying to pull his hand away. She whispered "Okay." Alen relaxed but didn't let go until he said one last thing.

But he didn't kiss her.

Aislin opened her eyes and looked at Jade.

Alen sat in one of the large, heavily studded chairs in the office. "Aislin. Maybe..." He leaned forward and let his hands swallow up the rest of his face that his unruly hair didn't cover. "Maybe I can tell you why I can empathize with Jade beyond what you feel is reasonable."

Jade sat up straight in her chair. "What?"

Aislin took the other chair. She looked around the room. Was she looking for James?

Alen gave Jade a long look, a look that was not forgiveness, but patient and full of remorse. He heaved a sigh and turned to Aislin. "This is why I do this, why I want to let Jade go. I left candles burning the night my dad died."

When he paused, the breathing in the room quickened as the realization settled into Jade. She refused to look at Aislin, but she wanted to. This information was no doubt unexpected, yet if he were to tell any two people about it, Jade knew he had chosen the right two. She and Aislin loved Alen like their own brother.

"It's okay, Alen," Aislin said. He needed the encouragement.

"We were off to the movies and he was going to sleep. He'd traveled far for work and had jet lag. I was playing with the nativity set, even though we weren't supposed to. We packed it for Christmas in the attic, but I liked to go up there. I unwrapped it and kept it hidden behind Majka's trunks so I could play. It was so old that instead of the plugin for the lights, it had little hanging lanterns. I would practice lighting matches and fill the little manger up with light. Some lanterns had wax and others were oil wicks.

"I'd imagine how it must have been back then, with only fire for light and warmth. While sucked into playtime, Majka called for me and I was so excited to go to the movies I forgot to blow the candles out. They said the fire started in the attic, but what started the fire was obscured. Destroyed. Majka never suspected it was me. But I played up there all the time..."

"I am so sorry, Alen," Aislin raised and went to him. He stood, slumping forward. She held him.

"James?" Alen's voice was all tears and pain. "Where are you?"

"He's been gone awhile; I don't think he heard your story." Aislin rubbed his back.

He hugged her hard and cried. "He's not the only reason I'm keeping your secret. You see, Jade? I'm doing it because I understand what it's like to make a mistake. A terrible mistake. It was a mistake, right Jade?"

Jade watched his pinched face and curls matting in a wet tangle. "Yes, of course, Alen, of course it was a mistake."

Aislin said nothing. She just held him.

"No," Jade ventured. "We won't have to tell anyone about these things. They can be our secret."

Aislin pulled away, moving her hand to his arm, and putting herself between them. "No, Jade. He was a child! What if it was Egon, Nick, who set that fire? Jade, how dare you think that this excuses your behavior or somehow makes you two the same? You can get chummy now? Children make mistakes, accidents happen. Sabotage is not equal to a child leaving a candle burning." Aislin's voice built to a shout.

"Alen," Aislin lowered her voice, but the fire remained, "entire cities have burned because of candles and lanterns. Many people have died, and it is tragic. I am so, so sorry you've carried this with you your whole life. I know it may never leave you, but you told me this in a context of forgiving Jade and I want to implore you—You know that what you did is different, right?"

"There is forgiveness for anyone who makes confession, who atones for their sins." Alen turned away, his voice flat and final.

"An accident isn't a sin." Aislin's voice dropped to a whisper.

He just shook his head and wiped his eyes.

Jade wanted to hold him, and she almost stood, but she could not handle his rejection. She sat and stared at her brother-in-law. A terrible, tangled, teary-eyed man who lost his father in a fire that he started. It was the same.

"It is the same," Jade said. "We both made mistakes." She wished to retract her words, but had to sit with them out there, had to be judged again by Aislin—the home-wrecker.

But instead of flying insults and the defense she expected from the woman she hated and envied even more; she got a motionless, heated stare.

Finally, Aislin exhaled and walked away, "I don't owe that woman any-thing." Jade heard the study door slam, followed by clattering footfalls.

Alen fell into the chair again, and although their eyes locked in a moment of sympathy, the volume of the desk made him feel a mile away.

"I am so sorry, Alen."

"It was a long time ago." He tilted his head back and squeezed his glossy eyes shut. When he looked at her again, a soberness appeared that silenced anything else she was preparing to say.

"Aislin has promised not to tell my mother or anyone else. And I promise, as well."

Jade tethered between belief and doubt. At least she understood Alen's in-tentions better. He was a Catholic. He could not pardon her, but if he believed God would, that mattered. It gave her a level of comfort she did not deserve. Her confession was all Alen required, and luckily it didn't need to be made to a priest.

It was just an accident, just like Edward's death had been.

They shared a heavy silence for a long time. Alen rose without looking at Jade in the face. "I'll be with the boys for a few hours. But I would rather not see you again before I leave."

Well, he didn't arrive with Aislin, at least there's that.

Jade remained in the chair in the half-dark, wondering where James was.

Three afternoons later, the echo of the intercom bell flooded through the house for the third time. It finally penetrated Jade's current state of rumination about Aislin. Aislin, Aislin, Aislin. Aislin had been closer to James in the end than

Jade ever dreamed. A residual closeness. It was around the time that he started writing the will that he had withdrawn the most. And now Jade knew Aislin's arrival in the desert wasn't just to write a memoir. Somehow, until she found the letters, Jade had completely missed that Aislin and James remained in love.

She opened one of the towering foyer doors. "Come in, please, Victoria."

Victoria's eyes darted around the room, finally resting on the bloodstain that required a professional to remove. No one had bothered hiring one. Jade stared at the spot, too, her eyes welling as she remembered that she alone was responsible for things like that. James—gone. And Alen would have been there for her before she broke them apart.

"Thank you for seeing me." Victoria walked further inside, stopping right on the spot the bridge had splintered. She didn't appear to notice Jade's preoccupation. Jade broke away before the tears could spill over. She looked at Victoria.

She watched the girl's gold eyes take in the stain again before they finally rested on her face. With pity? With anticipation? Expectation?

"Tea?" Jade offered, unattached to the response.

"Yes, please," said Victoria.

They arrived in the kitchen without ceremony.

Jade gestured to one of six barstools around the huge stone-slab table. Victoria slid comfortably into the chair. Jade just hoped to have some semblance of sanity, while Victoria called up her dead husband. They went through all the tea pleasantries before Victoria blurted, "He's here."

Jade didn't know why she expected a seance. She choked on her tea. "That's it? You don't have to conjure his spirit or anything?" She coughed, struggling to get the question out.

Victoria shook her head. "If you want to talk, please speak freely. He can hear you."

"James." Jade choked on the tea she'd already choked on. "You're here." She inhaled and cleared her throat. "So. I should have something to say."

Victoria stared at her with those golden eyes that, along with everything else on earth, made Jade nervous. Alen promised to tell no one. But he and Victoria were lovers. After the long years he pined for her, breaking up meant nothing. Jade had a hunch they would get back together again. *Didn't "tell no one" normally not apply to conversations between lovers? Unless the secret wasn't your secret to tell and you really believed that. Few did....*

"Jade, I don't mean to be rude, but I have a session in a little while, it's quite a drive."

"Yes, of course." Jade rolled her eyes. "I can talk to him anytime without you here, that is, if he is here at all. Otherwise, I am just talking to myself...."

James, do you have anything to tell me?" Jade worried this conversation could expose her, unless, of course, Victoria already knew. *Would she still be helping me if she knew? Un-freaking-likely.*

A week before, Victoria reached out to Jade and insisted she could help communicate with James. Alen and Aislin agreed never to tell anyone—not Victoria and not Hana. Absolutely no one else will ever know the facts about the accident.

The only reason Aislin promised to keep the secret was because James and Alen asked her to. And Alen, well… she eyed Victoria and wondered if she knew about the fire. Aislin keeping her secret was the main reason that Jade even believed in this ghost thing. Still, her mind flitted back to the bedroom during her confession. There was something there.

But deep inside, Jade wanted to believe that Victoria could help. She still thought Aislin and Alen were playing a game with her. Victoria seemed separate from all that. And she said James was trapped and needed to cross and that she could make that happen—with Jade's help.

Jade blew stale air out from deep in her guts. If that were true, how the hell could she deprive him of peace?

"I don't believe his ghost is really here." She said it to screw with Victoria more than anything.

"He said he understands, and he wants you to open your heart to him so that you can see him," Victoria's voice echoed off the tile. Her words came out confident and a bit too loud for the slow throb building in Jade's head.

Jade lowered her eyes. She watched the honey drip into her cup from a porcelain dipper. She tried to focus on her heart. It would not open. *My heart! What a laugh.* It had turned to stone inside her chest, and her body could not regrow the vital cells. Jade could no longer support a heart. She could not remember what it felt like, how it might have had rhythm once before he died. Before she killed him, breaking his rhythm. She got up and went to the window above the kitchen sink. Outside, the desert was limitless. Amid what seemed infinite dryness was a mother quail leading her children through the brush. Jade closed the shade on it all.

"He says he should not have been so absent, and he takes responsibility for everything that went wrong."

The hot tears that she was becoming familiar with scalded her cheeks. These weren't tears from her heart, these tears came from her nervous system, from a pulsing in her veins that constricted her diaphragm and lungs to the point of exhaustion and release. Adrenal fatigue, likely. Likely the bottle. A perpetual cycle, an internal ouroboros. She returned to the table and added whiskey to her tea. She offered the bottle up, and Victoria shook her head.

Could it maybe be like one of those movies where he could pass on into the light and I could feel a puff of air in my ear or over my hair? Oh, how she wished.

Victoria could see James. Jade hated it. What was he wearing? His funeral clothes? What he died in? Was he smiling? Did he smell? She smelled the air, and she could imagine cigarettes, but they were probably hers. She shook her head. That's ridiculous.

"Thank you, James. I am open. I really want to see you."

"He asks that you accept his forgiveness and all his words. He is sorry for not being there." Victoria paused. "We are looking for the light, but it doesn't come."

Jade rolled her eyes again. "I can't let him take responsibility for everything." She looked around the room and her voice echoed against all the beauty he had built out of wood and stone. "… James, I can't do that." *I have no salvation, no hope, if I let him accept responsibility for everything. How could I?*

"Would you condemn him to float here eternally? Please, try harder." Victoria lectured.

Why did Victoria want James to pass on?

"He's still lingering because he knows he wasn't always the best husband."

Alen surely had shared a lot, but maybe not all? Did he even feel bad telling the woman stories that weren't his to tell? Jade forgave him, for that was often how it was between lovers. Sometimes they got to hear all the details of your best friend's life. Could she trust Victoria?

Victoria prattled on obsessively about James' crossing over. "But what if I got it wrong and Jade's forgiveness isn't the key to the crossing?" She suddenly changed direction. "I guess it could be about Vitez—survivor's guilt. Or it could be about when the dicks at work said that they were putting his death under investigation? Unsolved reasons for death are quite common explanations for spirits to hang back. Besides the affair with Aislin, these are both good reasons he isn't crossing—."

"What?" Jade interrupted.

"Hm?" Victoria stopped speaking, her lips pressed together. "What part?"

Jade paused, thinking to choose her words carefully. She studied Victoria's face, feeling the muscles in her own tense from the neck up. Her heartbeat grew loud in her ears. She realized she might breed even more suspicion. She could allow no one to rattle her.

Or could she? Wouldn't that be a natural reaction even if she wasn't the guilty party? Perhaps. But she had something to hide, and that made all the difference. Her brow furrowed and tension migrated to her scalp.

"How dare you talk about my marriage? It is none of your business!" Jade covered her curiosity about the investigation with the point she would have been vexed about—the affair. She dare not ask questions about the investigation. Had she been naïve to latch onto a theory about unrelated vandalism?

The suspicion of foul play laid out before her by Victoria… Well, that was something to worry about.

So is the word affair, because….

God damn it, that gives me a motive that I didn't even have at the time.

Victoria's hidden agenda for wanting James to cross, however unclear, became unwelcome. Jade was done listening.

The structure of her heart was making its final metamorphosis, taking on the hardness of a diamond: unchangeable, unmalleable, no openness, not able to take a scratch by anything less.

And that was how Jade's heart finally hardened against the day and the rest of her life.

The rest of her life was in danger.

Even when Jade opened to accept his gift, his forgiveness—in that moment—she still could not see him. The stone that had become her heart cracked, but her shoulders squared. *Forgiveness has nothing to do with it, but I love my husband and despite the events, I won't let anyone diminish what we had.*

"Leave, now. I'm not ready to buy into the fact that three people I know can see ghosts. And talk to them. And that the ghost is James. I don't know what shit you're trying to pull or what you want from us, but please do not drag my husband's name through the mud and spread your crazy rumors." Jade's tone was even, yet it shot out with the breath of an icy wind, lungs heaving beneath her thick ivory and red angora shawl.

The ouroboros no longer interested in its ancient purpose—it continued eating its tail until its belly was tight against her neck.

Victoria left, apologizing to James for failing to cross him in some awkward sing-song voice that seemed out-of-character for the normally pulled-together woman. She crossed the kitchen and looked back at Jade once she reached the edge of the travertine floor.

Jade crossed her arms and turned away from the golden eyes with their accusations and some false pretense of do-goodness that meant absolutely nothing.

She almost started crying the moment she heard the door close. But swallowed hard instead.

What the fuck?

The cops suspected foul play.

Would the detectives come and talk to her again?

When?

Why hadn't they returned?

Her only hope was that they believed his death a random act of vandalism. A chill ran through her, and she recognized the sentiment of justice. Forever looking over her shoulder felt like punishment, but was it punishment enough?

Chapter 51 ✦ Victoria

VICTORIA WALKED AROUND THE DIRTY FOUNTAIN IN THE FRONT YARD. Her brown boots clanked against the stone.

That did not go as I planned. What went wrong?

She stretched her calf for a moment, an impossible cramp chasing the length of her leg. But in her head was the face of the girl, the fear of the girl, the words of the girl who chased Victoria through time. And nothing would stop her from trying to make it right for her.

In the long shadows of the window in autumn, impossibly translucent and opaque all at the same time, her visitor's face became known. Her eyes wide and haunting and almost hollow, but for the faint iris detected by only a shy, eleven-year-old girl.

And what Victoria remembered from then, twenty years later, may have changed. May have taken a new story, a new shape in her mind—for that was always the fabric of memory.

Since she never learned her name, Victoria called her Sybil, for she represented the psychic connection between Victoria and the land of the dead. She was the first ghost that had spoken to her, but there would be one other whose voice made it across the veil. Other ghosts remained silent.

Apparitions floated around each of the facilities that she tried to place her mother in. They were the reason she did not frequently visit the woman she missed so much. She had finally settled on a place that had the least intense of them, but it was also the saddest.

Ghosts were nearly everywhere. Their mouths opened with no sound. They came so close there should have been breath and Victoria expected it, but it never came, just like the words.

Open mouths, moving lips. Silence and frustration. They knew she could see them. Some tried to communicate with her one-hundred ways, but she seemed to be lucky they haunted their locations. They could not follow her home.

James stood apart.

Sybil had warned her about a man sucked into the dark. "You must help him," she said before her tears became an inky black shadowfall from an infinite source of sadness. "He will end up like me. Just like me."

Victoria had tried. But now what?

Alen was beyond her reach. She turned to see James, hovering above the bloodstain in his foyer as she made transverse paths across his cobblestones. His glorious fountain and all he worked for crumbling down. He waved.

She stopped pacing and climbed into her car. Circled the fountain and left Athelstan House behind her. Sad that she lost her lover, her future, and the chance at new friendships.

But telling the truth was too scary. They did not need her world full of dead. The only thing she ever wanted to do was protect Alen. Instead, she would have to forget him and leave all of it behind her.

Victoria set her course for the library, the only place she belonged.

Chapter 52 ✦ James

Jame saw the pale skin of Jade's crossed arms. He watched Victoria pace his fountain and waved before she drove away. He walked back into his kitchen, where Jade sat at the table and warmed her tea with more whiskey. Why did she even bother with water, lemon, or honey anymore?

He placed his hand on her pouring hand. Wishing he could stop her from drinking it. Jade's eyes, dulling from malnutrition and overconsumption, looked into his. She sat up straight in her chair, removing her wrist from his gentle grip.

"James?"

"I am here, Jade. My Jade."

She looked around the room. It was not yet clear to him whether she heard him, but she certainly could not see him. He was aware of the tightness in his chest, more mystery, still so much mystery about his senses.

Alen's voice echoed through the hall.

"Hi, Alen," James and Jade said together.

"I parked in the garage. The boys fell asleep in the car." He looked only at Jade and did not acknowledge James.

"Oh, that's good. Well, you won't be needed for runs to soccer or anything when they start boarding school. They have soccer there."

"You would do that to Majka?"

"What about your mother? It's not far. She can see them on weekends—whenever. We can all drive and see them. I'll miss them, too."

Alen did not respond.

"What the hell, Alen? Are you going to take care of them?" Bitterness stuck to her.

"I know. I know… I'm not. I can't." He shook his head and dropped it forward. In shame? "What've you been doing today?"

"Victoria was here, and she was going to help me say goodbye to James, or hello. She was going to cross him over."

Alen's eyes became enormous, but he did not speak right away. James thought he looked worried, scared. "And how did that go?"

"I kicked her out. You all are so full of shit."

"You know you're becoming a mean drunk, right?"

"Well, whatever." Jade rolled her eyes, but her chin dropped. James noted her shielded sensitivity.

"I just came in to say goodbye to you, anyway."

Her head jerked up at full attention.

"I was going to ask about rehab and a place for the boys. It appears you figured it out on your own. I'm glad you're sending the boys to school, away from you. It's as if James knew you were off your rocker, writing in the will that they should go off to school. You smell like shit. I can't stick around."

"He asked that you forgive me, you know."

"Of course—you would believe that he's really here when the story suits you. But no. No, not forgiveness. He asked that I not tell anyone about your fucking little scheme. Made me swear it. Made Aislin swear. I made her promise, too. I can't even look at you. How can I keep this secret if I have to look at you? If you don't check yourself in somewhere, I will contact Richard about the clauses in the will."

James went to slam his fist on the table to call order to all the bullshit, but in his inconsistent form, it just sailed through. "God! Damn it! Alen!"

No one heard him. His family was crumbling, while that promise should hold them together. The lack of his involvement drove James into a pacing and seething tempo.

And this thing about the cops that Victoria brought up…. James knew nothing about that. He could not even ask Alen about it because his brother could not fucking see him anymore. He could ask Aislin. Since when were they talking about his death like it was a case to be solved? How much did he need to worry about Jade being discovered? For all he could see and all the eavesdropping he was capable of, why did he not see this? James desperately tried to release the tightness in his chest, pursed his lips, and blew out nothing—so nothing changed.

He remembered the detectives at the wake and finally understood their presence. Still, nothing he could do about any of it.

Fuck that historian—James hated letting him get away with the part he played. But they had to stick to the plan. He had his children to think of.

He drowned in the guilt and his insane desire to protect his wife. And if that meant John Murray as well, so be it.

"Oooh, Alen, I'm so scared," Jade taunted. "What are you going to do? Take away the house? There's plenty for me. You know I can't live here, anyway. And I'm—" her voice caught on a tear or maybe a feeling of indignation. "I'm gonna go dry out. But not here. And the boys know, Alen. They know they are going to a different school; they know Majka will come see them on the weekends. Your mom already knows, too, Alen."

Her decisions were news to James, as well. *When did she decide all this? Where was I when she made these arrangements?* James constantly hated time.

"Okay then, where is this treatment center?" Alen asked what James wanted to know.

Her lips curled. "The ninth circle of hell."

James' heart, the non-heart that it was, broke and broke once more.

"Alright, fine." James watched his brother's hands fly into the air and turn to leave the room.

"Alen?" Jade called him back.

"What?! What now?"

"You know you should have told me that James still loved Aislin."

"What?" Both Alen and James said at the same time. Still, Alen did not hear or see James.

"You know he loved her. And he cheated on me. You knew."

James heard Alen's, "I didn't know," chorused with his own, "I did not cheat."

But James was still cheating. And although he had been physical with Aislin for less than a minute during his marriage before his death, a piece of his heart belonged to Aislin from the moment he met her. And it was possible for him to touch Aislin—intimately. He imagined her hair, her lips.

"Get ahold of yourself," Alen screamed at Jade. "He married you. He loved you."

The pressure of a demolition bucket pulled its way through James' core. More and more guilt spilled out at every pass. The metal teeth fought to take him apart. Upon his center, the excavator reached max breakout force, and the bucket torqued and poured his soul into oblivion. Alen and Jade were crying. James was not sure when their tears started, but it would not surprise him if they never spoke to each other again. Being empty of compounds that comprised tears did not deplete James' range of emotion. He was loathe to stay in the room with them any longer. Nor could he leave.

For a moment, he watched Alen. His brother had been unable to see him since the day he promised to keep Jade's secret. James did not know if that decision was the reason for this change. But James knew he was dead to Alen for the second time. And as Victoria predicted, this second death was more painful than the first. The secrets behind the death were too much of a burden to keep. James did not deserve his brother's love. He asked for too much.

Alen and Jade stood in the kitchen with their backs to each other when the boys walked in, rubbing their palms on their sleepy faces.

It was too late to say goodbye. But he knelt before them anyway, attempting to kiss each on the head, sending all the love in his heart. Then he simply sat on his travertine floor, knees to his chest, imagining the cold of the hard stone that he could not feel. His shoulders hunched over a torso tightly wrapped by his own arms, his hands somehow still able to grasp his own ribs. James began to rock. An ant crawled through him, one tiny little ant that he wanted to crush.

Epilogue

She, hapless one! both stretching out her arms,
and struggling to be grasped, and to grasp
him, caught nothing but the fleeting air.

—Ovid, *The Metamorphoses*

Aislin

IN Majka's home, James sat and listened to his mother's stories as Aislin interviewed her, took notes, recorded. Interviewed, took notes, recorded. They searched through piles of letters; Hana translated many of the ones she had written to Edward in Bosnian. Aislin wrote Hana's story, put the pieces in Hana's words.

Some letters were so fragile, they used gloves to handle them. Aislin brushed her latex thumb across the name and address on one with letters and numbers rubbed out.

"Hana Hadžić," Aislin said aloud.

Hana gently corrected the pronunciation of her maiden name. "Hajj-ich, in the center it is a j sound like jug. It ends with ch like chin."

"It's beautiful."

"My mother told me that her grandfather went to Mecca, this is what my name means. Perhaps I take a metaphorical pilgrimage, myself. Hajj is the real pilgrimage. Discovering the history of Islam in my family after a lifetime of following another god and having another name. The words have not yet come to me for this."

"When did you change it back?"

"Well. I was Petar until I married and became Athelstan. I used this post to exchange letters with Edward, and we wanted to use my name. My original name. To use it meant we connected outside of expectations. It was intimate. Our secret. Truly, had I used that name in my everyday life, things would have been different for me. I shall never know the differences. But I am grateful for the family that raised me when all else was lost. I think that losing my James now makes me realize how much I want to know more of my parents and their story. Do you know?"

Aislin believed she did.

Aislin's connection with James' mother deepened. Although she knew Hana used the book as a needed distraction and showed gratitude for this unearthing of her love life with Edward—sometimes it drowned out the present. She confessed to Aislin that she suspected her son was not at rest. Aislin tried not to look at James as Hana said these words. And James disappeared from the room.

Because he's not at rest, Hana. He's far, far from resting. Aislin rediscovered the days when she cried herself to sleep. The secret stirred her melatonin around until it changed form, became nothing but empty molecules.

"Maybe we can go to a grief counseling session together? I have been looking at some." Aislin asked.

"Hmm?" Hana looked at Aislin, but it was clear her mind had wandered.

"I was thinking of going to grief counseling, Majka. With Alen, too? Maybe the boys can go, too. They have camps to help children when they lose someone close."

"What happens there? Do I have to do anything?"

Aislin realized that even after losing Edward, Hana had never sought counseling. "Well, we talk to a therapist. We share memories about James with other people who have lost people, too. I went when my parents died. They made me, but I am glad I did." Aislin noticed her voice drop to a whisper when she mentioned her parents. She had to work to raise her voice so Hana could hear her.

"Okay Aislin, I can go for my Alen if he wants to go."

"I will call and see if there's space." Aislin said. She knew she would call to make private appointments, too. *Talk is important. And so is treading carefully when it comes to seeing ghosts. Oh my god, can you imagine?* She felt her mouth curl into a smile and rose to prepare for their new afternoon ritual of tea.

Time meant little. Finding out that Jade was responsible for James' death tore Aislin in half. She wept. She sat around, wondering if the detectives would ever sort it out. She remembered the day she had wanted to protect Jade from their uncomfortable stares. The day she welcomed them in, but really wanted to rush them off.

She knew their names. In fact, one had left his card for Jade to call them back when she felt better. She pictured the letters in navy on the white background with the Sheriff's Department logo, how it just sat on the kitchen island for days until it disappeared. She assumed Jade called them back.

She sat around thinking about her promise to not call them. Obstructing justice.

Her own guilt at letting the man she loved marry that woman gnawed at her from every corner. *But no one said I was sane, right? Healthy people don't take the blame when someone else commits murder.*

Who was to say she wasn't healthy? Wasn't she getting better? Couldn't she? She finally furnished the little apartment. Aislin was starting over. What was wrong with starting over?

They spent as much time together as they could. They were grateful Palm Springs was mostly sunny, speculated about his experience in a cloudy place like Gig Harbor. But each time the darkness pulled him away, he returned altered. The darkness came back with him; a flick of shadow in his eyes intensified. Aislin set up her own altar. But even long-burning wicks could not last forever. And she promised herself some self-care.

Ever increasing were the moments James found solid form. The light didn't change. He remained luminous, but in the short time frames before the sun fell, he remained able to touch Aislin. It began weekly—then bi-weekly, and then nightly—that he could hold her, that she could touch the light of his hand. Sometimes this light felt like the feathered back of a bird, the foam of a cappuccino, sometimes like the pressure of constant wind. They stayed together during the hours leading up to this time. Side by side on the bed, waiting for James to become solid. Then their lips would touch, and Aislin would sense his hand on her skin.

They made love during these times, James saying he could even feel her warmth. She would rehearse the letter she kept folded in her pocket, whispering the sensual words in his ear until they were frantic in their desperation for one another.

Some nights, they held each other and wept, unable to drum up additional energy. Somehow, this gift of touch meant that he knew of darkness more and more often. He drifted around, trying to get back to her. They longed for their magic hour.

On a cool morning in early spring, Aislin and James lounged in bed, the white cotton drapes open. The glaring sun hit him as it rose into the window frame. He was human-shaped dust caught in its rays. The light fluxed around him, suddenly bending with a small pull to another world.

Her mouth dropped open, a gasp of wonder and fear just audible to James.

She smoothed her goosebumps; she remembered him holding her the whole night, how his body contoured around hers. And now she realized the season was changing. He touched her cheek. She smelled sunshine, cigarettes, the burning of electric wires. Her overwhelmed senses sought the scent of her home: begged for the lavender in her pillow. Tried to settle down. He had never been physical an entire night—into the morning. Suddenly, and with nausea, she knew this change indicated something significant. He was leaving.

"Our time is slipping, Aislin. It seems like I am being carried into the darkness, a piece at a time. It is happening and I cannot change it," James kept his mouth next to her face. Breath that might have been hot, not there at all.

Once again, she rubbed away the chill that filled the air. The magic that kept him there, snagging the sun as it so often did. He was leaving her. The knowledge began to sink inside. "I know we cross this line, James. I always dreamt we could totally obliterate it and I am no longer threatened by crossing it. I'm overcome with guilt and gratefulness, at once."

Her voice was sewn from tremors. She admitted how her shame was never strong enough to stop loving him, and how, years back, the idea of being a home-wrecker had somewhat helped her to stop writing to him. Yet the truth—she'd seized writing him only after his letters changed in tone.

"Once I returned to you, I knew I had never really left. We were never just friends. We're exceptional friends. And now you're dead, James." She pushed her head into the nook of his shoulder. Her lips found skin that was not skin. Her palm rested on his chest. The contrast of her skin and his like chocolate and cream. Yet he was still made from dust. Not always opaque. Even when he was solid, he could still appear translucent.

Light filled her mouth. She could sense it on her tongue.

She now knew how light tasted: like grief, like love, like James.

"We both have so much guilt. Did I ruin Jade? With us, Aislin? Our love so strong and our friendship, this deepness has power. It makes me solid; it allows us to connect." He fingered her bare breast and took her nipple into his mouth. He kissed the other one, sliding his body on top of hers. Their eyes met. The white down comforter slid to the floor.

"Our love never ebbed, not even now, not especially in the end." His voice was deep as he pushed himself inside her. James found her hand. Their fingers tangled. Her breath was hot, but she did not know if he could feel it. They made love for a long time. Never slowing, drying, nor tiring. The sun climbed the sky of the east.

Aislin wanted to be with him forever, but he was not hers. "This feels like the last for both of us." She kissed him and pulled away to see his face. Aislin's heart swelled painfully against the walls of the new box she'd built for it. Impervious now to fire; made from rose gold, made from glass, with walls of hurricanes.

His eyes were still full of a life already lived. Tears came from her eyes. James did not have wet tears, but as they made love, streams of light fell against her skin and vanished like raindrops in the desert.

They rose to their feet, and he was unable to hold her again. Then, like a star, his shape wasn't a shape at all. It was only an airless vacuum. They tried to hold hands again but failed. The dust that had once combined to make James swirled into particles of mist and swirled again until he no longer stood before her.

Aislin took a deep breath and exhaled. Naked and alone.

Later that day, evening light changed the tone of the lavender walls. Aislin sat cross-legged on a mat and low table with Alen in her studio.

"I found something for you." She carefully smoothed out the piece of parchment James had used during a physical time.

Dear Alen,

Mortality has violated and interrupted our years together. Death is something our culture here has yet to meld with and understand. I hope that some year you might say "James lived" more often than "James died." I suppose, though, if our roles were reversed, I would miss the way you lived and that would be the same as grieving your absence.

Oh, my Brother, I am finally moving on from this middle place.

I had a chance to say goodbye to you, to see you at the beach, to understand how much my friendship and family bond meant to you. I am no longer scared of what is in that blackness, for I am passing from a place that has given me faith in all that is love and time.

Keep building, my good brother. Rodney is there for you. You know Aislin and Jade will be there for you. My boys love you deeply. Majka knows where the river goes—our blood—our bond.

Forever in love and brotherhood,

James

Alen looked up from the letter. A perceptible chill in his shoulders. He took a tissue from a nearby plant stand. Aislin put her hand over his. She had found the letter around lunchtime and called Alen at once.

"He's really gone then?"

"Yes, he disintegrated into light. It was like dust swirling in the sun, but I couldn't catch it." She was semi-aware that her lips parted. After a moment, she lowered her hand, not even realizing she had placed her fingertips in some settled dust. His dust.

Alen smiled. "How poetic."

"Yeah—" She smiled back with a girlish laugh. They stood and held each other in a long hug. Tears flowed to soak their collar bones. Relief emanated from their muscles. Worry slid away from their minds and hearts—replaced with a sense of peace that the man that they cared for was no longer affected by the trials of this life.

A foreign sense of wholeness and living energy took root. Little fragile roots, but roots, nonetheless.

Her new roommate—a tiny cat they called Saint Jimmy—skittered to a stop at their feet with a meow. She scooped him into her arms and buried her face in his fur.

Hana

Many years ago, in Edward's presence, Hana acquired a taste for smoked black tea. And as she enjoyed her early morning cup, that reminded her of burnt earth, it suddenly smelled stronger than she recalled. In the corner of her eye, a dust-filled light beam began to shimmer before the window of the breakfast nook. She turned her head to see the phenomenon with both eyes. The glowing dust swirled around in an undetectable breeze.

"James." She whispered. Sneaky thieves made of water and salt, almost stealing her voice. The light faded from the dust particles and disappeared altogether. "Goodbye, my son. Peace to your soul."

Hana's heart pounded fast in her ears.

Each breath moved both shoulders—but gently—normalizing the respiration rate of an organ that had resisted harmony for years, but had deteriorated since his death. She coughed a little, then her chest settled. Alveoli, bronchi, pleura, and five lobes filled with the oxygen that she needed—becoming her lungs once more.

James' mother let out a deep sigh and then her pulse returned to a normal, perceptible anomaly. The miracle of life. The end of her son's wandering surrounded her, and she desired a short walk. Her aching hand pressed the call light. After using the strength of both arms to push onto her feet, she placed her hands on her heart and lungs, repeating long, full breaths.

Rose appeared through the back door. "Hana? What is it?"

"Walk with me, please, Rose. I would like to know the earth beneath me."

"Of course, Hana." As Rose helped her collect a coat and scarf, Hana lowered her hands and hunched over the back of her solid kitchen chair. Her eyes glued to the place she was sure James had visited within a swirl of free light. That very place before her kitchen window was the place where he said goodbye to her. She understood his journey would continue in more peace than he had known on earth and that he would forever be a part of her.

James

June 1, 2014

Dearest James,

We get our ideas from the world around us. From music, from faces, from those that go by holding hands and others that shun an outstretched one. We get our ideas from the constant alpha that rules our mornings, plowing into the silence with sadness and endless possibility. From the omega that steadies our days and completes us. I get my ideas from you. I try to cycle your presence in my life. I hatch beautiful plans to live a saline life. Sans-James. Because you brought passion to me again and I realize now—that passion gives me life. I will discover love again; I will not allow myself to waste away without human touch.

I remember feeling you in the darkness, as I tried to pull you back out of numerous moments you disappeared. You—calling out that you love me, maintaining our truth that we will always be in love.

I remember the final time that the shadows put their claim on you. Yet it wasn't the darkness that came for you, James. You became dust; you became something both new and ancient. I hold hope that you found peace in that magical moment of light.

Will I rest 'till I know for sure? Will I ever know for sure? You return in dreams and I get to hold you. It will take time for this to change. It may never change.

Many months ago, you reminded me that your love for Jade was a solid concrete slab. And you wouldn't have had your boys without her. While I know this is true, I pretended I understood your continuing commitment to her, and your love. But the secret I keep—the promise I made to *protect her—haunts even my shadow.*

I remember your gravelly voice, the way the sun dropped, and your eyes caught it all. I remember the vow you wished to keep, "I won't let us be cut off in the middle of another sentence (or a kiss!) by another astronomical twilight."

You just had one more thing to say. I watched you, a pale version of your former self, exist with a translucency you only get from death. Your lips parted. "Aislin, I will love you always, always..." The sun encircled you with no regard to us. It was so different from our nights, where civil twilight became nautical twilight and then nautical twilight became astronomical twilight and I didn't even know there were so many twilights before you died.

May this letter be the last I write, still believing you might read it. Am I to arrange every word in just the way I think your previous sensibilities would approve, or do I have the strength to become myself?

Ever,

Aislin

He reaches out his hand. There is nothing in it. There will never be anything in it again. The sun sets over the desert. He has been walking for months on the same long sad road; but he celebrates because he can feel the end. The mountains are spotted with few trees. Bushes are on the south slopes, there is little growth on the northern slopes, yet there his eyes fix again and again as if drawn there by god—who he hopes it is, glowing in the western half-light. It does not matter that he may have been excommunicated had the church known of his past, religion could not define his spirt. His life is no longer. And his wild years did not define the man he had become in the end. They only leant flavor.

He has been dead perhaps eight months and during these long months he consummated the relationship with his soulmate. The months also unearthed the desperate deception of his life partner, a woman he loved deeply and married.

James looks out to the mountain. Wishing for his soulmate to have peace, sending peace to his mother and brother, love to his children. He pauses longer to send peace to the woman who can never rest. He sends peace to his own heart because her unrest tortures him, as well.

The ground is dry, but nothing cracks beneath his feet as he travels toward the mountain. No snakes slither out of his path or strike at him. The poison of a scorpion or the venomous bite of a Gila monster are dangers no longer.

He keeps walking even though the sun is down, and all the twilights pass overhead, walks until the deepest of them takes the last light. He keeps walking, for in the mountain, the gods are glowing like the moon. He walks the night, all night. The cacti and the needles do not stab his calves and the mesquite leaves his clothes alone.

He walks over the fingers of dawn light and turns around to be swallowed by the sun.

The End

Endnotes

1.   Rudd, W. N. (1909, September 14, 15, and 16). The Subdividing of a Cemetery Into Sections, Lots and Single Grave Districts. Retrieved March 5, 2017, from https://www.iccfa.com/reading/1900-1919/subdividing-cemetery-sections-lots-and-single-grave-districts

2.   Kübler Ross, Elisabeth. *On Life After Death*. New York: Celestial Arts 1991. Print.

3.   Eliot, Gil. *Twentieth Century Book of the Dead*. New York. Charles Scribner's Sons 1972. Print.

4.   Editorial Team Sevdalinka.info Editorial Management: Edina Klopić. Author: Avdo Huseinović (2019). Sevdalinka. Retrieved July 20, 2021, from https://sevdalinka.info/en/about-sevdalinka/

Note about Aislin's Journey and Suicidal Ideation in The Disconsolate

If you are having thoughts of harming yourself or know someone who is call 1-800-273-8255, 911, or text 988.

The information that follows does not replace a one-on-one relationship with a qualified health care professional and is not medical advice. I intend it as a sharing of knowledge and information from the research and experience of myself, the author, and my community. The author encourages you to make your own health care decisions based upon your research and in partnership with a qualified health care professional.

Having said the above, you may also notice that although I am a huge advocate of Narrative Medicine and many journaling methods, I will use the word talk a lot. Here are some things I have learned and leaned on:

a.   Know when you need help, know it's okay to talk about it, keep a list of people that know you have suicidal ideation: one doctor you trust, perhaps a pinky swear buddy. A pinky swear buddy can be on the other end and you always promise to call each other if you need help. Sometimes we need to get help for our pinky swear buddies because we don't want any suicide pacts happening! Be aware of when you need the extra reinforcements. Be ready to say, "I am struggling too, let's take the next step and call someone else."

b.   It might be hard for people who do not have suicidal ideation to understand what we're going through, but once you have people on your list and they have agreed to be there for you, trust that they will listen. Whomever is on your list—they know they are on there and what for—so if they get a call at midnight, they are ready to listen. Have the hotline number available too, because sometimes the people that love us are fast asleep, and they want to be there for us, but you know—sleep.

c.   Whatever helps you keep a foot planted firmly on earth, label it, identify it. Know that even if it's the waterfall of grief you have witnessed others go through after losing someone—that if we talk about it, we can get help when we need it. It can be anything: a memory, a tattoo that reminds you of who you are tethered to, or even get help from a Blue Box at Find Your Anchor (visit https://findyouranchor.us/)

Acknowledgements

Thank you. I wish to be the flight of a bird. I wish to land on each of your fingers and spend a few moments in chirpy excitement, telling you thank you for your part in this book. The people I have met may not always know how often I think of them and remember.

A flower and a kettle. You are the shining night of stars, whisperers of writing that helped me create the lines within.

You were the spark that kept me going. Feel the little bird claws on your finger and hear a song of my gratitude:

Jeffrey Bell—thank you for reading drafts, drawing the art (the beautiful border and the Palo Verde flower) and for those multiple nights of listening to me go on and on (and on) as I do. Bell of my heart, I love you!

Write Around Portland and Fly-by-Night writers! Erin Zinser, Susan Montgomery, Jan Krochina, Sara Fisher, Rob Sassor, and Linda Drach! I am so grateful for the last eight years of writing and sharing with you. Milena Petrovich and Kellie Ernst you are always Fly Bys.

Editors and beta readers, some of you read this several times and helped with different versions. All of the thanks. This book is what it is because of you: Carole Shorten, Corey Hartman, & author M.J. Bell! Annie Pisacano—I love having you as my writing friend. Cindy Johnson, Cheri Stowell, and Heidi Yu, Grant Miller, Bobby Eversmann, Suzy Vitello, Susanne Haught, Pia Pimputkar, (Erin, Linda, and Rob) and my IPRC classmates. Tara Lehmann for the marketing consultation. To M.F. Corwin—thank you for the beautiful book design and editing.

Thank you, family: Carole and David Shorten; Gina and Nico Cifuentes; Corey, Cody and Alexa Hartman; Janet Wong; Christian Frisk; Mow Kofol; Alex Wong; Lourdes, Aaron, Tiffany, and Tim Bell; April Elizabeth, Rick Shorten and Alix Foster; Sue Shorten and Patrick, Tim, Jojo, Carrie; Michelle, Scott, Pete, Andy and Jessica Shorten; Aunt Penny and Chris; Theresa and Chuck Byer; Bobby and Heather Nemeth; Richard Nemeth; Jamie, Collin, Rachel, Breanne and Hope; Sandy, Steve, Shannon and Pete, and Billy; Sara Obertino and your lovely girls; Erin, Randy, and the whole Gipson bunch.

Shane LaLama—thank you so much for the writing, support, and excitement. Nicole Raubenbacher—thank you for your friendship, leadership, and lending me the book that inspired the prologue. From Frances Wilson's study on epistolary romance, I was able to distill my understanding of how letters might profoundly impact their recipients. Thank you, Frances.

Teachers! All IPRC teachers in 2016, Coleman Stevenson who lent guidance with the Dark Exact deck over the years; Vennie White of CCC; Dick Fontaine of PCC; and so many thanks to my high-school creative-writing teacher, Kim Holland, who forgave me à propos my severe lack of censorship on an open-mic night and continued with encouragement.

Lovely friends and mentors have lent their ears to my writing (& aspirations) over the years, among them: Kari and Matt Gottschling, Tim Nelson, Kevin and Carissa, Tom Ono, Katie Grannan, Kristen Grantham, Alma Wells, Damion LaPier, Hannah Miller, Molly Thompson, colleagues at PSU & Gore, David Yates and your family, Jennifer Burks, Randy Sproat, Ryan Flett and Kelly Fulop, Mark Adams, Corey and Laura Uva-Gjerman, Jodi Butler, Kim Alcorn, Felicia Howe, Ben and Jana Moan.

Inspiration for writing about the Balkans came from many places, foremost, Zlata Filipovic, who published a diary of her life in Sarajevo. In 1992, Filipovic was the first to make a deep impact on me and opened me to so many things I was simply unaware of. She stayed with me as I went to the Coconino County Library in 2009 in search of a greater understanding of the Bosnia and Herzegovina, half of the heritage for James, who was born in my imagination that year. I was eagerly consuming more books from the Multnomah County Library after moving to Portland in 2013 and read and reread books and online articles about the region, ethnicities, music, and religions. I wanted to write and to recognize those who died. In the way of these words, we remember as Hana remembers, and her sons remember.

My wonderful Bosnian coworker, Amela, taught me how to say majka correctly, and gave me feedback about my characters and the relationships I described to her. She recognized the formality of speaking that I gave to James and Hana. Amela, thank you so much for your help and for your interest and excitement about this book.

I dedicate Helen and Aislin's searches to learn more about their family histories and traditions to my father, Thomas Nemeth. Thank you for calling me, Tom, I am so grateful for that time with you. And though your family came from many hills to the north of Bosnia (from Slovakia), the search for an ancestral connection that so many of us share is what propels James to prioritize the telling of his mother's story. Maybe someday I will travel to the Balkan's so I can write the story of Hana and Edward in letters. And travel to learn about my own.

I acknowledge Mary Downing Hahn who wrote my first-ever genuine ghost story. I read Wait till Helen Comes a hundred times as a child and the haunting story is a huge informer of my love for ghosts and spirituality. Thank you for that touching story.

In loving memory: Joshua Aaron Maust; Thomas, Mary, and Andy Nemeth; Fon Cordasco; Diane Gipson; Nancy Barnes; Ginny and Art Shorten; Louis & Martha Frisk and Al Rozzi; Patrick Jones; Kyle Matthew; Rafe Sweet; Angela Reuther; Dick Hardy. We are connected, and I will always hold space for you in my heart.

Love to you all.

Writing is the soul of Aislin and James' story. It's through writing I have woven a texture of lives from my core and unraveled them here... it took time to coil everything up. But the important thing is there is more inside me. The novel is not the end of writing and once I finally release it and let it fly to everyone (like the bird has done in thanks)—I want you to know that the trees are so full; the water is so clear; the sky is so blue because of words. So, I include those on this list that are not only the assistants of The Disconsolate, but the assistants of all writing that I will ever do.

And I suppose it's in the writing of thanks that I will endeavor toward the other side, to thwart becoming Werther and land in the soft arms of benevolence, whispering that there is always more.

Elizabeth Bell lives in Portland, Oregon with her husband Jeffrey, their cats Artemis and Tansy and spirit cat, Basil.

Her first novel naturally combines a lifelong fascination with ghosts and love for the epistolary. Religion and spirituality captivate her: the rituals, the communities, the questions.

B loves cooking, eating, playing Dungeons & Dragons, and collecting rocks from any location, but especially the Oregon Coast or the mountains and deserts of Arizona.

She shares a weekly writing practice with the Fly-by-Nights and has written online at Cat Over Clock.

Notes